Allies

Allies

IAIN ORD

Copyright © 2024 Iain Ord

The moral right of the author has been asserted.

Apart from any fair dealing for the purposes of research or private study, or criticism or review, as permitted under the Copyright, Designs and Patents Act 1988, this publication may only be reproduced, stored or transmitted, in any form or by any means, with the prior permission in writing of the publishers, or in the case of reprographic reproduction in accordance with the terms of licences issued by the Copyright Licensing Agency. Enquiries concerning reproduction outside those terms should be sent to the publishers.

This is a work of fiction. Names, characters, businesses, places, events and incidents are either the products of the author's imagination or used in a fictitious manner. Any resemblance to actual persons, living or dead, or actual events is purely coincidental.

Troubador Publishing Ltd
Unit E2 Airfield Business Park,
Harrison Road, Market Harborough,
Leicestershire LE16 7UL
Tel: 0116 279 2299
Email: books@troubador.co.uk
Web: www.troubador.co.uk

ISBN 978-1-83628-049-1

British Library Cataloguing in Publication Data.
A catalogue record for this book is available from the British Library.

Printed and bound by CPI Group (UK) Ltd, Croydon, CR0 4YY
Typeset in 11pt Minion Pro by Troubador Publishing Ltd, Leicester, UK

To my parents, Stanley and Margaret Ord, who lived through the trauma of war.

CHAPTER ONE

"We'll wake these hicks up good and proper!" Benedict squealed as he swung the steering wheel.

Bellucci remained resolutely silent, nursing both his characteristic irascibility and his unprecedented ambivalence.

But the driver was right. The arrival of the first contingents of the US 116th Infantry Regiment in the Devonshire town of Chalford was the occasion for perhaps the loudest noise ever heard in the 1,000-year history of one of Alfred the Great's original burghs.

It is true that the burgh had been sacked by Danish armies in 982. It had also been invested and stripped bare some six centuries later by Sir William Waller's Parliamentarian army.

It cannot be supposed that a horde of rampaging Vikings with their horns, war cries and penchant for drunken excess, nor Roundheads with their musketry drill, psalm singing and trenchant political debate, were the most discreet of visitors. However, the roars and screeches (the inevitable consequence of drivers unused to the convolutions of English roads) of upwards of fifty lorries and Willys jeeps, motorcycles, M3 Stuart light tanks, M3 armoured personnel carriers, and M3 37mm and M5 75mm anti-tank guns mounted on half-tracks bursting out of the tight lanes and into the streets that lassoed the market square, were of a volume to bring the venerable burgh into the twentieth century with the precipitation of an alarm clock, or the equally familiar sound in this age, an air raid siren.

Presented with the chocolate-box scene of cobbled market square complete with stone cross mounted on three well-worn steps, surrounded by the Chalford Arms Hotel, one pub, a baker's, tearoom, grocer's and butcher's shops, Major John Bellucci looked quite as morose as he had whilst staring through the windscreen at the narrow belt of tarmac winding between grey hedges. There had at least been a proximate cause for the latter, he being a native of the state of Kansas and used to having his gaze roam with the untethered ambition of the first settlers, greedily swallowing panoramas that stretched the retina like a piece of elastic. In comparison with such vertiginous freedoms, to endure the landscape of east Devon was as to be trapped in a maze.

But his mood stemmed from more than simple geographical displacement and exhibited unsettling contradictions for one in his position – someone who was, in his own mind at least, a career soldier, now presented with the opportunity his whole being yearned for: to fight.

"I can't get used to how tiny this country is."

This from his driver, Private Tyrone Benedict, as they negotiated the blind switchbacks on the approach to the square – switchbacks that caused the publicity photograph of the actress Madeleine Carroll, honorary 'daughter of the regiment', that had been propped up on the dashboard, to fall to the floor.

"It's just like some kid's toy... like them toy farms they make, with them little bitty sheep and cattle."

"My word, Private, I never realised what a poetic soul you have."

"Yes, sir. A tiny little country."

Benedict, a gaunt and spotty car mechanic from Tennessee, clearly wished to talk, or perhaps he was one of those men who, though naturally taciturn, when struck by some inspiration, must continue to reflect upon it, and are unable to keep those reflections to themselves.

"How come a tiny little country like this kept them Nazis at bay 'til we come in to help 'em?"

"I guess that English Channel had something to do with it," Bellucci replied dryly. "If it weren't for that, what, twenty miles of water between them and France, the English'd be bowin' the knee to Herr Hitler right now, you can depend upon it, son... Anyway, you might as well ask yourself how come an itsy bitsy little country like this is ends up rulin' half the world."

"Shucks, Major, that's quite beyond me."

"Backbone, Private. Those places, full of niggers and such like, ain't got the sense nor the backbone to stand up to 'em. Nobody had savin' us. That's what yer history teaches you, son. Now we's gotta come over here and save 'em like we did in '18. Can you make sense outta that?"

"I guess it's what we's made to do."

That was the irony of it. It was what Bellucci was made to do. True, he was a draftsman by trade. But he had joined the Officers' Reserve Corps in 1933, the year the President created the Civilian Conservation Corps, which recruited unemployed men to work under the martial aegis of the Organised Reservists. He was quickly promoted to commanding officer of the CCC in the Hiawatha National Forest in Michigan.

At first the novel thrill of command captured him, for he had always known he had that within him – he called it 'spunk' – to be a natural leader, but felt he had, at college, at work, been passed over for responsibility in favour of those – he designated them 'ass-lickers' or 'Yale mincers'– who had gained preferment on account of their background, speech and manners.

But the thrill of wielding the baton soon paled with a consciousness of the futility of instilling only a modicum of discipline in the ungovernable detritus of the dust bowl. He returned to draftsmanship only to find that he pined for the baton once again, and however much he might admire the finely drawn plan or elevation, that representation was not amenable to drill, and however much he might deplore the creations of Bauhaus or Frank Lloyd Wright, they were impervious to amendment by a barked command or a week's latrine detail.

"It's what we done left our families fer and come over here," Benedict added.

HIS family? Bellucci's wife, Dorothy, had left him two years since for a household appliance salesman from Utah, taking their two-year-old son, Herman, with her to Cedar

City. He had not seen the lad for eighteen months, and feared that under the mother's influence he would become what he regarded as 'a faggot', a term used loosely to describe any who did not live up to his prototype of masculinity.

And so, when the President ordered all Organised Reservists into active service for the duration of the war, Bellucci was more than happy to return to the home that was most congenial to him. He exchanged the honesty and simplicity of the well-pressed gaberdine of the US Army for that shabby civilian garb, frayed at wrist and turnup with uncertainty and indecision, patched at elbow with compromise, faded and stained with submission to unworthy authority. Posted to the 'Stonewall Brigade', the 116th, at Fort A.P. Hill, Bellucci was whole again.

"You reckon? Comin' here?"

"Well, I guess the President knows what he's doin'."

The major had not thought to wonder at the belts and flywheels that translated the will of the commander-in-chief into actions by the likes of himself. It was not for him to question an authority he looked upon, in contrast to that of the civilian corporation to which he had been subject, as legitimate, and, moreover, noble and manly. Yet now he found himself doing just that.

"You guess, do you? Had his head turned by that Churchill guy. The guy could talk the hind leg offa a donkey."

"But them Nazis gone and declared war on us, didn't they, sir?"

"That they did. But what do you think they can do to us? You think they can blitzkrieg their way into Washington DC? 'Course they can't. And they wouldn't have done it neither if Roosevelt hadn't bent over backwards to give Churchill anything he wanted."

"Ma brother, he says we ain't got no quarrel with them Nazis and Eyetalians. He says they's keepin' the Commies at bay and stoppin' 'em takin' over Europe."

"Well, your brother's a wise man. Ain't nobody with a lick of sense wants a bunch of reds tellin' us how we gotta live our lives."

"But the Brits done good up to now, ain't they, Major?"

The major's opinion of his allies, already so low it was doubtful if there was a lead capable of plumbing it, had, almost literally, sunk even further during the Atlantic crossing when their troopship, the converted liner *Queen Mary*, collided with its escort, the cruiser *HMS Curaçoa*.

"Done good? Why, son, you got no idea. They sent their little army to France, and first sight of a German tank they's high-tailin' it outta there, leavin' the Frenchies to it, and headin' for the beaches so's theys could be picked up and tekken on home. Shit, it was the biggest goddam evacuation in history, and they's celebratin' it like some goddam victory!

"And look what they done in the desert. Bagged a few thousand Eyeties that didn't want to fight, then old Rommel comes along and they's skeedaddlin' faster'n a possum with a rattler on his tail. Shit, boy, it was only the Australians that stuck it out in Tobruk or them Egyptian pyramids'd have Nazi swastikas on 'em by now."

"But they won at El Amalein, didn't they, sir?"

"Rommel was over-extended is all. That's why they didn't get their asses whupped yet agin."

They turned into the market square, and Bellucci raised his hand to halt the column, whose vehicles fanned out behind him, edging round the market cross, sending shoppers scuttling for places of safety.

"Krantz!" Bellucci bawled as he stood up in the jeep.

Corporal Krantz exited his jeep and came running across the cobbles.

"Keep the men and vehicles here while I go and find out where we gonna be billeted."

"Yessir."

"And make some goddam room and let me out!"

As Benedict reversed cautiously between the vehicles which were making way for him, he asked:

"Where's we headin' fer, sir?"

"The vicarage. Next to the church. Look fer the church tower. Gotta find me the vicar. What sorta goddam country is this when a major in the United States army has to take his orders from a parson?"

The sort of country Bellucci did not like. He was a man who, if he did not always know who his friends were, prided himself on being able to identify his enemies, both at local level and international.

This war had now injected an unsettling uncertainty into his world view. He had always nursed a sneaking admiration for Fascist regimes, foreign though they may be: for the way in which Adolf (Aydolf in his parlance) Hitler had imposed order on a society grown decadent under the Weimar Republic, undermined by an effeminate relativism and corrupted by the deviancies of a Jewish intelligentsia; for the way in which Franco had stamped on the Communists and anarchists who would have turned Spain into a chaotic talking shop. Even Mussolini had achieved good things, although Bellucci could not but think of the man as a buffoon.

England, on the other hand, he always saw as the enemy. The enemy in the revolutionary war, the founding myth of his country, and in the war of 1812; the country that had enslaved a quarter of the world in its empire. But not the United States of America! Not Uncle Sam, no sir! Uncle Sam was made of sterner stuff than would bend to the imperial yoke.

Bellucci was a man who looked the world squarely in the face, and, not deigning to wait until it came to him, and true to the motto of his regiment, marched forward to meet it. He did so in step and metronomically in time, looking not back nor to the side, and even the hint of a deviation was met with an inaudible stentorian bellow to get in step and dress ranks. The rifling of his mind sent its bullets unerringly to their target, and that target was any enemy of his country, defied to deviate on pain of onerous fatigues. His progress through a world of strange arcs and baffling convolutions was that of an overwound clockwork toy of a major in the United States army, the greatest army in the world, the mailed fist of the greatest nation under God's sun, yes sir!

Except that Major John Bellucci had never experienced that to which his whole life had been dedicated, namely combat. It was his dearest wish he be granted the opportunity to prove himself in what was, in his eyes, the only true test of a man. Then why this doubt? He was on foreign soil, with the anticipation of confronting his country's enemy, an outcome without which his life would have been a sham, as if he were an actor condemned to perpetual understudy, never to set foot on stage before an audience. Every breath he had taken had been with a view to a situation such as this, and if history had not gifted him it, he would have been no more than a chocolate soldier decorating a Christmas tree. Why then, this feeling which was, to one so straightforward and downright as he, the most frustrating of all, of ambiguity?

His enemies were his country's enemies, his friends his country's friends, which he defined as those nations who did what Uncle Sam told them to do, his incarnation of that avuncular gentleman being an imperative one. But here was a situation in which his country, the good old US of A, because it was plain and downright and backwoodsman like himself, had been duped by a nation more sophisticated and cunning of ancient lineage, and that huckster and flim-flam man Churchill, into coming to the rescue of their goddam empire. His country, the greatest country under God's sun, had been tret like some goddam Huck Finn. It had been conned into hazarding its wealth and the blood of its youth on the last throw of the dice by the sleaziest down-at-heel river gambler, his cuffs frayed, holes in his boots, and possessed only of the coin of cunning.

First Roosevelt persuaded the House of Representatives to approve the Lend Lease Bill, abandoning the stance of absolute neutrality the nation demanded, and the security zone was pushed ever eastward to protect the convoys. All this was done in defiance of American public opinion, polls having shown a majority against financial aid for the British, even after the Nazi invasion of Norway. Then after he had said as late as 30 October 1941 that American boys were not going to be sent into any foreign war, Roosevelt had been seduced by an old corruption, and against the wishes of the US people, committed the seed of the greatest country on God's earth to coming to the aid of that corruption when it had once again bitten off more than it could chew.

If Bellucci had not been constrained by his rank, he would have shared a platform with Lindbergh and Congressman Nye and the American First Committee, standing against Lend Lease and the repeal of the Neutrality Acts. The bitter irony was that Bellucci, as an officer in the US military, was subject to the will of the commander-in-chief, the representative of American democracy, the greatest democracy in the world, and found all his inclinations resistant to that will, yet nevertheless bound to perform it.

"Get outta the way, can't yer!" Benedict yelled. "Goddam injun." 'Injun' being the term Benedict used indiscriminately for anyone not manifestly white or black.

It was a further paradox for the major that, in his opinion, war was the best thing that could happen for his country. The USA, once so strong and wholesome, was tending to a state of diversity and degeneration. That diversity, of which his racial antecedents, even if he chose not to admit it, were part, resulted in a dilution of the national will and purpose. It sapped the resilience, the sheer stubbornness, that had enabled the first settlers to tame the wilderness and subdue those savages that occupied the old frontier. The collective will that had forged a continent was being eroded by the increasing confidence of races that had hitherto been subservient to those Americans who hailed from Europe.

The newspapers were full of stories about the criminal activities of zoot-suit-wearing black and Mexican teenagers, particularly in the wake of the murder by the 38th Street gang of Jose Diaz at the Sleepy Lagoon. Such youngsters, with their love of jazz (monkey music in Bellucci's opinion) and unconventional clothing and, not least, their flaunting of segregation and lack of respect for authority, threatened the fabric of his country, and he, being a military man, could see no effective remedy for those ills, other than a war that would require the delinquents to relinquish their outlandish attire and adopt not only the uniform, but also the principles of those conservative elites the army represented.

Of course, the Nazis had declared war, but for Bellucci, as with many Americans, in the aftermath of Pearl and the Japanese capture of the Philippines, Guam, Wake and the other US possessions in the Pacific, it was the east that was the critical sphere of operations from the point of view of US interests. But Roosevelt had been seduced by the Brits into committing resources to Europe, and, even worse, delaying any invasion on the pretence that they were not yet ready, to concentrate on the recovery of the sideshow that was North Africa.

*

They were before the vicarage, a substantial property of fifty years or more whose brick was of a rich red colour. A dozen sash windows with oriental blinds flashed in the sun as Benedict drew up on the gravel drive, just in time to avoid hitting a square planter overflowing with hostas.

Bellucci rolled down his sleeves, concealing the death's head tattoo on his right forearm.

"Stay here while I speak to the vicar."

As Bellucci was about to shut the door his driver asked: "You nervous, Major?"

When Bellucci looked enquiringly at the private, he went on:

"I won't knows how to talk to these folk. I know they speak American, but it ain't the same as us, is it? I done read that book they give us (he referred to *The Short Guide to Great Britain* published by the US War Department as an introduction to the eccentricities of the strange land they now inhabited, and which cautioned the GIs, amongst other things, against criticising the Royal Family, the food, beer or cigarettes, or saying that they won the last war, or boasting about what they were paid) and I can't see how Is'll ever understand their money, if'n I live here twenty years, with them hu'pennies and tuppenny bits."

"Ain't Bob Hope explained it to yer well enough?"

"I guess not."

Bellucci had also read the *Short Guide* and was deeply suspicious of its assertion that the Brits did not want just a wartime alliance but a friendship that survives the peace and becomes a force for shaping the new world.

Likewise the film *Welcome to Britain*, which he and his men had viewed, narrated by Burgess Meredith and featuring Bob Hope. In addition to lecturing them in pious terms about not wolfing down food when invited to tea because the poor locals could not afford such lavish hospitality, the film proceeded to warn them that there are fewer social restrictions on coloureds in Britain, and even to interview General Lee, the chief of supply, who assures the viewer in silky terms that the black has been promised full citizenship, and they should all respect each other. For Bellucci the whole thing was nothing more than an experiment bound to end in disaster.

He said:

"It's threpenny bits, son. And I advise you to study hard or these folks whose empire we come here to save is gonna cheat you outta every dollar. Don't you forget, we's richer than they is, and they'd like nuthin' better than to redress the balance."

Bellucci's boots crunched across the gravel, and he found himself facing a stout door boasting a lion's head knocker and topped by a fan window around which purple wisteria wound. Feeling much the same discomfiture to which Benedict had confessed, but swallowing it down and feeling it burn through his innards like a mouthful of bourbon, Bellucci rapped the knocker against the door. Within a couple of seconds, as if the occupant had been lying in wait, Bellucci heard a click and felt the door move away from him. He dropped his hand like a pickpocket caught in the act, secreting the guilty implement in the pocket of his trousers.

He found himself staring down into the lightly rouged face of a middle-aged woman, forty at least, its complacent fleshiness framed by a profusion of chestnut curls. She wore a tweed skirt and a cream-coloured blouse whose understatement emphasised the string of enormous beads that encircled her neck. She smiled uncertainly but with discreet comprehension, as if she had been expecting to see him but was surprised nevertheless.

"Ah! You must be…"

"Major John Bellucci, ma'am, 116th Infantry Regiment, at your service."

"Ah yes, Bellucci… Italian… Delightful."

"I guess, ma'am. Some ways back."

"Please, forgive me. Do come in."

She turned briskly and he followed her over the threshold, getting immediate whiffs of floor polish and dog.

"I was told to see the Reverend Villiers."

"My husband is in the study, working on Sunday's sermon."

She opened the door to her right, and Bellucci was ushered into a room of wonderful light and airiness, in which the sun and brilliant white paintwork conspired to sting the major's eyes. The vicar sat at a desk in the big bay window. Books bound in every imaginable hue clung to the walls either side of him.

The Reverend Villiers was a small-faced, sallow man, his jet-black hair parted severely down the middle as if someone had been disturbed in an attempt to bisect his skull. There was a brief delay before he became aware of the American's presence, then he shot from his seat with the precipitation of an overly eager schoolboy at the entrance of his master.

"Major Bellucci, sir. I was told to report to you on my arrival."

"Of course, of course."

The vicar threw down his mother-of-pearl fountain pen, sending a tiny spray of ink over the blotter, and advanced on Bellucci, the two wings of his cardigan flapping loose about him, and wiped his palm vigorously on his corduroy trousers. He was dressed less for the study than the garden. A hand of unnatural whiteness was thrust towards Bellucci's midriff. It felt like a bird's wing in Bellucci's vice-like grip.

"I was just working on Sunday's sermon. Mark 13."

Bellucci had no use for religion, but, as a leader of men knew its value in convincing those he led that God was on their side, and that howsoever reckless or inadvisable their actions or hopeless their position, the close relationship – or even equivalence, down to the top hat and Stars and Stripes – of God and Uncle Sam would save them from harm.

Although not of a religious bent, Bellucci had nevertheless often been heard to utter, or formulate in his own mind without articulation, the phrase 'God bless America'. In his mouth it was not merely a plea to an almighty he did not really believe in. It was also an instruction to a deity who, if He did exist, must be American, and an assertion that, whatever that country chose to do, God would bless America.

Bellucci looked at the vicar with a bemusement guilty in its ignorance but nevertheless bridling at the fact.

"Well, might the Lord say of this our age 'watch ye therefore; for ye know not when the master of the house cometh, at even, or at midnight, or at the cock-crowing, or in the morning. Lest coming suddenly he find you sleeping.'"

Bellucci, who had no conception of what the Gospel writer meant, nevertheless agreed insofar as his own experience allowed, reflecting on the punishments he were likely to inflict upon any sentry caught sleeping at his post.

The vicar spoke in that high-pitched singsong that some Britishers had, and that Bellucci was pleased to regard as effeminate. Beside the reverend's bright fragility, he felt himself to be a lumpen being, one altogether more primitive, and was obliged to remind himself that the parson was the representative of a culture, that while effete and decadent and far less vigorous than his own, possessed a rich store of corruption, garnered over the centuries and calculated to tarnish the purity and simplicity of anything transatlantic. When it was his turn to speak, his voice sounded unnaturally loud, fit to shatter the fragile porcelain in the bureau to which his gaze was directed.

"I was told to report to you, sir, and you would tell me where my men could bed down."

"Of course," said the vicar. "I will show you directly. Might I first ask, for we have had very sparse information, what sort of troops you have under your command?"

"Infantry mostly, but only five companies as yet. Also Quartermaster detachments, signals, bomb disposal squads, pay and salary clerical men. Plus MPs – that's Military Police. We also have some communication and postal units."

At this point their discussion was interrupted by a crashing from upstairs, with the sound of a banging door and a child's wailing interspersed with increasingly forlorn pleas of "Arthur, Arthur."

"I do apologise, Major," said Mrs Villiers. "That is Arthur, one of our two evacuees from London. Not having any children of our own we had wanted to take one of the Jewish refugees – the Kindertransport. The way the Germans treat the Jews is really quite barbaric. Mr and Mrs Chalmers took on Manfred, and he has settled very well. But it was not possible in our case, so we were determined to do our bit when the evacuation started.

"He's always been a difficult charge, Arthur, not like our other one, Isabel, who has settled perfectly into the country life. Of course, when they come to you they are often in a dreadful condition, with nits, lice, some young girls with no nightwear. Had never seen an inside toilet. Quite shocking. It opens one's eyes to the terrible conditions some of these children have to grow up in, and makes one determined to ensure a better future for them. Rather tongue-tied and suspicious as well of course, but that's only to be expected. And of course, they don't understand why they've been sent away, thinking perhaps that their parents don't love them anymore, the poor dears. And the things some of them have witnessed…

"But Arthur, just when it seemed he was finally settling in – the language he used to come out with at first you wouldn't believe… well, of course you would, being a soldier, what am I saying – but now he has gone backwards. I don't know if you've heard of the Bethnal Green tube tragedy, Major?"

"Er, no, ma'am."

"Well, I'm not sure myself whether it was bombed or whether there was some sort of panic, but 173 people, including many children, were killed. And one of them, sadly, was Arthur's mother. He's up there now, being attended to by Mrs Burns, one of our ladies, who is a Londoner herself, and has experience of the bombing. We can just hope… well, time is a great healer. I'll go and see to them."

"Yes, ma'am."

Mrs Villiers bustled out of the room with a compound of tweedy gusto and practicality.

"You were saying, Reverend," said Bellucci, the storm from above having abated.

"Yes. I've been given instructions as to the broad categories into which your men might fit, and where they're to be billeted, and I trust that is acceptable to you. The senior officers are to be housed in the Devonshire Hotel, which you will find at the end of Sherborne Road. Junior officers are to be billeted in the Manor House, just behind the market square. I assure you they'll find the accommodation most comfortable. Other ranks are to be housed in Nissen huts in Farmer Westwood's field on the western edge of town."

"Nissen huts, Reverend?"

"Semi-circular huts of corrugated iron. I am assured there are separate washing and toilet facilities and each is equipped with a coke-burning stove to keep the rigours of our English winters at bay. I believe some men from the British Catering Corps are on hand until you get things ship-shape. How many men do you have, Major?"

"Seven hundred and fifty, Reverend, with another 600 to come in two weeks."

"That many, indeed. We were forewarned of little more than half that number."

"We have our own bell tents, if the need arises."

"Oh, I trust that won't be necessary. A number of my parishioners have volunteered to have your young men in their homes – put them up, you know, not just have them for tea, although I am certain that invitations of that nature will also be extended to them."

"Thank you kindly. I should warn you, Reverend… Villiers… that although there ain't no black troops amongst my men as yet, they'll be arriving in the next few months, and… it were best I speak to you on that… mebbe a little later."

Bellucci realised his discomposure was not so much due to the subject matter of his speech, as an unconscious attempt to ameliorate his Midwest drawl. The realisation brought shame and an instinctive pugnacity in its wake. Everything about this goddam country made his flesh creep.

"Well, they will be very welcome," said the vicar, smiling his suave, complacent smile.

But the vicar had entirely misunderstood the intent of Bellucci's words, and the latter thought, *We'll see just how welcome the niggers are when they get here.*

"I have to caution you that the farmer, a Mr Westwood, was none too pleased about his land being taken for your use. Pugnacious fellow, rather cross-eyed. If he should say anything to you, please take no notice."

"We'll pay him no mind."

The vicar went on as if he had not heard him:

"It's a bit windswept, I'm afraid."

Can't these people utter a sentence without an apology in it? thought Bellucci, who never apologised for anything. In his view, to apologise was the worst thing of all, un-American. Just as the United States of America never had anything to apologise for, since whatever it did must always be right, neither did he, that country's proud instrument.

"Better if we had found you something in the valley, but there's the risk of flooding. And I daresay you hardy frontiersmen will not mind a bit of wind off the sea."

Bellucci smiled wanly. That was another thing with these people: you always felt they were laughing up their sleeve at you.

The vicar went on:

"But let me say what a reassurance it is to have you chaps on our shores. When I think back to the dark days of '40 when the RAF were doing battle with the Luftwaffe over our very heads, and Herr Hitler was readying his troop transports to invade. Then we had but our faith to sustain us, and while that may have been enough for some of us, for others, alas… We are not all blessed with a sustaining faith; one could tell who was and who was not just by looking into their eyes, although doubtless there were some that put a brave face on it in the grocer's queue, but once their doors closed behind them were liable to give way to the most natural of fears. One of my parishioners told me she would wake in the night to the sound of jackboots marching up and down outside her cottage.

"And then the bombs started falling. We may be some distance from Portsmouth, but it's widely believed the Luftwaffe jettisoned their unused bombs on us when returning from raids on Bristol, particularly the 3 January raid, when a bomb fell on Cordwainer's Row, and one on Lampton Street, and a couple of incendiaries on the new estate. Eleven people were killed in all, including Kate Middlewich and her daughter. Yes, our public shelters proved quite inadequate, lacking proper mortar, and the fire service was stretched to its limit. Some people blamed Mayor Markle, but that was most harsh… The sewage was lying in the streets. Most dreadful. Even last September in Lonsdale Road five people died.

"Yes, you chaps are most welcome. Coming on the fall of Singapore and the sinking of the *Prince of Wales* and *Repulse*, it was as if the Good Lord had answered our prayers for deliverance. Indeed, answered the prayers of the civilised world."

"Please take no notice of my husband," said the vicar's wife, who had re-entered the room, "he is inclined to be somewhat discursive. It's a habit he has endeavoured to curb, after many subtle and not so subtle hints, in his sermons, but, alas, once out of the pulpit, those words are inclined to flow rather freely."

"My dear, I was simply extending a welcome to the major and his brave men."

Bellucci's emphatic chauvinism squirmed in the presence of this effete civilisation like a woodlouse exposed to the air by the removal of its stone.

"What my husband is trying to say, Major, is that we in Chalford, who, we must remember, have had it easy compared with the experience of many of our cities, are very grateful for your help, and are sure that with America at our side we cannot but overcome the barbaric shadow of Nazism."

It was more likely, Bellucci thought cynically, that Uncle Sam would be in the vanguard and the Brits quivering behind.

The woman, who seemed to be her husband's equal in discursiveness, if it meant rambling, went on:

"We shall do everything in our power to make what must be a difficult and novel experience for your men as comfortable as we may. Since the announcement that American troops would be arriving on our shores, we have been racking our brains for the means to make you welcome and I am sure we shan't disappoint."

"I am afraid disappoint is what we shall inevitably do, my dear," the vicar corrected. "We simply cannot provide the comforts your men have been used to at home. Almost four years of war have taken their toll…"

Was that some sort of implied criticism, Bellucci wondered. It was maddening how he could not read these people. They might speak the same language, but it might as well be Mandarin as far as he was concerned.

"Although the body may be lacking, the will most certainly is not. We have provided ourselves (the cardigan flapped negligently in the direction of the bookshelves) with a copy of Mr MacNeice's *Meet the US Army*, and cannot but agree that if this war with all its consequent horrors and privations is good for anything it is the bringing together of the sons of the two great English-speaking nations, that the moral authority of our shared pacifism may prevail over militaristic nations that see in war an end in itself."

These airy platitudes quite passed over Bellucci's head.

"Well, Reverend, the way it was told to me our camp's gonna be a home from home and anything we need'll be given us – newspapers, cigarettes, even movies – so we don't want for nothin' and if the army don't look after us, the ARC sure (he successfully resisted the temptation to add 'as hell') will. So don't you good people mind none about that."

The vicar's wife clapped her hands together, quite startling Bellucci.

"Oh, what a gentlemanly way you have of talking, Major. It's so sweet. I hope our young fellows learn from your example. The way some of them speak these days it really is too coarse."

"Why, thank you kindly, ma'am."

"But no, you shan't escape us that easily, Major. We ladies have been hard at work preparing for your arrival. Our WVS under the redoubtable Mrs Cadwallader have set up a welcome club for you and your men, and anything that goodwill can provide will be 'given unto you' as my husband would say. We are already planning your first tea party."

"Well, that sounds just swell, but we don't want to put you out, ma'am."

Bellucci's smile was a wry one.

"Not at all. And the offer of accommodation in our humble homes, including this one, stands. They are more than welcome. Our ladies would be quite down in the mouth were you to disappoint."

"Well, that's mighty kind of you."

The vicar said:

"Well, Major, you have the look of a man who needs to be rescued from an excess of feminine hospitality. If there is anything you need, any little word I can put in to grease the wheels, just let me know. And please tell your men they will be most welcome at our services. The times for Matins and Evensong are on the board in front of the church. One thing we have learned from our recent tribulations is that the word of the Lord is the greatest comfort of all, and I am sure your men must feel that quite as much as any of us.

"And any who wish to simply visit the church, to sit in quiet contemplation, in which they may find some solace as the prospect of conflict looms, are welcome. There is much to admire in St Edward King and Martyr… Am I right in thinking you don't know the sorry story?"

"Of course the major doesn't—"

"Well, Edward inherited the throne on the death of King Edgar. However, his younger brother Ethelred coveted the throne, and in 978 the king was murdered by Ethelred's retainers at Corfe. And after the body was interred, the late king was regarded as a saint.

"I don't like to boast, but the church is quite the most splendid in Devon. That is on account of it being the abbey foundation. One can still see part of the original cloisters. The apse is twelfth century. And you must see the fan tracery, so delicate one wonders at the artistry of these ancient folk. And of course, the great bell itself, Old Tom. It is said that Old Tom was a villager who led the defence of the church against the Roundheads…"

Bellucci coughed discreetly, or as discreetly as was possible in a man in whom discretion was one of those cardinal sins that came under the giant umbrella of 'un-American'. The vicar recollected himself.

"Now, I suggest I show you the field where your men can camp, and then your officers' billets. It's just a short walk. No need to take your motor…?"

Bellucci suddenly realised he was being asked a question.

"Jeep?" he suggested.

"Jeep, yes. All these new words we have had to learn since this conflict arose. I never imagined the language we had grown up with to be so inadequate."

Bellucci, anxious to escape this urbane verbosity, which suggested ever more strongly to him, effeminacy, donned his cap and, after tipping it to Mrs Villiers, was led by the vicar out into the hall, where the latter grabbed coat and hat and walking stick from the stand by the door, and they exited the house.

*

Forty-five minutes later, Bellucci and Benedict were heading back to the market square. The vicar had not been wrong when he described the field as windswept, the major reflected. He had been conscious as he tramped across the thankfully well-drained earth, of a salty tang in the air, as if it came unimpeded straight off the Atlantic.

They turned back into the market square, only to find that what had been a bare expanse of cobbles occupied only by an abandoned market stall, with one or two housewives carrying baskets, now had the air of a circus big top. At the centre of all were their own vehicles, but entirely surrounding these were more people than Bellucci had imagined the town to contain.

The jeeps in the foreground were engulfed by a swarm of schoolchildren, aged perhaps from ten to sixteen, the boys in short trousers, with caps on their heads, most sporting lurid scabs on their knees as if they were badges of honour, the girls in bonnets, and many of both sexes draped with cardboard gas mask cases. He heard one boy shouting at a sergeant through the windscreen:

"Hey, Mister Yank, you got any sweets on yer?"

And another:

"You got any gum?"

To which the GI responded:

"You got a sister, mister?"

"Yeah, she's twelve and always pickin' her nose."

Three of the GIs inadvisably decided to dole out candy and were immediately surrounded by raised hands and screams. Someone tried to restrain them with a:

"Hey, you nippers, stop that." But to no avail.

Some blushing girls were eyeing a group of GIs who had got out of their vehicles to stretch their legs, and who, under this close scrutiny, posed languidly with cigarettes between their lips in imitation of Paul Henreid or Gary Cooper. One even put his fingers in his mouth and whistled at them.

The high-pitched voice of a schoolboy pierced the general hubbub:

"Show us yer gun then."

To Bellucci's horror, one of the urchins attempted to climb up the tailboard of a lorry, from between the canvas canopy of which appeared the faces of GIs, some appearing to encourage the adventurous youth, who had to be restrained by a private pulling at his jacket and causing his school cap to fall to the ground. The boy, with a 'Hey, mister, wha'd ya do that for?', picked the cap up, dusted it off, wiped a drool of snot from his nose, swung the case for his Mickey Mouse gas mask around his body, and walked disconsolately away with this Parthian shot:

"My dad's in the Eighth Army. He's been fightin' Rommel, and he's gotta bigger gun than you. He's got a Bofor's gun."

Bellucci's gaze swivelled round to where a knot of his men were engaged in animated conversation with two young women carrying shopping baskets. Both girls wore heavy coats, the more matronly one a floral headscarf, the attractive younger one a blue hat bound with ribbon. Neither appeared to be wearing makeup; perhaps they did not have it in this country. One of the privates offered them gum. The attractive girl giggled, while the older squealed:

"Oh you're not, Em!"

She appeared reluctant to accept the gum, as if it were the very apple from the Garden of Eden itself, but then put out tentative fingers and drew a strip from the pack.

A group of three signalsmen were accosted by two elderly matrons, one spreading wide her arms in what may have been a gesture of welcome. Unfortunately, it was lost on the three men who, whilst smiling politely, were casting envious eyes in the direction of the two young women.

A middle-aged man in a sports jacket with leather patches at the elbows, his cap pulled down tight and ears protruding at the sides, was lighting up outside a building with the sign of a crown hanging from a pole, and named the King's Arms, which Bellucci identified as the typical British pub. The man raised his face from his cigarette and stared at the soldiers milling about the square. Another man, without jacket but sporting a waistcoat with watch chain dangling from its pocket, and chewing on the stem of a pipe, had just exited the pub and was saying to the first:

"Look at this 'ere bleedin' shower. Call theirselves soldiers. Look at 'em, Alf, 'ands in their pockets, chewin' gum. They wants sending over to Africa and get theirselves a taste of real soldierin'."

"Tha's roight," said the other, "and a bit o' smartenin' up. Spit and polish. Discipline is what they wants. Ain't they never seen a woman afore? Don't they 'ave women where they come from?"

"Well, they don't have no sergeant major, that's fer sure. That's what they wants. Somebody that'll put the wind up 'em good and proper. No way to run an army, if you ask me. And they expects to beat the Germans. Gawd 'elp 'em."

They come over here to save this shithole and its precious empire and… It was all Bellucci could do to stop himself walking over and smacking the two of them in the face. This was going from bad to worse. Facing the Wehrmacht could, he thought, only be an improvement on this.

*

Back in his study at the vicarage, the vicar resumed work on his sermon whilst Mrs Villiers loitered on the pretence of arranging a display of carnations in a glass vase. After some minutes of contemplation, she said:

"I must say that if the major is anything to judge by, our American friends are frightfully polite and not at all what one might expect from watching these gangster films. Definitely more of your Ronald Colman than Jimmy Cagney."

"You've seen *Random Harvest* too many times, my dear. And I believe Ronald Colman is English. Personally, I do not care for the man; his face is too close. He seems to lack charity."

"Really?"

"And to occupy more space than his frame entitles him to. The study seemed to positively expand when he left."

"You are too harsh, my dear. He's just shy."

"Certainly, he is uncomfortable as a social being. That I suspect is down to absorption in his work. But you must also remember that we would not judge our own troops, brave boys that they undoubtedly are, by their officers."

"Really, Frederick, I would have thought you would welcome this opportunity. You might quite double your congregation."

"That would depend on which faith the major's men espouse. Certainly, the more people I might reach with God's word at this perilous hour the better, but do not let us, in our open-handed anxiety to welcome the doughboys, as I think they are known, be blind to the dangers inherent in our situation. Surely Mrs Cadwallader, with her restless vigilance for our morals, has impressed those dangers upon your WVS ladies."

"Indeed she did, and in the most lurid and sensational terms a meeting of the WVS would admit of. However, it is clear she has a lower opinion of the morals of the girls of this town than I have. She does not take into account the effect of a good Christian upbringing as the foundation for sound moral principle. Our gals are not going to throw that off for a smart uniform and an American accent, however many Clark Gable pictures they've seen."

"I sincerely trust you are right, my dear," said the vicar, crumpling up his latest attempt at Christian exhortation and throwing it in the waste paper basket.

"But you forget the land girls, who have come from backgrounds we cannot imagine, but may assume are less grounded in scripture than our young women. Moreover, even we ourselves are not immune from the ills that beset the city. Think on Ted Barkiss going about whispering in everyone's ear, 'You don't need any coupons when you deal with me', and Mrs Ford passing her forged clothing coupons."

"Oh but, Frederick, that was an innocent mistake. Really, to hear you talk you would think our little town a perfect Sodom and Gomorrah. A few Americans are unlikely to corrupt us."

"But what might they do when they clap eyes on the land girls?"

"I confess I am concerned about that. Corduroy breeches, ill-fitting jerseys and no baths allowed are unlikely to put off young men so far from the influence of their womenfolk. One can only take comfort from the fact that there aren't many."

"Half a dozen at most."

"And if there are rumours, the Rep might always step in."

"Comforting as that may be, my dear, the fact is that the more inaccessible the land girls are the more the American youth are likely to gravitate towards our own. What is more, what will be the effect on the morale of our brave soldiers were it to get back to them that while they're risking their lives, their sweethearts, or even – God forbid – their wives, were excessively friendly to these pampered Americans? You and your ladies must be ever vigilant to minimise all risks, and I am always of course on hand to offer spiritual counsel should the need arise."

"Let us hope then that the need does not arise," said his wife.

And the vicar, who often felt himself oversensitive to satire, did not know whether he should feel insulted by that remark. His response was to turn even gloomier in his predictions. As his wife departed to see how matters were progressing between Sally Burns and the recalcitrant Arthur, he said, as much to himself as to the lady's departing back:

"This is a community built on centuries of continuity. On order and tradition and the security derived from knowing one's neighbours and their antecedents. One cannot help fear its disruption in times such as these. And such a precious relic, once lost, cannot, I fear, be regained."

CHAPTER TWO

"And there was one of 'em whistled at me."

Emily France, and her friends Lucy Watson and Joyce Foster, were walking along Simpson Lane early that warm spring evening bound for the first house at the Gaumont.

Emily smiled a satirical smile.

"Are you sure he weren't whistlin' for his dog, Joycie?"

"He was whistlin' at me."

Joyce, who at twenty-one had progressed beyond the age at which her bulging flesh could be looked upon indulgently as puppy fat, and whose complexion bloomed with spots, adopted a vaguely offended air, as if unsure to what degree she should be offended, perhaps uncertain whether Emily had implied blindness on the part of the infatuated GI. Indeed, Emily herself was not sure whether she had intended the greater insult.

"I saw them when they come," said Lucy, patting down her curly brown locks in the manner she employed on being approached by a customer in the draper's shop where she worked, "walking down the street in their uniforms."

"And you went all mazed arter them."

"No I didden. But they was so 'andsome. So smart. Not like our boys in their rough khaki and hobnailed boots. Their uniforms was tailored."

"And they know how to wear them, if you know what I mean," said Emily.

They did. They knew it was not just the well-pressed gaberdine, but the assurance of the men in it, that contrasted so starkly with the Tommies, farmers' boys and short-sighted clerks, who wore their battledress like burlap sacks into which they had, like so much grain or a harvest of apples, been poured.

"It's like Hollywood has come to us."

"I know," said Joyce. "I looks at 'em and I tries to see who they's like. One was the spit of James Stewart. And… there was a Clark Gable, and a Gary Cooper. Only they was younger, so that's even better."

"They even know how to smoke better'n our lot," said Lucy, with a hint of the forlorn in her trilling contralto.

"Don't let Jim Fenton hear you say that. Where's your loyalty?" said Emily mischievously.

Lucy sucked in her full lips, bright red with the lipstick Emily coveted, hers being derived from chopped and strained beetroot, and adopted an archly aggrieved expression.

"I didn't say I'd wait for him, did I? There was no understandin' nor nothin' of that sort. Anyway, where's yours for Tom Dawkins?"

At that Emily simply laughed, and they joined the queue at its end in front of Peelers greengrocer's. From where they were, they could not even see the cinema entrance in Sherborne Street, and Emily hoped, rather fancifully, that they were not standing in a queue for a long overdue delivery of bananas.

"I said we should've gone to the second house," said Joyce. The second house was always more popular with the women, the men tending to gravitate towards the pubs.

They waited fifteen minutes, during which time the doors opened and they slowly wound their way around the corner and got their first view of the colonnaded stairs, the commissionaire in his braided uniform at the top, framed by the glass cases displaying stills from the picture.

In the nationwide hierarchy of cinemas, the Gaumont, which had opened its doors on a cut-price version, almost a pastiche, of Art Deco splendour, some ten years earlier, and situated in a small town in Devon, was pretty near the bottom. Consequently, Chalford audiences were only now being treated to the heroics of Noel Coward's *In Which We Serve*, with which London audiences had been familiar for months. It was not the sort of film the girls would normally have frequented, their taste being romantic melodramas, but in these days there were few, even amongst young girls, who were immune to the flag-waving impulse.

They were still at the back of the queue, with only one middle-aged couple, the woman sporting a fur stole for all the mildness of the evening, behind them.

"Hello, girls!"

The American twang rent the stillness of the night, like a bolt of electricity, telling of energy, of life, of modernity, of glamour.

There were five of them, all in a uniform that was not the typical American uniform, with white helmets with the initials MP and the same initials in white on a black armband on the left arm. On their shoulders they bore insignia in green with crossed pistols in gold and the motto 'Assist, Protect, Defend'. They wore gun belts with pistols in holsters. Two were tall, another short and stocky with an Errol Flynn moustache. One of medium height took the lead in speaking to them; he was blond, his face slightly flushed, and with full, fleshy lips that drew out the vowels, sent them arching and spinning like a lariat, and finally lassoed them in true cowboy style.

"Howdee, young ladies. Can you tell us boys so far from home, what this here movie is all about?"

Emily, who thrilled just to hear his words, especially the bewitching syllables of 'movie', found herself taking on the responsibility for replying while her two friends simply stood and gaped.

"The big picture's about the navy," she said, conscious of the incontinent breathiness of her voice, and endeavouring to rein in its high spirits. "It's about a ship, a Royal Navy ship."

"That gets sunk," said Joyce.

"Well, that don't sound much of a movie to raise the spirits," replied one of the GIs, who was very tanned with bushy black eyebrows and a grin that revealed impossibly white teeth.

"Yeah," said another, "how come they don't make a movie about sinkin' German ships?"

"I... I dunno," Emily said lamely.

"Strikes me like the sort of movie Herr Hitler's gonna wanna see." This from one of the taller men, who wore spectacles and had the air of a librarian, an impression compounded by his relative absence of a tan. But even librarians in America seemed to possess glamour, Emily reflected.

"Let's hope he ain't in the audience," said the short one.

"He'd better hope he ain't," said the second tall one, hunching his ample shoulders as if squaring up to the German dictator, a smile of malicious glee elevating prodigies of cheekbone.

The first spoke again:

"The way I sees it, ma'am, you Brits gotta be more like us. We don't make movies about our ships gettin' theirselves sunk. 'Tain't right."

"It's defeatist," said the librarian.

"Sure, defeatist, that's what it is. But that's just the way we sees it. We don't mean to come to your country and tell you what you should do, you understand."

"I should hope not," said the woman with the fur stole.

"No, ma'am, don't take it personal, we's just here to do our dootee. But I ain't doin' the gentlemanly thing. I should introduce myself. I'm Larry. Military Policeman Larry Schultz at your service. Excuse the German name. And this here's Duke. He might look ornery, but don't you pay him no mind. We call him Duke, but he's really Rudi Dolenz." He indicated the other tall man.

"Hey!" the latter objected. "I can speak for myself, can't I?"

"Well, go on then."

"Like he said, Rudi." The man had a slow way of speaking and the long drawl of his accent made him sound almost retarded.

"And I'm Stan... MP Stan Deacon," said the librarian.

"Luigi Risi," said the short man.

"Eugene Larkins," said the fifth.

"So you're all policemen?" Emily asked.

"Sure are, ma'am. Military Police Platoon 116th Infantry Regiment."

"But… but you're still soldiers?"

"Sure is. Just the soldiers that makes sure other soldiers behaves theirselves when they come to nice places like this is. They don't always appreciate what we do fer 'em, though."

Here the other four all laughed, as if it were a shared joke.

"Are… are you from New York… or Los Angeles," asked Joyce, as if these were the only two places in the whole of the United States.

"Los Angeles," replied Rudi, correcting her pronunciation. "Our platoon is based in Chicago, but we's from different places. I'm from Boston. Larry here, he's from Georgia. Stan, he's from North Carolina. Luigi from New York, and Eugene's from the Midwest – what's that place that ain't on no map?"

"Sure is on the map. Hastings, Nebraska."

"Ooh, just like the place on the south coast," said Joyce.

"You mean there's a Hastings in England as well?"

"Ees… Where the battle was."

"Oh, sure. Well, Stan and me, we met up when we was doin' our trainin' at Fort Riley Kansas. Then Larry, he joins us from the Provost Marshalls General School in Fort Myer – that's how come he's such an expert in the law an' all…"

The blond laughed heartily.

"Assist, Protect, Defend, that's me."

37

"...And then we met up with Rudi and Luigi at Fort Custer just afore we come over the pond."

"So what are we to call you three lovely ladies?" asked Stan.

Joyce, whose naive prattle had begun to embarrass, giggled like a schoolgirl, and Emily winced.

"I'm Emily, and this is Lucy and this is Joyce."

"Well, I'm mighty pleased to meet y' all."

"I guess we sure have been lucky," drawled Larry. "There can't be three prettier young ladies in all of England. And we just happened along here. Would you care for some gum?"

His excessive politeness verged on satire, but Emily was smitten nevertheless. There was something bright and metallic about his blue eyes and blond hair, something that reminded her of sunny, crisp days on the beach at Weymouth, so that when she looked at him, she could almost imagine the fresh, antiseptic smell of ozone on the breeze, the briny tang on her tongue. Blond hair and blue eyes can be chill, even dead traits, but in him the eyes in particular were full of life, drowningly deep and vibrant, and possessed of the attractiveness that knows it is attractive but is charming with it.

Larry took a pack from the top pocket of his jacket and offered it first to Emily who, blushing furiously, put out a delicate forefinger and took a strip. He then offered the pack to Lucy and Joyce who did likewise. Emily endeavoured to execute the unfamiliar task of unwrapping gum with the refined gestures she thought appropriate to a young lady, at the same time acutely conscious of Lucy staring at the item that lay between her thumb and forefinger as if it were a puzzle of a cunning sufficient to baffle the Brains Trust.

"Here, see." Larry took the strip, slit the paper with his nail and withdrew the gum, handing the latter back to her.

Joyce, meanwhile, was examining the procedure with an attention so acute as to suggest she was packing parachutes and her own life depended on the process. Emily found herself chewing with an unladylike vigour.

"Swell!" cried Rudi. "We wanna see you all chewin' gum and eatin' Hershey Bars. Just like in the good old US of A."

Emily laughed uneasily, nervously fingering hair which was drawn up in a side comb, and shooting a glance that she just restrained from being loathing but nevertheless was freighted with reproach at the two friends who had undermined her pretences to sophistication. She even felt resentment at the Americans, despite being overwhelmed by their exoticism, and determined henceforth to merit their interest and deserve their respect, even if it meant distancing herself from Lucy and, particularly, Joyce.

"You look to me," said Larry, "like the sort of gals that'd like to stretch their pins… in a dance."

The pause was ambivalent as to the deliberate suggestion of something other than dancing or the embarrassed attempt to contradict an unconscious suggestion of the same kind.

"Welllll, yess," said Emily, uncertain as to whether she was receiving a personal invitation.

"When we've had our fill of digging air raid slit trenches and endurance marches we wants a place of recreation where we can let our hair down."

"Don't you have anywhere at your camp?" Joyce asked, her ill-complexioned face naively open.

"Sure we do. But they're kinda strict about young ladies. They means to ship 'em in by bus, but they's gotta be vetted first, so I guess that means only the prim schoolmarms. And I'm kinda sick of dancin' with Gene. The doc says it's bad for my toes."

Emily felt compelled to cut Joyce off mid-giggle.

"There's the Astoria… in Charles Street… Just ask anyone."

"That's more like it, sister. Folks are sayin' you Brits don't know what jitterbuggin' is."

"And you ain't heard of the lindy-hop neither," said Luigi.

"We know the waltz, the foxtrot and the rhumba and the palais glide," said Joyce.

"Sister, you ain't seen dancin' 'til you seen the jitterbug. And the best jitterbuggers in the US Army is right here in this old town – me and my pal Luigi."

Joyce giggled again, probably at the use of the word 'jitterbuggers', to the implications of which the Americans were oblivious.

"Hey, whattabout me!" complained Eugene.

"Sorry, Gene, but you ain't got the smooth moves me and Luigi got."

The couple in front vacated the kiosk, and they were obliged to separate as the girls fumbled in their handbags for change, and the GIs had to allow the middle-aged couple to go before them on pain of much displeasure if the face of the woman, anticipating queue jumping, was anything to go by.

"Hey, you gals!" Larry shouted. "We'll look out for you at the Astoria."

"We go on Friday and Saturday nights!" Emily shouted back, attracting the middle-aged lady's scowl of disapproval.

"Em!" Lucy whispered in her ear.

"What?"

"You shouldn't."

"What?"

"Encourage them."

"Don't be so Victorian. It's only a dance. Don't you want to know what the jitterbug is?"

"It sounds rather rude," said Joyce.

"Well, you don't have to come," Emily retorted, rather hoping that her friend would take her at her word.

"I suppose it can't do no harm," Joyce said as they handed their tickets to the girl at the door to the auditorium and followed her weaving torchlight into the darkness as the opening credits to Pathé News blared out.

CHAPTER THREE

Larry flopped down on the bed in his Nissen hut fully clothed, twenty minutes before lights out.

"How'd ya like that movie? It ain't no wonder the Brits can't win Jack shit."

Gene, sucking on a Camel while pulling off his boots, replied:

"I can't understand a goddam word they say. That captain, uh, uh, uh, he was talkin' like he had a baseball bat stuck up his ass."

"That last speech was quite moving," said Stan, his long legs dangling over the end of the upper bunk.

"The only thing it'd move in me is my bowels."

"How come the officers speak different to what the sailors do?" Luigi asked.

"Ratings. The Brits call them ratings."

"Okay, smart ass, you know all about it, so how come?"

"I dunno. I guess it was the school they went to."

"They all went to the same school?"

Stan leaned out over the edge of the bunk.

"No. But it's like back home. Some guys go to Harvard

and Yale, other guys just hang around the street and get no education at all."

"Like Duke."

"Just like Duke."

They all laughed.

"Yeah," said Rudi, "but who got the music, eh? Who's the guy you all gotta come to to get a little swing?"

In the hut, which had little room for anything apart from the twenty two-tiered bunks and the stove at the far end (the warm end, as opposed to the other which housed those last to arrive), they had managed to excavate sufficient space for the gramophone which was standing on an upturned packing case, the side of which had been removed to accommodate a stack of records, next to Rudi's bunk.

"Sure," said Luigi, "you can't sing, you can't dance, but you got the gramophone."

"That's right."

"What you guys so happy about? You think we's at a party here?" said Randy Temple, from one of the bunks by the stove. The words were accompanied by a spray of saccharine shrapnel, Temple being engaged in munching on a doughnut he had bought from the PX[1]. Temple, an acerbic sharecropper from Tennessee who spent much time lamenting his separation from his thirteen-year-old bride, was addicted to doughnuts.

"Cos he's got hisself a lady friend is all," replied Stan, nodding, as if illustration were required, at the magazine picture of Betty Grable, showing off her famous legs to good effect, on the wall above Duke's bunk.

---

1   An American army service store

"Who?"

"Larry."

"He's got hisself three," said Gene.

"Aw shucks, she's just a girl I got talkin' to in the movie queue."

"Queues! If queues could win the war the Brits would have it won by now. Jesus! They queue for everything."

"That's 'cos everything's rationed," said Stan.

"Anyways," said Larry, as if he had not heard, "you was talkin' to her same as me."

"Not the same as you, buddy, no way."

"What, an English girl?" Temple asked.

"Like he smuggled hisself an American goyl into the country in his kitbag. Sure, an English goyl, asshole," retorted Luigi.

"Ain't no call to be like that." Temple's stock in trade was the aggrieved, the put-upon. He applied the preparation, sometimes with a spoon, sometimes a trowel, sometimes a spade. "I got a right to speak my mind. Ain't I got a right to speak my mind? All I say is I hope you got a peg or something to hold over your nose. They stink."

"Whadda you know about it, Temple?"

"They all stink in this country. I goes into a store, I goes into a bar, and there is this stink. Everywheres I go there's this stink."

"You goes into a store, and there's this stink, you goes into a bar and there's this stink. You never think you might be the stink?"

"Aw, come on. Do these people never wash?"

"And like you're so particular," said Stan, stretching

out his long legs and removing his boots. "Remember these people been at war nearly four years."

"Yeah," said Larry with derision. That was typical of Stan. Always defending the Brits. You would think he was one of them.

Temple went on.

"Yeah, and they never tire of remindin' us, neither. Like we bin sittin' on our asses all that time. And they look at you in that way as if to say, 'Well, how come it took you so long to come and fight our war for us?' It's right what they say, the English flag is red, white and blue, and yella!"

"That ain't fair, Temple," said Tommy Kosminsky, a diminutive private from Tennessee. "What about El Alamein?"

"No, Tom, Temple's right for once," said Rudi. "That's just what they think."

"Yeah," said Larry, "why is we here? This ain't our war. North Africa don't mean shit to us. Just 'cos Churchill wants us to."

"Nothin' here matters to us," said Gene. "We wus attacked by the Japs. We should be goin' after those slanty-eyed sons of bitches, gettin' back the Philippines and our other places they took, 'stead of bein' stuck here. What's England to us? Let them go fight it out among theirselves, I say."

"The Nazis ain't so bad. I'd rather fight the Brits," added Temple.

"So the hell would I," said Mickey Reilly, his pug face squeezed into a crumpled ball of distaste. "My folks come from Ireland. We bin brung up to hate the Brits. Give me half a chance and I'll be off over the sea to join the IRA."

"What's the IRA?" Luigi asked.

"Irish Republican Army. Irish freedom fighters."

"I ain't never heard of them. I thought Ireland was free. They ain't in the war."

"Then you ain't heard how they brought terror to the streets of England in '39?"

"What with?"

"Bombs, of course. Until that lily-livered government in Dublin gone and interned their country's heroes!"

"You guys seem to forget that Hitler declared war on us," cautioned Stan.

There he goes again, Larry thought.

"Sure, but he ain't gonna invade New York, is he?" Larry retorted. "We just gotta protect our ships and let them Nazis fight it out with the Russkies since the Brits ain't up to the job."

"Yeah," said Temple, "if the Nazis wants to invade England I'm all for clearin' out and lettin' 'em do it. The only shootin' this guy wants to do is back home in Tennessee with ma old rifle and ma dawgs. I don't want no medals—"

"Ain't nobody gonna give yer any."

Temple went on as if the interruption had not occurred.

"...I just wants to come home with a few rabbits and hogs. Don't make no sense us bein' here, no sense at all."

"Does to Larry, now he's got his eye on the ladies," said Gene.

"You all got your eye on 'em."

"Not the fat one. Anyways, you got yerself a gal, Larry. You wanna leave the field open to us unattached guys."

"I just said I might see her at the dance, is all. Anyways, my gal's an ocean away."

"You're right, let's us make hay while the sun shines. You hear them jokes they tell: 'Heard about the utility drawers? One Yank and they're off.' We'll never get ourselves another chance like this. All those gals, they're either free or their fellas are away fightin' or on the seas. What more can a guy want?" said Luigi, leaning over the side of his bunk and grinning down onto Larry Schultz.

"A woman that takes a bath once in a while."

"Better a doyty dame than no dame at all," said Luigi.

"You tell him, fella."

"The dirtier the dame the better is what I says."

"Just listen to yourselves," said Stan. "Is this the way for Americans to behave when they're in a foreign country."

"Hey, preacher man," Larry said, "it's 'cos we're in a foreign country we can do what we wants."

"Aw but it ain't the way a fine southern gentleman behaves," mocked Temple with an accent straight out of *Gone with the Wind*. "Y'all got to mind yer manners now."

"Those girls," said Stan, stretching out his long, thin neck over the top of his bunk as if to get as close to Temple as possible without actually moving his body, "their guys are away riskin' their lives."

"Sure, fer their country not ours. And they don't have to go with us, do they?"

"Anyways," said Larry, "we'll soon be fightin' fer our lives. And fightin' fer this, their goddam country, when we ain't got no business fightin' fer anybody but ourselves. So I say we're entitled to what pleasure we can git. T'ain't as if we wus forcin' ourselves on 'em."

"Yeah," said Gene, "this is our chance – maybe our only chance – to have us some fun."

"Yeah," said Luigi, "like the man said, what we doin' in this goddam war anyways? Let the Brits fight it out with the Krauts and... and they and the Russkies can all kill theirselves and we just get stronger by doin' nuttin.'"

"I doan like them Nazis," said Rudi in his slow drawl.

"Nazis ain't so bad," said Gene.

"Like, son?" Temple retorted. "Shit, you doan have to like 'em. Shucks, they ain't gonna hurt us none. We's stronger by far'n what they is. What we riskin' our lives fer here? I wish I'd listened to ma baby brother and done what he done and dodged the draft, is what I wish."

"How'd he do that?"

"Just lit out. Hid hisself away in a shack. Nobody cared to look fer him."

"So what we doin' here?" Temple went on. "We had us a revolution to get rid of them Brits. Is it freedom that some guy in Washington orders yer to come out here and risk yer life to save someone else's ass? If I takes up ma gun it should be to protect ma own property, not somewhere's halfway across the goddam world. That's the American way. That's the freedom we fought for. We don't fight for no-one but ourselves. We don't take orders from some no-good Yankee pinko in the White House. Shit, I wish I'd done what ma brother done, and what ma pappy done afore him, when we had to save their asses in '18. What Roosevelt done ain't democracy, bringin' us here to fight the Brits' war. Shit, folks didn't even want us to send the Limeys aid, but he gone and done it. Let's take a vote on it. Who thinks we shouldn't be here?"

All save Stan and Rudi raised their arms. Rudi said lamely:

"Aw gee, I dunno."

"You dunno," said Temple contemptuously.

"Aw shaddup, Temple, I'm sick o' hearin' yer goddam voice." Rudi hurled a sock in Temple's direction.

"Democracy ain't gonna get us outta here," said Larry. "It didn't do us no good when we voted to keep us outta this goddam war. So we'd better just make the best of it. Like the man said, make hay while the sun shines. And come inspection you better make damn sure all that sugar is by your bed, Temple, or you'll live to regret it."

CHAPTER FOUR

From the balcony of the Chalford Arms Hotel, Major John Bellucci had a view of the entire town, looking out over the red-tiled squat roofs that were dominated by the square tower of St Edward's church, to what to his eyes was a hill with ruined walls on the top, but was the remains of the motte and bailey of Chalford Castle, built by Guy de Lusignac, one of the followers of the Conqueror, and over the green fields towards the hint of eminence that was Dartmoor to the north and the hint of blue that was sea to the south.

It was the time of year when the scene could be regarded as at its most attractive, the sky a ceramic blue, with the Saturday morning sun gilding the ochres and greys and pinks of wall and tile, turning the grass into a vibrant tessellation cemented by hawthorn hedges whose gnarled branches shimmered with the first mirage of lime green buds, and falling in tiered majesty on the copses of oak and beech, sculpting the grey trunks in a sacred light evocative of the pillars of St Edward's church itself.

But for Bellucci the scene bespoke a cramped disorder.

Compared with the precise grids and ruled lines of an American town, Chalford was a chaotic jumble of streets that wound and twisted and returned contrarywise, leaning in on themselves as if to snap shut their jaws upon the unwary traveller. Some of these people, he noted, lived in cottages thatched with reeds, the sort of hovels the meanest sharecropper back home would disdain to inhabit. And beyond the town there were no straight roads, no open vistas of field, rather tiny belts of tarmac that wandered with the aimlessness of a drifter oppressed by the time on his hands, and those fields the size of handkerchiefs, hemmed in by high walls of hedge. It was as if the landscape had been designed by the village idiot for the purpose of frustrating traverse, commerce and the well-ordered life.

He stood at the rear of the balcony, draped with Union Jack and Stars and Stripes, together with Mr Henry Markle, local solicitor and mayor, Mrs Markle, the vicar Mr Villiers and Sir Cuthbert Greaves, a hook-nosed lugubrious man in dress uniform, dripping with braid, who was introduced to him as the lord lieutenant (pronounced 'leftenant') of the county, as if he should know what this meant.

Only Bellucci and Mr Markle stood, the latter at the front of the balcony, preparing to address the crowd, the other three sitting, the lord lieutenant with his leg stretched out to accommodate the preposterous sword, buffed to a perfection of shine, he wore at his belt. Did he think to counter the German Panzers with that toothpick? Bellucci was reminded of that class of southern gentlemen of the Civil War era, an anachronism confronted with the march of progress.

Withdrawing his contemptuous gaze, Bellucci saw Mrs Markle staring up at him as she patted down her permanent wave with a hand on which the flesh bulged over an enormous diamond ring. She, like most of the women in this country, had an unhealthy pallor as if they never saw the sun but lay on a sick bed all day, although Bellucci had to admit that Mrs Markle had nothing of invalidity about her.

Below them the marketplace was as full as a movie house on the first showing of *Gone with the Wind*. Bellucci's own men stood at ease and in loose groups together with what was presumably most of the population of the town. Indeed, on his journey to the hotel, breasting the attempts at handshakes and slaps on the back, Bellucci noticed that many of the shops had 'closed' signs in their windows. The cobbles of the square, the steps of the market cross, were draped with people in holiday mood, all the roads out of the square were blocked, and the throng pressed right up against the doors of shops, so that even had any been open, it was doubtful how anyone might enter.

Mr Markle, a dapper, balding man in a frock coat, with a receding chin shaved and lotioned to a sheen, was beginning his address to the crowd who had gathered for this 'welcome meeting'. His voice was deep and sonorous but had those rolling vowels and clipped consonants that suggested to Bellucci a consciousness of superiority whose corollary was his own inevitable inferiority. He was not at all sure he had not scowled when addressed by the mayor and lord lieutenant on his arrival in the hotel foyer.

"Ah, Major! How are you and your men settling in? No difficulties, I trust?"

Bellucci assured him there were none, save for the unheralded appearance of a farmer at the field in which his men were encamped. The men were assembled for hand-to-hand bayonet fighting drill under Corporal Clark, and Bellucci was watching their progress. He then heard shouting from the hedge that bordered the road, and that had been supplemented with a six-foot-high fence topped with barbed wire for the duration of their occupancy.

"Hey, you Yanks!"

He was a scruffy individual in a worn sports jacket. From beneath a cap of checkered pattern peeped the flattened nose of an unsuccessful boxer and a chin of greying stubble. A moth-eaten terrier, tethered by a piece of string, stood at his feet and barked in time to the words.

"Moi family done farmed these here fields nigh on a 'undred year and ain't nobody been able to turn us off 'til you came. Thinks yer smart, don't yer, with yer tanks and guns, thinkin' I don't have the money to go to the law. Nor do I, but I knows a trick or two, you just see if I don't. Moi boy, he's with the Eighth Army, and when he comes home we'll show you a thing or two."

The old man cackled like a dotard, his false teeth rattling like castanets.

"All yer good fer is poncin' about in yer smart uniforms. You ain't real soldiers. Toy soldiers is all you is."

"Old Westwood," said Mr Markle. "He's quite harmless. Bark worse than his bite."

The lord lieutenant, looking down his long, haughty nose, said:

"Not quite the village idiot but not quite the full shilling either, eh? Obsessed with his land, which he'll get back soon as the present emergency is over, of course. Does he think the Nazis are going to respect his right to his damn fields? There's always one, eh?"

Bellucci was suspicious of this 'eh?' which the lord lieutenant tended to use in preference for a period. Was he supposed to respond to it, as in a question?

"Doesn't see the big picture the way we do. Strategy and all that," Mayor Markle added.

Bellucci felt repelled by the man's complacency. What did some hick politician know about war?

The worthy began:

"Good people of Chalford, I'm delighted that so many of you have taken time out from your daily cares to welcome Major Bellucci and the men of the 116th US Infantry Regiment who have travelled across the ocean to strengthen our arm against the Hun hordes who have enslaved the continent.

"It is indeed fitting that the two great democratic nations of the world have thus joined forces to banish evil from the face of the earth. We are two nations so closely allied in blood and kinship (had he not heard, Bellucci wondered, of the millions of immigrants of non-Anglo Saxon extraction to the US, including Germans, Italians and Irish who would cheerfully have seen Great Britain consigned to flames?), and even more so in tradition. Two nations grafted from the same stock, as it were. The United States has sprouted from the trunk of this old land, grown and flourished, and whilst we two nations have had our differences in the past, as families do, it was only a matter of time before kinship and our common love of liberty brought us together once again, as in 1917, to rid Europe of militarist tyranny."

The mayor was, Bellucci noted, like many British, more inclined to claim kinship than the Americans were to reciprocate.

But his attention was distracted by an unfortunate episode, as a man's voice rang out from the crowd:

"Yeah, you Yanks was three years too late then, an' all!"

As members of the crowd turned on the man, calling 'Shut up!' and 'For shame!', Bellucci seethed at the ingratitude of these people who seemed to expect the USA to help them whenever they bit off more than they could chew.

Markle meanwhile seemed disinclined to ad lib, and, having allowed the uproar to subside, carried on with the script he held in a somewhat palsied hand.

"Let us not forget that the founding fathers of American democracy wished for nothing more, before sword was drawn from its scabbard, than to enjoy their birthright as free Englishmen. They saw themselves as following in the hallowed footsteps of Messrs Pym and Hampden, those great upholders of parliamentary democracy in the Civil War, in their determination to champion the cause of representative government in a world in which, as now, the continent of Europe was swathed in a dark pall of tyranny.

"Let us two nations, in fraternal embrace, stand together in defence of those principles we hold most dear: respect for all men whatever their race and creed; respect for the right of nations to live in peace with one another; and, above all, respect for the liberty of each individual.

"If there be any in this land who still doubt the sacrifice of blood and coin we have made, let them look upon Major

Bellucci and his gallant men who, in the great tradition of American arms, have answered their country's call, who did not hesitate to cross the hostile ocean to place their strong arms at our disposal (some subdued laughter from his audience at this point), their lives on the hazard for the mutual security of our nations and a better world for those benighted wretches on the continent; a world in which each man has a say in his own destiny. A right not to be hauled from his bed in the dark of night and thrown into a concentration camp. A world in which man may speak without being informed upon by his neighbour."

Bellucci, who had been staring down at the mayor's shoes, the tight leather of which bulged out on the sides to accommodate his bunions, travelled through bafflement at the mention of Pym and Hampden (like most Americans he believed the USA owed nothing to any other nation, and had sprung into being like Athena, fully armed, from the head of Zeus) to a state of semi-coma when assailed by this storm of platitude. He stifled a yawn and moved back a right leg that was beginning to feel the heating effect of the sun. He had never expected to find himself too hot in this country.

"Let these boys, so far from home and missing parents and sweethearts, know the warmth of a Devonshire welcome. Take them not only to your hearths but to your hearts, you mothers whose own sons are fighting. Treat them as you would wish your own precious blood to be treated were they far from home. Never let it be said of us here in Chalford that we didn't know how to extend the arms of welcome, offer a hand to dry tears or a breast to lay their weary heads upon."

Bellucci reflected that not the least distressing aspect of war was its capacity to inspire oratory, and clearly Markle was not immune to that temptation. He should have a care what he wished for, as some of his men were inclined to lay their weary heads upon any female breast, and there might be more than one lady in this town willing to accommodate them.

"Three cheers for the Yanks!" someone shouted.

"Yes," Markle went on, "let me just remind any of you who have not yet volunteered to accommodate our allies to sign the book in the church hall, then let us raise our voices in welcome. Three cheers for our new guests, the US 116th Infantry Regiment!"

Three cheers rang out, reverberating against the tall windows of the Chalford Arms Hotel with three hip hip hoorays, whilst Bellucci's mouth grew drier still with the anticipation of his own ordeal. He had addressed bodies of soldiers of the size of the crowd, but never a body of civilians. Soldiers he could address, because he spoke their language, and if his oratory was not of Senate standard they would understand, and even esteem him the more for being the blunt soldier he was.

As Markle waved a chubby pink paw to invite his response, he wished he had furnished himself with a bourbon from the bar, or had at least learned his words by heart. He pushed his body against a weight of apprehension, and, guts churning within, took a step toward the balcony. The sun was bright, something he had not reckoned with, and he briefly wished he had worn his shades, but there was no glare from the dun and matt clothing below him. Nevertheless, he felt dizzy and disoriented. The first words were almost blurted from his mouth.

"Er, thank you, Councillor Markle," he began, clinging to the edge of a planter full of begonias for support. "I... I am a soldiering man and no great speechifier, so you'll pardon me if I only say a few words—"

"We'll thank you an' all!" some wag shouted out.

"...er, just a few words to thank the councillor, the vicar, all you good folk, for this welcome. I can say on behalf of my men, we're all mighty grateful, and... look forward to meeting you good folks where we can, just so long as that don't interfere with us doing our dooty... I beg you to remember that we're here for a purpose, and that purpose is to ready ourselves for combat and get in shape so's we can get to grips with the enemy soon as possible."

As soon, he thought, *as Churchill stops tying up the US forces in pointless sideshows.*

"Of course, we gotta get used to your customs, so if we have problems understandin' things – like your money – I'm sure you good people'll bear with us. We're very grateful for all you mean to do for us, and know you wish to help. But remember that you can best help by letting us get on with the task we have come here to perform... Er, thank you."

Bellucci turned, acutely conscious of the flush to his cheeks and anxious to gain a seat out of sight of the crowd, who were acknowledging his speech with a gentle ripple of applause conspicuously lacking enthusiasm. Glancing to right and left, he saw smiles of a decidedly chilly character and hands that moved mechanically to the clap. All had the air of a child taken to the fair but forbidden the rides. The lord lieutenant roused himself.

"Quite right, Major. A soldier's job is soldiering, what."

Again, Bellucci did not know whether he was expected to reply to this 'what'.

Mr Markle meanwhile had risen to his feet and was thanking Bellucci for his words 'both warm and sobering', whilst encouraging the crowd once again to extend to their guests a good Chalford welcome.

As Bellucci rose he saw that below in the square the welcome had already started as men were going among the GIs and hauling roughly on their arms or offering them some of the disgusting cigarettes the Brits smoked. Elderly matrons were approaching the same innocents and trying to entice them from the world of martial drill and boot-blacking to that of moth balls and lavender and that dreaded lubricant to all social intercourse in this country, the English tea.

Bellucci reflected cynically that there were more hazards in war than President Roosevelt could ever imagine.

CHAPTER FIVE

"Now, ladies, we of the Chalford Women's Voluntary Service must set to with a will if we are to match the martial efforts of our young men in foreign fields, and those of our young ladies in native fields and forests."

Thus announced Mrs Cadwallader, who, with her husband, Henry Cadwallader, owned the estate of Dovecote Park, north of town, and who was known as a minor authoress of romantic fiction of a kind that some described as cloying, although from neither her manner of speech, or any other attribute apparent from normal social intercourse, would she have struck the uninitiated as in the least degree sentimental.

Her rousing treble, so often heard to good effect in St Edward's church, where she gave thanks to God for that formidable larynx whose descent was inclined to drown out the voices of her neighbours like species of bird assert dominance over their territory by means of song, immediately silenced the ladies' chatter.

Sadly, she reflected, the church hall did not possess the acoustic resources of its parent building, and her voice, rather than be heard to best advantage, reverberated with harsh cadences from walls adorned with aircraft identification pictures left over from an ARP meeting, the old ARP 'Women Wanted' poster so often the butt of prurient humour, one advising that Potato Pete made good soup, and those exhorting its visitors to be wary lest the German Chancellor be crouching under their table.

"Let us gird ourselves with the vision of our founder, Lady Reading, at this new challenge that has come over our horizon, with the advent of the soldiers from across the Atlantic. Let us have ever before us our motto, 'The WVS Never Says No'. Let us bring to our aid all the ingenuity with which we have faced our multifarious undertakings. Let those who look on our doings not think us fit only for organising whist drives, collecting paper, tin and cotton reels, for harvesting rose hips and chestnuts, for weaving camouflage nets."

Of the thirty women who sat on the cane seats listening to Mrs Cadwallader, some, she was pleased to note, appeared rapt by her ringing if discordant tones, yet others seemed by their demeanour to suggest they might take this sort of thing from the Prime Minister, or even from Mr Markle, but found it tedious in the extreme when it came from one of their own.

Many of those ladies were adorned in whatever their clothing coupons could extend to, or failing that, what 'make do and mend' might furnish, in skirts made from amputated dresses, blouses of butter muslin or contrived from curtains, whereas Mrs Cadwallader felt her position demanded she address them in her WVS uniform of bottle green vivified by beetroot, and sober felt hat.

"It seems," she went on, "the number of troops that have descended upon us has exceeded expectations (here she was unable to restrain herself from shooting a glance in the direction of Mrs Villiers, who coloured and bridled somewhat), and we must look to our own hearths for their repose. We must search our consciences and ask: can we, who have sacrificed so much, not offer those homely comforts to servicemen far from home? True, it is not a responsibility members of our organisation should bear alone, but we have this opportunity to give a lead to the town, and we have had many instances to show that where we lead others follow.

"I have here a ledger (she thumped the pink succulent flesh of her hand down upon an imperial volume) in which we are called upon to state which properties might accommodate Americans, and how many each may take. Of course, those housing land girls are exempt. This I shall pass round so all who are minded may subscribe their names, and if you need to discuss the matter with your family, I shall leave it on this desk until Friday. I trust, within the week, we shall have shown the Americans that we are willing to take them (she resisted the temptation to say, 'to our bosoms') to our hearths."

Mrs Cadwallader, whose respiratory system was, despite her prodigious larynx, never the best, drew a much-needed breath, then added:

"We at Dovecote Park are more than happy to accommodate four of our transatlantic allies... their officers, you know."

"That's all very well for you, but it's not all of us has a house the size of Dovecote Park." This from Mrs Alder, the butcher's wife. "You can put up four of 'em and never see them dawn 'til dusk in that great place of yours. In our place we'd be squeezed in like we was all in an Anderson shelter."

"I don't say everyone can take—"

"And what's this about their officers?" asked Sally Burns, the switchboard operator and wife of Arthur, the Labour councillor, who had moved from London to escape the Blitz, in a tone as laced with suspicion as if she had just uncovered some dastardly Nazi plot. "We just have to take who we're given, is that it? It's just like the evacuation. Don't worry, I've heard tales of how it was when the buses arrived here, and they was all lined up on the village green like horses at an auction, with them as has the money giving a nod and a wink to the billeting officer and getting the pick of the litter while Joe Soap was left with them as was covered in vermin."

"I hope you don't accuse any of the ladies here of such practices, Mrs Burns. As you know, I took in three very deprived children, and you well know what Mrs Villiers has to cope with in young Arthur," said Mrs Cadwallader, although at the same time uncomfortably aware of the fact that it was the poorer sort who were more needful of the 10s 6d for the first child and 8s 6d for each subsequent child paid by the government upon registration.

It was not the first time Mrs Cadwallader had heard Mrs Burns express opinions which were, in her view, frankly bolshie. Surely even Sally Burns was not so stupid she could not appreciate that the American officers would seek and be entitled to the best accommodation. Did the woman really want her to come out and express a fact that, though obvious to them all, would of necessity be unpalatable to many? Were they at Dovecote to take grubby little privates while the major was to have an unheated pantry in a leaking cottage?

Mrs Burns seemed to subside in the face of such a challenge, uttering only an unintelligible mutter.

"We must all take who we're given, Mrs Burns. For myself I do not have so low an opinion of the United States soldiery as you seem to have."

"Why don't you take them then? Frightened they'll smash your fine china or muddy your carpets, I'll bet."

Mrs Cadwallader felt her face settling, or rather slumping, into its resigned look, like a giant hand putting aside the tarnished coin of this world and anticipating its reward in Heaven.

"Really, Sally, must we descend into this unseemly tone?" said Agatha Wills, the GP's wife, a middle-aged, taut-bosomed woman of sour demeanour who, although very low church in Mrs Cadwallader's eyes, nevertheless evinced the appropriate respect for the latter's position.

"We's all supposed to be equal, ain't we?" Mrs Burns retorted. "Only the way I sees it, we's all equal and you ain't."

"Do we have to shout at each other like a group of washer-women?" asked Mrs Markle.

"I wasn't shouting."

"I think, Mrs Burns," retorted the GP's wife, whose putty-coloured complexion was an ill advertisement for her husband's calling, "your attitude does this organisation little credit. If, as our chairwoman says, this community looks to us ladies to take a lead, it ill serves them to descend to this sort of slanging match. In fact, it would encourage those who have mocked our efforts in the past."

"I think it's asking a bit much of some of us," said Lucy Flint, a teacher who was married to the local constable. "Those of us who've already accepted evacuee children and are now called upon to do the government's job – or the American government's job - for it. As Mrs Alder says, it's all very well for you, Madam Chairwoman. What would you have us do, tell the children to go bed down in a hay rick?"

"As I said, no-one will think ill of any who feel unable to accommodate the soldiers. Particularly those who have already accepted evacuees."

"Who's gonna see to their meals and wash their clothes is what I wants to know," said Lily Foster, the postmistress. "I ain't got the time to spare for looking after them."

"I am sure," said Mrs Cadwallader in a tone of some exasperation, "that the United States Army is capable of seeing to these matters."

"We can accommodate three young men at the vicarage," said Mrs Villiers.

"You'll understand why we must decline," said Agatha Toms, English and history mistress at the local school, "with our two girls."

"Well, that lets me out as well then," said Lily Foster. "We got our Sally, ain't we?"

"Your Sally's only fifteen," said Agatha Wills.

"Well, it's old enough, ain't it? You don't know what them Yanks is used to in their country. It ain't the same as here, you know."

"I'll take two," said Mrs Fincher of Keenleyside Farm.

"The bigger 'n' stronger the better 'til they gives me a land girl."

"I think," said Mrs Cadwallader, her vowels burgeoning with excess of solemnity, "that the American soldiers are here to train and in due course liberate Europe from the Nazi yoke rather than relieve the labour shortage on your farm—"

"Well, the government gone and took my Tom, didn't they?"

"Yes… well, we must all examine our consciences, and no-one will incur any censure if they feel compelled for whatever reason, be it space or propriety, to decline the request."

"Hear, hear," said Agatha Wills. And Mrs Cadwallader felt grateful that some at least of 'her ladies' knew what was due to her.

"And now let us proceed with the setting up of a welcome club. As you will recall, I suggested we designate ourselves a welcome club for the duration. In that regard I've been in contact with some of our sister organisations in areas that have already played host to Americans and Canadians."

She neglected to mention that on her responding to the question of whether Chalford was to play host to Americans or Canadians, the prevailing tone had been one of commiseration rather than congratulation.

"They've kindly suggested that we might like to hold dances. It is generally the case that American bases hold their own dances, and the Red Cross make arrangements with organisations such as ourselves to supply the names of suitable girls to partner the Americans. However, our

Americans are not yet in a position to accommodate that sort of entertainment, and in its absence I think this hall would recommend itself as a suitable venue, with the aid of some gramophone music and a tea urn. We should have to be vigilant lest any of these young men seek to smuggle liquor into the premises. Any donations of gramophone records would be most appreciated, particularly from you younger ladies who may have the sort of music the youth of today seem to prefer (the vowels of the latter word being drawn out with the disrelish of a tooth being pulled). But no unseemly dancing, of course."

"We should erect a sign saying, 'no jitterbugging,'" volunteered Mildred Gregg, a prim spinster of some fifty years, about whose sparrow-boned form hung an aura of doomed romance and unlikely subversion. She had married beneath her, only to have her love, Albert Prinker, the blacksmith's apprentice, fall in battle at Passchendaele. Mrs Cadwallader wondered that Mildred Gregg had heard of this jitterbugging.

"Whatever that may be when it's at home. It certainly sounds fairly reprehensible. It was also suggested we establish contacts with the American Red Cross, and through them, those of you who are willing might invite some to tea at your houses. I will leave a list pinned to the notice board."

"I think some of them might be after more racy entertainment than a cup of tea and a bath bun," said Sally Burns.

Mrs Cadwallader, reflecting that this was just the sort of comment she might expect from that lady, polished her vowels to a spectacular state of orotundity and replied:

"Well, in that case they will be sorely disappointed in Chalford is all I can say. We should not judge these young men by our own standards."

"Oooh, hark her!" cried Sally.

"What I mean," Mrs Cadwallader replied, inwardly regretting her words and cursing the need to palliate them, "is that there is in any group of young men a disparate spectrum of personality, and many being far from home, might be reassured by matronly solicitude, a warm fire and a hot beverage. The army cannot provide everything."

"Kiss me goodnight, Sergeant Major," said Sally sarcastically.

Not knowing how to take this intervention, Mrs Cadwallader went on:

"It strikes me we should do all we can to take the minds of these young men off things, so that they are not inclined to dwell on what the future might hold.

"Furthermore, it might be useful to have some introductory talks to help them adapt to life in this country. On the blackout, for example, or on the monetary system, which I am informed they find most challenging.

"I thought we might even invite Professor Sachs (this gentleman was a former professor of history at Bristol University), to give a talk on the history of our area."

"What about invitin' them Yanks to give us a talk on what they's been doin' for the last three years when we been at war?" suggested Alice Jones.

"That's not at all helpful, Alice," said Agatha Wills.

"If we start with a talk on currency and see what level of interest we get," endorsed Mrs Villiers.

"And the idea of inviting these young men to tea is a perfectly splendid one," said Mildred Gregg. "If they are prepared to take pot luck, they would be more than welcome."

"Hear, hear!" said another.

"Well, that's just the spirit I would expect," said Mrs Cadwallader. "If the warmth of a welcome can compensate for the paucity of victuals, we ladies of Chalford will not let them down."

However, when she was walking back from the hall in the company of Mrs Wills, she was by no means so sanguine.

"I am really quite depressed by this evening. Is this what three years of war have done to us? We who have always met every challenge with ingenuity and enthusiasm. And yet tonight there was such a sad mood of negativity."

Even the peal of bells from St Edward King and Martyr, the ringers led by the sure hand of Jed Linley, who had rung Great Tom to herald the relief of Mafeking, as well as mark the passing of so many in conflicts past and present, whose imperious tones rarely failed to lift her spirits, as suggesting the superiority of the Anglican church over the bell-less Methodists, did not have their usual effect.

"Never forget, Cynthia, there is a silent majority," said Mrs Wills, with a sour look on her kaolin-white face. "It's the likes of Mrs Burns and Mrs Alder have brought you low. That Mrs Burns is most frightfully common. Our organisation has done much good, but I do so deplore its levelling tendency. When we should all be pulling together, to be faced with this... bolshevism. It really is the limit."

The lady novelist had always experienced difficulty imagining the lives of her lower-class characters. It was difficult for one who had never wanted for anything to picture the moral dilemmas to which one might be subject if one's guts were aching with hunger, and yet such was the currency of the Victorian melodrama.

"Yes, I do not ask that the woman always agrees with me, merely that she keep a civil tongue in her head."

And, she might have added, accord her the respect and... yes, even deference, she considered her status in Chalford society merited.

As she traversed Cordwainer's Row, she tapped the ferrule of her walking stick on the pavement. There was no discernible tune in the tapping, although the tenor of the act was unmistakably martial.

"What are we fighting for if not that sort of... decency, and proper respect? And I fear the arrival of these Americans will disrupt our way of life in ways we cannot as yet imagine. They are, after all, notorious for their disrespectful and bolshie temperament."

CHAPTER SIX

"If I get outta this and live 'til I'm eighty I'll still have sand comin' outta me 'oles."

So said Private Tom Dawkins of the 8th Battalion, Durham Light Infantry, known to his friends as 'Cockney', he being the only southerner in a platoon otherwise composed of Northeasterners and Scots, who regarded all from south of the Tees as Cockneys.

Having spoken, Tom returned to opening a tin of bully beef with a clasp knife, and the only response to his words was the mewing of the kites circling above. His stomach told him he was hungry, but his mind advised that as soon as the bully was inside him, he would, for sheer fear, be bringing it straight back up.

Jack Ferris, Tom's closest mate, sitting in a lotus position before their sangar, regarded him with slitty eyes red-rimmed with sand-blast, from beneath his mop of hair bleached by the sun and coated with dust, it being too hot to wear helmets. The worn features were common to them all. Jack Ferris stared out of a sun-ripened face on which what had once been plump and smooth flesh was now sunken and chamois-leather dry, its lips chapped, and plagued by flies that descended upon any moisture with a ravening appetite. This was the coastal zone and, unlike the deep desert, there were flies aplenty. From that point of view at least, they all longed to be back 'on the blue' as their slang referred to the desert.

Jack scratched hard at the bandage on his left hand, on which a cut on an old shell casing had developed into the notorious desert sore, necessitating a course of M and B tablets to prevent it becoming, as many did, septicaemic.

There was no laugh from Jack, no smile, not even that token acknowledgement of the feeble attempt at humour that might be expected as camouflage for one's fear. He simply stared about him at the other sangars and bell tents screened by camouflage netting.

Could it be, Tom wondered, that Jack no longer felt fear? Could the fear have been leeched out, with the sweat and the juicy life of him, by the sun, the endless strain and, most of all, the things he had done and seen this past year?

It was March 1943. They had come all the way from Cairo, after years of shuttling back and forth over the desert, through the hell of Alamein, retaking Mersa Matruh then Sidi Barrani, and after all that suffering and dying, now reached Mareth. They had thought Alamein would be the end and had begun to relish the chase of the retreating Germans, only to find that a dangerous animal was always liable to turn on you and snap its jaws.

Now they were facing Mareth and had seen nothing like it. It was a North African version of the Maginot Line, running all the way from the sea to the Matmata Hills.

On this, the coastal sector, was what was known as the Wadi Zigzag, because nobody could pronounce its African name. The wadi was a dry riverbed that formed one huge anti-tank ditch, with enfilade fire along its length from concrete pillboxes and gun emplacements. Once over the wadi they would be confronted with an anti-tank ditch twelve feet deep and fifteen feet wide before they got to the main defences. The whole area was sown with Teller mines, the German anti-vehicle mines, shrapnel and AP mines. The briefing they had received, in which this information was imparted, was as dispiriting as anything they had heard since Alamein.

Tom's nerves grated on the silence. Fear was one thing, but silence made it that much worse; your fears were fertilised by silence and grew thick and spiky and impenetrable like a patch of gorse. But there was one subject calculated to snap Jack out of his reverie: politics.

Jack, the pitman from Durham, never shirked a political argument, even when he and his interlocutor were of a similar political persuasion, so that Jack and Stevie Morris, the Scots docker, would worry the subject of socialism or communism – Tom, whose interest in politics was lukewarm, was never sure what to call it – to a grisly, fur-shredded, blood-soaked death. To talk would be good for them both. A little provocation, a little prod of the exposed nerve, and all would be well again.

"We gotta rely on our officers to see us safe home. They've been trained to lead, haven't they, in Sandhurst. All we gotta do is follow."

As Tom calculated, Jack's head jerked up, like the leg when tapped by a hammer at the knee. His turned-up nose slightly raised, like the hound scenting the fox. His eyes, that had been dulled under brows bulked up to awnings from the sun, now ignited. The sparks of yellow light that were in their grey depths stirred once more, and he spoke in that low guttural that seemed designed to imitate the growl.

"Trained to lead us from disaster to disaster. Like it was in the forst war. Nowt's changed so far as that's concorned – we're just the cannon-fodder."

"We won at Alamein, didn't we?"

"Just like the forst war," Jack repeated as if he had not heard, his tone ominous, comminatory.

Keep him talking, don't let him slip back into that maddening silence.

"In the first war the officers was more likely to cop it than we were. We're all in this together. An officer's just as likely to take one as us."

"Ay, so you say."

Again, that lapse into silence, as if it had not been the real Jack that had spoken but some imposter, lacking the passion, the sparkling irascible life. There were those that on first acquaintance with Jack Ferris might be offended by his irascibility. But they quickly learned that the splenetic outbursts were emitted from the man much as sparks from a grinding wheel; it was just his nature. He was the perfect soldier in that confrontation came as naturally to him as breathing, and putting on a uniform and fighting Germans was simply an extension of his normal life. That made the quiescence verging on sedation that characterised this new Jack all the more alarming.

Something wicked surfaced in Tom to inspire provocation.

"You seem to be losing respect for your betters, Private Ferris."

Jack's face was roused all of a sudden, as if it had come to attention.

"How many of us poor sods has to die before we rid wasels of 'our betters', I ask. It was wor betters what sent us oot here with those fuckin' A13s (the lightly armoured British tank that proved no match for the German Mark 3s). And those Honeys weren't much better (the American M3 Stuart tank). Did they think we was gonna knock oot a Panzer with their pop guns? Why, man, the shells just boonced off 'em. You had to be within 800 yards of a Kraut to knock him oot and arl the time their 88mm has a range of two mile.

"Is it gonna be the same this time, those of us as is lucky enough to gan home to a country fit for heroes, and arl we gets is more unemployment, shoddy hooses and folk like Chorchill runnin' the country. He fucked up in the forst war, so wadda we dee, put him in charge of this, would you fuckin' credit it."

"Well, he's done c… good."

"Ah, I hord yer!" Jack's eyes were now sparkling. "You nearly said 'canny' there, didn't yer? Ha ha! I'll teach y' to speak Geordie yet. You'll gan home and forget yer Cockney ways."

Tom laughed. It was true. A twelvemonth in the DLI and he was picking up the northern way of talking.

"Well, Churchill's done a good job, hasn't he? Nobody but him could unite the country."

"Why no. If he's doin' so well why'd he have to fight off a vote of no confidence in the Hoos of Commons after the fall of Tobruk? Wavell and Auchinleck were good generals – look at how the Auk torned the tide at Sidi Rezegh. They knew what wor limitations were, and he sacked them because he wanted us to win battles we weren't capable of winnin' because we didn't have the equipment. Just so's he could get the glory of it. He arnly accepted Monty because the bloke did what Chorchill telt him.

"As for him unitin' the country! Divvent ye believe it. He's hated by the workin' class."

"I'm workin' class, but I don't hate him."

"I don't say arl. The workin' class in the toons. Pitmen and shipyard workers. Why, man, he hates the unions. In the General Strike he threatened to resign when Baldwin wanted to negotiate with the strikers. Because he doesn't want us ordinary blokes havin' the power the union gives us. We try to take a little power for wasels, we're the enemy to him just as much as the Gormans. You gan to any pit, son, naebody'll have a good word to say for Winston Chorchill. He's a Victorian, and he's in charge of a modern country fightin' a modern war. We'll vote him oot forst chance we get."

"Well, there you are then. The country's changed since the first war. Look at the Labour Party, running the country under Ramsay MacDonald."

This time the provocation was quite unintentional. Tom had forgotten that Ramsay MacDonald represented another of Jack's sensitive spots. He began to feel like a dentist, probing along the jawline and ever so often stabbing a nerve and eliciting that spasm of pain and outrage.

"Ramsay MacDonald!" Jack exploded. "That traitor what sold oot the workin' class, that was the Labour fig leaf for a Tory national government that cut the dole! If I saw him in the street I'd spit on the bloke."

"Well, Atlee seems to know what he's about. And from what I hear he's as good a chance as Churchill of winnin' the next election."

"Whadda y' hear?"

For the umpteenth time Tom wondered whether this irascibility was what contending for your livelihood with the rock and the earth did to a man. Probably not, as not all pitmen were like that, and the man he now saw approaching over the sands, tossing away his cigarette butt as if in disgust, the Scotsman, Stevie Morris, was a docker, and thoroughly as ready as Jack to square up to the world, particularly if that world spoke with an English accent.

"I hear plenty talk about politics when you and him are around."

Stevie's sunburnt thighs towered over them, his figure slightly hunched. There was about the Scot a formidable suggestion of power in abeyance, as of a wild animal that has just been tranquilised. He announced:

"I'm fuckin' parched." His blue eyes fell on the hob of stones cemented with dry sticks and topped with a four-gallon flimsy, its top removed.

"We got ourselves a brew on," Tom said unnecessarily. Their water tasted of the petrol residue in the tank so the brew can was always on the boil.

"Char!" Stevie said contemptuously. "I just been havin' that dream again. The one where we're ridin' through Cairo in a gharry, throat dry as fuck, and you're anticipatin' it, you ken. Then the gharry puts us off in front of the Hurriya Bar, and we push oor way through the bead curtain and there's three Stellas lined up on the bar, cold as a heeland February, with the drops on the outside—"

"Shut up fer Christ's sake," said Jack. "We're a lang way from Cairo now."

"...And then we troop oot ter the Berka to see the lassies, yer ken."

"Well, that's one good thing the army's done for us," Tom added mischievously, "givin' us all the French letters we want."

"Fat lot of use you make of it... keepin' it arl fer yer lass back hame, whasser name? Emma?"

"Emily."

For all his complaining Stevie took a metal mug and added condensed milk and two spoonfuls of sugar to his brew. He draped a dirty handkerchief over his face to keep off the flies.

"Tiffin?" Jack asked.

"I got me the shits something chronic."

"Jack here'll soon cure you of that with his talk of Churchill and Ramsay MacDonald."

"Ay," said Jack. "I'll bung yer up good and proper."

"He's just been sayin' how his two heroes has made Britain the great country it is."

"Hadaway and shite," Jack said. "Bastards arl of them. Them and their kind."

Tom laughed until the exclamation stalled with the dry adhesiveness of his throat. Nevertheless, the exasperated amusement with which he often regarded his friends concealed admiration. He had never met two men so concerned with others, with righting injustice, as Jack and Stevie. His father had never cared for anything save himself and his own; had never expressed any interest in politics. He had a sudden sense of his own impoverishment and thought with blame of the older Dawkins. And yet that concern his friends felt was never expressed directly. Only through the medium of hatred and loathing of politicians, of Tories. It was almost as if that concern had to be camouflaged, as something embarrassing, or even as if it was simply an excuse for that hatred, that loathing.

"I know a fella," said Stevie, scratching his buttocks then settling himself on the sand in front of the sangar, "thought hisself the bees knees with the women. After work he couldnae wait to be away and suit hisself up and be oot on the toon. You'd see the guy, walking doon the street, reekin' o' the cologne, carnation in his buttonhole. And then you twigged, you'd never see him wi' a lass on his arm. Turns oot he niver had the courage to ask one of 'em oot. You're the same, Jack, ma mon."

"Whaddaya mean? I got meself a wife and bairn."

"I dinna mean that," said Stevie, his soft lowland Scots a gentle insinuation. "I mean politically. You believe things but you dinna take them to their logical conclusion."

"And what's that?"

"Communism. Have I not told ye 'til I'm blue in the face? All the Labour Party will get is sops to the working classes. The only way to get true change is for the working class to seize control of the means of production. Then there'll be nae mer class, we'll all be pullin' in the same direction."

Their conversation came to a halt with the thunderous roar from a formation of medium bombers, probably Bostons, passing overhead. Stevie took a packet of Players from his pocket and, after offering them around, performed his favourite trick of throwing one into the air and catching it in his lips.

"Aren't we pullin' in the same direction now?" Tom asked, conscious as he did so of the naivety of the question.

"Dinna kid yersel. Churchill wants to protect the power of his class. Look at the anti-strike legislation."

"We are at war!" Tom protested.

"Look at the imprisoning of the miners of Betteshanger."

"Didn't Morrison order their release?"

"You still see magistrates finin' strikers."

"Only because we're at war. Anyway, don't you want an independent Scotland?"

"Ay. Because only when Scotland's free of the English yoke can we achieve the classless society we want."

"That's bollocks," said Jack. "Scotland's got class same as England. And tarkin' aboot nationalism is a distraction from the true struggle, which is a struggle between classes not countries."

"Tell that to the crowd at Hampden Park," Stevie said.

"Before you two put the world to rights we've got the little matter of a war with the Germans."

His friends did not want to be reminded of it. Nor did he. He had intended this political debate to be a distraction from the battle to come, and now he had ruined all his good work. The eyes of the two men regressed beyond the sangar, with its roof of canvas cannibalised from a disabled Bedford, its revetment of sandbags, beyond the tents and the milling men, the perimeter of flattened barbed wire they called mattress wire.

Tom knew what they faced: a first war battle like Alamein, hand to hand, bayonet in the guts. His father kept chickens in their back garden, in a coop protected by wire that was coming away from its frame. As a child he had been at the window when a chocolate-brown fox, with a proud bushy tail, slinked into the garden, and while the chickens squawked and fluffed themselves up in panic, pushed his snout through the wire and took one of them in his jaw. And with a knowing, almost sardonic look, the fox went about his business, in a singleness of purpose that was the eye to the hurricane of panic-stricken flapping. He should strive to imitate that fox. For the world was one in which there was prey, and there were predators, and he must be one or the other.

'All things wise and wonderful' they had sung in Sunday school, 'the Lord God made them all.' But also 'Tyger, tyger burning bright in the forests of the night'. Now was no time to be a lamb. He must be the tiger if he was to get back to Chalford, to Emily, to fulfil his destiny with her, and make their children, that his seed might breathe the air of the future and not perish in these barren sands.

He knew how those children would look. When he closed his eyes at night he saw them. A boy and girl, with moon faces milky white, and their eyes pale blue like the summer evening sky, freckled with innocence, but knowing him; knowing him by some filial instinct deep within them in those places where the blood flowed and the breath diffused and the heart reigned; flower of his seed that could only be engendered of her.

Emily was the lodestar, fixed and immoveable, that drew him on. She had been the cause of the only argument he ever had with Jack, when the latter had talked disparagingly of 'the girls back home', referring to letters in the papers from GIs thanking local girls for dancing with them, and implying that more than dancing had been going on. After that, even the irascible Jack knew not to touch upon the subject. Tom could believe such things of 'girls', but not his Em.

But now, having come through the hell that was Alamein, they were facing death once again.

Alamein was when he first knew the crippling terror of fear, of risking all by walking into a hail of bullets and shell, a mere shard of which might leave Em and his da with nothing but a memory of him. And he had prayed he might survive; but he prayed to no God. He prayed to Em.

He had survived and thought himself safe. What a ridiculous feeling in a war. But Alamein had been everything, hadn't it? It had been the make-or-break battle, and he had come through the ordeal with nothing more than a few days in the 9th British General Hospital in Cairo. And now they faced a challenge every bit as great: an attack on a seemingly impenetrable fortress.

"Do you think God is on our side?"

Jack and Stevie looked at him with amazement. They had never talked of religion. He doubted if either were religious. He himself, although he had always attended church at the insistence of his mother, had never given religion much thought. But you didn't, did you, not until you were faced with something like this?

"Whether he is or isn't, lad," said Jack, wafting the flies from the mess tin he held as close to his mouth as he could while he ate, "he won't protect you from the bullets and shrapnel. Many's the man that prayed to God and is lyin' stiff as a board on the sand. The arnly God worth prayin' to is luck."

"Ay," said Stevie, "and dinna forget the religious leaders on the continent support the Nazis."

"Why?"

"Because they're all of them conservative, and they see the Nazis as their bulwark against communism. It's aboot power, yer ken. The Pope and them lot'll support any regime that supports them. They hate Communists. So they support the Fascists. Same as the Catholic Church supporting Franco's Fascists agin' the Spanish peasants in the Civil War. So much for the poor inheriting the earth. Once yer have power, you use ony excuse to cling onto it. It's the same in religion as everythin' else. Life is a struggle fer power, yer ken. It's to have control over people, make them do what yer want, make them think the way yer want them to think, even if that's to think they're somethin' less than what you are."

"Like this army," said Jack.

"Ay, yer nae rang. Seems to me the bloke that's moral is the one that acts agin' his ain self-interest – but that's as rare as hen's teeth."

"But that's what we done, isn't it?" Tom said. "Us, Britain, I mean. We could easily have thrown in the towel and sided with Hitler, and we wouldn't have had none of this. He didn't want war with us, did he?"

"Ay, I guess yer right at that," conceded Stevie. "But

come tomorrow look to yersel' and yer mates, son, not to ony divine help to protect yer. If there is a God, he's just lettin' us get on wi' it."

It was just as much the chilling matter of Stevie's words as the thought of going through the hell of Alamein again that made Tom shiver. *Don't let me funk it*, he thought, *but even more so, don't let me die.* If his friends had not been about him he would have wept.

CHAPTER SEVEN

Larry Schultz, with Rudi and Luigi behind him, jumped out of the jeep in which they had cadged a lift, in front of the Astoria dance hall.

"Thanks, buddy," said Larry.

The jeep driver, who, like them all, just wanted to keep on the good side of the Military Police, simply scowled, then accelerated away in a spray of gravel.

Larry turned towards the shabby white stucco of the frontage, to which posters had been liberally affixed, advertising 'Saturday night is dance night. Waltz away your troubles to the music of the Al Simpson trio.'

"You sure this hop's on tonight?" Luigi asked.

The man had a point, Larry thought. He had expected to see a queue halfway along the block as would greet him on Saturday nights outside the Palais de Dance in Macon. Three bucks it had cost him for that lift. He hoped his money had not been wasted.

"That's what the poster says. Says it's been started half an hour. On account of the goddam blackout. Let's go."

The GIs paid their entrance fee and were directed

through a double-padded door opened with satirical courtesy by a middle-aged man wearing a tuxedo who paid much attention to their footwear – no doubt to ensure that no-one wore hobnailed boots.

Larry was pleasantly surprised by the sight that greeted him. Okay there was no swing band, only a trio and a brylcreemed MC, also dressed in tuxedo, with a carnation in his buttonhole. But there were spotlights hanging from the exposed beams of the ceiling, which changed colour as they turned, and a mirrored ball that scattered its moonlight beams on the dancers, the kaleidoscope of coloured lights weaving between the figures, causing them to stutter between static corporeality and obscurity like the figures in an old movie. There was a sprung floor and settees down the wall, and tables immediately before the stage.

But best of all was the fact that of the thirty or so patrons, less than ten were men. The women, sitting at tables nursing glasses of lemonade or orange, or standing by the wall like exotic climbing plants in their pastel ball gowns, in boredom or hauteur, or in isolated cliques of feminine confidence, grew alert at their entrance. It was for all the world like a squad of soldiers coming to attention. Larry Schultz had entered many dance halls but never had he felt like he did now: an acute pleasure at being the centre of attention that swiftly mutated into an uneasy sense of being something very like prey.

A blonde girl in an olive-green dress unglued herself from the wall and flounced past, her skirt bouncy and showing shapely legs, marred only by the unsteadiness of her hand in applying the charcoal or gravy browning to counterfeit the seams of her non-existent nylons. Her glance fell briefly on the GIs and then sheared deliberately away.

This was what they had been warned about by Major Bellucci when he addressed them on parade, his close-cropped head, so nearly resembling a bowling ball, rattling in its rack as he barked:

"Now, some of you men will want to spend your recreation time fraternising with local women. Ain't nuthin' wrong in that, just so long as you knows what it can lead to."

Larry could not help smiling. Surely they were not going to get a lecture about the birds and bees from their surrogate father.

"The brass hats is worried how you innocent young Yankees is gonna be subject to the attentions of Limey females that want nuthin' more than a ring on their finger and a ticket straight to the good old US of A. This country ain't like back home. It's a poor country, and these gals see you as their ticket out o' this mis'rable place and they's gonna do all they can to sedoos you."

By now the smiles had become all but universal, and some sniggering was breaking out.

"You ain't so innocent I need to draw you a picture. But what they is after is your pay packet and a ticket to the US. They think you is all millionaires livin' in Hollywood. And if you's hooked, don't you go thinkin' it's gonna be easy. The authorities don't want you returnin' home with foreign wives when there's plenty of American gals waitin' fer you.

"And some of these Limey gals ain't so clean as they might be. I don't mean in the way of washin'… but in the way of disease."

By now Larry's throat muscles ached with the suppression of his laughter. It was not just the matter of Major Bellucci's speech as the effect it had on the martinet, whose cheeks which, if they were inclined to ruddiness as a consequence of constitutional irascibility, now blushed through sheer embarrassment.

Larry had seen the latest edition of *Stars and Stripes*, the forces newspaper, which carried a cartoon showing a GI in the clutches of a girl in front of a wall on which the V in 'V for Victory' had been replaced with VD. It was said that prostitutes, or 'suitcase girls', were haunting country areas attempting to entice GIs.

The major went on:

"Information movies are gonna be shown, and a doctor's gonna speak to you as soon as can be arranged. The condoms you can buy on the PX – good American condoms – are soon to be available for free."

Here, to the major's fury, a cheer went up from the ranks.

So far, the precautions had not yet arrived, but Larry doubted whether matters would progress as quickly as to require them. Sure, he knew nothing of British women, and had always regarded the race as a whole as prim and proper. Back home you knew how far you could go with girls, and in a small town like his most everyone knew their neighbour's business, so to get what you wanted you had at least to convince the girl you were likely to marry her, even if it was not a downright engagement. And engaged was what he was to Barbara; it was the only way he could get her into bed – not that they used a bed, just the back of his father's old Chevvy.

But in a strange country you were loosened from these conventions. When folk feared for their lives they threw off old restraints; consequences were no longer so important. And if these girls were anxious for a meal ticket to the States, they would be willing to put something on the hook, otherwise that old catfish, he wouldn't bite at all. And once the bait was taken, there would most likely be a posting elsewhere, and he need never see the girl again. And why shouldn't he take his pleasure where he could? He was gonna put his life on the line to save this goddam country; it was only fair he get something in return. Yeah, if he played his cards right and came through it unscathed, this war could be the best darn thing that ever happened to him.

"Where's all the guys?" Luigi asked. Two men, both in their forties, Larry guessed, had come up to them and shook their hands, but the preponderance of females in the hall was striking.

"Can't all of them be gone to war," said Duke.

By this time Larry had spotted her, and she spotted him. It helped that they were together, the same threesome as in the movie queue: the plump, spotty one, the nervous, withdrawn girl with the feathery hair, and her. Emily was her name, taller, rather gawky, passively appreciative in her regard of him. The other two might hold out the promise of an innocent fumble terminating in a bleating retreat, but she, Emily, promised something more. He did not know how to describe it, save that it was the nearest these people approached to class, to sophistication.

And sophisticated Barbara had never been. Down to earth, practical, was Barbara, and everything she did the product of cold-blooded calculation. She saw in him a future, his job in insurance, a big house with two cars, regular holidays in South Carolina or the Keys. Barbara was up front in more ways than one. You knew what she wanted, and you knew precisely what she would give to get it.

These women, Emily in particular, represented mystery. He would like to tap that mystery, solve the puzzle, and then he would be able to return to Babs and… who knows, appreciate her more. There could be an attraction in down-to-earth practicality, but only if you have sampled its opposite. That was what these girls with their wide eyes represented. You didn't live with them or marry them, but like the hummingbird on the hibiscus, sample what they had, and then you're gone.

They were moving together toward the girls in unspoken concord, and the other girls stared at Emily and her friends with undisguised hostility.

"Well, howdy," Larry and Luigi said simultaneously.

All the girls seemed to blush, the ugly one a horrid hectic under the spotlights as the band played 'Night and Day'.

"Say, where's all the guys?" Duke asked in his slow drawl.

"They heard we wus comin' and lit out," said Luigi. "Can't stand the competition."

"They're in the pub," said Emily. "It's unmanly for them to come here before the interval."

"They're scared to ask us to dance," the dumpy one said.

"Without getting a few pints down them," Emily added.

"Well, we ain't like that, is we, boys?" Larry said. "Care to smoke?"

He took out a packet of Camels and handed them round. The girls took one and he lit each in turn from his silver lighter, his going-away present from Babs – well, that and a quick pounding in the steamed-up Chevvy.

There followed an awkward silence before Emily asked:

"What sort of music do you like?"

"We likes boogie-woogie," Duke drawled.

"You got boogie-woogie here?" Larry asked.

"I don't think so."

"That's too bad."

"Eight beats to the bar, that's what we like. And this will suit us just fine." Larry's hand, holding its Camel, swept around the hall. "Plenty of room to shake those limbs. That's what we need, yes sir."

"We can do the quickstep and the foxtrot," said the spotty girl, before she stopped abruptly under their indulgent stares.

"You don't know Cab Calloway?"

"We know Victor Sylvester." The spotty one again.

"That's enough, Joyce," said Emily, rather tartly. "Our American friends will be thinking we know nothing of what's going on in the world."

Larry noticed that her accent had modulated slightly, the consonants terse and clipped, as if she were trying to camouflage the lilt of her natural accent.

"That all you got on that BBC of yours?" Duke asked.

"Yes. They think American music isn't suitable."

"It's too rude!" piped up her naive friend.

"Rude?" said Larry. "Well… I guess it is rude at that."

And they all laughed.

"Some folk say the same in the States. Bible-bashers. They think it's gonna make us all immoral or cause a revolution. Monkey music is what they calls it. But what the young folk want the young folk gets. Ain't no twenty-year-old wants to creep around a dance floor like his gran'pappy done."

"Yeah," said Luigi, "what's it with that BBC? They all talks like they's got somethin' stuck up their… Beggin' yer pardon, ma'am."

The girls may have blushed. It was difficult to tell in the spotlights. But Emily bent her head, and Larry noticed the discreet smile that tugged at her lips. Lips that looked like they had been painted with beetroot juice rather than lipstick. Lips that opened with a discreet modesty on her perfect teeth, like a flower opening on the sun, unsure as to how long that sun would continue to shine. Barbara never did anything with discretion or modesty, it was not in her nature; she did all boldly, without shame. There was nothing hidden in her, all was on the surface. That was where the charm lay in these girls. The smile did not say it all, it kept something in reserve; the lips remained to be conquered, and for a while they would hold out, just long enough to pique your curiosity, maybe long enough to excite to a frenzy, then they would hurl themselves at you in their anxiety to surrender.

"Yeah," Larry said, "we done had enough of that BBC of yours. They give us radios, one for every hundred of us guys. Classical music, Victor Sylvester, and that – what is it? – Eye Mar – you know with that woman with the high voice."

"'I can do you now, sir,'" Joyce squealed, doing a passable impression of Mrs Mopp.

"It's ITMA," said Emily.

"What?"

"It stands for *It's That Man Again*. Tommy Handley. Every Thursday night. And TTFN is 'ta-ta for now'. And EIEAMS is 'ee if ever a man suffered.'" Joyce did her schoolgirl giggle.

"There's *Music While You Work*, and Vera Lynn's *Sincerely Yours*," Emily added.

"Well, we done had enough of it. So we got our own American Forces Network now. AFN not ITMA. Proper music: Glenn Miller, Benny Goodman, big band stuff. Yeah."

"I know," Emily said. "I listens to it sometimes. When Mum and Dad are out."

"Well, there you are. You's more than halfway there to doin' the jive. You got it in your blood. I can sense it."

Emily dipped her head with the ingenuousness that he was beginning to find increasingly beguiling. For a moment or two he forgot the existence of the others, addressing himself with a passionate exclusivity that was only partially calculated, to Emily alone. And then, as if to compensate for his unseemly interest in her, he turned to the other two and said:

"I'm sure all you gals has what it takes, yessir."

"I never miss *Dancing Club* on the wireless," said Joyce, "and we get the *Radio Times* so I can follow all the steps in the drawings."

"Well, I don't reckon they do what we does in their dancing club."

The words were interrupted by the MC speaking through the microphone.

"Betty Thomas, you are my next partner and the next dance is the chrysanthemum waltz."

"Chrysanthemum waltz, jeez, what the hell is that? Beggin' yer pardon, gals."

"Hey, Larry, why doan you go speak to that guy? Get him to play something with a bit of beat to it," said Duke.

"Sure, I'll catch him when he lets go of that dame. Just you wait, gals. You wanna good time, we'll show yer how. Luigi here got hisself that down home face, but he has the sweetest moves you ever seen, ain't that so?"

"He's tellin' no lie, ma'am," the little man said.

"But we don't know how to do these dances," Lucy said.

"I'll show yer."

But Larry ignored Lucy and took Emily's hands in his. Soft hands, sweating slightly. He felt a charge run through him and involuntarily glanced downward. She had nice legs. He would have to get her some nylons. That line of gravy stain or whatever it was looked goddam ridiculous. They said these girls would do anything for a pair of nylons. He didn't think this one would do *anything*; she might do a little. But he would have to promise her more than a pair of nylons; or if not promise, then lead her to believe that more was on offer.

She would believe it, he was sure. These people were so poor and innocent. Not like Barbara or the girls back home; they were too goddam savvy by half. You promise them anything, then, oh boy, you had to deliver. Maybe it was the same with these girls and their guys. But they were so starry-eyed, a Yank could shoot them any line he wanted. That was what he was counting on.

He led her in a hold like that for a waltz, his arm around the small of her back, feeling the warmth pulsing through the thin material of her dress, the curve that began to rise toward her buttocks.

"Right. Three quick steps to the left – that's *my* left, see, quick and quick, then back again. That's what they call the rock step, yeah. Then we do the same again, quick and quick and back. Then next time, quick and quick, and go under my arm and turn on the spot, while I go back, and then we come together again. Got that?"

"I think so… It's fast, isn't it?"

"Sure is."

He glanced behind to where Luigi had grabbed Lucy and was taking her through the same routine, whilst poor Duke had been left with the ugly one who he was throwing about like a rag doll.

"Now, we does it on the spot. The same steps, quick and quick, like stampin'. But I get you in this hold – the handshake hold they calls it. And after we done the steps once I pushes you away, see. Then we does the same again and I takes you in my left hand, still your right. Then we turns side on and goes past each other, back to back, still doin' the steps. Then we both kicks out, me with my left and you with your right foot. Then we turns and goes back again, each time doin' the kick when we turns, and on the fourth time we comes together. Keep those feet goin'."

She was breathing heavily, the material of her dress filling out in a way that led him to believe her boobs were bigger than Barbara's. She uttered some little gasps and stared at him with bright, wide eyes that shimmered in the spotlights. And that mouth opening on those white teeth.

"We'll have to practise a spell, then I'll go up and get that fella to play us somethin' with a bit of spirit. Whaddaya say, fellas?"

He looked behind to where Luigi had his girl in something like a wrestling hold and Duke stood by like the big dumb ox he was while his girl dissolved in a fit of silly schoolgirl giggles.

"Miss Emily, you and me, we's gonna get along just fine."

CHAPTER EIGHT

They met on George Street, where the bus stop provided a convenient camouflage for Emily's true purpose. She took out her compact and admired herself in the mirror before replacing it in her handbag and snapping the catch. Thankfully there was only one other person in the queue, a middle-aged farmer's wife in a dirty floral headscarf whom Emily did not know.

The jeep that Larry arrived in deposited him, at her suggestion, some yards up the road opposite the bandstand. He got out, and turning back to the driver, made a gesture with his finger to his throat, then turned and walked away. With his white helmet topping everything else in the street, figures that seemed squat and primitive in comparison, she was able to watch as he weaved his way through the pedestrians with a sinuous lope that drew admiring glances from ladies and awe-struck schoolboys, which he accepted with a wry smile, as if it were no more than his due. She felt her own self-esteem swell within her at the thought that this man, so admired, was coming to meet her.

His smile of recognition was appreciative, she was glad to note, having devoted much time to her clothing and makeup.

She had scoured the house for every last vestige of soap, so she could give herself a good wash, and then had her hair set in sugar water with a combination of pin curls at the front and barrel curls at the back.

She wore a grey utility suit of a kind that had only just become available under the scheme to mass-produce quality, if unadorned, clothing, at reasonable prices.

She was pleasantly surprised by the quality of the fabric, and the perfection of cut that nipped in her waist and subtly moulded her shoulders, the cutaway front artfully disguising its aim of saving on material. And even if she was permitted only the regulation three buttons on the jacket, the reflection she presented in the window of Tait's haberdasher's, with a side comb behind each ear, had much to admire.

Her ensemble was completed with a dark blue hat, imitation leather platform shoes and a large clutch bag.

In her desire to achieve that perfect look, a desire she had never felt when meeting Tom Dawkins, she had obtained a bright red lipstick from under the counter of Mr Gadd's shop in Cordwainer's Row. This she applied with her mirror in an alley behind George Street.

Her cheeks boasted a foundation of calamine lotion, over which cornflour starch had been applied to add shine. A light rouge was achieved by melting down her old lipstick ends in a saucepan and mixing with cold cream. A little fingertip dusting of soot had to suffice for mascara as they had run out of boot polish. That, together with a hint of Eau de Cologne and she would not, she thought, be out of place modelling for the Yardley's 'No Surrender' advertisement.

"You sure look swell, Miss Emily," he said, as his appreciative glance wandered from her face down to her legs.

She found herself blushing, and unconsciously dipped her head, cursing herself at the same time. She was acutely conscious that she had a rendezvous with, not Tom Dawkins, the only son of Ted Dawkins, the owner of the pitifully few acres known as Naughton Farm, but a sophisticated member of the forces of that country that had given the world Hollywood; a man who looked as though he had stepped straight out of that flickering screen that was their window on a larger world, rather than the pigsty or byre.

She wanted to project the image of one of those sophisticated women in the movies, a Katharine Hepburn or Joan Crawford; a woman who would be a fitting escort for an American soldier, not some gauche schoolgirl who knew nothing of the world. She found herself regretting she had not lit up before he arrived; a cigarette between her lips always made her more self-assured.

He was in his MP's uniform, but this time carried a white baton. He saw her looking at it.

"That's just for keeping the troops in order. Don't worry, I don't use it on the natives. I shoulda brung you some flowers, but—"

She laughed nervously.

"It doesn't matter. What did you say to the man that drove you in? I saw you pointing to your throat."

"Just pointin' out he should put his tie back on. I could've had him put in the cooler, but it don't go to antagonise guys unnecessarily. MPs is unpopular enough as it is."

"Why?"

"'Cos we's MPs. 'Course some like to hand out beatin's and check everyone's passes – not me and my buddies, you understand. So that gets the whole corps a bad name, get it? Nobody likes the idea of the army interferin' with their free time. But, fact is, there ain't no free time in the army."

"Is that the sort of thing you do, like ordinary police?"

"That's the sort of thing I do – enforcing regulations. That and other things: traffic control, criminal investigations, catching deserters, security of the HQ, enforcement of off-limits areas and blackouts."

"Like an ARP warden?"

"I guess. A bit more than that. So. Where do you wanna go?"

This was something to which she had given a great deal of anxious thought.

"Let's go to the British restaurant."

"The British restaurant?" Larry said, with a certain amount of awe that may have been arch. "That sure sounds grand. What happened to rationing?"

"It's not that grand."

She led him towards the British restaurant that had been set up in the hall of the infant school. These local authority-run 'restaurants' were furnished by the Ministry of Food and staffed by the WVS, to provide basic, cheap fare (the price was capped at five shillings) for those whose workplaces lacked canteens.

"Well, you look like you wouldn't be out of place at the Ritz, if you don't mind me saying so."

She didn't mind at all. She was suffused by a pleasure that brought a bloom to her cheeks. The fingers that touched the door handle tingled as they had when, as a child, she had thrust them into snow. Tom never paid her compliments or commented on her dress. She could have turned up to meet him in the best dress money could buy or a siren suit like Churchill, and either way he would not have batted an eyelid.

The only qualification to her pleasure, one that served to tighten the tension in her stomach and boost those charges of electricity that ran through her, was the anxiety lest she be recognised by one of the WVS women who staffed the restaurant, and who might tell her mother that Emily had visited the premises in the company of a GI.

The door opened on a hall the size of a tennis court, packed with tables of various sizes from those able to seat two or four to those that might cater for sixteen or more. At the far end was a serving counter and at the side a door through which women emerged bearing plates on trays. The smell of overcooked vegetables and dirty dishes mingled with cigarette smoke.

Emily's eyes scanned the women at the counter. One was in her fifties with a bowed figure as if she were used to leaning on a stick, the other younger, who moved the dishes with dextrous movements like those of a postmistress sorting post into its respective dockets. To her relief she did not know either. They would know her mother, of course, but as long as they did not know her no tales would get back home.

The people sitting at the tables were shop and office workers on their lunch break. This was the reason she had chosen this time for their rendezvous, hoping they would be less conspicuous. But she had neglected to consider that the more people, the greater the likelihood they would know her – or Tom. She recognised Anne Ketch, who she had gone to school with, and two girls who worked the searchlight battery at Pinkstone Point. As far as she knew they did not know Tom, or that she was walking out with him.

When the waitress came round, they ordered the choice of the day, an odd term in Emily's view, since there was no choice at all; it was pie or nothing. When the waitress departed, Emily was unable to suppress a yawn.

"What's that fer?" he asked.

"Just tired, that's all."

"And what's it that Miss Emily does that makes her so tired, when she's not looking beautiful and showing the world how to dance, that is."

Larry Schultz had obviously not learned the English habit of conversing in whispers, and he reacted with a naive smile to the looks of disapprobation that were turned upon him.

"Beautiful? No…"

She felt herself blushing furiously, and wishing she had some means to hide her face beyond staring at the Formica tabletop.

"Sure you are… So how do you spend your time?"

"Oh, Mum always has plenty for me to do. She has her 'make do and mend' parties. Mendin' the blackout curtains. Spring cleaning is her thing at the moment. And there's always the washin', though it's not so bad on yer hands at this time of year; winter they's red raw."

"Ain't you got no washin' machine?"

She found herself colouring again, thinking of how she, her sleeves rolled up to reveal arms whose whiteness ended abruptly at her wrists, as if she were wearing red gloves, would have to agitate the washing with the dolly, remove it with tongs, then put it through the mangle, or sometimes scrub the really dirty items on the washing board, and looked down at her plate as she replied:

"No, we jis' got ourselves a copper."

She went hurriedly on:

"And zewin'. And mending laddered stockings – even if they ain't silk, we gotta mend them. Proper Mrs Sew-and-Sew, I am… I'm waiting to go into the ATS."

"The what?"

"The Auxiliary Territorial Service – they do things like driving and cleaning for the forces, to free the men for fightin'."

At this point the waitress returned and, with a quick appraising glance at Larry Schultz that Emily rather resented, negligently dropped two plates with pie and mash on the table. When she had gone, he asked:

"Is that what you want to do?"

"Hardly. Sleepin' in a frozen Nissen hut with a load of other girls and drivin' Tilly trucks around all day. No fear. But I haven't got much choice."

She didn't know why she said that. Perhaps it gave the impression she knew more about the world than she did. That was what the likes of Veronica Lake were like, after all – worldly wise. But she wasn't reluctant. For one thing, her call-up would provide the excuse to persuade her mother to allow her to wear Tampax instead of the disgusting rags the older generation shoved in their pants.

"I want to have some money of me own," she said. "Girls as are workin' can afford things. Some of 'em come to us and want to buy our clothing coupons.

"Single women between twenty and thirty are conscripted, so we have to go into the ATS or the WRNS or the WAAF – that's navy or air force. But most of all they want women to work in munitions or the ATS, and I don't want to go into munitions, even if they do get an allowance of makeup. I've heard too many tales of the Canaries in the first war."

At his blank look she went on:

"That's women munitions workers what was turned yoller or blown up makin' bombs. Best jobs is in the parachute factories where you can get yer hands on the off-cuts of silk, but them's like gold dust. I'd rather go into the WRNS or the WAAF. They looks so much smarter than the ATS."

"Yeah, I seen them about. Say… are you sure this is beef?"

His handsome mouth had a lopsided look of distaste.

"You can't be sure these days."

"I guess not. This chow certainly takes some gettin' used to. And the pastry tastes awful funny."

"It's probably made with mashed potato instead of wheat. On account of the rationing. I can't tell the difference no more."

"Gee. We're lucky, I guess. It must be tough on you folk, this rationin' an' all."

"Ees. You get so you can't stop thinking about food.

We gotta use that powdered egg. Tastes like rubber. You can't get proper white bread no more – we has to put up with that National Loaf, all grey it is, like chewin' leather. And National Margarine that tastes of fish. You even needs coupons for offal now. Dad's in the pig club, so when they kills their pig we has pig's trotters, pig's ears, everythin'. I keep thinking of the breakfasts we used to have before the war – three rashers of bacon, two eggs, fried bread, sausages. I haven't seen a banana in ever so long."

"I love the way you say that."

"What?"

"Banarna."

She laughed.

"I'll get you some," he said.

She did not know how to respond to that so went on:

"Mum's joined one of those herb committees. Gert and Daisy told her to do it on *The Kitchen Front*. You know what we had yesterday? Boiled nettles on buttered toast – and there was precious little butter!"

"Nettles!"

"Ees, stingin' nettles like you find in the hedges, only they don't sting no more when they're boiled."

"You mean your ma, she goes pickin' these nettles?"

"It's called foragin'. The government's producin' all these leaflets encouragin' folk to do that sort of thing. She makes me and me brother drink rose hip syrup to keep the doctor away, she says. You gotta take the hairs out the inside 'cos they makes you bad."

"Gee, that's kinda crazy."

"We was lucky to have butter. Mostly it's drippin' these days."

"Drippin'?"

"Fat. On account of there's no butter."

She went on, hardly touching her pie in her desire to keep the conversation going.

"The WRNS is awfully choosy. You have to have someone in your family that's in the navy. I'd like to go into the WAAF, do plotting or work on the barrage balloons, but they said they'd only take me in the ATS if I wouldn't go into munitions."

"Will you have to move away from home?"

Was there a note of disappointment in his tone, she wondered, or was it just her wishful thinking? She was becoming uneasily conscious of the glances of the office workers turned in their direction.

"I dunno," she said distractedly. "I sometimes think I'd like to join a searchlight regiment, where you work as a range finder, but Ma and Da aren't keen – some of them are in out-of-the-way spots and the batteries are mixed."

"Mixed?"

"Men and women. You have to learn a lot – map reading, aircraft recognition; I wouldn't mind that. I was good at maps at school. There again, you have to do route marches. I know one girl that done it and she says they give them fur coats. I might do it just for the coat."

She laughed rather lamely.

"You had much bombin' here?"

"Not like Pompey and Bristol. They took a real pastin'. But sometimes they goes off course and gotta get rid of their bombs. Only last January, Lampton Street was hit and eleven was killed. And in '40 there was three streets hit, six killed, includin' my ma's cousin Lily, and they narrowly missed the school. It don't bear thinkin' about. But we get off lightly."

At this point the waitress returned, a cigarette depending from her lower lip. She cleared away the dishes, looking in reproach at Larry Schultz's plate which still had half of its pie uneaten. She swiftly returned with a tray bearing two coffees and two plates of spotted dick with custard, the latter coated with a skin that showed it had been standing for some time. The American looked incredulous as this concoction was placed before him, but raising his head, met the eyes of the waitress which seemed to dare him to make some critical remark. He remained silent until she had gone.

"Yeah, I guess you folks has really had it tough. But you're not goin' yet? Into this ATS, I mean."

"Oh no, not 'til next year."

She felt as if she were bathing in the warmth of his desire to keep her near him. But her nervousness inspired a volubility that was at the same time acutely self-conscious.

"Lucy can drive. She wants to be a driver in the ATS. I don't know what Joycie wants to do. She'll have some little dream, but she keeps mum—"

"Well, I don't care a fig for them. I'm only interested in what you're gonna do."

Again, she felt herself blushing and looking away, cursing herself. A man in a pinstriped suit was staring at her, and she wrenched her gaze back to Larry who was saying:

"But I guess I shouldn't be saying such things. For all I know a lovely lady like you might already have herself a young man."

"Oh… I… No-one special."

His question had caught her off-guard, and she was conscious that her hesitation may have revealed more than she intended.

"Well, that's just fine and dandy. This war's changed a lot of things. People meet new people, people they never expected to meet in their lives."

She felt the spotted dick sticking to her tongue and throat as she asked:

"And you… do you… have anyone? Back home, I mean?"

"No-one special. I dated a few d… gals… just to the movies, y' know. Say, this coffee, how do they make it? It ain't like any coffee I ever tasted. It ain't boot polish in hot water, is it?" His handsome mouth formed a rictus of distaste.

She laughed.

"You never can tell."

"Should've just asked for water."

He was regarding her with a fearful intimacy, and she swiftly wiped her lips in case any custard adhered to them. His eyes were an azure blue, and his gaze possessed a candour that Tom's had never done. Whenever she pictured Tom – and this was increasingly infrequently, for over the past year she had found herself struggling to remember what he looked like, and now she had no desire to picture him – he was always looking away, to right or left or over her shoulder. It may have been shyness, but the impression it left was one of shame or indifference. He did not look directly at her as this man did, open and unafraid.

But the thought of Tom made her feel guilty. Now she was looking away, not wanting to face that guilt. Rather she would meet the eyes of the American, so bright and candid and unsullied by... what? War weariness (and this the weariness of two world wars, the first of which had maimed Tom's father mentally as well as physically, the second of which loomed over the horizon as they met), and the dreary inevitability that Chalford represented.

And by the memory of parting. When Tom told her he had been called up, the Emily she had been had clung to him, thinking her life was ending (how little did she then know!).

In Tom's grey eyes could be read weariness, strain, fear. And something dull, lumpen, stolid, reminiscent of the clay of his father's fields, of the beasts that thronged his byre. By contrast there was in the candid blue irises of the American, an airiness, a self-confidence and assurance that quelled her own fears and doubts – doubts that had surfaced briefly on his abruptly changing the subject from his former girlfriends.

"And what's it like, living in America?"

Her need to say something that would distract from the frankness of his stare led her to ask something, or to ask it in a way that was, she realised, naive and gauche, the very thing she was determined to avoid. Her market town parochialism seemed to haunt her at every turn and frustrate all her assays at sophistication. She felt again the urgent need to light up but was unable to do so when still eating her pudding.

"I can't say. It's all I've ever known... Different to here."

She sensed something in his reply that went beyond mere confusion and hinted at reserve. Was it that he did not want to shatter her illusions, or did not want to be seen to boast to an inhabitant of this impoverished island, ground down by war?

In for a penny, in for a pound, she thought.

"Oh, tell me, do. What's your house like? What do you work at? What's the weather like?"

"Whoooahhh!"

And then, as if sensing her discomfiture, he laughed.

"Take it easy, will ya!… It's hotter than here, that's fer sure. Too hot at times, but you gets used to it. If you live there all yer life you know nuthin' else."

"Where do you live?"

"I live with my mom and pa near Athens city in Clarke County. That's to the east of Atlanta on the edge of the Blue Ridge Mountains. You know the song, 'The Trail of the Lonesome Pine'?"

"It sounds wonderful."

"It sure can be."

He proceeded to sing the first few bars of the romantic melody. She felt herself blushing and looking away towards the restaurant counter as his light tenor, for all it was muted, drew the stares of those on the next table.

"Hiking in the Chattahoochee Forest in the fall, taking in the colours of the pines is the best thing in the world."

She was unable to stop herself giggling, though uncomfortably conscious of the schoolgirl impression it must create.

"What?"

"That's such a funny name."

"Well, it's no funnier than Ly-sester."

Again, she laughed, and looked up to meet his broad smile.

"It's Leicester. Georgia... isn't that where *Gone with the Wind* was?"

"Sure is. Don't you go thinkin' of me as some Rhett Butler, now. Good old Dixie. I can smell the yellow jasmine just thinkin' about it."

"You miss home?"

"I guess I do," he said, as if the thought surprised him. "I would love sittin' out in the back yard on long summer nights just listenin' to the mockingbirds in the cypress."

"Yard? Don't you have a garden?"

"Sure... it is a garden... Miss it 'specially when we's doin' a route march in the pourin' rain."

"Do you often do that?"

"That and more is what we do. Twelve-mile endurance marches, wearing impregnated underwear, carrying full kit and pulling four carts per company, ten-mile speed marches. All that on top of the callisthenics, the machine gun and barbed wire infiltration courses, bayonet fighting. It ain't no picnic, no sir... But England does have its compensations."

She looked away, hiding her blush of pride, and tried to change the subject.

"Do you have skyscrapers?"

"Sure do. First was in 1908, with the Southern Mutual Insurance Company Building. Yes sir, we got it all!"

"Do you drive a car?"

"Soon as I got a job I got myself a '36 Chevvy. What you got here ain't nuthin' but toy cars compared to a Chevvy. She sure can roll. And we got freeways."

"What's freeways?"

"Big roads. Not like the little bitty roads you got here. It's just so much bigger, far as the eye can see. Unlimited skies."

"I often thought things here was too small."

There it was again, or did she just imagine it, that look of unease in his eyes.

"And what do you do? Your job, I mean."

"I'm in insurance. The Southern Mutual like I said before. I sells policies to unhappy wives plannin' to bump off their husbands."

They laughed. She liked his laugh. It was a hollow, low, throaty sound, as if it came from deep within him. But at the same time there was something guarded about it, as if he couldn't give himself wholeheartedly to the emotion but had produced an allowance of that laughter that was, for all its apparent generosity, carefully measured out.

"What are the women like in America?"

"Well, I guess plenty of guys'd say that da... women, are alike the whole world over. But no, there's differences. They're more open, up front, back in the US. Women here – I guess they're more reserved."

"Have you met many, here?"

He smiled. Her jealousy must have been apparent. Again, she cursed her naivety.

"We got invited to one of them WVS welcome club tea parties, and the hostess she was some real schoolmarm. We even had to bring our own potato salad and chocolate cake."

"Chocolate cake," she said dreamily.

"But no, we ain't met many gals. Just you and your friends."

"So I'm more reserved."

The way it came out it was almost an accusation.

"I don't mean that in any nasty way. I mean it in a nice way. It's nice to be reserved."

She sought to restrain the broadness of her smile.

"Okay, you done all the askin' and I done all the answerin'. So let me ask, what do you English women think of us American boys?"

She thought for a moment. It was like being handed the collecting plate at Evensong: how much could she afford to give away?

"You're smart."

"What, cleverer than your guys?"

"No, smart, smartly turned out. Much smarter than our boys. You take care of your appearance, and don't look any old how. You got better manners. You know how to treat a girl."

"And Englishmen don't?"

"It's as if they take us for granted. Of course, until you came they didn't have any competition."

"Well, a little honest competition never did no-one any harm, did it?... Hey, is that the time? I gotta be on my way. My pass is only until three. Say, I'm free Sunday afternoon, how about you?"

"Yes."

"Swell. What say we meet up and mebbe go for a little walk, eh?"

"We can walk by the river. It's nice and quiet there."

She found herself blushing, and had to stop herself from openly wincing at the thought of what she had said.

His smile told her that he was not oblivious to the

implications of it being quiet but was gentleman enough not to allude to it. A true southern gentleman. But to have the tongue of a gentleman was one thing, what about the mind? She just hoped he did not think she had meant it that way.

"I don't mean…"

"Sure you don't."

"We could go to the pub."

What was she doing? She was talking like a man inviting a simple-minded girl to walk out with him. When it should be the other way around.

"No. I like quiet."

A knowing smile tugged at his lips. Again, she had to stop herself wincing.

"What say we meet up at three o'clock?"

"Yes. I'd like that."

Her tone stuttered with reservation. She was wondering whether she had committed herself to more than she had intended.

"Where can we meet?"

"Do you know the police station… by the bridge?"

The stretch of river on either side of the bridge was the most frequented, and, unlike that further up by the old rowing huts, was popular with people of all ages. Part of her told her that this was the very place she should avoid, lest she be seen by her parents' friends. It was by the rowing huts that a girl and her GI beau belonged. But she was still reluctant to define herself in those terms. Larry was, she tried to tell herself, nothing more than a good friend, and she offering him no more than did the WVS ladies who took GIs to their homes.

"I can find it."

For a second or two she felt distrust, even fear, of that suave, assured smile, so redolent of cinema screens.

"See you at three then."

And then with a sweep of his jacket, with a lithe fluid motion that contrasted so strikingly with the lumpen, leaden movements of Tom Dawkins, he was gone.

She was reaching for her cigarettes when she became aware of the man in the pinstripe suit, a mackintosh and homburg hat in his hand, standing over her. He spoke, a sweet mellifluous tenor at variance with his words.

"You should be thoroughly ashamed of yourself, young woman."

And before she had a chance to reply, he was gone, and the door creaking on its hinges. She glanced up to see if her shame had been witnessed and saw the girls at the man's table staring in her direction, two of them openly smirking, a third looking away, haughtiness impressed on her doughy face, like the head on a Victorian penny.

She wanted to rise and go. But she wouldn't give them the satisfaction. Instead, she withdrew her cigarette and box of matches and lit up, staring back at them through the grey smoke that she trusted hid the burning of her cheeks.

What gave them the right to look down on her? Hypocrites was what they were. Why, for tuppence they would gladly swap places with her. They were just furious that no GI would look at them.

She thought of Sunday and her walk by the river with Larry. And she found that her reserve and doubt had quite vanished. They couldn't tell her what to do, these ignorant people who had lived their whole lives in this market town, and who looked down their sanctimonious noses, begrudging her a vision of something more. What was it Larry had said? A vision of unlimited skies.

CHAPTER NINE

The spring sunshine polished the blade of the river as Larry Schultz walked down the path with Emily on his arm, on this, the occasion of their third such tryst.

The water curved in a gentle arc so placid that the sunlight struggled to pick out anything like a current, anything beyond the bubbles that lay like strings of beads and merely hinted at flow, the ripples that burst and disappeared as insects fell into the water, anything beyond the twigs and fallen catkins that idled away the afternoon, mimicking the people that strolled past on both sides of the river, smart or casual as the fancy took them, but always relaxed and opulent of time.

They walked down a tunnel of branches bedecked with the first lime green shoots of spring, the first spectral shades of pussy willow catkins overhead, with the occasional crocus peeping out from the grass by the side of the path. The air was limpid, bright with that brittle brightness of early spring, with the merest breeze to impart a hint of tartness. Beneath their feet the mud of the path had been cast by the recent sunny weather into a relic preserving in relief the prints of horseshoes that had passed that way in the wetter season.

They passed middle-aged couples in their Sunday best hats, some trailing dogs, young men without jackets or ties, or elderly women hiding from the sun beneath parasols, until they reached those more secluded reaches of the path frequented by young lovers.

Larry, and apparently Emily also, he was gratified to note, preferred that bank of the river where clumps of willows often shielded the walker from view of all but the cows grazing in the fields.

The river was deep enough to accommodate smaller boats, even the Markles' yacht. Emily pointed out its sleek lines to Larry as the father ordered his son to take the wheel, and the gangly youth leapt over a coil of rope in his alacrity.

"He took that boat all the way to Dunkirk in 1940. Says he was lucky to escape with his life."

"Gee, ain't that something."

"Every time anybody grumbles about some byelaw he says, 'We've all got to do our bit. If I hadn't done mine the lads I brought back might be dead on Dunkirk beach.' That's typical of his sort. They use it to bully you with."

"What's his sort?"

"Posh folk. Thinks they's better than what you are."

"There you go with that class thing. What is it about this class?"

"Don't you have no classes in America?"

"No."

"But you know who the rich are? And who the poor are?"

"Sure."

"And only rich people can become president and in the government… And the rich hands their money down to their children?"

"Sure. That's the American way."

"And the rich runs your country same as they runs ours. But nobody takes much notice of that sort of thing no more. We don't doff our caps to the likes of Mayor Markle and Mr Villiers no more. But some of 'em still think they's better than the rest of us…"

"There you go again."

"We're all pullin' together now. And we're not supposed to get more'n our ration, though I bet Bob Alder has something under the counter for the vicar's wife. And we votes Labour now 'stead of Tory and Liberal. The old world's gone. Only there's some doesn't know it yet."

"Well, I can't rightly say as I understand. This country's a mystery to me."

"That's 'cos we've been around longer than America has. Anyway, you lot all come from here, didn't you?"

"I guess. Ways back, so's no-one can remember. Now we got Irish, Italians, Polaks, you name it."

"No English?"

"I guess they's just Americans now."

"Well, how can you understand what they're sayin'?"

Larry found her naivety engaging.

"They talks English. You gotta learn English soon as you step off the boat, otherwise there's no gettin' on."

"So you aren't all one country like we is. And they all mix together?"

"No… well, kinda, but the Italians is got their own

areas, and the Irish and the Germans and Scandinavians. It's like…"

"What?"

"Well, you gotta look out fer yer own."

"So how come your friend Luigi isn't fightin' for the Italians?"

"And I'm not fightin' fer the Germans, is that it? Well, 'cos our government tells us we gotta fight for the US of A. That's the price we gotta pay fer livin' in the richest country in the world, I guess. Then you got the niggers. They'll be comin' here soon enough. Watch out for them guys. They'll be all over you white gals like a rash. Don't have no self-control, don't niggers. Anyhow, we didn't come here on a nice day like this is to talk about niggers and class. You sure dolled yourself up good and proper. You look more like Veronica Lake every day."

Larry gazed unashamedly down Emily's body as she twirled about to display her lemon-coloured Utility frock decorated with cornflowers. But Larry was less concerned with the elegant lines of her clothing than what lay beneath. He looked with carefully crafted censoriousness at the gravy-stained legs with their pencil-drawn seam.

"Isn't it straight?" she asked. "The seam, I mean."

"I guess. How do you do it?"

"I tied the eyebrow pencil to me dad's bicycle clip to keep it straight. Anyway," she said coquettishly, "a girl shouldn't be givin' away her secrets. And a man should know better'n to ask."

"I gotta get you some silk stockings. Legs like that deserve to be properly tret."

"Really? Can you?"

"Sure. I can git you chocolates an' all. Only I get you the stockings and you gotta let me help you put them on… it's only fair."

She looked shocked, and for a second he feared he had misjudged her and gone too far too fast.

"Oh, you are a caution. Look, you made me blush. You are wicked, you Yanks."

She smiled archly. He was relieved to discover that hers was a show of propriety only.

"And how do you know so much about us Yanks?" he said, mimicking her archness. "I hope no other Yank's been hangin' round you."

"'Course not."

She blushed, but it may have been from the implied compliment.

"I didn't mean nothin' by it."

He was impressed by her naive contrition.

"Hey," he said, taking her hand in his. "You sore? I was only… what's the word?"

"Teasin'."

"Sure. I was only teasin'."

As she turned on him her smile that was so like a child's reprieved of offence, she tripped on an exposed tree root and plummeted forward. His grip on her hand slid up her arm and he held her. Her shoe had partially come off, and as she struggled to slide her toes back into the shoe, he pulled her towards him as surreptitiously as a pickpocket, so that when the shoe was back on their bodies were all but pressed together. They were alone on the path. The last people they had seen, a young couple throwing a ball for a dog, had passed them a few minutes since.

Emily looked up into his face with startling frankness, her brown eyes quivering with sunlight sheen.

"Will you forgive my teasin'?" he asked. "If you kiss me I'll know I'm forgiven. I won't be able to sleep otherwise."

She glanced nervously about her, up and down the empty path, and laboriously at the brake of willows in whose shadow they stood, as if to test the efficacy of its screen. Her expression was one of indecision, but he told himself it was nothing more than that salve to conscience that women – those that weren't broads, that is – applied before such a congress.

"What's the harm in a little kiss?" he pressed.

"None," she said with a deliberate asseveration as if she were surrounded by a whole regiment of Salvation Army asserting the contrary.

He fell on her, his lips subsiding into hers that received them, clumsily, uncertain at first, but succulent and hot, and then with a growing passion that made her hands claw at the back of his neck, drawing him into her. He released her to take a breath and did his best to wipe the lipstick from his face with the back of his hand. He must remember not to wash that hand before he had shown the boys his trophy.

"That was sure good."

He looked at the girl, all flushed and breathless. Had she ever been kissed before? Did those English guys do nothing but hold hands?

He was about to do it again when another couple appeared on the path ahead. It was Luigi and Lucy, the former with his arm draped unashamedly around the girl's shoulder.

"Hey! Fancy meetin' you guys here!" Luigi said.

"Yeah, fancy," he said, unable to camouflage the lack of enthusiasm. "Didn't know you had a pass."

"I don't tell you all my business, do I?"

Lucy looked sheepish and avoided Emily's gaze in particular, dipping her eyes beneath the brim of her floral bonnet, as they moved level and stopped.

"Sure is nice here," Luigi said. "Lots of that lovely vegetation."

Lucy blushed and squirmed with embarrassment under the arm that was still draped across her shoulder.

"Listen, we gotta get on. See you back at the camp," Larry said.

"Sure. We know when we ain't welcome, ain't that right, doll. Don't do anything your old uncle Luigi wouldn't do, eh, big boy."

Larry and Emily turned and proceeded in the opposite direction, Larry throwing the occasional glance back over his shoulder until he was sure the path was clear again.

"Say, are those two goin' steady? Whaddaya know." As if he didn't know. "You ain't worried we met them?" he asked. These English seemed ultra-sensitive about their reputation.

"No… she isn't one to gossip. You know what they say about people in glass houses."

"What do they say?"

"They shouldn't throw stones."

"I guess you British gals think us Yanks is fast, yeah? And that ain't the way you do things. You think we's too fast maybe?"

She did not answer.

"Well, you know, we're a young country. We're goin' places, we don't like to hang around."

At that she gave a sharp laugh, more like an embarrassed choke than a laugh. *Yeah*, he thought, *she don't mind fast, she's just too uptight to admit it even to herself.*

"But it ain't just that, you know. We's just here for the duration. We ain't gonna be around long."

At that she looked up sharply, and he had her.

"You gotta make the most of me, baby."

He laughed and pulled her to him. Her almond-brown eyes gazed up into his with an innocent plea that tugged at his loins as much as it ravaged his heart. He wondered what she would be like in the sack. Did some tigerish kernel lurk beneath that prim facade, was her naive enthusiasm and girlish gushing camouflage for something more adult? He was sure there was much passion, but would she, when it came to it, choke like a blocked machine gun? He realised that what attracted him to her was that not knowing, that challenge of tearing her out of her starched drawers and seeing not only what she looked like shorn of the Utility dresses, but how she would behave.

A harsh critic, one of them there bible-bashers, might say he wanted to corrupt her. But he didn't. He wanted her to corrupt herself out of her desire for him. He was sure she had another feller, serving with the forces. And her family would disapprove. He had heard the mutterings from the locals, along the predictable lines of 'over-paid, over-sexed and over here'. But in love it's survival of the fittest. And the way the war was going, there might not be many Limey boys to come back to these lovely ladies.

The thought that she would risk everything she had, all her relationships with family, friends, for him, was flattering. The pride he took in that fact was inseparable from his curiosity as to how far she would let her passion take her. It was like watching a boxing match between her proper self, legs together, guard up, and that other self of which she occasionally showed a glimpse, wild and passionate, throwing haymaker after haymaker. Did she have what it took to urge the latter onto victory? Sure she did; with him in her corner, it was a dead cert.

So curiosity, sexual pride and simple lust urged him on to the same end, like fans shouting for the same football team, and embellished this girl's considerable physical charms with nuances that continually surprised him.

She asked:

"Does England feel any more like home?"

He almost froze in his tracks. Surely she was not nursing hopes that he would settle down in this poor, ramshackle excuse for a country? That would be even worse than taking her in tow across the Atlantic.

He wondered, in an empirical way, how she would react when he ditched her. Of course, he would do it as gently as he could. He had no wish to cause ructions, what these Brits called 'a scene'. That would reflect badly on him and on the regiment. After all, he had as good an excuse as any guy who ever ditched a gal. He was going to war.

For how long, he wondered, after he was back in the States, would she yearn for him? For how long would she snatch up the morning's post in search of the letter that never came? For how long look out of the window every time she heard the train whistle, and wait in vain? When she married someone else, would she be thinking of him as that ring was slipped on her finger? When she bedded her husband? When she gave birth to her first child would she be thinking what their child would have been like? When she was on her deathbed, would she still see his face? It felt like pride not blood coursing through his veins.

This question of hers was worrying. But maybe he could turn it to his advantage.

"Sure does. Baby, anywhere you is is home to me, don't you know that?"

"But we've only known each other a few weeks."

"A few weeks is all it takes. Don't you feel the same?"

"I… I think so."

"That ain't very flatterin' to a man. Sure you do. You English gals is just shy of sayin' it."

"American girls aren't shy?"

There she goes again, talking about America.

"Not like you English… You do it so much better."

She laughed, and at the rippling chime he felt relief. They were hard work these English girls. But now it was time to turn up the heat some.

"There's more and more transports arrivin' from the States. Land being requisitioned for trainin' all the time. And… I shouldn't be tellin' you this, but we been down to the beaches to train with DUKWs."

"What's DUKWs?"

"Gee, I shouldn't say, but trucks, doll. Like the CCKW, but trucks that can go in water, how about that? To land on the beaches, you get it? So I don't know how much longer we gonna be here. If the invasion's gonna be this year it's gonna have to be soon."

He felt guilty saying it because there was little chance of an invasion until the following spring, but he could not help being gratified by her response.

"Oh surely not. Not yet."

"Sure now. You don't invade Europe in the fall. You gotta go in the spring or summer, before the snows set in, so's you can move your men and equipment."

"What if it doesn't snow?"

Her naive blitheness annoyed him. He had always imagined Europe having a climate like Minnesota.

"It's gotta snow, ain't it?"

"It doesn't always snow here. I don't know about Europe."

"Sure you don't. Well, the generals can't rely on that. We may be movin' is what I'm sayin', and faster than we think... so time for us is short."

"I see."

"Do you...? Come here."

They stopped beneath the overhanging branches of a willow and kissed again.

"You do... care for me, don't you?"

"Yes. You must know I do."

Then an inspired thought. It may be a shot in the dark, but...

"You ain't got someone else... some English boy that's away somewhere, have you?"

"No."

That second of hesitation told him that his shot had struck a bullseye. His guess, made with an ulterior motive, had been right after all. But she had denied it and it served his purpose to go along with the denial.

"Well then, there's just you and me. And I'm crazy about you, baby."

"I don't know what you mean, I don't know why you're saying this."

"Sure you do. You're a good girl... an honest girl, I know that. But these times we're livin' in... they change us. People can't behave the same as they did before."

"Why not?"

He felt exasperated, and disappointed.

"I can't help feelin' you ain't as keen on me as I is on you."

"No... that isn't so at all, but... I don't understand what you're saying."

Was this girl naive or downright simple?

"What I means to say is, we're at war. We gotta make the most of the time we got. Real time, not like here where we can't do what we want for fear somebody's gonna catch us and tell tales round town, you get me? What I'm sayin' is, I could get me some furlough for a weekend. We could go away somewhere, to a quiet little hotel somewhere... near the sea, maybe."

"Oh... that."

"See, I don't know how much longer I'm gonna be here. We might get orders to move any time."

"Move where?"

Waves of exasperation rose within him. Either she was stupid, or she was stalling for time.

"To the Channel ports. To Scotland or wherever. For the big push. And you might never see me again."

"You won't come back?"

He felt like slapping her.

"Sure, I'll come back... if I can," he added significantly.

As she thought about it, he added:

"You might not even want to see me... if I'm badly wounded. Scarred. Or I might lose an arm or a leg."

"No, no, don't say that. Don't say it!"

She turned to face him, grabbed him about the upper arms with a grip that was surprisingly strong.

"Baby, we gotta face facts."

"Whatever... you're like, I'll always want you... want to see you."

"Sure, sure," he said in his best mollifying tone. "There's some gals... but you're not like that, I know. It might be different here, but in the States, if a gal loves a guy... they do it, you know... If she loves him." Again, the significant postscript.

She still had hold of his arms and gazed up into his eyes with the dumb submission of a cow. He had her at last.

"I do... I do love you... it's just so early, I'm not sure I'm ready."

"Babe, none of us is ready. I ain't ready to go to France or wherever and have the Nazis shootin' at me."

She winced at that. Hitler's firepower was working vicariously in his favour.

"Let... let me think about it... just... I can't say now."

"Sure. Only we ain't got much time, you know that."

"I know."

They walked back along the path. Larry felt satisfied. He had sown the seeds and he knew he had her. It was only a question of how much more pressure he had to apply. Maybe he could get Luigi to drop a hint in her ear, a suggestion of a move that would be enough to push her over the edge. Goddam, he hoped she was worth it. But he didn't want to go through life and only have slept with Barbara.

They were walking slowly, arm in arm, and had just gone past the junction of the riverside path with that which led from the woods across the water meadows.

"Weeell, fancy that. Emily France."

He turned to see a blotchy-faced girl about Emily's age wearing a fierce red lipstick and a carefully manufactured expression of pleasant surprise. From one arm trailed a curly-haired terrier on a lead. Her other arm was through that of a lugubrious young man in the blue uniform of a British WOP AG.[2]

"I can see why you're dressed up to the nines. And who's this then?" the newcomer asked in a piercing vibrato that hinted at asperity.

Larry turned on the charm in an attempt to defuse the situation.

"Private Larry Schultz, US 116th Infantry Regiment, at your service, ma'am."

"Ooooh, not at my service, by the looks of it."

The word 'service' was heavily loaded. She went on.

"Schultz? Consorting with the enemy, Emily?"

The air gunner studied the dog's backside with evident embarrassment.

"He's our ally," Emily replied with a stubborn pout.

"Of course, dear," the girl patronised. "Consorting with the allies then. Me, I prefer them home grown. I thought you did, too. While the cat's away, eh – the Tom cat!"

---

2   An RAF wireless operator/air gunner

She exploded in a hideous cackle.

Emily's pretty face grew taut under a baleful smile, her rouged cheeks sunken. She gripped his arm with a surprising power, propelling him forwards.

"Come on!"

"All's fair in love and war, that's what I always say."

She exited with the bouncy gait of a cartoon character, dragging her airman with her.

When they had gone a hundred yards and neither Emily's face nor her grip on his arm had slackened, Larry asked:

"Friend of yours?"

"April Knight? Nasty little baggage, she is. Never misses a chance to stick her nose in someone else's business. She seems to think... seems to think me and... a boy I know have an understanding. When he's no more than a friend... I never said nothin' that made him think otherwise. I'm not that sort."

"Who is he, this friend?" Larry was unable to prevent himself loading the word with irony.

"Tom... he's in the Eighth Army."

"Does he write to you?"

"Yes...but as I said... we're like brother and sister."

The little minx. He knew it, of course, but now she had been forced to come clean. And she didn't like it. Even when she dropped his arm, he could tell by her brisk step and her taut gait.

"She's no better than she should be. Gives herself airs. She's just jealous 'cos no Yank ever looked at her twice... It doesn't matter to you, does it?"

"Not at all."

The only effect the intelligence had on him was to inspire a certain contempt for a girl who had a boyfriend – and for all she said, he did not doubt this Tom was a boyfriend – fighting for his country while she was walking out with him behind Tom's back.

Not that he gave a damn about these absent Brits. He was quite happy to take advantage of the situation. More than happy, since any vestigial guilt he may have felt for what he intended to do was expunged like chalk from a blackboard. He was, as the Catholics said, absolved.

It occurred to him that, although he had never thought of himself as cynical, maybe that was what he was, and it took this country to make him see that all a girl was after was a guy with a good job, a nice house, with 'prospects', as they said. A life in a country that existed on the big screen, and only existed there. And all this 'love' was just so much hogwash. A part of him felt sorry about that. But it wouldn't be him that would be sorry so much as her. She, and others like her, would be the price this country would pay for dragging them over the pond to risk their lives in a war that was no business of theirs.

CHAPTER TEN

Mayor Markle was in one of the offices off the council chamber in the town hall in the company of Grimsdyke, the wizened clerk to the council, when Major Bellucci entered.

On catching sight of the major, the mayor rose with the precipitation of one standing to attention and cursed himself for a display that no doubt confirmed to Bellucci an authority he seemed already to have arrogated to himself. He really must be more assertive in the presence of their American visitors. However, assertiveness was no easy matter when faced with Major Bellucci. It led him to speak abruptly to his clerk.

"Major, what can I do for you? Get on with that, Grimsdyke."

The clerk shuffled off with a thick file under his arm and a recalcitrant pair of spectacles on a chain bouncing under his chin.

When they were alone, Bellucci said:

"I need to speak to you about relations between my men and your citizens."

Bellucci appeared flushed and combat-ready. In any normal man this might, the mayor thought, be taken for anger. However, he had never seen the American officer other than flushed and combat-ready.

Mr Markle sank into a leather upholstered armchair that accepted his weight with a wheeze and gestured to Bellucci to take a chair on the other side of the desk. The opulent leather that expanded around him, and on which he outstretched his arms, had always impressed him after the manner of a throne, and now more than ever was he grateful for the appurtenances of his office.

Ever since he had first spied the chubby, beringed finger of political ambition beckoning to him, Henry Markle had modelled himself on the most distinguished politicians of the day – at least, those of a conservative persuasion. Initially his model had been Stanley Baldwin who, with his man-next-door lack of pretension he regarded as embodying that meritocratic trend in the Conservative Party that enabled men of his own background to aspire to the highest offices of state.

The country was travelling in an egalitarian direction, and he, Henry Markle, was determined to be one who marched to the tune of the times, particularly when its refrain accorded so well with his own advancement. With his chunky frame and large head, he was by no means dissimilar to Baldwin, and had taken to smoking a pipe largely in emulation of the former prime minister, although he felt the appendage added to his gravitas without the need for Baldwinian comparisons.

Now, however, comparisons with Baldwin served him rather ill. The man was part of the pre-war world, as obsolete as the wing collar and spats. With an irony that Markle could not fail to appreciate, Winston Churchill, who had, in the '30s, seemed quite as obsolete, an enfant terrible embodiment of an otiose aristocratic privilege, was now the only star in the firmament; the embodiment of national resistance.

It was true that Mr Atlee, with his bank manager unpretension, let alone Lloyd George and Ramsay MacDonald, the illegitimate sons of farm labourers, spoke more to Markle's bourgeois heritage than Churchill, but they were liberals and socialists, and nobody embodied the spirit of the nation more than Churchill, for all they called him in the ration queue. The pipe was out, and Henry Markle could often be found puffing on a cigar.

The mayor was a self-satisfied man, used to the deference of his fellows, in the bank, in the shops, the lounge bar of the Red Lion, where he took care to produce the cigar. They might not agree with the regulations foisted upon him by central government, but they knew the plight of the nation required such measures. And since Dunkirk, and his actions in taking the *Mary Bell* across the Channel under hostile fire, his prestige had risen to an unprecedented degree. Say what you like about the British, they knew the respect due to their elected leaders.

The same could not be said of the Americans, who, although they were not Communists or Levellers of any complexion, quite the reverse, were yet rebels at heart, instinctively opposed to any authority, however legitimate; who twitched in reflex to any suggestion of the common good; who stood on guard at the gate to their smallholding, their shotgun ready for action should federal authority hove into view.

Markle had been terrified sailing to Dunkirk. But Major Bellucci scared him in a way that no devilish machinery of Mr Hitler could – in a face-to-face way. A man could, he realised with dismay, brave shot and shell without flinching yet be brought up short, tongue-tied and cowed by another human being.

In Major Bellucci the Mayor of Chalford was brought within spitting distance (an apt metaphor indeed) of a lack of deference that verged on contempt and was combined with an overweening confidence in himself as representative of that arrogant nation. The mayor's blossoming self-esteem withered and died when the major muscled his way into his personal space. After all he had been through, that should not happen.

"You're not a military man, but it don't take no military man to understand…"

Markle felt his anger swelling. What did this 'military man' know of the terror that grips you when you hear the unearthly wail of Stukas diving on your unprotected craft? He had never seen a man cut in two by a shell, his upper body perfectly intact, writhing on the sand while he pumped blood from the carcass that remained of his groin.

Or guilt. It was his guilt that started it; his guilt that ended it. The survivor's guilt, they called it. He had survived when so many his age had been sucked into the mud of Passchendaele or churned up in the Kaiser's Spring Offensive. That and the fact that he owned the *Mary Bell*.

He could never have imagined that his pride and joy could bring him into such mortal danger, and provide inspiration for the nightmares that still brought him, screaming and drenched in sweat, to the surface of consciousness, a surface he saw as choppy waters, capped in a hell of burning oil that ate its way in his direction holding out the alternatives of drowning or immersion in a bath of fat that would melt the flesh from his screaming mask of a face, leaving him a grinning skull, bobbing like an apple of nightmare and licked by waves of fire.

"Do you hear me, Mr Mayor?"

Markle fumbled with the ink stand, teak and inlaid with mother-of-pearl, a gift of his constituency party, in a desperate attempt to achieve some self-esteem.

"Petty grievances shouldn't stand between men and their dooty."

Duty. Yes, it had been his duty after the Admiralty had made that announcement requiring particulars of all self-propelled pleasure craft between thirty and a hundred feet. He had not known how hard a duty until he and his nineteen-year-old son, Nicholas, and Les Craigie, the eighteen-year-old sea scout who would crew the *Mary Bell*, took leave of his wife, Amanda, and daughter, Helen. Hugging them, legs quaking beneath him, his soul ballasted with dread and the conviction he would never see them again, and worse, that he was taking his son to his death, the grief of it hardened in his throat and he had to turn away lest they see his tears. He read the pain in his wife's face: the pain he had authored. But love could be something worse than pain. Was there not, in those green eyes, reproach for him taking their son to a place where his life could be forfeit? He thought of Agamemnon taking leave of Clytemnestra after sacrificing their daughter Iphigenia.

Off into the fog. And when the fog lifted, particles of soot falling like black snow, the sea littered with burning destroyers, minesweepers and MTBs, palls of smoke from burning oil tanks, a caterpillar of men stretching for a mile along the Mole, while Heinkels circled like vultures and Stukas fell upon their helpless targets.

Compared with that, what were the major's gripes?

"Citizens. You mean the girls. Well, of course we all—"

"Not the girls. I guess nobody's told you. Last night one of your farmers drove his herd of cattle into our field where they trampled my men's tents into the ground and damaged important items of equipment, including anti-aircraft guns, before we managed to round them steers up and get them back out."

Henry Markle would not have believed that Major Bellucci's voice, intimidation being its characteristic timbre, could be the more intimidating, but now it quite surpassed itself in the comminatory, growling like a tank exchanging the metalled road for a dry stream bed. In his discomfiture he made a pitiful attempt at humour.

"No, I hadn't heard – no pun intended."

A degree of bewilderment subtly modulated the major's anger that, thus stalled, did not seem to know whether to submit to some appeasement or go on and augment itself to something even greater. The major's fingers thrummed on the tabletop, a morse code of pent-up fury. The walls of bone that comprised his maxilla and mandible were now defined by the adjacent muscles as something positively cyclopean.

In every man Markle knew there was some spark of shrewdness behind the eyes, some indicator of calculation, but not in the major; only that bullish will that would head-butt its way through life. That will, if it ever stood easy, did so only in the form of disgust and scorn. The wrinkles at each temple spoke not of an habitual smile, but of the sardonic focus on what he no doubt saw as the pettiness that surrounded him, and were he to laugh it would be in the contemptuous bark of the fiercest dog in the neighbourhood.

The mayor gave an uneasy laugh and hurried on:

"This is no time for levity, I see that. Unfortunately, these things happen in the country. A walker leaves a gate open, or the rope that holds the gate becomes frayed... Obviously I am very sorry for the consequences for your men, and I hope it did not cause them..."

"This was no accident, Mr Mayor. I believe this was a deliberate act of sabotage to the United States war effort on the part of one or more of your citizens."

"Oh come now, Major. You cannot seriously be suggesting there are Nazi agents in our town. I know we are all warned about it – careless talk costs lives and that sort of thing – but this is really rather fanciful."

Bellucci sighed in a manner that Markle found quite insolent. The mayor was used to men whose gaze rarely fell upon you while they conversed, rather roamed hither and thither in a way he found respectful, but Major Bellucci's brown eyes pinned you, like those of a robber who had you back against the wall up some alley.

"I don't say Nazi agents. I say townsfolk. This isn't the first example of this kind. My men have been shouted at in town, we've had a brick thrown over the fence with a piece of paper saying, 'Yanks go home.' There was nothing wrong with the fastening, I checked it myself. And it was loosed after dark when there'd be no walkers about, and so's the cattle could come rampagin' through the field where my men were bedded down for the night. We were goddam lucky none was injured."

"I'm sure there was no such intention—"

"That's as may be, Mr Mayor. I don't say there was. But you and your council gotta getta grip on these folks. My men didn't choose to be here, and don't wanna be here. But we're here for the good of your country. We don't expect gratitude. But we don't expect to be tret like this neither. Folk in this town don't like the idea of my men walkin' out with your women. But we got us a job to do, and they gotta let us get on and do it."

"Oh yes, Major, quite," said Markle, in his most placatory tone. "But this is a difficult time for us all, and while I realise there have been some - I do not say disagreements, but some slight failure of meeting of minds - I am sure this doesn't in any way represent popular feeling here in Chalford. No, I am convinced the actions are those of one man. And I think I need look no further than Mr Westwood, whose land was requisitioned for your use."

"Well, you rein him in, Mr Mayor. Get him told good and proper. Bring the law down on him if you need to."

"Certainly. I am sure that on reflection you'll agree our town has done its utmost to accommodate you and your men. I know that a number of them have been entertained by our good ladies of the WVS."

"The ladies have been most hospitable," Bellucci replied with an uncharacteristic equability, but the hint of a subversive smile.

"And the dances at the church have, I understand, been a great success in breaking the ice."

Again, that enigmatic smile from the American.

"Well, they have, Mr Mayor. I say nothing about the fist fight that broke out when one of your young men took exception to my men dancing with local girls."

"Well, we must expect that sort of thing, Major."

"That's as may be, Mayor. But I don't expect a herd of cattle tramping my men's tents into the dust. Please ensure this sort of thing is not repeated."

"You may rest assured, Major. I shall do everything in my power to smooth relations between your forces and our locals. I apologise unreservedly, but leave it with me, and think no more of it."

"I hope I don't have to. Or it'll be on your conscience."

As the major left, Markle writhed in fury. Conscience.

He had hauled himself from the cockpit, ears still ringing from the bullets that pinged off the metal, that drilled into the wood panelling like rivets, desperately looking for his son. And then grasping Nick as he rose from the deck, a thing of beauty, an oil-smeared incarnation of relief. But all the time conscious that they had lost their way and were beam-on to the waves. Then he saw the lad Les Craigie, floating upright nearly a cable to port, the swell breaking over his pale face, the staring wide eyes, the broken eggshell skull smeared with pink.

Henry Markle had always craved responsibility. Responsibility implied power, and having others rely upon his exercise of power was, he had learned early in life, flattering to his ego. Perhaps that was why he wanted to skipper the *Mary Bell*. To be at the helm, with others relying on his skill and nerve.

Never had he imagined that his position in Chalford society, his penchant for a life on the ocean wave, might impose an irresistible moral imperative to be responsible for the life of another. Useless to say that in wartime we are all without exception responsible for one another. What if the searchlight operator were reading the *Picture Post* when he should be attending to his duty? What if Mr Smith were not as punctilious as he ought about his blackout? What if Mrs Smith hoarded food? They were all, in a great way or small, responsible for each other. What of he or she who bought off a spiv like Ted Barkiss? As they said on the information film, 'say to yourself, it all depends on me'.

But none of this casuistry could bring back young Les. Useless to blame Herr Hitler when he was a thousand miles away. Here in Chalford was only Henry Markle. The responsibility began and ended with him and left him dearly wishing he had done as he had, unintentionally, in the first war: kept his head below the parapet. And if absolution beckoned in the question of what would happen to the nation if they all kept their heads below the parapet, it was only to be dismissed with the self-pitying plea of 'why me?'.

He had thought the worst that could happen to him would be to lose Nick, and it would have been. But the loss would have been his own. He was forced to bear witness to grief that was all the more harrowing for being understated: the stoic if glassy-eyed acceptance of a calamitous implosion. If the Germans had come, Henry Markle would have stayed to fight them, but when he saw grief suck in those hollow cheeks, apply paste to the sunburned skin, and undermine Frank Craigie's bowlegged stance, he wanted to turn and run like the guilty thing he was.

He stood at the window and watched Major Bellucci hurl himself into his jeep, for the first time in his acquaintance feeling contempt for the man. His complacent assumption of superiority was an American version of Colonel Blimp; the embodiment of all that was archaic and retrograde in the military establishment. The idea that we could go on doing as we had always done and come through because of some transcendental principle of entitlement was what, in his view, had led to some of the worst disasters of the war, from Dunkirk to the fall of Singapore.

The least you could say of the British, he thought, *is that we know how old and tired we are. The Americans are young, vigorous, think they know all the answers. But they don't even know the questions.*

As his golfing partner Tony Bland liked to say: 'We Brits know a thing or two.' That was why we had not succumbed to Fascism like Germany, Italy and Spain. Our love of liberty, distrust of dogma and the demagogue had served us well. As had our tolerance, love of fair play and sense of humour. Any army goose-stepping through an English town would be laughed to shame.

Markle could only hope it remained that way, because war tended to bring to the fore men who relished the brutality of the struggle, who gloried in its capacity to license inhumanity and liberate mankind from the discipline of civilised behaviour.

CHAPTER ELEVEN

Tom was shocked to hear Jack say:

"Funny, I never thought of meself as a windy, or superstitious or nowt. But I don't think I'm gonna make it through this night."

"Dinna talk stupid," said Stevie. "You gotta make it. You owe me a couple of packets of Passing Cloud."

"One of you lads, gan and see me old missus. Tell her… oh, I dunno… tell her somethin'… Tell her I was thinkin' aboot her… and it was quick."

"Any mair o' that talk and I'll knock yer lights oot and we'll both of us be up on a charge."

Tom laughed. But laughing was the last thing he felt like. He had never heard Jack speak like this. He had thought, after the briefing they had been given about Mareth, that he could not be any more unnerved.

The CO addressed them from the top of an upturned crate. They were to attack today. The 8th Battalion, including their company, A Company, were to take the Ouerzi Fort with Scorpion tanks. The Italian Young Fascist Division held most of the line, but the German 90th Light

Division guarded the critical parts of the sector with the 15th Panzers in reserve. That, together with the formidable defences and the natural advantage the defence possessed in the wadi, made the attack a terrifying prospect.

They were in the assembly area by an old Bedouin trail in the Wadi Zeuss. Under a vast night sky Tom felt like a tiny insect glued to the ball of earth. Never had he felt so insignificant. The moon was coming up and its eerie light turned Jack's face into something unearthly. Tom had heard of death masks being made of famous people after they died, and the term suddenly appeared in his brain, an unwelcome accretion to his own fear.

The previous day Tom was writing his last letter home when he saw Jack look up from the game of chess he was playing with Stevie on the latter's portable board, and at those troops who were LOB, or left out of battle, as they formed up and marched away. The expression on his face was one of grim envy and a sour fatalism, perhaps even nostalgia. He did not expect to see those men again.

Tom returned to the letter to his father. He had already written to Emily, a blithe missive full of the sort of Pathé News patriotism he felt she expected to hear and was camouflage for the dread that all but paralysed his brain. It was effectively the same letter he had sent before Alamein, and like that, characterised by the misspelt, ungrammatical stuttering that reflected his unease with the medium. On paper he was like the soldier who is thrown from the deck of the troopship into the sea unable to swim.

Tom was acutely self-conscious of his own incompetence with the written as well as the spoken word, never more so than when writing to Emily, who, even if she was not more literate than himself (it was difficult to judge, because her letters rarely reached him) nevertheless possessed a much neater hand, with elegant swooping loops to her letters. His father's view of education had been, 'What's the good o' all that larnin'?', a refrain that had run through his school years, and justified the elder Dawkins' refusal to 'waste good money' on books, and his perennial injunction not to 'waste his time' on 'readin' a load o' nonsense' when there were tasks to be performed about the farm.

It was only after the clichés were spent that, the sobs gathering in his chest, he added something more personal. 'Dear Em,' he wrote, 'I am thinking of you all the time and it's only the thort of you is keepin me goin. I hope to come home to you soon as may be, when we gets old Hitler beat good and proper.'

And indeed, it was only the idea of Emily France that held his competing emotions in some form of equilibrium. The thought of his not being there when the troop train pulled into Chalford, not falling into her arms, but have her stand there, desolate, while the other men pushed past her and were swept up by their sweethearts. That was the emotion that charged the panic in his breast; that had his chest heaving as if it could not swallow enough air; that called to him to get up and run off into that shimmering horizon, whose ochre hills called to him with their promise of innumerable funkholes, with the prospect of the sun glinting off the sea, and the salty tang of it calling him home. The panic that made his inexpert hand more inexpert still, that made him feel like weeping at the thought of what he was putting on the hazard, was balanced, but only just, by the opposite scale, wherein lay her contempt of him should he fail in doing his duty to defend his country, his town, and most of all, her.

It was with relief that he sealed the letter to his girl and took up that to his father. For all that they had been thrown together by the death of his mother from a stroke when Tom was eight, father and son had never been close. But it was inevitable, he sometimes thought, that virtually all his experiences, his very thought processes themselves, should be moulded by his father; that he should be a copy of his only surviving parent. The thought filled him with dismay. For the last upon which his tender leather had been beaten was a hard and unforgiving one indeed.

Tom had known as much when his father, his heavy hand pressing implacably down upon his shoulder, ushered him into the parlour where the dead body of his mother lay in an open coffin, lit by three candles in jam jars, and, as gently as he was capable, eased his head down to look into the ghastly face, whose whiteness mirrored that of the lilies that lay on her sunken chest. Tom had never known if his father had meant to shock him, or to show him that life was hard and what death was like. But whatever the motive it failed. Because Tom barely recognised the marble bust, with the eyelids closed upon the vivid green eyes and the mouth slumped down like that of Jackie Carson, the village madman who accosted all the boys with slavering shouts of 'You Johnny!' It was not his mother; it was only a death mask.

What should he say to his father when those words might be the last that passed between them? Just the same old Pathé News clichés. They would roll up the enemy and send them packing. What else did they have to say to one another? They had not parted on good terms when he joined up, as Tom had enlisted before replacement workers were required for every farm. Tom had written a few times since, and as his father was even less forthcoming with the written word than the spoken, had received only one reply, a brief note in unsharpened pencil, bereft of punctuation and bemoaning the fact that the War Ag inspector had given him a grade C.

He did not know if his father missed his mother; he never spoke about her. His father had never asked what he wanted out of life. When informed he was walking out with Emily he had simply said, 'Mind you don't get her in the family way, my boy, or you're gonna have to pay fer her.' If the elder Dawkins was on his deathbed, his son could imagine him saying nothing more impassioned than the instruction, 'Don't you forget to feed them chickens, boy.'

It was strange, but Jack Ferris, though only seven years older than Tom, seemed more of a father to him than his own dad. Perhaps that was because Jack had a wife and kids. Or because they had the experience of the war in common. But sons do not usually have to go into battle with their fathers by their side and have to look out for them as well as for themselves.

Visibility was good, and the chill of the night coming on, descending from the sky with its godlike moon upon an earth that still retained some of the day's heat. They marched off, followed by a convoy of jeeps carrying two-inch mortars and their supply of hot cocoa. After two hours they reached the FUP, marked with white tape.

They had a few hours before the attack and settled down, with some lying on their packs and trying to get some sleep. They did not dig slit trenches. Tom, after wetting his handkerchief and wrapping it around his face to protect it from the dust, sat up for a while with Jack and Stevie, but saying nothing. Tom envied those who could sleep, while he sat restlessly pulling at a loose nail, his mind rehearsing the mantra, 'Let me come home to Em.'

His stomach gurgled, his pulse thrummed at his temple, and at each involuntary movement of his body he was conscious of the muscles tensing and relaxing. He was more acutely aware of his body than he had ever been, and regarded that body with an eccentric sentimental protectiveness. His mind was a sentry, primed to extreme vigilance in defence of the organism it inhabited.

Stevie had fallen asleep, but his oblivion was rudely interrupted by the arrival of the truck that brought up the scaling ladders they needed to cross the wadi. As Stevie started awake, surprise and outrage on his face, Tom laughed, an unnatural explosion that possessed a component of hysteria.

The truck's arrival brought down on them a vicious enemy artillery stonk. The truck was hit, bathing them all in a jaundiced glare. Caught in the open, without any trenches for cover, they could only cower, making themselves as small as possible. Tom drew his legs up and tucked his head between his thighs, drawing his knees over his ears. But the whine of the incoming shells would not be gainsaid, piercing the flesh and bone, and driving its unmanning eldritch screech deep within the tissue of his brain, as his body shook to the cleaving of the air and the thudding of shells.

When it was over, he took a deep breath, drawing the gritty evening air deep into his lungs, feeling as if he had held his breath for hours. He drew up his head against the protest of aching muscles. Through blocked ears, behind the stippled darkness, there was more screeching. A shape was created out of the darkness. The man's form coalesced, hopping comically, for his left leg was gone, severed at the upper thigh. But the man's castrated howling for his mother was not comic. A man tried to wrestle him to the ground, but he fought him off, and he had to be brought down by another whose cries of 'Medic! Medic!' competed with the man's screaming in which all reference to the mother was now lost, confounded in a maelstrom of shock.

Strangely, as if he had blacked out for a minute or so, the next thing Tom knew the man was gone, and he was struggling to his feet. He was light-headed, and staggered. His body was drenched in a sweat that immediately chilled to the touch of the cold air and he began to shiver. He examined the dark shadows about him and to his relief found Stevie and Jack, both looking ghastly beneath a coating of sweat-streaked sand.

The truck had overturned, but the scaling ladders were intact, and they were ordered to unload them, a laborious task since each ladder required eight men to lift it. The ladders were then loaded aboard the Scorpion tank that was to accompany them to the wadi.

The Scorpion, which Tom had never encountered before, was a flail tank that could only move at a walking pace when using its flails, which were designed to clear mines, and which flung up clouds of dust that stung the eyes and reduced visibility to a few yards. Their company were to march in threes behind their Scorpion. Tom, Jack and Stevie walking behind the tank as a three could only console themselves with the thought that they had not been the man chosen for the suicidal task of walking in front of the Scorpion as a guide, bearing a lantern.

A barrage of 25-pounders started up in support of the attack on their left, and their own machine guns fired over their heads. Half an hour after the barrage started, they set off in their threes. They followed a white tape and crossed the start line, a painstaking progress interrupted when they flinched and dived for cover as one of their Scorpions set off a mine.

The frightful roaring night was a gravity that pressed him in on all sides at once, so that the evacuated can that was his being felt itself crushed, inevitably, irresistibly, at the same time as it seemed to balloon outwards, to form a wall against which the shock waves reverberated, making the bricks to ring and mortar to crumble away.

They continued to advance, the German tracer passing harmlessly over their heads. They crested a ridge and could see moonlight glinting off water. It was the wadi, thirty feet wide and with dauntingly steep sides, running full after the winter rains. As they manhandled the scaling ladders from the Scorpions, a couple of shells landed amongst them. Tom dived behind a stunted bush, the only cover available. But four or five men were caught in the blast, including Freddy Bastin, the Battalion boxing champ. As the wounded were tended to, and told to scrape out shelters for themselves, dark rumours began to spread and Stevie readily took them up.

"That's oor barrage. The fuckers is fallin' short. If I survive this I'll gie someone a kickin' fer this, you just see if I dinna."

They climbed down to the wadi and waded knee-deep to the other side, where all were accounted for, and climbed out using the ladders. Beyond the wadi was a patch of mined ground on the way to the anti-tank ditch. The sappers got to work, swinging their detectors from side to side. But they quickly gave up on the task, complaining to the captain that there was too much ordnance about, and their earphones were rendered useless by the barrage.

The enemy opened up with a fierce stonk from which Tom and the others took cover. But the sappers were caught in it and lost their corporal and a good few of their men. They could do nothing but go on and try to traverse the uncleared minefield.

They moved out in single file, Tom tense, his breath wrestling in his throat. *Don't let me die.* Or if it had to be, let it be quick. He did not want to live for hours in agony with his legs gone from under him, his life blood seeping into the greedy sand.

Then to his right, flashes and screams. There were calls for stretcher-bearers. Tom stood stock-still, the cordite irritating his throat, not wanting to put a foot beyond that precious spot of safe earth on which he stood. That which was the essence of him retreated deep within his skull, and sat there, tense, vigilant, prickling with its own vulnerability.

But they had to go on. Tom was walking behind Jack and Stevie when Applethorp, the man on his right, stood on a mine. Tom ducked, fighting the instinct to fall flat on the ground, and instead crouching in as much of a ball as he could manage, as shards of shrapnel tore through his neck and wrist. Pain flared up his arm and burned into the base of his skull. He could have called for a medic but didn't want to be left alone like the poor buggers they had passed in their dug-out scrapes, and without Jack and Stevie. So he bit on his lip and wiped the flesh and blood from his face, and rose groggily to his feet.

But they had to take cover again, as the explosion had attracted a fierce concentration of artillery and mortar fire. The company 2IC dropped, and someone tried to drag him to cover under the lip of the wadi. In the light from the artillery flashes Tom could see it was Stevie. His friend was trying to drag the man by the legs when something hit him, he spun round and collapsed on top of the other man. Tom scuttled over to the two men, moving at a crouch, a numbness seeping up from the wound to his wrist. By the time he arrived there were a couple of stretcher-bearers already dragging them back to the wadi which represented the only cover.

"We'll take care of these! Get back or you'll be on a charge!" one shouted.

"I'm all reet, son," said an enervated voice, the ghost of Stevie.

After they had moved on a hundred yards, they were stopped by an intense artillery bombardment and machine gun fire that was behind them, and Tom hoped Stevie's cover was good enough.

They reached the anti-tank ditch. They spanned the fifteen feet with two ladders. Once across they were grateful to be able to shake out into proper attacking formation. Within minutes they had reached a road, and the captain judged that Ouerzi should be just beyond it. They were sending up a Very light to signal reaching their objective as a stonk of their own artillery sent them scuttling for what cover they could find. Thankfully they incurred no casualties.

Briefly they settled down, Jack coming across to ask Tom what had happened to Stevie.

"You wanna get that seen to," Jack said, pointing to Tom's cheek.

"I'll be all right."

It was his wrist, from which he had pulled a couple of pieces of shrapnel, halfpenny size, that bothered him. It hurt like the blazes, and if he was unable to fire his Lee Enfield he would have to go back. Oh, how he wanted to do just that. But he could not leave Jack. Not to his imagined fate. So they tucked into bully beef and biscuits and said no more.

First light revealed, about 500 yards ahead, an enemy strongpoint protected by a 20mm. As Bostons and Mitchell twin engine bombers flew through puffs of ack-ack to pound the enemy positions, the Captain rounded up the wounded to take back to Battalion HQ. Tom's temptation to go wrestled with guilt at leaving Jack in his state of fatalistic depression. So he kept his head down and watched with a desperate nostalgia as the wounded trooped off.

"You should gan wi' 'em, y' silly bugger," Jack said.

"Tek any chance yer can to get oot o' this."

"Oh, it's not so bad."

They were dug in, and their job was to hold their position while the Royal Engineers crossed the wadi, so that the 50th RTR could take their machines across. They spent an hour filling sandbags. In the evening they got a welcome supply of food, even some Maconochie stew, and settled down for the night amid rumours of a German counter-attack, Tom fielding Jack's recriminations for his failure to leave with the wounded.

At midday they were warned that the expected counter-attack was imminent and the 2-pounder anti-tank guns were ordered up, and targets for the three-inch mortars registered. A man from the Bren gun group had been injured so Tom was ordered to take his place, which he did with some trepidation, concerned that the injury to his hand would prevent him changing the magazine or rotating the release lever catch in front of the magazine to unlock and change the barrel if it became hot during sustained fire, since he had been given the job of the number 2 who loaded the gun and carried extra magazines.

The enemy must have registered their position, and soon they opened up with heavy stuff directed at the wadi to their rear (Tom thought once again of Stevie) and lighter stuff at them.

Slowly enemy tanks and Panzergrenadiers began to appear through the shimmering dust of early afternoon. The sun-glare was rent by the shattering noise. Tom glanced to his left. He could see Jack standing, rifle at the ready, a hundred yards away. There was heavy fire to their left where the 6th and 9th held the position. Then two

Mark IV Specials and a Mark III entered their company area, shelling them with 'flying kit bags' whose noise gave them ample time to duck down into the slit trench. The German fire was concentrated on their tanks, and it sounded as if the 50th RTR was taking a pounding.

The Bren fired, the casings chattering as they bounced off the body of the gun. Frank Lomas, Tom's Bren gunner, was aiming for the tank commanders, and caused one of them to duck down inside his tank, his field glasses thrown from him, until the Germans replied with fierce bursts from their machine guns, and they could only duck for cover. Between the bursts of gunfire, Tom could hear screaming from his right.

Their own artillery must have been called up by the forward observation officers, and started to pound the German tanks, shells falling uncomfortably close to their positions, so that they were forced to make themselves as small as possible in the bottom of the trench.

"If I get blown up by our own artillery, some bugger's gonna cop it," Frank said. It sounded as if he were whispering, but the movements of his mouth were those of shouting.

The shelling grew in intensity. The enemy tanks were firing their machine guns constantly. You couldn't distinguish the sound of exploding enemy shells from those of the 25-pounders' counter fire. The air was streaked with scars of red tracer. In a brief lull, Frank spotted the Panzergrenadiers moving up, but couldn't engage them because the machine guns opened up again. There was a loud rumble as one of the tanks overran 14 Platoon's position, getting right in amongst them in spite of the Bren gun fire, and turned its 75mms on their slit trenches. Bullets whipped and zinged into the revetment above their heads. To right and left, gun pits burst into flames as the open boxes of cordite charges burst, belching out eruptions of black smoke. Number 2 gun was hit, the shield crumpling like a ball of paper in a fist. Frank grabbed the Bren shouting:

"I'm not standing for this."

He got no further. A machine gun bullet tore into his face, sending fragments of bone and teeth flying, and he fell back on Tom, a hideous grin where his face should have been. Tom could hear a 68 grenade being fired and someone trying to respond with a Bren gun. There was a squeaking and grinding of the tank's wheels, and he wondered if the Germans were turning and withdrawing. But to his horror he realised that the tanks that had entered their position were trying to crush the slit trenches by turning neutral above them. There was nothing any of them could do; the tanks had smothered the entire position with machine gun fire.

There was a hideous scream from his left. Tom risked a glance over the top of the slit trench to see the German tank turning, the rear of its caterpillar tracks passing over the slit trench where Jack was. As the cloud of dust ground up by the tank's tracks sank, with a sickening lurch of his stomach he saw the body slumped on the parapet, a bib of blood over the front of the tunic.

"Jack!"

He was half out of the trench and heading for Jack's body through a hail of grenades and Bren gun fire when he heard the order.

"You, man! Man, your fuckin' Bren! Now!"

The bullet struck him in the thigh, spinning him around, so that through the searing pain he saw the bright blue sky and fluffy white clouds rotating about him, tasted the grit on his tongue, and then the thud of earth. He looked up into the sun, but its heat was as nothing compared to the conflagration engulfing his leg. He heard screaming, a sound that was part of the kaleidoscope of light whose shards fell upon his retina, and as the startled face of a medic appeared above him, he realised that he was the source of the noise.

CHAPTER TWELVE

Mrs Knight entered the grocer's shop in Clergy Lane, the toes of her scuffed court shoes catching on the edges of the cracked lino. She found herself facing Mrs France, her chubby and blotchy forearms planted proprietorially on the counter by the scales, a ready smile of welcome beneath her freshly laundered cap.

Mrs Knight reflected on how that smile had changed. Until the autumn of 1939 there had been something optimistic and bountiful about it; now, although to all intents and purposes the same, there was an apology in it, perhaps even something abortive behind the regret, as if she had failed in her capacity of grocer to provide for the needs of her clientele, and the actions of German U-boats were entirely peripheral to the breach of this unspoken compact between grocer and customer.

But there was something altogether more sepulchral in Mrs France's gaze, before which the customer's resolution faltered.

"Oh, Mrs Knight. Have you heard the terrible news?"

Mrs Knight's empty shopping bag grew heavy in her hand.

"What?"

"Alice Squire's Jack's gone down with his ship in the Atlantic. Torpedoed. All hands lost. Didn't you see the closed curtains?"

"Jack Squire."

She repeated the name as if she required the incantation to call him to mind. She didn't. A gangly lad, who as a child had been inseparable from a catapult he would fire indiscriminately into the trees by the river. She could see him now, a mirage in the medium of water, gasping and fighting for breath; not a man's face, but a child peering between the twin forks of his catapult. She could allow herself the image; her son was in the army. But the intelligence did nothing to impede her resolution.

She bore no grudge against Mrs France. There were of course the usual rumours that Mrs Markle and Mrs Cadwallader would have certain items secreted for their use beneath the counter. And perhaps there was a certain arrogance that came with the bestowal of the woman's bounty.

And a quite unmerited pride in her daughter. True, Emily France was a bonny girl. But that was no reason to look down on those whose daughters, like April, sadly, did not possess the same gifts of figure or face. Yes, she was due to be taken down a peg or two.

"I must call in when we shut," said the grocer's wife. "If she's receivin'... I just wish I could keep her something back... but it's the law."

The law for some, Mrs Knight thought. She resented this assumption of an obligation on her to call in on the bereaved lady. Who did she think she was?

"How old was he?"

"Twenty."

"Twenty. Those Nazi…"

"Yes… just missing they say, but…"

A shudder passed down Mrs Knight's spine.

"Well, life must go on. What can I do for you, Mrs Knight?"

"Do you have any tripe?"

"Sorry. I sold the last an hour gone."

"I'll have my 8oz of cheese, please."

There was a rumour the cheese ration was to be reduced to 3oz and she wanted to make sure she got her entitlement.

"…I'll have my tin of dried egg, please, and 4oz of bacon."

"Won't be two ticks," said the shopkeeper.

Mrs Knight withdrew her ration book from her purse and pushed it across the counter for stamping, but Mrs France had already departed for the cold room.

She also needed some jam, but she was registered with the Cochranes for that because their preserves were of better quality. She would also get her jar of Camp coffee and packet of Brown & Polson blancmange from Cochranes'.

Mrs France returned with the items already wrapped.

"Is there anything else?"

"Oh yes. A jar of Colman's mustard if you have any."

As Mrs France's gaze roamed the shelves, Mrs Knight pondered how best to approach the subject, easing up her hat and patting the marcel waves in her hair. She was a woman who relished confrontation, so the most obvious option of a direct accusation was the first to occur to her. But she instinctively felt that a disingenuous approach was likely to strike home with more force, provoking in Mrs France not a defensive posture but rather the natural concern of a parent for a wayward child and, indeed, the patriotic feelings proper to the occasion. It was important not to mention her own daughter, as malice would be suspected.

Mrs Knight handed over her bag. When she spoke, her words were spiced, not so much with malice as with a consciousness of performing a sort of justice, as if it devolved upon her to right the natural balance of the moral universe.

"That was a smart young man I saw on your Emily's arm the other day."

Mrs France looked up from stamping Mrs Knight's book, startled.

"What young man?"

"American. Tall. Good-looking. You could eat your dinner off his boots."

"What American?"

"Oh… I hope I haven't gone and put my foot in it."

Mrs France made that dismissive gesture with her hand that Mrs Knight associated with those occasions the former was obliged to confess to the lack of a desired commodity, and which she now saw extended to the reception of a disagreeable intelligence as well as the imparting of one.

"I can assure you, you haven't put your foot in anything," said Mrs France, beginning to bristle for all the subtlety of the attack. "You must be mistaken."

"Oh, no mistake, Mrs France. I'd know your Emily, wouldn't I? I've known her since she first went to Sunday school."

Mrs Knight felt rather sorry for Mrs France, standing there with a glaze of bewilderment on her ruddy features. But she couldn't resist the opportunity to twist the knife.

"Nothing's happened to Tom Dawkins, I hope."

CHAPTER THIRTEEN

"Let everyone who wants one have a beer on Good Old Uncle Sam!"

Not everyone in the saloon bar of the Black Bull that Tuesday evening was grateful for the offer. Sam Westwood, sitting in his familiar seat by the fire, scowled into his pint glass, which had no more than half an inch left in the bottom. But he was damned if he would accept a drink from the Yanks. They came to this country throwing their money about (and the blond one was literally throwing the money his imperfect grasp of English numismatic eccentricity judged correct on the counter) as if all Englishmen were in need of American charity.

The tattooed forearms of the landlord, Tom Curtin, set to with a will to pull the pints.

"Ruddy doughboys," Westwood said in a dismissive sibilance strained through the tobacco-stained moustache whose fringe depended over his upper lip.

"That's very kind of you," said Frank Lightwater, jumping with some alacrity up from his game of table skittles with Jack Flint by the door to the saloon bar.

"We don't need none of your charity, Yank," Westwood added surlily, in admonition of Lightwater.

"You needed it when we sent Lend Lease, though, didn't you," said the one called Temple, wiping the froth, with some disgust, from his upper lip.

Westwood gave a smile that was half snarl. Temple had clearly not forgiven Westwood and his drinking companion Abraham Barkiss for their welcome. In attempting to sit in the inglenook he had been informed mischievously by Westwood that that was old Barnabus' seat, and it devolved upon Tom Curtin to say:

"Don't you mind him none. Old Barnabus's been dead these five year. And he havin' bin in South Africa didn't mind no furreigners, less'n they wus the Boers what shot a hole in his backside."

Now the landlord's distinctive diplomacy was employed again.

"Don't you mind him."

"Yeah," said the tall one with glasses, "they told us every pub has its philosopher, and I guess that's what he is, right enough."

"That's 'cos we's been standin' up to 'itler, an' been bombed and starved fer it while you lot's been watchin' on 'til they Japs gone and blew up yer navy."

"That's enough, Sam," said Professor Sachs. Sachs stood at the bar nursing a half and resting his arthritic frame on a silver-topped walking cane, his right hand holding the lead attached to his Springer Spaniel, Cromwell. "They're here now and they're our allies, so say no more about it."

Westwood, whose respect for Oliver Sachs derived less

from the latter's expertise in English Civil War levelling movements than his social status, acquiesced in a scowling mumble. For much of his surliness stemmed from the fact that he would dearly have liked a pint at the expense of the Yanks had his pride admitted of it.

Sam's friend Abraham Barkiss was another who harboured no such scruples and rose from the settle with the aid of his ash stick, to join the Americans, the professor, Lightwater, Tom France, the grocer and Colonel Bland at the bar.

"Thaat's right kind of you, young zirr," Abraham said, his milky eyes staring almost vertically upwards at the blond one out of their deltas of wrinkle.

"Think nothing of it. I reckons I could get me a taste for your English beer. Sure do wish you'd get the stuff chilled though."

"It's the way we likes it," said Lightwater.

"Oh sure. No offence."

"Criticisin' our beer, now."

"Take no notice," said the landlord. "He's just mad 'cos you lot took his land."

"It wasn't their lot, it was the government," said Bland. "And we've all got to make sacrifices for the war effort," he added sententiously. The phrase was common currency, particularly, Westwood reflected, amongst those whose sacrifices were comparatively few.

"Sacrifice," rejoined Westwood. "'Tain't nuthin' but sacrifice. First I's gotta shoot my best Ruby Reds on account of that there foot and mouth, then I can't sow my tatties that was already chatted on account of the rain, and now I gotta hand over moi land so this 'ere lot can chew gum on it. You just remember, Tom Curtin, I'll still be here when these Yanks is up and gone."

"That's what worries me," said Curtin.

"That ain't funny."

"From what I hear you're not doing badly," said the professor. "The prices of wheat, barley and oats are rising steadily. You get premium payments for your milk. And the Ministry of Food buy from you at higher rates."

"Not wheat, they don't," retorted Westwood. "And we has to touch our forelocks to the War Ag, tellin' us how to do our job, what we've done since we wus in short trousers, threatenin' to take what little land I got left."

"Well, you're on the War Ag Committee, aren't you?"

"Much good it does me, I'm still down the queue for a tractor – even a Fordson, ne'er mind a Field Marshall. I still gotta do what that thurr inspector tells me, and 'tain't right. Not with moi own land. Gotta watch they films, keep records o' milk yields. Can't make butter nor cheese wi'out their say-so, gotta get a licence to kill moi own pigs and have some copper stand over us while I does it. And half goes to the government. 'Oh, you's just using sixty per cent o' your land, Mr Westwood, that's only a B, you gotta do better than that.' Grow flax for parachutes, they says. Flax, on moi land. And who's gonna pull it up? We ain't got no weather forecasts no more, so's we doan even know when to get the hay cocked."

"Well, you should be glad the Yanks have taken part of your land," said Bland.

Westwood looked daggers at the colonel.

"Farmer Westwood is our very own Old Tom Cobbleigh," said the professor.

When the Yanks looked blankly, he went on:

"It's a song in these parts. Don't ask us to sing it for you."

"Whyever not? I likes a zing-zong, does I. 'Tom Pearce, Tom Pearce, lend me thy grey mare.'" Lightwater was clearly beginning to feel the effects of the ale he had drunk rather precipitately, as if in fear the offer might be withdrawn.

"Tell 'em," said Westwood, "how laast time we had such as them in these parts (he waved a tobacco-stained forefinger contemptuously in the direction of the Americans) they wus banged up as prisoners of war in Princetown gaol."

"No, I don't think I will," retorted Lightwater. "Since they's good enough to buy an old man somethin' to wet his whistle, I'll tell 'em as how there's a tavern on the moor, zee. And they got a fire in the bar 'as been lit for nigh on an 'undred year, tee hee."

"Why?" asked the blond Yank, his head bent at an uncomfortable angle to avoid scraping the old oak ceiling beam with its attached horse brasses.

"I dunno," Lightwater said and cackled once again.

"So when do you think we're gonna see this second front everyone's talkin' about then!"

The question was posed by Tom France to the five Yanks.

"Ay," Lightwater agreed. "'Pon a time we'd be scanning they barometer fer an high pressure and an easterly so's we could bring in the harvest, now all folks wants to know is when that there invasion's gonna start."

"You don't suppose General Eisenhower tells everyone his plans, do you, Tom?" said Bland satirically.

"Don't see why not. They're Yanks, ain't they."

"Well, I can assure you they tell us nothing," said the tall one with glasses, taking a couple of steps backwards to avoid a ceiling beam and release his head. "It's the same as it is in your army. We're the last to know anything."

"Well, we're glad you're here anyhow," said Tom Curtin genially.

"Oh yes, you's glad," said Westwood. "If Uncle Adolf was to walk in here and order pints you'd be glad of that."

"I think they'd prefer a pub that serves German beer," said Bland dryly.

"You got pubs that serves German beer?" the short Yank asked, with an unbecoming enthusiasm.

"Just jokin'."

"Well, you got nuthin' to worry about now we're here," said the blond.

"Oh no," said Westwood with heavy sarcasm, "we couldn't do nothin' 'til you Yanks come. Held out against the Luftwaffe, beat them Jerries at Alamein, we did, without no help from you."

"What about them ships we sent you?" said the one called Reilly, his face flushing bright pink.

"Bah! Half of them couldn't 'ardly float. Anyway we paid for 'em, didn't we? Paid through the nose. And if it hadn't been for your president you wouldn't have done nuthin' 'til 'itler gone an' declared war on yer."

"Yeah, well, we wasn't at war then, was we? Why should we come in and 'elp you anyways?"

At this point two men entered the snug. Westwood smiled at the sight of his son, wearing the uniform of a private in the Eighth Army, and squinting to right and left as if expecting to see a sun that had followed him all the way from North Africa.

"Da."

"Here."

"What's goin' on here?" Dick Westwood asked, regarding the Americans with the sort of suspicion appropriate had they been clad in the uniform of the Waffen SS.

"Just the Yanks causin' trouble."

"Don't you mind your pa there, Dick," said Curtin. "It's him what started it."

"Started what? And gimme a pint of mild."

Dick walked up to the bar and put his hands proprietorially on its surface as if disputing its possession with the Yanks. When the pint was pulled, he said:

"One fer me da. And one for 'im an' all."

His thumb indicated the other man, squat and bow-legged, who wore the uniform of the Royal Engineers.

"Who's this then?" Barkiss asked.

"Fred Tile from Seaton way."

"I can answer for myself, Dick."

"What's it all about then?"

"Nothing," said Bland amicably.

But Temple was not prepared to let it go. He said:

"Your pa there was wonderin' why the good old US of A didn't drop everythin' and come bale you lot out like we done in the first war."

"Take it easy, ·Temple. Don't start nuthin'," said the bespectacled one.

"I ain't startin' nothin'. He done started it." He pointed at Westwood. "I says what business we got here anyways?

'Tain't nothin' to do with us. Let the Germans have Europe. Let them have the British Empire. We had our fight with your empire and we good and licked you. Now you're wantin' us to come in and save you. So's you can rule half the world and have them injuns and niggers slavin' fer you? We believe in democracy and freedom and here we is fightin' fer yer empire."

"I think, young man," said Oliver Sachs authoritatively, "you'll find that while your republic continued to uphold slavery, Britain was the first country in history to abolish the vile practice, and our navy did its best to stamp it out, including boarding your slaving ships, at the cost of over 1,500 British sailors' lives. Abolishing female infanticide and suttee, bringing peace and Christianity to places that have never known them, incorruptible governance, sound and honest administration, and improvements to the lives of ordinary people through medicine, irrigation and transport is no slavery. Indeed, there have been instances of peoples applying to join the Empire. You will also find that most of the democracies in this world are British dominions or territories, or in the case of the USA, an ex-territory."

"The... the US of A is the freest country in the world," Temple spluttered. "Ain't none freer."

But the professor went on:

"Your attitude is perfectly hypocritical. What is your country if not an empire built by white settlers and taken with considerable violence from natives, who, rather than succour and aid, you now coop up in reservations? Hitler himself compared the activities of his army in Russia with your expansion over your continent. What is Manifest

Destiny but a call to imperialism? And one of the reasons you rebelled against the crown was that the British tried to prevent you encroaching on Indian lands. One hundred thousand Loyalists thought so much of your republic they immediately decamped to Canada."

"I don't see you doin' no fightin'," said Dick, ignoring Sachs as if the contribution of academia was of no account. "I just sees you proppin' up the bar. You waitin' fer those poor Russkies to knock out 'itler so's you don't 'ave to get yer pretty uniforms dirty?"

"And from what I heard," said Tile, "you lot been spendin' all yer time tryin' to have yer way with our girls."

"Well, what fightin' you been doin'?" asked Temple. "Seems most folk in this town don't know the meanin' o' war."

"Hey, young fella," said Barkiss, "we've had twelve in this town been lost, and we just come from the funeral of Jack Squire whose boat gone down in the Atlantic."

"I been in the Western Desert," said Dick.

"What, runnin' away from Rommel?" Reilly taunted.

Dick started toward the American at this point, but Bland grabbed him by the arm. Dick stopped, looked down at Bland's hand, and contented himself with:

"No, givin' him a good hidin'."

"What good's the desert anyways?" asked Temple. "It's all so's you can save yer empire."

"So we can safeguard our oil supplies through the Suez Canal," said Bland. "Otherwise we can't fight this war."

"Yeah," said Reilly derisively, "it's true what they says about the Union Jack. It's red, white and blue… and yella."

As Dick struggled to draw his arm free from Bland's grasp, saying, "I oughta knock your fuckin' lights out, Yank," Fred Tile said:

"Never mind, Dick, from what I heard the Germans think all their Christmases has come at once now the Yanks is 'ere. At the Kasserine Pass you lot run faster than that Jesse Owens."

Tile was referring to the disorderly retreat of the US 1st Armored Division at Sidi Bou Said.

"You goddam lyin' bastard," said Reilly, striding towards Tile.

"I doan want no fightin' in my pub," was the contribution of Tom Curtin. But as he spoke it was already in vain, and a gleeful Sam Westwood shuffled to the edge of his seat to watch the fun.

Reilly's punch was a haymaker that proceeded with a deliberation that owed much to the four pints he had downed, towards Tile's jaw. The sober newcomer eased himself out of the way of the blow and drove his fist into Reilly's midriff, doubling him up so that he collapsed onto the footrest below the bar.

"Now, gents, must I call for the constable?" said Curtin.

But Temple had already advanced on Tile, evading the bespectacled Yank's restraining grip. Temple was as drunk as Reilly, and his punch as telegraphed, but Tile had not seen him coming, and turned right into a blow that caught him on the jaw and knocked him backwards onto one of the tables, spraying a shower of blood as he went.

Temple had barely righted himself from the blow when Dick was upon him.

"I'll show you who's yella, Yank!"

Sam jumped up and roared his son on:

"Go orn, you show 'em, lad!"

Westwood junior threw his pint in Temple's face, and as the dripping visage tilted in his direction, struck him firmly just below the ear, and sent him sprawling over Reilly and Tile.

"I'll go for the constable," said Bland, whose days of fisticuffs were long behind him, although he still bored people with extravagant tales of the brawl in the Nefertiti bar in Cairo in '17. As he exited the pub, Tom Curtin interposed his ample frame between Dick and the short Yank who were squaring up to each other.

"Any more punches thrown by anybody and they's barred."

The bespectacled Yank had Reilly in a bear hug, while the Irish-American wrestled to extricate his pinned arms and twisted his livid, contorted face from side to side. The tall blond, who was attempting to raise a dazed but still splenetic Temple from the floor, said:

"We don't want no trouble. But next time somebody insults the US Army they'll get trouble good and proper, y' hear."

As Reilly was manhandled through the double doors, the latter's head swivelled round and he said:

"It's only fer fear of gettin' put on a charge I didn't bash your head to pulp, mister."

Dick was forestalled by Tom Curtin's warning finger, and he deferred to it, or at least to the tattoo of the anchor decorating the landlord's meaty forearm.

And as the Yanks exited the pub, Sam Westwood sniggered into his empty glass and greedily eyed those fuller glasses the departing men had left behind. But seeing where his gaze lay, Tom Curtin immediately swept the glasses up and deposited the contents in his sink, returning to wipe the bar with a self-satisfied smile.

CHAPTER FOURTEEN

Mrs France had little opportunity to raise her concerns about her daughter and the American soldier. She rarely spoke to Emily these days, save at mealtimes, and it was as they were gathered about the dining table, Mr and Mrs France, Emily and her fifteen-year-old brother, Eric, that the subject received its airing.

Mrs France was nevertheless forced to wait until her husband ceased lamenting that the accumulator had gone on the wireless, on the very night Henry Hall and his orchestra were on, and updating them on the progress of the pig (he owned a share in a pig kept on Tom Style's allotment and fed on Tottenham cake made of vegetable waste).

In spite of her anxiety to express her concerns for her daughter, the good lady was these days inclined to be indulgent where her husband was concerned. It had been considered by her parents that in choosing Tom France in the name of a passion that is as fleeting as it is overwhelming, she had married beneath her. But now at long last Tom was showing people what he was capable of: their status as guardians of the all-important rations recognised, he appointed chief ARP warden and admitted to Chalford golf club. And ever since her husband had been elected to the town council, she had felt herself a cut above the ordinary, and that something more was due to her than she had for twenty years been used to receiving.

Once having deferred to the man responsible for raising her social standing to heights it had never previously attained, however, Mrs France was not a woman to sweeten a pill.

"What's this I hear about you goin' with some Yank?"

Emily looked up from the plate, smeared with the remains of the Woolton pie of broccoli, swede and carrots but minus the cheese whose ration had run out, she was pushing from her prior to a precipitate exit. There was on her face a subtle shading of resigned precognition upon the undercoat of outrage.

"Who told you that?"

"Never you mind who told me that. What do you say?" her mother snapped as she slammed the National Loaf down onto the breadboard.

"It were that April Knight, wasn't it? Spiteful little piece she is. I know her game."

"I don't care about her game. I want to know about your game."

"You goin' with a Yank? Can you get me some chewin' gum?" piped up Eric.

"Take yourself off to your room, Eric," said Mr France.

"Aw, must I?"

"Now!"

The door closed behind Eric, although Mrs France listened in vain for his tread upon the stair.

"Well, what you gotta say, girl?" Mr France asked severely.

"Ain't no harm in it. I was only bein' friendly."

"How friendly?" her father asked in an ominous tone.

"I don't see that it's gotta do with anybody else."

"We're not anybody else," said Mrs France. "We're your mum and dad."

"What's the harm in it? It was only a dance… and… a walk by the river."

"One walk?"

"Once or twice, what's it matter?"

"What about Tom, girl?" said Mr France. "You never think of him? Away fightin' to keep the Nazis from our door and here's you goin' behind his back with some Yank. You should have more sense, girl."

"More sense and more decency, is what I say," added her mother. "That ain't no way for no daughter of mine to carry on."

"You didn't want me walkin' out with Tom in the first place."

"I was just thinkin' of you. You could've done better than Tom Dawkins. Why, you could have set your cap at Dick Bentley that works in the bank."

"He's only a clerk, Mam."

"It don't make no difference. He don't work with his hands. Even got hisself a car now he's been passed unfit for service. He was sweet on you and you didn't give him time of day."

"Well, what's done is done," said her dad. "You made your bed and you gotta… ahem."

Here the admonition of Chalford's chief ARP warden stalled in embarrassment.

"What I mean is, Tom's relyin' on you. Relyin' on you bein' true to him. Leastways bein' open and honest. Have you told him? You do still write to him?"

"Often as he writes to me."

"So you have told him?"

"No, why should I? It's only a bit of fun."

"Fun… Is that what you call it?"

"Fun, yes. What's a girl supposed to do when all the men are away fightin'?"

"Behave herself and act decent," said her father. "We got ourselves a reputation in this town…"

"Is that all you're concerned about?" Emily, flushed and half risen from the table, retorted.

"Ain't it enough? Tom Dawkins, he's a good lad, well thought of. Even if he works with his hands."

After years of having been made, in many subtle ways, conscious of what Mrs France had sacrificed in marrying him, this was the furthest Tom France dare by way of admonishment of his spouse, and she in her turn was prepared to overlook it, particularly in the circumstances.

Mr France went on:

"What happens when he comes home, eh? You ever think of that? There's plenty in this town that'll let him know what's been goin' on."

"Like April Knight."

"Whoever it is," said her mother, "there's no blame attached to her. All the blame and all the shame's lyin' at your door, my girl. I'll never have believed it of you—"

"You did, though!"

"We brought you up to have respect for yerself, and here's you throwin' yerself at the first Yank who comes along."

"I didn't 'throw myself'. And he's perfectly respectable. He's in insurance."

"I don't care what he is, my girl," said her father. "You gotta be straight with Tom Dawkins. You don't want him no more you gotta tell him. But don't think folk in this town's gonna look kindly on you, when he's away doin' his bit, and his sweetheart's carryin' on with some Yank."

"I'm not... his sweetheart."

"Well, everybody thinks you is."

"Anyway," said Emily, her rouged lips tensed in a moue, "there's plenty of girls is seein' Yanks."

"I don't care what plenty of girls is doin'. I just care what *our* girl is doin'. What you see in 'em, anyway?" asked Mr France. "They's not proper soldiers, shufflin' about, chewin' gum like they was in a dole queue. Our British lads not good enough for you, eh?"

"No, they ain't if you must know."

"What!" her father exploded.

"It's not just me," said Emily, her face suddenly fearful, her gaze askance as if seeking some escape route, and sitting back down as if she wanted to put the table between herself and her irate father. "All the girls say it. The Yanks is... handsome, always well turned out... and they know how to treat a girl."

"Oh, I know. They're free and easy with their nylons and all the things they has and we ain't seen since this war begun. I dare say they're free and easy with a lot more besides."

"What do you mean by that?"

Mrs France was disappointed to see that her husband's anger had subsided, the flush on his face receding to leave its tracery of red capillaries, and there was a resignation in his tone as he said:

"They're young men far from home. They just wants to have fun, and when the war's done they're back to America, leavin' broken hearts in their wake, don't you see that?"

"Lucy Brooks' Yank has proposed to her."

"Is that it?" Mrs France said. "You girls has had your silly heads turned. And you think you're all bound for Hollywood on the arm of Cary Grant. You ain't got the sense you was born with."

Mr France added:

"What I hear is the Yank army won't let their men marry English girls unless…"

"Unless what?"

Tom France rose from the table and, walking to and fro before the window with his thumbs running down the insides of his braces, added:

"Never you mind. Tom Dawkins is solid, dependable, not some here today, gone tomorrow Yank. You could do a lot worse. And he don't deserve to be tret like this."

Mrs France was beginning to feel frustrated by the increasingly despondent tone adopted by her husband. And their daughter was growing in confidence as a result.

"I don't mean Tom no harm, but a girl's gotta follow her heart—"

"You don't means you's fallen for him?" asked her mother. "You ain't gone and done nothin' you should be ashamed of, have you? Don't you be stupid enough to give yerself to a feller that'll leave you in the lurch first chance he gets."

"No, Ma, course not. Like I said, it's just a dance or two. They sure know how to dance, those Yanks. Not stiff as boards like our lads. Where's the harm in that?"

Later, when Emily had gone to her room, Mr and Mrs France were sitting before the fire, the former repairing the hinge on the metal hood of his bicycle blackout lamp. Suddenly Mr France said in a lugubrious tone:

"Where we gone wrong, eh? We been good parents haven't we, Marj?"

"Yes. It's just a different world. When you was at the front in the first show I wouldn't have dreamt of lookin' at another feller."

But of course there hadn't been hundreds of Yanks billeted in the country in the first show.

CHAPTER FIFTEEN

"You should know, ladies, that you can't trust a nigger."

Major Bellucci's opening words to the Chalford WVS took Mrs France aback.

She looked around the village hall and found her fellow ladies evincing similar surprise. When invited to a talk to prepare the town to receive the anticipated influx of black troops this was not what they would have expected, even had their previous experience of talks by men not been confined to Reverend Villiers on birdlife by the riverside.

But Major Bellucci was in typically combative mode. If the US Army were all like him, Mrs France reflected, the Germans were in for one hell of a time.

Mrs France, however, was less concerned about Major Bellucci's nature than that of Larry Schultz. She had learned the name of her daughter's beau the previous evening. She found her daughter sitting at her dressing table mirror engaged in a minute examination of the complexion of her left cheek.

"You mustn't give yourself to a man who, however honourable his intentions, might be whisked away before he gets the chance to propose."

"Of course I won't. But this is war, Mum. Men are being killed all the time."

"War or not. It's all the more important the proprieties are observed. Wars don't last forever, and when they're over, people still think the same way—"

"Well, they'll have to change the way they think. There's plenty girls whose fellas won't be comin' back—"

"We don't want you to end up in the same boat as plenty other girls."

There followed an interval of that excruciating silence that punctuates the dialogue of parent and child.

"Is that all you and Dad care about, the way things look?"

"Act your age. That's what you should be caring about, my girl. If he asks you to marry him, well, that's one thing, although we wouldn't like it one little bit. But you're in twice the danger any other girl is—"

"What girl?"

"A girl going with an English lad. He might up and away and you never see nor hear from him again. And then there's Tom."

"I didn't ask—" her daughter began. But it seemed she was not in the mood for another confrontation on this subject.

Emily said she would think of Tom. But Mrs France, who, on account of Emily's youthful vibrancy, and the peculiar combination of physical self-assurance and hesitancy that reminded her of her own youth, had always favoured daughter over son, no longer trusted her daughter. The empty-headed girl was infatuated either with this Larry Schultz – even the man's name sounded like a treachery – or the Americans in general, with their swagger and their ample bounty. She dreaded the thought that that infatuation might lead Emily to a life on the other side of the Atlantic.

But her daughter's emigration might be the least of it. Young men can be very persuasive, especially ones from far across the sea who dispense perfect smiles and the sort of luxuries some girls had never seen.

Major Bellucci's ample form landed on the desk in front of him, the impact of his hands causing its timber to squeal in protest. His bull head stretched forward on its thick neck as he challenged them thus:

"I don't want to alarm you good ladies. But it's my dooty to warn you what's gonna happen. I'll wager you ladies has never seen a black in your lives."

They had to admit it was true.

"The only blacks I've seen are Paul Robeson and Sabu," said Mrs Squires in her quaintly rhapsodic voice.

The rest muttered their agreement.

"What of you, Mrs Burns?" asked Agatha Wills. "You used to live in London, didn't you? Were there any blacks there? One imagines all sorts of things in London."

Mrs Burns looked up from her lap, surprised by the personal question, and displaying a glimpse of that fearful, even shrinking, something, Mrs France had noticed in the Cockney lady's less guarded moments.

"I seen one or two come off the boats, and then they'd go straight into the pubs 'til they sailed again," said Sally Burns. "There was a bloke lived darn our way that was…

swarthy, like – said his folks come over with the Armada, but nobody believed him."

Major Bellucci smiled condescendingly.

"See, that's just what I mean."

"But really, Major," said Mrs Cadwallader, "we might not have seen one, but they're just the same as us, save for the colour of their skin, surely."

The major appeared taken aback by this suggestion, but quickly regained his condescension.

"Well, that's just where you're wrong, Mrs Codwalla ma'am, if you don't mind me sayin' so. I've lived 'mongst niggers most my life, and they ain't to be trusted. No sir. That's why we don't let them do the fightin', just the fetchin' and carryin', so think no more on them than you would think on a mule."

"Are you suggesting they constitute some sort of threat?"

It seemed to Mrs France that the major's condescension, or possibly his inability to pronounce her name, had provoked Mrs Cadwallader to her most magisterial, the vowels rolling off her tongue with more than even their usual orotundity.

"Don't you ladies worry none about that. Just take care and don't go treatin' them same as you would us. Never was a nigger didn't carry a knife about his person. So don't go invitin' them into your homes like you done us. Don't turn yer back on them. And make sure you ain't alone with them where there ain't nobody else about. But I'm sure you ladies is far too sensible for that."

Mrs France was confounded by a mixture of incredulity and alarm. As if Emily stepping out with the Yank wasn't bad enough.

"Really, Major, you make these people sound worse than Nazis," said Mrs Villiers, squirming in outrage so that her cane chair squeaked in protest beneath her. "To hear you talk you would think they weren't human beings at all."

"They ain't, ma'am, I tell you. I've lived amongst them all my life, and I tell you watch out for them. And don't let your daughters go near them. They takes their pleasure where they can, like a dog or a horse. Back home they knows what they'll git if they goes anywhere near a white gal. And white gals knows they's to steer clear of them. So you tell your womenfolk, good and proper, steer clear o' them niggers."

Mrs France could not believe what she was hearing. Here was the US Army bringing into the country people who seemed scarcely less of a danger than a regiment of German Stormtroopers.

"Rather than scaring us half to death, Major," said Mrs Cadwallader, "perhaps you can explain exactly when the black troops will arrive and what they will be doing here."

"Certainly, ma'am. They's due to arrive in two weeks' time. They'll form part of the Quartermaster and Service Corps. Don't worry. They'll be kept well away from you good folk. They're to be billeted in tents in a field some ways from the town."

"Pardon me, Major, but the field your troops occupy is not 'well away from the town.'"

"You misunderstand me, ma'am. They ain't gonna be billeted with my men – that is, with the white troops. No sir. They's gonna be put in a field by theirselves, away from my men."

"That seems most peculiar. Should you not have your troops all together... in case of some emergency?"

"No, ma'am. My men won't mix with them blacks. They's kept separate in everything. We can't stop them comin' into town – I only wish we could. So we'll have us a system for my men to go to the dance hall one night, and the blacks another. Same with the pub. But that's something I'll have to talk about with Mayor Markle."

"My husband will want a full meeting of the council if such a thing is to be contemplated. The pub landlords and the owner of the dance hall will need to be consulted," volunteered Mrs Markle. "And I cannot promise there will not be opposition."

"Whites one night, blacks the other. Really, the very idea," said Mrs Villiers.

"It does seem an extraordinary method of proceeding," said Mrs Cadwallader.

"Folk won't like it," said Sally Burns. "I tell you, they won't like it. This is Devon, not... I don't know... Tennessee."

"Well, it ain't nuthin' to do with them," said Major Bellucci, getting heated.

"Have you dreamt this... this... policy up all by yourself, Major?" said Mrs Cadwallader, after the manner of a schoolmistress who has discovered some of her pupils bunking off.

"No, ma'am. This here's the policy of the US Army. Ain't to be no mixin' of blacks and whites. And we don't encourage fraternisation of the locals with them neither."

"With whom?" asked Mrs Cadwallader in a provoking tone.

"With the blacks, ma'am," said an increasingly exasperated major.

"Well, I don't know that I care to hear of people treated in such a fashion," said Mrs Cadwallader.

"Quite right, Mrs Cadwallader," agreed Mrs Villiers. "A human being is not to be treated as an animal."

"Well, the Nazis is animals, ain't they?" the major retorted.

"This is ridiculous," said Sally Burns. "Treating your own people like that. I don't see why any of us should stand for it neither. My Arthur'll have his say when it comes before the council, I'll tell you."

Mrs France, on the other hand, was more than happy that people who seemed barely civilised and posed a threat to the young women of the town should be kept as far away as possible. Rather, she was alarmed at the suggestion that the blacks should be allowed to mix freely with the locals. She might have to impose some sort of curfew on Emily. At least the white soldiers would not be out at the same time as the blacks, and she would not be tempted to leave home.

"This here's the policy of the US Army, ma'am. Don't you treat them blacks like they's whites. They won't thank you fer it, and the army won't thank you fer it."

Later, when the major had finished haranguing them, and the sound of his jeep was receding along the high street, Mrs France sought out Mrs Cadwallader and Agatha Wills, who were deep in earnest conversation in the entrance to the hall, where a photograph of the King peered over the latter's frail shoulder.

"Why, Mrs France," said Mrs Wills, "you look as if you've seen a ghost."

"I only wish it were a ghost, I shouldn't mind half so much. But I've got my Emily, and there's many another young girl in this town, and now this here major's bringin' a load of blacks here that would, well... you know... as soon as look at them."

"I don't think you can blame the good major for that, Mrs France," said Mrs Cadwallader dryly. "I think from what he said he would rather have had Nazis under his command."

"Well, why have 'em then?" asked Mrs France, annoyed at the great lady's facetious irrelevance.

"It has been forced upon him from above," said Mrs Cadwallader with a sigh whose significance was lost on Mrs France.

"Well, I don't like it one little bit, and them as has pretty daughters as is likely to be jumped on by these blacks ain't gonna like it either. I'd like to know what Mr Markle and the vicar got to say... We'll all wake up with our throats cut, I shouldn't wonder."

"My dear," said Mrs Wills pedantically, "if your throat was cut you wouldn't wake up at all."

"There's no call for levity. Seems to me our whole town's at stake here. The whites is bad enough, but blacks..."

"My dear Mrs France," said Mrs Cadwallader, with a projection sufficient to carry all the way to Mrs France's own shop, "their colour has nothing whatsoever to do with it. I concede that I have never met a black, but then neither have you, and whereas Major Bellucci has, the man's prejudice is as plain as the nose on his face. And I must say I don't care for this term 'nigger'; it's not at all seemly. What he told us was nothing more than scaremongering—"

"Tommy-rot," agreed Mrs Wills.

"...to ensure that we keep our distance from these people who, no less than the whites, have come to these shores to aid us in our hour of peril."

"Our hour of peril was three years past and they wasn't here then."

Mrs Cadwallader continued as if she had not heard:

"I cannot imagine what he hopes to gain by it since these people are in his army. Save that he clearly wishes us all to abide by his segregation policy—"

"And we will, won't we?" said Sally Burns, who had just re-entered the hall accompanied by Mrs Villiers, and in a provocatively loud tone. "Of course we will. We jump when the Yanks bark their orders. We don't want to rock the boat. Tom Curtin'll be happy enough just so long as he's got someone to sell beer to!"

"Well, why shouldn't we?" Mrs France asked. "If they's as dangerous as what he says, they should be locked up 'stead of bein' able to walk around this town like howsyer-father."

"Oh yes," Sally retorted, "lock them up for the colour of their skin."

"No-one's talking about locking anyone up," said Mrs Villiers. "That's not the British way and not the Christian way. I'm sure the US authorities will look after their own, and we must trust them to protect us. But whether we can countenance the sort of arrangement the major proposes..."

"'Course we can't," asseverated Sally. "It's monstrous. It's uncivilised."

"But are they civilised?... The blacks, I mean," said Mrs France.

"Don't be so stupid."

"Stupid, am I?" Mrs France felt herself grow livid with anger.

"There's no call for that," said Mrs Cadwallader in a withering tone of admonition calculated to quell any save, it seemed, Sally Burns.

"I think there is call for it. She doesn't know the first thing about them."

"It's all right for you, you don't have a daughter," Mrs France retorted, and felt a glow of pleasure to see Mrs Burns wince in response.

"As I see it," said Mrs Wills, "it's entirely a matter for the Americans. We're not called upon to bar anybody—"

"Yes we are!" said Sally. "When the whites are in town."

"And vice-versa," said Mrs Wills. "But the point I'm making is that no-one is asking *us* not to associate with them. If the white Americans don't wish to do so, then that is a matter for them."

"No," said Sally vehemently, "it's just plain wrong."

"I must say that for once I'm inclined to agree with you, Mrs Burns," said Mrs Cadwallader in her ringing tones, as if she were some peculiarly plangent judge delivering a final verdict.

"We shall see what the council makes of it," said Mrs Villiers. "And my husband also."

"Do you think he will denounce it from the pulpit?" Mrs Wills asked.

"That, I think, would be tantamount to a declaration of war on our allies. And since we are engaged in a fight to the death and apparently need their strong arm – strong white arm, I should say – we must be circumspect."

"Well," said Mrs France, "if none of you are prepared to protect our girls from these people, I'm sure there's plenty as will."

Uncertain as to what she intended by that remark, and not a whit mollified, Mrs France turned swiftly on her heel and left the building. As she walked home, she did so fearing that her beloved Emily, having escaped the clutches of good old English Tom Dawkins to fall into those of a Yank with a German name, should not fall into some worse ere long.

CHAPTER SIXTEEN

Reverend Villiers, his wife by his side, took his seat in the front row as the chairman, Mayor Markle, called the meeting of Chalford Parish Council to order.

It was an extraordinary meeting of the council, and was open to the public, the fact having been advertised by notice posted, as required, at least three days earlier under the glass cover of the parish notice board, situated on the green by the memorial to the dead of the first war.

As a consequence, there was a marked disparity between this meeting, which filled the parish hall 'to its rafters' in Mrs Villiers' words, and most council meetings, which normally consisted solely of Mr Markle, the quorum of three members and the town clerk, Mr Alfred Appleby. Those such as the vicar and his wife, to whom deference accorded the facility, occupied seats on the floor of the hall, the others standing down the side aisles. To one side of the bench on which sat the council members was a desk, on which Mr Appleby sat scribbling in an ancient leatherbound ledger.

The mayor rose to his feet, his chain of office swaying, and rapped with his gavel.

The purpose of this extraordinary meeting – Mayor Markle rehearsed the words of the notice – was to consider the request by Major Bellucci of the US Army, that the facilities of the town be made available on alternate days, and exclusively, to white and black US servicemen respectively.

The major himself was not in attendance, but many of the residents of Chalford most certainly were.

The meeting was declared open without the formality of a reading of the minutes of the previous meeting, and a veritable forest of arms sprang from the floor. The mayor, rubbing one finger between his neck and shirt collar (the day was a warm one and the hall possessed the stuffy atmosphere of a box room deprived for many years of ventilation) intoned:

"Before I invite comments from the floor, perhaps we should hear first of all from the vicar."

Mr Villiers was grateful for the courtesy, conscious that his diffident arm might otherwise have gone unnoticed amid the thrusting boughs, and rose from his seat, turning his body to address simultaneously the bench and as many of the attendees as possible.

He stood, the notes that were his aide memoire shaking slightly in his hand, and raised his voice in a conscious attempt to transcend that mellifluous and, as some would say, soporific tone with which he had lulled so many of his congregation over the years, and which his wife chaffingly described as daring them to nod into oblivion. This was a speech he had agonised over as much as any sermon. He had always tried, with what some may consider unrealistic optimism, to fashion each sermon in the hope it might effect a positive change in the heart and soul of at least one member of his congregation. Now he must use all his oratorical skills to move a whole community to the rejection of a monstrous ideology.

"Mr Chairman, I have no wish to be critical of other nations, particularly one which is our close ally. But the proposal the major has made does strike me as most unchristian. Not that the blacks are being penalised in any way, as I see it. However, for a nation to go to war and one part of their army to say to the other that it does not wish to mix with them, is both unwise, and contrary to the sort of community in which Our Lord would wish us to live.

"'By this shall all men know that ye are my disciples, if ye have love one to another.' Is this not the greatest gift of the many the Lord has bestowed upon us unworthy mortals? How can any man love another and say that he will not go to the same public house as him, or walk on the same street, or serve beside him?

"You may argue that any institution has the right to decide such things for themselves, and if the Americans do so decide, it is not for us to gainsay them. But we are asked to be active participants in this. Some might say accomplices. And we, as citizens of this town, have the right to petition our elected council as to whether we be compelled to accept such a regime. In deciding what your stance will be you might think it is a fair proposal, allowing as it does for access to the town's amenities by blacks and whites equally. But I want you to be in no doubt, that it is an insult – and I have no hesitation in saying it – an insult of the worst kind imaginable to the coloured troops who will soon be arriving in this part of Devon."

"Hear, hear, Frederick," his wife muttered from beneath him.

"This town has a long history, fighting for liberty against the Spanish Armada, Napoleonic aggression and the Kaiser. And never in that history has it engaged in the sort of segregation the American authorities are now proposing. Look into your hearts, ladies and gentlemen, and ask yourselves if you had a son in forces in a foreign land, whether you would wish them to be – I believe the American term is 'corralled' – in this fashion, that they might be shunned by their fellow troops who see them as polluting.

"Our missionaries in India have long been appalled by the treatment by higher caste Hindus of their fellows who they describe as 'untouchable', an attitude which seems to have its roots in the same aversion to colour we see in this case, and I trust they've done their best to discourage such a reprehensible tradition. And yet we are being asked, as one of the prices we must pay for American support, to practise in our own land, just such a mischievous, indeed vicious, regime.

"It seems clear to me that those who accede to this proposal thereby tarnish themselves, and it would reflect badly upon our otherwise unimpeachable town, were we to do so. Do not, I beg, taint our history of service to the cause of liberty by agreeing to this shameful manner of proceeding."

"Well said, Vicar," someone shouted as Mr Villiers resumed his seat, grateful to know that he had some support in the hall beyond that of his wife. Not that he doubted that many in the town would think as he did.

Nevertheless, he was fearful that – what was the phrase? – realpolitik, would result in the council bowing to American pressure. To what extent, he wondered, had the town been 'softened up' by years of privation and fear that it might be willing to capitulate to the Americans?

The vicar became conscious of a loud coughing from the floor. Predictably it emanated from Mr Warburton Clegg, the Methodist minister, whose jaw beneath his bald pate reverberated with the effort so that he resembled the skull of Yorick in the hands of a peculiarly vigorous Hamlet. Mr Villiers was unable to prevent his lips forming a slight smile. The vicar's low-church counterpart was always quick to perceive an insult, usually where there had been no intent to administer one, and was no doubt angry that Mr Villiers had been given first shie at the coconut, as it were, and wanted to make sure the insult was not compounded by his being overlooked for the second shie.

"Er… Mr Clegg," said the chairman.

Mr Clegg rose from his seat and, after he had swivelled round through 360 degrees of blue, distempered wall, surveyed the heads around him with sympathetic condescension. He spoke in a drawling bass.

"I will be brief (was he being uncharitable in interpreting this as a dig against him, the vicar wondered).

"These Americans who have now come among us claim to be Christians. Indeed, I am led to believe, pride themselves upon their faith.

"Even those who live their lives in ignorance of the word of the Lord are familiar with the parable of the Good Samaritan. But what they might not be so familiar with is the question to which Our Lord told the parable by way of answer. 'What must I do to gain eternal life?' The Lord said, 'Love the Lord your God with all your heart and with all your soul and with all your strength and with all your mind. And love your neighbour as yourself.' And then the expert in the law asked, 'Who is my neighbour?' It was in answer to this question that the Lord told the parable.

"What, I ask, is that parable but a plea for understanding and sympathy between nations, creeds and, dare I say it, races? The hated and vilified did what the priest and the Levite turned aside from with distaste. What false concept of purity makes these Americans act as they do, that they should shun their fellows, who might live in the same town as they, even in the same street, for their colour? Shame on them, I say.

"Do not let anyone say shame on us. Rather, attend to the words of scripture. 'Go and do likewise.'"

Pithy and powerful, Mr Villiers reflected, conscious of the sin of envy. And he, who had spent a lifetime endeavouring to conquer the affliction of verbosity, wondered how the fellow achieved it so easily.

The chairman now invited comments from the floor, an invitation whose folly was immediately apparent, it being gratefully accepted by so many that it was impossible to hear what any said. Mayor Markle's gavel slammed down upon its block, and with a face which combined solemnity and reproof in various shades of grey, he required them that wished to speak to raise their hand, and he would call upon them one by one. The forest of arms sprouted anew, some of their owners even hopping up and down like schoolboys over-eager to impress their master.

It cannot be said of the mayor that he was egalitarian in his choice. Mr Villiers reflected that he appeared to demonstrate a form of agnosia hitherto undocumented by medical science, namely the inability to perceive the owner of the frayed cuff, the rolled-up shirtsleeve and the fingers soiled by dirt or motor oil. The lady he called upon first could never have been accused of displaying any of those distressing attributes.

"Mrs Cadwallader!"

The lady arose with a screeching of chair legs, hauling her ample frame, clad in a dark blue twinset, upright and calling in aid her formidable lungs.

"Good citizens of Chalford, the vicar and minister have spoken well and we must be guided by them as to our Christian duty. It does not sit well to treat people as the major would have us do, and to put a landlord in the position of having to refuse to serve a black – or indeed a white – soldier in his bar, because of the colour of their skin. But we are not free agents in this. We are the servants of His Majesty the King, and we are at war, and if the government requires us to bow our heads before the dictates of the US Army, then that, howsoever distasteful, is what we must do. The only thing that can trump morality is the need for survival. Were we not at war then the matter would be different, and I for one would be the first to inveigh against such a suggestion. But we have been asked to make many sacrifices in the cause of victory, and this must be accounted the latest of the number if we are not to mar relations with those that have crossed an ocean to fight in our aid."

"That is the argument that will carry the day," Mrs Villiers whispered.

"I fear you may be right, my dear."

As the great lady subsided, the chairman's finger next lighted upon the town's most distinguished academic, Professor Sachs. The professor, blinking myopically into the sun that streamed, dust-laden, through the sash windows, and with thumbs thrust firmly in the pockets of his waistcoat, spoke up:

"Ladies and gentlemen, we have now survived the greatest trial our nation has experienced and have come through it with our way of life intact when many nations have succumbed. Those that invoke the spirit of the Tommy fighting for what he knows in the form of old cobbled towns, thatched villages and ancient byways do not lie, sentimental though it may seem.

"We have prevailed because of our essential unity, a patriotism that binds us as the ties of kinship. A sense that however much we may quarrel with our neighbour, however much we be divided from him in wealth or politics, that which unites us, the fact that our ancestors shared space with our neighbours from time immemorial, our respect for the institutions of government those ancestors put in place, our shared faith, our respect for our king, provides a sense of belonging that will always prevail against those that seek to impose their alien way of life upon this land. We may deride myth and ritual, but they are the cement which binds us as a race, together. They provide our sense of identity and link us to generations that have gone before, without which we are disembodied, schizophrenic, an orphan society.

"We are not sundered from one another, as these Americans that have come amongst us are, by competing allegiances, antagonistic traditions, and that is why we shall prevail.

"These Americans might think that the prodigality of their factories is all that is needed to vanquish the Hun. However, had we not stood firm, they would not have the opportunity they now have. They shall soon see that it takes more than economic might to prevail. It takes the moral force of a tradition rooted in history, in a soil in which its ancestors are buried, reacting in defence of that soil.

"Pity these Americans if you must, for the lack of that which sustains us, but do not submit to their dictates in preference for those of the Nazis. What are we fighting for in this war if not that we be allowed to manage our own destiny in accordance with our principles? One of those principles is that those of a different race be not persecuted and reviled. It is the case that some people feel the need to look down upon another class of people distinct from them – indeed define themselves by who they feel entitled to look down upon. If we countenance what the major proposes, are we not doing exactly what Hitler is doing to the subject races of the Nazis?"

A chorus of voices rose, even before the professor had finished speaking, and broke on the adamantine shore of Mr Markle's gavel as it descended thunderously seven times.

"Colonel Bland!" shouted the chairman.

The colonel stepped briskly to his right in order to face the bench, and with a back of military straightness bellowed:

"I've never met a real black myself, you understand, but I know the Arab of old. And if these blacks are anything like them they ain't to be trusted. Sneaky and with a decided cruel streak is yer Arab."

"They're not Arabs, they're Americans!" shouted a female voice, whose withering contralto may have belonged to Sally Burns.

More shouting and banging of the gavel. As its reverberations subsided, hands were raised and the chairman looked along his bench towards Mr France, who was the object of vigorous hand gestures from his wife. Mr France, nervously polishing the lenses of his spectacles, spoke up at a volume more suited to a venue twice the size of the hall.

"Well, what I say is, what's it got to do with us? Let the Yanks do what they will. Ain't no skin off our noses if they wants to keep black and white apart. After all, it's what they does on a chess board, ain't it?"

This latter witticism appeared to form no part of Mr France's brief, as a consequence of which Mrs France glowered up at her husband, who engaged in a minute examination of his spectacles.

Mr Villiers felt his heart sink. If this was to be the level of the debate…

Again, the clamour of voices, although this time the chairman was able to dispense with the services of his gavel as he pointed to Tom Curtin, the noise gently subsiding as if in deference to the man's calling. The landlord, with his shirt sleeves rolled up and hands waving restlessly before him as if in vain search for a bar on which to lean, said:

"I agrees with Tom France. It comes nearest me this, since I gotta have whites one night in my pub, blacks the next. I don't mind servin' blacks—"

"I bet you don't," said one, although it was unclear if this was a criticism of the landlord's indiscrimination or his cupidity.

"Like I says, I don't mind it. I ain't never seen a negro, so I don't know what they're like. But I don't mind it, see, 'cos it seems to me they done this so's blacks don't fight with the whites, and I don't want no trouble in my pub. We had enough of that the other day when a couple of our lads squared up to the Yanks. There y' are."

"Predictable," said the vicar under his breath.

The next called was Dan Squires the garage mechanic.

"These Yanks like the major know these blacks, and they don't trust 'em. Else why would they be doin' this, eh? How do we know these blacks aren't going to get drunk and try and ravish our women?"

The vicar's heart sank further, and he was debating with himself whether he should attempt a response. But the chairman was compelled to take note of Sally Burns who was jumping up and down as if about to lose control of her bodily functions.

"Oh, for heaven's sake! I've never heard such nonsense in my life. These people are the same as you and I. The whites don't like them because they've kept them under their thumb for years. If they had their way they'd bring back slavery. And here we are aidin' and abettin' them. Shame on those that agrees to this!"

"Mrs Burns is quite right!" said another.

"Hear, hear," another.

The gavel was called in aid once again to such thunderous effect the storm of voices fell away before its resonating authority. Mayor Markle's face resembled a radish.

There followed more of the same, with contributions from Dan Taylor, the landlord of the Swan, who suggested that his clientele, who were on the whole a 'better sort' than Tom Curtin's, might not take kindly to sharing a bar with a 'load of darkies', followed by four of the same clientele who assured the chairman they did not mind in the least doing so, and if Taylor objected they might take their custom to the Black Bull.

Mr Markle then called the meeting to order and invited the views of those councillors who had not yet been heard before the vote was taken. Arthur Burns, the Labour man, and husband of Sally, was adamant there should be no compromise with 'the Yankee military machine' that occupied this country and seemed intent on staying put until the Russians, by dint of great sacrifice, won the war for them. A wiry man, twitching with the energy of frustrated indignation, and the marked squint which made him unfit for active service, he said:

"Ask yourselves what we're fighting for. It must be more than simple survival. We're fighting for a better world for all, not just the peoples of Nazi-occupied Europe. Is it right we should countenance the sort of oppression the white Americans practise against their black brethren? If we stand for freedom and decency, those benefits should be available to all, not just those of the same skin colour. Can you look yourself in the mirror every morning if you treat someone like we are asked – demanded even – to treat these black Americans?"

Mr and Mrs Villiers joined in the loud ripple of applause in which that emanating from the vicinity of Sally Burns was loudest of all.

"I don't see it, don't see it at all," said Cathcart Wainwright, the town undertaker and a Tory of the old school, to be greeted from the floor with:

"Well, put yer flamin' specs on then!"

"Order please," admonished the chairman. "Mr Wainwright."

"I really don't see that it's any insult to blacks or to whites for that matter. It's simply a matter of keeping them apart so that they don't go at one another. Eminently sensible in my view."

"Quite right," said Cuthbert McQueen, a retired stockbroker possessed of a cyclopean head he nodded to the accompaniment of every other word, thus resembling a particularly unsteady Easter Island statue. "The question is not one of ethics but one of public order. Those who would have us reject Major Bellucci's request will, in addition to incurring the wrath of the Americans, condemn our town to frequent outbreaks of disorder and violence of a sort we have never witnessed before—"

"What about when Tom Ireland laid into Mickey Sims in the Swan?" from the floor.

"Order... order," brayed the chairman.

"And, if I may finish," McQueen went on, "we simply don't have the resources to cope with it. Two constables are quite insufficient to deal with one large public order disturbance, let alone if they occur on a regular basis. The constabulary would be forced to solicit reinforcements from Exeter, and they would be given pretty short shrift. In case people haven't noticed we are suffering a shortage of manpower."

"Eminently practical," said Mr Cadwallader who, in marked contrast, which was capable of inspiring great mirth, to his wife, was possessed of a thin, reedy enunciation. "As has already been pointed out from the floor by none other than my good lady wife, we are not free agents in this—"

"What are we havin' this meetin' for then?" came from the floor.

"Realpolitik," the vicar whispered, his voice too low to convey the resignation he felt. His wife turned to him with a look of bewilderment on her face.

"As I said," said Mr Cadwallader, piping his resignation, "we may be able to debate it, and have the power to reject the proposal. But let me assure you the next thing that will happen is that we come under pressure from higher up and are reminded in no uncertain terms of our duty to the war effort and encouraged to reverse our decision in terms that will brook no opposition."

"By whom?" someone asked.

"The War Office, I would imagine. The cogwheels of democracy may still turn, but make no mistake there is little scope for democracy in wartime. The government of the nation demands a coalition, and we also have to do our bit for the greater good.

"In a war we are not able to take the moral high ground and hold it; to use an apt analogy we do not have the resources to do so. Mr Burns has referred to the Russians whom he seems to regard as more congenial allies than the democratic USA. I would remind him of the monstrous tyranny that country represents. Remember we came into this war because Hitler invaded Poland, but so did the reds, and many Poles have been – what is the phrase? – liquidated, as a result."

"There may be some truth in that," said Arthur Burns,

"but the distinction is that the Russians are not occupying this country and importing their unsavoury practices to the town of Chalford."

"You tell him, Arthur." This from Mrs Burns.

"Nevertheless," Mr Cadwallader went on, "if Hitler and his thugs come marching down the high street they will not applaud us for taking a stand against Major Bellucci, their yoke will not fall upon us more lightly because we have taken a stand for, well…"

"Decency," someone yelled.

"Order! Order!"

Without further ado the vote of the council was taken by means of a show of hands. Those in favour of Major Bellucci's proposal were invited to show. All save Arthur Burns and two others raised their hands.

Reverend Villiers' head was lowered. He even felt tears prickling the back of his eyes. He was conscious of his wife's arm around his shoulder.

To murmurs of disgruntlement or satisfaction from the floor, the result was announced and duly recorded. Henceforth Chalford was to be a segregated town.

"You'll look back with shame on this day!" someone shouted as the sports jackets and works overalls, the twinsets and the War Ag coats trooped out of the hall and into the blinding sunlight. And yet another:

"You do this and there ain't nuthin' 'twixt you and them Yanks."

"This is a black day in our history, my dear," said the vicar as he exited arm in arm with his wife. "I fear I shall feel, the next time I set foot in our dear church, that it is somehow less holy than heretofore."

CHAPTER SEVENTEEN

When Grover Carson first set foot in England he was pleasantly surprised. It was true that, as his well-read friend Errol had said, 'There ain't no blacks in England', but the country was not the frozen wasteland he had pictured it to be, and the fact that there were no blacks did not mean that conditions were worse for them than back home; rather the reverse was true. He was not required to stand in a separate queue for the bus than white people, or to step off the sidewalk when a white person was passing.

When he enlisted, he knew virtually nothing about the country in which he was to be based. He knew only that it was far away across the sea, that it was cold and rained a lot, and that the white Americans had fought a war to gain their freedom from the British. He was still confused by the difference between Britain and England. Errol had done his best to enlighten him, telling him that after their defeat in the white man's War of Independence, the British had rescued the blacks who supported them from the American slavers and resettled them in Canada. 'Then they done boarded American ships and rescued what slaves they could.' This all sounded good, although Errol's insistence that England never had a summer, and he would freeze to death if he did not wear his greatcoat, less so. Likewise, 'They talks English, but funny.'

He met Errol on the boat coming over. A man with more poise, more self-assurance than he had ever encountered in a black, but in whom any approach to swagger was redeemed by the roguish humour that resided in large, liquid eyes. There was something portentous about him, rather like an Old Testament prophet, but Errol nevertheless possessed a cheeky irreverence that was wholly incompatible with the Israeli judge.

He was standing at the rail, staring down at the grey swirling water in the wake of the vessel that was about to embark upon a seventeen-day voyage. A voice, deep and gruff like that of the teachers at the black school he had attended in his hometown of Atlanta, Georgia:

"What you doin' there, boy. Thinkin'? Don't you know this is the army you is in now? The army ain't no place for thinkin.'"

He looked round, and found himself facing his interlocutor's chin, expecting the stern face of rebuke, only to find an impossibly wide grin of pearly white teeth and eyes of mischievous sparkle.

As they sat in the truck that took them and six other men of the 1514 Quartermaster Truck Battalion from the general depot at Taunton to the Chalford OCQM post, it was Errol, who hailed from Montgomery, Alabama, who posed the pertinent question.

"What you here fer, boy? Why'd you join up? Or was you drafted?"

"I enlisted."

"Well, ain't you the clever one."

"Didn't you?"

"Guess I did. Ain't no sense to some of the things a man'll do."

"I was drafted," said Clark Endean, another of their number, who looked little more than nineteen, as he gazed out at the passing hedgerows as if anticipating ambush. "And I was mighty fearful that when I come here, I'd be mixin' with whites, and it'd go hard with us."

"No fear o' that, boy. Savin' fer Captain Harris, we's all to ourselves, all neatly tinned up so's we can't contaminate the environment, just like them rations we's handlin'."

"The en... what?" Endean asked, his expression one of naive pain.

"En...vir...on...ment... means what's out there."

Errol turned back to Grover and asked:

"So why did yer? Enlist."

Grover Carson was twenty-six years old, of a lithe fluid physique, and a strong arm that had won him a reputation as a pitcher for the Atlanta Black Crackers, a baseball team in the Negro Southern League. He lived with his widowed mother in a two-up, one-down in Sweet Auburn, one of the neighbourhoods into which blacks had retreated in the aftermath of the Atlanta Race Riot of 1906.

"I guess, I didn't wanna be left behind. I wanted to see me some of the world... and I guess, I thought hows I might be tret better when I got back home, bein' a vet."

Errol broke into a raucous laugh that threatened to turn into a choking cough.

"Well, I thought I'd figure me who was the stoopidest, you or me, and it turns out we's just the same. That's just how I done figured it. Thought they might treat us better in this here army. But they done treat us same as they allays done."

"Least we gets somethin' in our pocket at the end of the month," said Leroy Clark, a sullen, rather lethargic fellow from Mississippi, "not like back home where the unions keeps us walkin' the streets, beggin' a day's work sweepin' the floor, or a dime to 'go fetch that, nigger.'"

"Still, we ain't stoopid as some as I've talked to," Errol went on, ignoring Clark as if he did not exist. "'I wanna fight fer my country,' they says. You ever heard anything stoopid as that? My country. Like they was General Patton."

"Well, what's wrong with that?" said Mitchell Wiley, one of the older members of the battalion, who stared back at Errol with eyes that started from an ambush of luxuriant brow. "That's what I done, and I'm proud of it. I figures it's only by provin' ourselves, in combat if need be, that our situation's gonna git better."

"Man, you's old enough to know better. Ain't you though? They ain't gonna let us fight, and things ain't gettin' better. You think just 'cos there's a war we ain't gotta step off the sidewalk to let a white pass? Ain't they told us enough lies? They done told us we wus free, and we ends up sharecroppers workin' like slaves for the same masters. Else we's convicted of fare dodgin' or talkin' to a white woman and we's leased out to chain gangs and worked to death. I lost count of how many of my folks dropped dead in the service of Federal Prisons Industries Incorporated. So much for the 13th Amendment."

"I's old enough to know times is changin'. What you say to the Double V campaign? Victory fer democracy at home, and victory abroad. I say we all of us has a stake in this here war."

Errol's face was a monument to scepticism.

"Man, you bin seduced by them Double V girls. Them men in suits at the *Pittsburgh Courier* just wants as many of us blacks to join up so's we can do the dirty work while the white boys is gettin' all the medals, and when the war's done they gonna say we done nuthin' to help."

"What about the President bannin' discrimination in the defence industry?"

"He only done that 'cos Randolph and Walter White marched on Washington and wouldn't call off the march less'n they got what they wanted. He done it out of shame. What use is that gonna be after the war when we don't need no defence industry?"

"We's allay gonna need defence."

"Is they gonna stop lynchin' any black that looks the wrong way at a white woman? No they ain't. Is they gonna stop stonin' any black that swims in the wrong pool? You bin invited to tea by Eleanor Roosevelt or somethin'? What democracy we ever had? I never bin any place didn't have a grandfather clause[3] save on the sea we passed to git here. You wants to be some kinda hero, when the whites won't let us fight, and all we're good fer is to fetch and carry? It's a goddam wonder we wasn't on some raft towed behind the white ship."

"Either o' you had yerself a job?" asked Leroy Clark.

---

3   A constitutional device enacted in some southern states to deny African Americans suffrage.

"Just cleanin', diggin'," said Errol.

"They done said to me, if there's one white fella outta work, you gotta choice, nigger, relief or the rope, which'll it be? In the end I got me a spell in the pen fer beatin' up on an officer of the law."

"So maybe we ain't so stoopid after all," said Grover, "when the whites won't let us work long as one of them's outta work. Maybe it's the whites shouldn't've enlisted when they's got theirselves a pay packet back home."

"Well, you ain't as stoopid as you looks, nigger," said Errol, showing to their full advantage his array of porcelain white teeth. "And neither am I. What do I do? I reads. I goes into the nigger room in the library and I improves ma mind."

"You lookin' fer a AGCT class one?" Leroy Clark asked. "Even if'n you gits it they ain't gonna make a nigger like you an officer."

"What good'll that do yer?" Grover asked. "Seems to me like it'll do yer more harm than good."

"No, you ain't as stoopid as yer look. Yeah, whites see me with ma head in a book, they're gonna think, 'Is this here some sort of uppity nigger that's tryin' to get above hisself, that's best off hangin' from a tree?' But I don't do it where they can see, and I don't carry me no books. No, I slouches in good Uncle Tom style and they don't pay me no heed. 'Cos they don't know what a learned nigger I is. Yessir, I's proud to get me the lowest AGCT[4] grade there is."

Here he broke into his raucous laughter once again, smiting Grover between the shoulders and almost

---

4   A US Army General Classification Test to assess intelligence or other abilities.

impelling him into the lap of the man who sat facing him.

Then the vehicle lurched, drawing suddenly to a halt. From the front came the words:

"We're here, boys. Buckingham Palace."

The driver jumped out and unfastened the tailboard. Grover was the first out, jumping down onto the tarmac and stretching his cramped and aching knees.

He found himself on what looked like a runway for aircraft. To his right were four buildings, two that resembled hangars, the third a low, small-windowed barracks-type building, the fourth smaller and resembling an office.

A short bow-legged negro waddled across the tarmac to greet them as the others jumped down from the truck.

"Is this all I got?" the man asked.

At Grover's look of incomprehension, he added:

"I was expectin' me twenty men."

"Well, we's all you got," said Errol, jumping from the truck and bringing his kit bag around in a wide turning circle that struck Grover on the shoulder and Wiley on the forearm.

"And I got me a smart-ass what talks back. Bring yer kit and follow me."

The corporal led off to the barracks and they trooped behind, over tarmac so broken it could not have seen any aircraft take off in the last decade.

The barracks was spacious, with room for fifty men in double bunks, two stoves at each end, and the walls adorned with a dartboard and pictures either of a personal nature, or featuring Double V girls.

Three men sat around a circle of cards on the floor, two more reclined on bunks. A battered wireless stood silently upon a table at the far end. Both stoves were lit, and the accommodation appeared to be anticipating Errol's most pessimistic forecast of the English climate. The room smelled of damp socks, cigarette smoke and carbolic.

"Grab yerself any bunk that ain't been tek. If you gets one that is tekken you better be ready to fight fer it. Sergeant O'Rourke will be in to see you new men. Chow ain't 'til twelve."

Grover didn't like the sound of Sergeant O'Rourke. His experience of the Irish was that they hated blacks more than anyone else, an animosity that dated back to the Irish lynchings and beatings of blacks in New York during the 1863 Draft Riots.

"Best chow I ever had," said a man sitting bolt upright on his bunk. "It's like I never tasted chow 'til I joined the US Army."

Errol threw his kit bag onto the nearest bunk. As the upper bunk above Errol appeared unoccupied, Grover claimed it with his own kitbag.

"Any of you guys got a gramophone?" asked one of the men playing cards, without deigning to look up.

"No," Errol replied.

"Radio?"

"No."

"Shiiit."

"You don't have no radio here?"

Errol looked in the direction of the contraption on the table.

"That ain't never worked. Them whites got radios. We got shiit."

The man who had been staring at their boots all the while, now looked up as if to confirm for himself what they said was true. His eyes were wary and furtive, as if the subject of popular entertainment for the armed forces was one of top secrecy.

"They didn't tell me when I enlisted that I'd git no jazz in this country... Name's Tom... Tom Grainger."

The newcomers reciprocated by introducing themselves, as did three of the existing inhabitants of the hut, two of the card players remaining mute and immersed in their hands. Grover climbed on top of his bunk, and Errol sat beneath him, loosening the laces of his boots.

"How long you bin here?" Grover asked.

It was Grainger who replied.

"We just bin here four days. But we bin in England six months, ain't we, boys?"

None of the others replied. There was a silence. Grover asked the question he sensed they all, especially Errol, wished to ask, but refrained from appearing naive.

"What's it like?"

"Colder'n back home, but good. Whites here they don't treat you like they does back home. Don't look at you in that 'What you lookin' at, nigger?' way. Treats you respectful like. Shiiit, we even had ourselves an invite to the house of some old biddy made us tea and cakes, didn't we, Art?"

"Sure did," said Art, one of the cardplayers, glancing up with an open, ingenuous face, and then looking shyly back down at his hand.

"'Don't you be tekkin' advantage of them English,' O'Rourke says to us. ''Cos they've never had no niggers here they don't know how to treat you. None of yer tricks, now, y' hear,' he says. They stares at you, 'cos they ain't seen no blacks before. The kids wanna touch yer skin. One of them kids he even aksed if I was made of liquorish. Liquorish! But they don't mean nuthin' by it. They's kinda funny, the English.

"There's a white infantry battalion billeted in the same town – calls it Chalford – you gotta watch out fer them. But we ain't allowed in town same time as they is. Ain't no 'whites only' signs here. 'Sceptin' fer them infantrymen, we left Jim Crow[5] behind on the other side of that ocean, boy. I was even invited by their minister to join the local Methodist congregation, which I'm cogitatin' on, 'cos I's a Baptist myself. Where's you from?"

Grover replied that he was from Atlanta, as did Clark Endean, and Errol from Montgomery.

"Well, I's from Greensboro," said Tom, who seemed to have garnered all the rations of garrulity that were dished out to the original tenants of the hut. "So we's all of us escaped lynchin' to fight fer our country."

"I don't think you should talk so lightly about lynchin'," said one of the card players, whose ponderous baritone sounded as if it belonged to someone twice his size.

"Quite right, Abe," said Tom. "I apologise."

Then to the newcomers:

"His great uncle was lynched on account of lookin' at a white woman the wrong way... so let's change the subject. I hope you don't mind me ramblin' on some, it's just these lot don't talk overmuch... It's like holdin' a conversation

---

5   Laws in the southern American states which enforced racial segregation.

with Lot's wife… so I says you come at a good time fer you. If you'd a come three months ago they'd have worked you all to the ground… See that Abe there, he was six feet tall afore they got to him!"

Abe was about five feet three.

Tom broke into a cackling laugh that would have done justice to an old crone in a horror B movie.

"How come?" asked Mitchell Wiley.

"On account of the Torch landin's in Africa, 'course. Shiiit, we wus run ragged. Here at Southern Base Section we wus under Colonel Thrasher, and shiit, didn't he thrash us good and proper!" Another consumptive cackle.

"Yeah, Class i and iii supplies, twenty-seven pounds per man per day, Type A Field Ration: food six pounds; clothing and equipment one and one half pounds; petroleum products fifteen pounds; solid fuels three and one half pounds; and miscellaneous (he pronounced it 'miskellaneous') one pound. All of that worked out in square feet per man per day. We wus deluged in manifests."

Another man spoke up:

"Every little bitty thing from home they got. Nickel candy bars, best brand of cigarettes. Comic books and magazines."

Tom went on:

"And we had to mark each can with strands of wire, one strand for 80-octane gasoline for wheeled vehicles, and a strand spanning two bars for 87-octane for tracked vehicles. One barber set per company, and a thirty-day supply of fly paper and rat poison. Man, they thinks of everythin', and I mean everythin'."

"That there guy Patton was the worst," said Art. "With his individual, reserve, beach reserve and B landing ration. A hundred and thirty-two pounds per man. I wonder they could stand up, I truly do."

"So when they comes to invade Europe you won't have time to take a shit."

"When do you think that'll be?" Grover asked.

"Shiiit, not this year. Ain't no army gonna invade Europe when the winter's comin' on."

"Gee, when does winter start here? It ain't even summer back home."

"It's preparation, boy! 'Sides, they's hopin' the Russians'll get the Krauts beat before they's gotta risk the lives of American white boys."

"You said it, yessir," said Errol.

"Anyway, what you boys do anyhow?" Tom asked.

"Whaddya mean?"

"Well, it's like… I sings, fine baritone. They calls me the Black Sinatra. And Abe there he knows baseball figures, every average there is, way back. Georgy, he plays the piano, though we ain't got one. So wadda you fellas do?"

"I don't do nuthin," said Errol, portentously. "I's a learned nigger."

They all of them, even Abe and Art, laughed at this.

"I plays the sax," said Leroy.

"Well, we can have us a band, if'n only we can get us some instruments," said Tom. "Whaddabout you?" he asked Grover.

"Oh, I don't do nuthin."

"Listen to him," said Errol. "Don't pay him no heed. Tell him, boy, tell him what you can do."

221

"Oh, it's nuthin.'"

"It sure is somethin'," said Errol. "He's boxed in his time, middleweight, ain't that right? But what he is is the best goddam dancer you ever did see in your born days. He can jitterbug them white guys off the floor... I seen him do it, yessir."

"Well, let's see some of your moves, boy," demanded Tom. And for the first time since they arrived in the hut, all eyes were on the newcomers.

"Oh, I can't. I needs some music."

"Well, sing, Tom," said Errol. "Come on, we'll all join in."

So Tom commenced singing 'Boogie Woogie Bugle Boy', the others joined in, and Errol got up to partner the embarrassed Grover.

Slowly, fearfully, Grover started to move to the beat, his feet leaden and clumsy. Tom's singing was taken up by some, and others clapped and stamped their feet on the boards. Errol took the lead and started to pull and weave Grover through a jive. As the clapping rose in volume his steps grew lighter, more assured. His self-consciousness fell from him as he immersed himself in the beat, and his movements grew more fluid, so that he threaded the air with a lithe grace, the balls of his feet barely touching the boards of the floor that sprung beneath him and impelled him on.

"Wowee!" Tom shouted as the song ended. "Man, you glides, and them feet, they's nuthin' but a blur. Wait 'til you gets on a proper dance floor."

"Do they have dance halls here?" Grover gasped.

"Sure they do. They ain't like back home, they ain't got

no proper bands. But man, when those English gals sees you… But you take it easy with them, they don't know nuthin' about the jive. They's kinda old-fashioned, you get me."

"Oh, I don't…"

"What?"

"I don't wanna cause no trouble. 'Sides, there ain't no black gals."

"You dances with the white gals."

"You mean they'll dance with me?"

"Sure. They'll be queuin' up to dance with Black Lightnin'. It ain't like back home. Man, you'll have yourself one hell of a time. Yessir."

But Grover wasn't sure.

CHAPTER EIGHTEEN

Emily sat opposite Larry in the button-backed leather armchairs in the entrance hall of the Red Lion Hotel in Elterbridge, awaiting the arrival of the jeep that would take Emily back to Chalford and Larry to his base.

The hotel was mock baronial in style, with the eyes of stags cut off in their prime staring down at them from the wall, flanked by two shields bearing an armorial crest that, predictably enough, featured a stag. A huge sweep of oaken staircase led up behind them. From her station behind the desk, the receptionist, a forty-something blonde, eyed them with the scepticism with which she had received their introduction as 'Mr and Mrs Schultz, lately married', a hostility in which cupidity seemed to contend with a desire to request sight of marriage lines, and cupidity won out.

"When can I see you again?" she asked, hoping that the words did not betray her insecurity.

"It's like I said, doll, we're really busy. The big push is just around the corner, and we gotta get ourselves ready."

It was as he had said when he urged her to this weekend, but he had not been too busy to fit that in.

"We can't tell when we might get posted to some port,"

he said as they picked their way through the cow pats and mole hills in the field that led to the long barrow by the road to Kingsmere.

"Will I not see you then?" she asked, a little tremor in her voice mimicking that which tickled her spine.

"They don't tell us nuthin', babe. I said to the major, I said, 'There's some of us got gals here, and we needs to know where we stands.' He says, 'You'd best be ready to say yer goodbyes 'cos you might not get much notice.'"

"But you'll come back for me?"

She found herself nervously patting at the victory roll hairdo that had been the result of much combing, pinning and curling, and which had been somewhat disarranged by their recent activities.

"Sure, doll."

She wanted desperately to raise the subject of marriage, but every approach she imagined to that subject seemed clumsy. She felt like a predator stalking prey over broken glass and eggshells. In the end, out of sheer frustration, she blurted out the first thing in her head.

"Will you take me to the States?"

"You wanna see the States?"

He made it sound like he was some travel agent.

"Not just see… you and me."

"I sure will. Ain't nuthin' to beat it in the whole wide world. You'll just love it, babe."

"And make me your wife?"

"Hey, ain't the guy supposed to be the one to ask?"

Yes, she thought, *you are, but I might be waiting until Doomsday for you to propose*, and she was immediately remorseful for the unkindness of the thought.

"Don't joke, Larry, not about this."

And then since he did not reply:

"Will you?"

She had no resource but her remorselessness.

"Sure I will."

It was what she wanted him to say, but not the way she wanted him to say it. The words should have been spoken with alacrity. Indeed, the plea should have come from him, down on his bended knee, eyes full of entreaty and fear. Instead, they were given with every impression of one backed into a corner.

"You do mean it, don't you?"

"I said so, didn't I?"

She must have still looked sceptical, for he added:

"The Schultzes don't say nuthin' they don't mean."

An appeal to family tradition was not what she had imagined a proposal to be like. But now she had him on the back foot, and she wanted to take advantage of it.

"Well, why don't we get married, now before you get shipped out?"

"Would your pappy sign the papers?"

"I can persuade him."

"And I gotta get the permission of my CO – and they don't give that out with packs of cigarettes, let me tell you. They only give it – what do they say? – if it's in the interests of the prosecution of the war."

"How can our gettin' married be in the interests of the war?"

"Gee, I don't know. That's how these folks talks. And if they do grant it, there ain't no special treatment."

"What do you mean?"

"Things like accommodation, travel subsidies."

"I'm not interested in that!"

"I know, babe, I'm just sayin' is all. And they won't pay for your passage to the States—"

"But won't you—"

"Sure, babe. And they won't grant you automatic US citizenship. The army don't like it. To their way of thinkin' it's takin' American men away from gals back home. If the press was to hear of us boys fallin' head over heels for you English gals, why, there'd be riots in the streets. And... I guess... they's worried there might be a shortage of menfolk when this war's done."

"Oh, don't say things like that!"

"Doll, we gotta face these things... I don't know of any case they've given permission to marry 'cept where it's gonna 'bring discredit to the service' – and you know what they means by that."

"No, what?"

"Where there's a baby due... see what I mean?"

She remained silent. He went on:

"So ya see, we gotta make the most of the time we got, 'cos if we's posted you might not see me afore we gets shipped out to Europe. 'Course, when the war's over, I'll come back fer you... if I can."

"Oh, Larry, don't say it."

"Oh, don't worry, babe, I'll be fine. I ain't the stuff of heroes."

"No, don't say it. I hate to think of what you might have to face."

"It's just..."

His blue eyes gazed out over the fields and the bunting

of May blossoms. And she marvelled once again at the golden glow of his skin, warm and burnished, that was so unlike the skin of her compatriots.

"What?"

"Nuthin'... it's just... if I was injured, would you still want me?"

She flung herself into his arms at that, and as she nuzzled into the gaberdine of his shoulder he said:

"We don't wanna have no regrets... when it's too late. When we could have... gotta know each other."

"Oh, Larry, it's just that... I'm afraid."

"What's there to be afraid of? I love you, kid."

"You do?"

"I said so, didn't I?"

"Have you ever done it before?"

"'Course not... and now I found myself the woman I loves I don't wanna ship off to God knows where, and maybe not come back, without... showing her how much I loves her."

"It's just if something goes wrong."

"Whadda ya mean?" he said, and it seemed to her as if he was being deliberately obtuse to frustrate her.

"If I end up pregnant."

"Babe, I got me somethin' that'll take care of that. They gives them out free in the PX."

"But what... if things went wrong, and I was going to have our baby... and you..."

She waited for him to help her, but he stood like a man on a beach watching the incoming tide, depressed by its inevitability.

"...you were killed, and I was all alone!" she blurted out.

"Hey, what is this?" he said with chilly insouciance.

"Well, what people will think of me! It's all right for you men, but us girls, when we get in the family way and we haven't tied the knot… in a place like this, you gets yourself a name. People turns their noses up at you. It must be the same where you come from, or are there no unmarried mothers in the land of the free!"

They climbed a stile, he helping her with a gentle hand. But he appeared quite unmoved by her words. The only sign he gave of sympathy was when he took her hand again, but he held it lightly, even rather loathe, as one would a kipper one was buying from the local fishmonger.

"I told you, babe, ain't no call to worry. The thing I got from the PX it takes care of all that. And it's army issue, so it's gotta work good. And I am comin' back. Those Nazis ain't gonna hit old Larry Schultz – why with a name like I got I'm practically one of them."

For all her anxieties she had to laugh. And he did too, the sunburnt skin around the corners of his eyes crinkling like wave-dressed sand. God how she loved him. Her love was hard and pitiless like something stuck in her throat.

"Well, don't go saying that round here."

And so they booked into the Red Lion as a newly married couple under the severe gaze of the receptionist, who had no doubt taken sufficient bookings of a like nature to be able to tell the bogus from the genuine.

It had not been the romantic idyll she had pictured. She was tense, trembling as she took off her stockings, feeling gawky and inadequate with her thin, shapeless legs, worrying lest any residual gravy browning might come out on the sheets. Feeling ashamed of her underwear made of the muslin cloth in which their butter came wrapped. She dived into the ice cool of the sheets to conceal her nakedness, but it availed her nothing as he peeled them back to reveal her flesh, and she squirmed under his gaze. The whole process of applying the 'Johnny' as he called it, was so ludicrous she would have laughed out loud had she not been terrified. And what followed was more pain than pleasure, so that when he flopped exhausted by her side, she just wanted to grab her clothes and run, barefoot if need be, for the nearest bus stop.

"Babe, that was great!"

She responded with a wan smile.

He lay flushed and satisfied by her side, and she felt resentment that the old wives' tales, which suggested that sex was something for men's pleasure only, seemed true.

But her tenderness returned, and she felt a gratitude that she had been the cause of such pleasure for him. And tentatively hopeful that this flawed congress might be the means of binding them together forever. Or were those other old wives' tales, that men were only after one thing, and when they had got it, would leave a girl in the lurch, true? But no, not her sweet Larry, with his long, wiry, almost hairless body, flinty hard but liable to twitch in response to her own, with his blue eyes searching out her eyes, and his smile of perfect white, to which she could not but reciprocate.

But now she was not so sure. He was restless, and it was as if he eagerly anticipated the vehicle that would separate them from each other. There was something remote, even offhand about him, and he responded to her concerns, not as he had formerly done with lively interest, but with something approaching indifference.

"Can't you make time, even for me?" she asked, acutely conscious of just how abject she sounded.

"It ain't up to me, babe. You know if it was, I'd spend all the time I could with you."

He spoke the words, but the conviction was lacking, in him and in her. The words 'they're after only one thing' recurred in multiple-part harmonies in her head, sometimes strident and accusatory, at others tolling like a passing bell.

"Aren't you free on Sunday, after church parade?"

"Sunday we gotta work on the anti-aircraft battery."

"What do you need that for if you're moving?"

"How the hell do I know? Anyways I didn't say we wus movin' fer sure. They don't tell us nuthin'."

"But you've always been free on Sundays."

"Sure, but it's like I said. There's things we gotta do now… things is comin' to a head, can't you see that?"

There was exasperation in his tone, but even that exasperation was indifferent, exhausted, depleted.

He had had her, now he had lost interest. Was it the same for every man after they had bedded their girl? They lose interest and, flapping like a canvas in a gale, can only be tamed by the tent pegs of pregnancy being driven into the ground, holding them reluctantly in place?

"Don't you want to marry me?"

"Sure, babe. I just wish I could up and marry you here and now, but them army brass won't allow it."

"Some do though. There's a girl, Jenny, that got married to her American sweetheart."

"Well, that must be like I told you – she got herself pregnant, otherwise they wouldn't have allowed it. Or maybe her guy was owed a favour. That's the way it works sometimes. But they can't do it fer all, on account of what the folks back home'll think. But once this war's over I'll come back here and there ain't nobody can stop me marryin' my best gal."

But perhaps it was only her insecurity that made her uncharitable. They were in the midst of war, after all. Could not this change in him be attributed to a natural fear of having to be a part of that fistful of grit thrown at the Germans' Atlantic wall? She felt chastened. She should not pester him with her concerns at a time like this. And she turned to look at him, his face with the tan that had first struck her as a living, glowing thing, now seeming faded like silverware the maid has neglected to polish. She felt pity and sympathy welling up inside her, and a fierce desire to bring back the burnished wonder of him. She spoke, without first knowing what she would say, wanting only to bring him comfort.

"I hope, darling, that you'll think on this weekend… when you're taken away from me. That you'll hold it in your heart and it'll give you some comfort."

"Sure, babe," he said, and there was a brightness to his indifference that chilled her.

CHAPTER NINETEEN

Sally Burns had known she was coming to the school; an announcement had been made that the next WVS meeting would take place there rather than the village hall because the latter was required for training of ATS girls in map reading, aircraft recognition and anti-gas drill. She should have asked her doctor to give her something for her nerves. But she never thought she would be as bad as this.

The meeting had been underway for fifteen minutes. And for ten of those minutes Sally had been standing outside, in the school yard, her limbs shaking, her heart beating frantically, the sweat soaking her armpits and groin. Every organ of her body, every artery, bone and sinew wanted to execute the manoeuvre whereby she would turn around and walk back through the gate, away from Chalford Infant School.

It was not her determination to have her say on the subject of the blacks that stayed her, nor simple pride, an emotion she had little truck with at the best of times. It was the consciousness that if she did what her body and mind were screaming to do, she would never be able to come back and try again. This was her one chance, and if she failed in it, any future attempts would prove that much harder. And if they were to adopt children, since she and Arthur were unable to have their own, this was something she must inevitably face, either here in Chalford or elsewhere. Because it was not this school in particular, it was any school.

The toe of her shoe tapped like a telegrapher's key on the step that led to the door, the loose buckle threatening to disengage. She leaned against the revetment of sandbags, facing the panes of glass leaded with blast tape. Dare she risk going in and, perhaps, collapsing in some heap of quivering flesh on the floor, throwing up in a corner, and all that in front of women whose cogitations she had been used to criticising with withering scepticism? Many of whom would remember, with a grudge, the way she had opposed the motion for a fundraising dance in aid of the 'Wings for Victory' campaign in support of Allied bombing, on the grounds that it was immoral to fund that which would lead to the deaths of women and children.

They would sympathise when they knew the cause. But before that, some would think it, even if they did not say it, that it was to be expected of one of her class, that lack of backbone.

The yard was bad enough. She had led them across the tarmac of the yard with its hopscotch chalk marks, to their deaths. Her trembling fingers reached up to her brow, to touch, she expected, not the felt hat she was wearing, but the hard rim of the tin hat.

She had become a voluntary part-time ARP warden

in April 1940, coming on duty after she finished her shift at the bottle factory, and in August became a full-time warden based at the post in the butcher's shop in Queen's Road in Canning Town, that ran at right-angles to their street, Rendel Road, under post warden Ted Andrews.

She was a quick learner, and it did not take her long to absorb the information crucial for an ARP warden: the names of the residents of their area; which were old and infirm; which shelters they used; where the hydrants were; and where the rest centre was. She was trained in anti-gas procedures, fire drills, smoke drills for entering a burning building, using a stirrup pump or sand to put out incendiaries, splinting a limb, disinfecting a gas mask, and carrying a casualty on a stretcher. She also received the benefit of lectures on the smells of different kinds of gas such as mustard gas, the standards of shelter protection, and the effects of a high explosive detonation in the form of outward and suction waves.

There had been the three of them, her and Ted and Jack Fletcher, the ship-scraper and part-time boxer with the crooked nose, drinking tea and completing the group situation reports of incidents called in that would be sent to the local ARP headquarters... But no, until then there had been only light raids. So they had the cards out, playing brag on the counter, the smell of blood and offal rising from the sawdust beneath their feet.

"It ain't fair, that's what it is," said Jack.

Sally wholeheartedly agreed.

"You would think it'd be different in war, but it's the same as always, the poor gets the worst of it and the rich comes up smellin' like roses."

She was referring to the fact that the German bombers were concentrating on the East End, and it was the poorest inhabitants of the capital who were suffering most.

"And there's them toffs in the West End gettin' off scot-free," said Jack, "sittin' in their shelters quaffin' champagne and what have you. Ain't no justice in the world, ma girl."

"And we's sittin' ducks an' all. Ain't hardly a shot been fired in anger. We's just supposed to sit here and take it."

Until this time, anti-aircraft fire had not been allowed over the capital in case it brought down British fighters.

"The Palace was hit," said Ted.

"No more'n a scratch."

"Least they stayed here. King and Queen. When they didn't 'ave to. Give them their due. And we can hit back now. They moved a load of them ack-ack guns what's been defendin' the airfields up. We can give as good as we get."

"Yeah," said Jack, obviously speaking from personal experience, "worst thing of all is havin' to take a pastin' and not be able to throw a punch back."

"Nah," said Ted, "worst fing is they don't even say what we is goin' frew. Papers ain't allowed to report there's been a raid and what the casualties are until four weeks is gorn. So all we gets is 'London can take it', and people ain't even allowed to know what we is takin'."

No, she was wrong again – what was the matter with her memory? – it can't have been that day. Because this was the late afternoon of Saturday 7 September 1940 – no ordinary September when the East End would head to the fields of Kent for the hop picking. It was what would come to be known as 'Black Saturday': the start of fifty-seven continuous nights of bombing.

The yellow stand-by warning sounded and alerted them to the fact that there were bombers within twenty-two minutes' flying time. They threw down their cards, extinguished their cigarettes, donned their helmets and went out to patrol the streets.

The police were already out on their bikes, placards on their front and back that read, 'Air raid warning. Take cover.'

The siren, or 'Moaning Minnie' as it was known, went off at twenty to five, indicating that the bombers were twelve minutes' flying time away. The sky was a bright blue, and suddenly formation after formation of bombers, in V shapes, the sun flashing off their polished metal, were etched across it and coming in from the north, like the flocks of starlings she had seen over the Essex marshes. Coming in along the Thames, punctuated by puffs of smoke from the anti-aircraft guns. And then came the thump of bombs.

Her heart contracted. She had been waiting for this day; waiting with dread in her innards, fearing…what? Fearing fear itself.

The bombers were targeting the Royal Albert and Victoria Docks, the economic heart of the East End, where Tate & Lyle had their sugar refinery, Spillers their grain mill. The docks where her late father, who had no union card, would stand outside the gates every morning hoping for the casual labour that would 'keep the wolf from the door', so that her mother would not have to pawn her wedding ring or clothes for food or, worse, have to go begging to the Public Assistance Board. The docks were only a couple of streets down from Rendel Road.

Sally's mother, Eileen, lived in a two-up, two-down terrace in Rendel Road, a quarter of a mile from where Sally and Arthur lived, together with Sally's sixteen-year-old brother, Donald, who was waiting to join the Auxiliary Fire Service, and twelve-year-old sister, Edith, known as Edie. Arthur, who was unfit by virtue of his eyesight for active service, was on duty with the fire brigade.

Rendel Road was always Sally's first call. She found her mother calmly sitting by the fire listening to Arthur Askey and Stinker Murdoch on the wireless, her dog, Patch, a wire-haired terrier, with his head on her slippers, and Edie urging her mother to vacate the house.

"Hello, dear, you got time for a cuppa tea?"

"Of course I haven't, Ma. We're in for a bad time. You gotta get to the shelter."

"Oh, I don't think so, dear. I think we'll just stay here and hide under the table like we done last time."

"Oh no, Ma," Edie pleaded.

"This ain't like last time, Ma. This is a big 'un. You gotta get out and go to Invicta Road."

These terraces with their narrow back yards rarely had their own Anderson shelter. If they used a shelter they went to the communal domestic shelter in Invicta Road, one street beyond Rendel up from the river.

She saw her family safely to Invicta Road, joining the spate of families, children in their arms, old people chivvied on by their young, carrying coats or bundles of blankets, or in one case a bird in a cage. At the shelter Sally ticked off the names of the residents, then returned to encourage others to get to the shelter as fast as they could and checked on those who opted to remain in their houses.

Then she helped the firemen, manning a stirrup pump, trying to put out the eighteen-inch incendiaries that ignited on impact. But stirrup pumps were of little use. For every fire dampened down another four or five sprouted as if without cause; as if the city were reacting to the bombing by spontaneously igniting in hysterical sympathy. And when she looked up and around her, through the smoke and ragged teeth of ruined buildings, the whole river seemed aflame.

At 6.10 the planes left, and the all-clear sounded like the outrushing breath of relief. It was the first big raid. People had yet to realise that the incendiaries were merely the prologue to the main performance, that they lit beacons to guide bombers to their targets. And when they came they returned, again and again.

She went on her round to look out for the falling bombs, the land mines, the general-purpose bombs, which ranged in size from 110lbs to the giant Hermanns or Satans that were as much as 400lbs, parachute bombs that could destroy a whole street. Then she would telephone the emergency services, guide those in the open to shelters and administer first aid. It was only in the brief intervals between these activities that she appreciated the scale and terror of the evening's events.

The early evening was alive with the whistle and crump of falling bombs. Her brain froze under the power of that scream. The whoosh that could suck the air from your lungs and leave you without a mark on you, but stone dead. Then the suction and compression of the air pulling and releasing her, driving the breath from her body as the masonry and bricks fell about her and the shrapnel danced on the cobbles. It was as if those cobbles themselves were rising and falling, the ground heaving, as if the earth itself were one giant fairground ride that ended in a vomit of earth and debris. The frontage of a warehouse seemed to expand, the bricks separating one from the other, but slowly, as if in some slow-motion film, before it came crashing down. Ack-ack shells burst overhead, and shrapnel fell like deadly rain out of a sky bruised yellow and orange like the atmosphere of an alien planet. Her eyes that at one minute seemed about to be sucked out of her head returned to a stinging reality.

In those brief respites from the roaring of falling shells and the sound of collapsing buildings, the night rang to the clanging of bells as fire appliances rushed past desperate householders trying to flag them down. The banks of the Thames were engulfed in a sea of flame, so that night glowed as bright as day, as the Germans targeted the Surrey and Royal Victoria Docks and the Woolwich Arsenal. The North Woolwich Road became a river of molten tar holding up fire appliances and ambulances. Panic engulfed Silvertown after the Beckton Gasworks was hit, with rumours that the Nazis were dropping mustard gas. Streets were blocked by flames high as a cliff face, and the air reeked with the stench of burning rubber and tar, and sugar from the crust of molasses that lay on the river and burned like hell itself. Terrified rats fled burning warehouses like a plague. And all the while the inhabitants crouched under tables and in under-stair cupboards or even under bridges, caught unawares after becoming used to nuisance raids that took a toll only on their sleep.

At 3am the raid was as heavy as ever. The dead and dying lay on the pavement, legs and arms and severed heads like parts of the broken toys of a wilful child. Frantic parents searched for their young, calling names that with each repeat grew but more forlorn.

And she was sure that she would not survive that night; the next bomb must surely get her. For in those days everyone had their special bomb, the one with their name on it.

The all-clear sounded at 4.24 in the morning, after eight hours of bombing. As always, the ARP wardens and fire brigade were the first on the scene, the heavy rescue squad yet to arrive to cut off the gas and water supplies to prevent explosions and save those who were trapped from drowning.

Sally went to check on her mother and Don and Edie as soon as she was able to do so, running along the street, past dazed people cloaked in blast dust, screaming disorientated children, and Civil Defence volunteers searching for survivors. People scrambled amongst buildings that had become heaps of matchsticks, their eyes staring and their movements frantic and desperate, or else exhausted and haggard, grimly negotiating the piles of rubble, sloshing through the pools of water from burst mains. One of the volunteers held up an authoritative hand for silence, and from beneath the mangled concrete she could hear screams that reminded her of a rabbit she had once seen caught in a trap.

People were having their injuries assessed by the First Aid Party, and then queued for the stretcher party to transfer them to a first aid post: a young girl with her face swathed in bandages, holes only for the eyes; a man with a luggage label bearing the initial M for morphine tied to his braces; another the label bearing the inscription X, for internal injury. One of the first aid workers bending over a stretcher, holding a rag to someone's face and saying, soothingly:

"Breathe deeply, dear. This'll take the pain away."

It was waiting in Martindale Road for her, her worst nightmare. A baby lying on the cobbles, the livid red and white of its head, like a burst melon, appearing garishly through the coating of brick dust. An old woman plucked her by the sleeve, and shouted into her ear as if she were half a mile away:

"Get somethin' to wrap it in! Get somethin' to wrap it!"

She tried to answer, but her throat was dry and impacted. She pointed at a torn curtain, and as the old woman, one stocking hanging down a flabby white leg, bustled through the debris, she tore her face away, and ran back up the street, immediately forgetting what she had seen. It was only in the months that followed that the sight of the burst head of the baby would return to visit her by night, and by day also.

To her relief she found number 22 Rendel Road intact. Her mother and brother and sister had returned from the shelter as soon as the all-clear sounded. They had been lucky, many of the houses around them had sustained damage, their roofs missing or walls collapsed in a scree of bricks.

She was immediately called away to deal with an unexploded bomb at 8 Martindale Road. Signs saying

'Danger. Unexploded Bomb. No Entry' had been erected blocking off the road. The bomb would either have a time delay fuse or it would be a dud. There was no way of knowing which. There would have to be an immediate evacuation of all buildings in a 600-yard radius. It was the responsibility of the ARP wardens and police to arrange that evacuation. Meanwhile, if all went well, the bomb disposal men would lift the bomb by pulley and take it to Hackney Marshes where it would be detonated.

A tide of families, clad in overcoats and carrying cases, was already making its way out of Rendel Road on that Sunday morning when Sally returned to her mother's house.

She strode into the hall, keeping her helmet on.

Her mother and Edie were at the kitchen table, sitting over a pot of tea. The wireless was on, playing dance music.

"Ma, there's a UXB in Martindale Road. You gotta get out. Get yourself ready now."

She expected to see fear, or even resignation in her mother's face as she looked up. She saw neither, and that was perhaps even more frightening.

"Where's Don?"

"Upstairs."

"Don!" she called.

There was that look again on her mother's face. The absent dazed look she had first noticed when her father, Tommy, died of consumption eighteen months back, but which had appeared ever more frequently since the bombs started. Occasionally she would see, like a glimpse of sun through cloud, something of the vibrant, funny woman, fond of dancing and loving her trips to the Palais, her mother had once been. But now those glimpses were rather of a child than a woman; a child who knew more fear and loss than a child should.

"What's a UXB?" her mother asked.

"Unexploded bomb. You gotta go now. Grab everything you need. No time to mess abart."

Her mother turned off the wireless and looked around her on the floor.

"What are you after?"

"My shoes."

"They're in the hall where they always is."

"That you, sis?" Don shouted from the top of the stairs.

"Unexploded bomb in Martindale. Come on, you gotta clear art."

"Righto."

Her mother raised herself from the armchair with a resigned sigh, eliciting a questioning look from Patch. She went into the hall and exchanged slippers for shoes.

"Do I have time to go to the lavvy?"

"Well, be quick about it."

While her mother went through the back door to the privy in the yard, Sally went into the kitchen to check the hob was not lit. Her mother had never gone out and left anything on the hob, but Sally felt she could not be trusted these days. With a roll of thunder, Don pounded down the bare treads of the stairs.

"You make more racket than the Luftwaffe, you do."

Donald gazed at her through the unruly comb of hair that fell over his eyes. The gaze was a level one, and it seemed to Sally that she had not noticed the change from her staring down into his freckled cheeks and sparkling green eyes, to her having to meet them flush with her own. The exploits of Herr Hitler had, she thought, decoyed her gaze away from the deterioration in her mother and the maturation of her brother.

"Cor, we ain't 'alf copped it. I was just art to help. Satans, I reckon."

She couldn't help but smile at the matter-of-fact nonchalance that aimed at maturity, but, fell short of the mark.

"Grab what you need. You'd better get yer skates on."

"Where's Ma?"

"In the lavvy."

At that their mother appeared. That dazed look again, glancing down at her shoes as if she could not remember why she was going out. Sally watched her mother's face, impassive beneath its faint blush of powder. She reached for her coat from the hall stand. It caught on the peg, almost knocking over the top-heavy stand, and Sally had to reach out a hand to support it while the coat was drawn free. Edie scooped up Patch.

Then she said:

"Oh, I don't think so, dear."

"Ma. This is a UXB."

"Are we goin' to Invicta Road? I'll take that blanket then, case it gets cold."

She looked towards the blanket that did duty as a blackout curtain.

"You can't take that. The whole area's gotta be evacuated. You gotta go to South Hallsville School in Agate Street. To the rest centre. They got a basement, which is bein' used as a shelter by them as is bombed art, and an evacuation point for them as has lost their homes and has to get buses."

"We ain't lorst our home."

"I know. But you still gotta go."

Her words lacked the conviction she needed to impart. She didn't wish to be drawn into an argument. She had come to dread these confrontations with her mother that sparked not so much arguments as a frustrating breaking of her will upon the rocky shore of maternal resistance; a dumb unthinking stubbornness that was stubborn for its own sake.

"Oh, I don't know. It ain't safe. And it's smelly, dark and cold. Havin' to do yer business in the bucket. All those folk crowded in. And those benches. Play merry hell with my back, they do. And last time Ella Toms took the box I was usin' fer me feet. There's nothin' wrong with her. Not like me and my back."

"Ma! That's the shelter. You ain't never been to the school."

"I'd much rather be in my own home."

"Tommy and Pete'll be there," Don said.

"Well, I don't care about Tommy Parker or Peter Wright," her mother replied testily. "They ain't nothin' to me. I'd much rather be with folk I know."

"Ma, you know everybody. Your friends. Jessie Byrne that takes in washin'll be there, and the Bakers and the Sims," Sally said. "You like Sal Baker and Jean Cummins, the fishmonger's wife."

"Stinks of fish, he does."

"It don't matter what he smells like, Ma. You're safer there."

"Oh, I don't know, dear. I wanna go to Elsie's. She'll take us in."

Elsie was her mother's cousin who lived in Shoreditch.

"Don't be daft, Ma, how can you get there?"

"We can walk easy enough."

"It's too far."

Was it really? It was less than a mile. But with all the wreckage of the bombing, the burst mains and the blocked roads… Don would be there, but… he'd never done anything like this. He didn't have the training, he didn't know the hazards. If they walked to Shoreditch she would have to go with them, and that would take her away from her duties. She might be accused of neglecting others in order to escort her family who could more conveniently be put up at the school. Some would say it was typical of a woman to let her emotions get the better of her and put her own before others. That was why they should never have let women become ARP wardens.

"There's some goin' to the Tilbury. Or sarf into Woolwich Tunnel, or up to Epping Forest to camp art," Don said.

The Tilbury shelter was housed in an old railway warehouse.

"Don't be stupid, Don. The Tilbury stinks. How can your ma get up to Epping Forest? You're goin' to the school."

"I doan wanna get mixed up with them evacuees and get meself carted off."

"Lor, Ma, is that all yer worryin' about? Nobody's gonna cart you off. But it's safer art of here. There's an unexploded bomb. And the bombers'll come back. They're targeting the warehouses and the docks, and we's right in the middle of it."

"You sure, Sal?"

"Yes. Trust me, Ma. It's safer than goin' to Elsie's or darn the tunnel. It's what they're tellin' folk to do. They wouldn't tell folk to do it if it weren't the right thing, would they?"

"Yeah, let's go, Ma. If Sal says it's okay, it's okay," said Don.

If Sal says it's okay.

"Well, all right."

"I'll join you later, Ma."

It was the reassurance she always gave so glibly. And her mother accepted it for the truth, notwithstanding all the times she had said it and had never appeared. And her job gave her the excuse.

It was not out of callousness or lack of sympathy, rather the reverse. She who had looked up to her mother, admired her resilience, particularly since Dad died, could not bear to see that woman, who had been the pillar on which she had leaned all her life, dissolve into fear. She could not bear to witness the pale, drawn tension, the little tics and winces every time a bomb screamed down, the tears that leaked down the ritually rouged cheeks; or worst of all, on occasion, hear the screams that issued involuntarily from her mouth. Or have to pretend on her rising not to see the pool of wet where she had been sitting, nodding innocently on hearing her mother say, 'I don't wanna come here no more, it's so damp.' To hear the words and wonder whether her mother really believed them.

"Well, come on there, Ma. Don't stand there jawin'. I got work to do."

Edie carried Patch, Donald the big suitcase, and as they trooped out through the hall Sally caught a glimpse of her mother and sister and brother in the hall mirror. It was the last proper sight she would have of them.

Faces. Faces she thought she had forgotten would sometimes appear with startling clarity in her sleep, and she would start awake, trembling. There were the Gateses and the Turners, the family with the retarded boy, five children all gone. The Robertses from Crown Street: Mrs Roberts and her husband, a stoker in the navy, the two grandparents who lived in the room below, the grandmother thinking they were still fighting the first war and stuffing her ears with the plugs issued by Charles Key, the local MP, and the four children. On the wall of their hall they had a picture of Jesus, cradling a little child on his knee.

Mrs Roberts informed her that her husband had built a brick shelter in their back garden and they would go in that. At this point the old woman, who had discarded her ear plugs, now commenced wailing and saying she couldn't stand it.

"I don't wanna be buried!" she screamed. "Ain't no Kaiser gonna bury me."

The youngest girl commenced a wailing saying she wanted to stay in her own home, and Sally had to threaten to call the police before they came with her, up Queen's Road past smouldering ruined houses, the mother with the youngest child on her hip, the others holding the hands of their grandparents. Came meekly led by her, Sally Burns, to their deaths.

And those others: people whose homes had been destroyed, whose tangible memories had been erased, with nowhere to sleep, no clothes or food or ration books. Faces graven with the knowledge that this was what war was, not the rhetoric of politicians. Fathers clutching suitcases containing their treasured possessions; mothers expanded with clothes, because it made sense to wear as many as possible, cradling babies in their arms; children, gasmasks in cardboard boxes around their necks – all following her like the Pied Piper, plying her easy assurances of their safety from the bombs that fell each terror-stricken night.

She checked them in as they stood in the passage. They sat on cases and bags, pregnant women on camp beds, the children on forms, staring blindly at the wall in front of them, some with torn and filthy clothes, some only in pyjamas or nighties, with slippers on their feet, faces blackened with smoke, unconscious of the indignity. Some were bleeding from wounds and oblivious to the fact, often resisting attempts to tend them. Families clung together, knees shaking, faces wide-eyed and glassy. Some were hysterical, screaming and screaming until someone slapped their face. Others called out names, asking where such-and-such was. Men sat cursing foully. Old toothless men or women sat alone, white with fear, mumbling to themselves, or asking when the buses would arrive.

What could they do for them? When she offered them a cup of tea, together with the buns provided from a WVS canteen, or a Salvation Army blanket, to be greeted in some cases with angry refusal or a thrusting of the cup away, or a tearful pathetic gratitude that made her want to weep, it only served to emphasise her impotence.

With a naive and self-serving faith in the assurances the authorities gave, she told them the buses would be there that night. And even hardened dockers or known criminals regarded her with the trusting eyes of puppies. But no bus arrived that Sunday, and in the evening the bombs came again, and the refugees wailed and screamed in that crucible of Bedlam.

Sally reassured her mother it was best to stay there until the unexploded bomb was defused and the bombing ceased, or the buses arrived to take them somewhere safer. She had begun to see in this an opportunity to have her family evacuated, even if only temporarily, out of the reach of the bombing she anticipated would continue. Away from her home, she hoped her mother's nerve would give and she would be only too glad to jump on the first bus that arrived.

But the buses still did not come, and the anger and frustration built, some determining to leave, others simply cursing and swallowing the knowledge that the bombers would return.

There were 600 of them in the school when the bomb fell at four o'clock on Tuesday morning.

"Are you quite all right, Mrs Burns?"

She started at the voice at her ear. Turning she saw Agatha Wills, pert and abrupt as always, but evincing real concern.

"I… I just took a bit of a funny turn, that's all."

"You look white as a sheet."

"Well, come on in then." Mrs Wills, like many of her class, had a schoolmistressy practicality about her. "You'd best have a sit down. If there aren't any seats I'm sure someone will give up theirs when they see you are unwell. When the deliberations are over we can have ourselves a nice cup of tea, and I'm sure you'll feel much better."

"I'm not sure I should go in."

"Oh, don't be silly," Mrs Wills said. "There's always someone who turns up late. There's more frightening things in the world than Mrs Cadwallader's opprobrium, you know."

Didn't she know it? And it was a relief to yield herself to Mrs Wills' arm, which guided her over the threshold, past details of corridor she dare not examine too closely. In the rubble there had been a chart of the alphabet with pictures for each letter beginning with an 'a' for apple, and, most poignant of all, drawings done by the children – she remembered a rabbit with floppy ears that hung down to its feet, and the schoolbell that must have been rung for decades to get the children into class… She could not go on.

Then Mrs Cadwallader's sonorous voice, as she found herself guided to, and subsided into, a seat.

"We can feel justifiably proud of all we have achieved with our welcome club, and though not all of our transatlantic brethren have been unable to resist the attractions of our tea urn and gramophone, I think it undeniable that we have cemented an excellent relationship – dare I say it, bond – between the community of Chalford and the Americans."

Sally had not even been aware of wondering why she had come to this meeting with a sense of urgency. But her leader's words served as a timely reminder, and the sense of purpose swept in on her like a wave, its ozone tang a sovereign remedy for her fear and nausea.

Someone saying how the American servicemen she had invited to tea had arrived with tinned peaches and a couple of oranges.

As the woman's voice ended in an attack of embarrassed self-effacement, she found herself speaking, and regarded the gymnastics of her lips and larynx with surprise, as if she had found herself speaking in tongues. And indeed, that was what it sounded like, for there was little of the usual confidence or combativeness about her oratory. Rather she began by enunciating her words with a tentative quaver, and, like one defusing an unexploded bomb, afraid to press on any vowel or consonant for fear it may set off the mechanism of death. And then, more disturbing still, she tried to compensate for her lack of fluency, and only succeeded in impaling her words on a needle of shrillness.

"It's all very well for you to say that, but what about the blacks? Are we to extend our welcome clubs to them?"

There followed an uneasy silence, and she was not sure whether that silence reflected the matter of her speech or the manner of it. Then Mrs Cadwallader said sonorously:

"You make a very valid point, Mrs Burns. We have not, as you know, extended the benefits of that particular form of hospitality to the negroes in the Quartermaster Battalion."

For once the august lady appeared to be at a loss for words, and in attempting to progress the discussion exhibited that which had never before been heard to emanate from her lips: a stutter.

"I... er... we, as you know, are unfamiliar with the American blacks – indeed any blacks – and as such it might be a trifle premature—"

"We were unfamiliar with the whites." Sally, having recovered her composure, was in unforgiving mood.

"Yes, indeed. But they were… I think… perhaps, more like us. With the blacks… well… one doesn't know how to talk to them."

At this point Lily Foster, the postmistress, came to the rescue of the beleaguered champion of Chalford WVS.

"If what Major Bellucci says about them is true, we don't want them in our houses. I'm sure I don't want my throat cut."

"I'm sure Major Bellucci is simply exaggerating as far as that is concerned," said Mrs Villiers.

But Mrs Foster was not to be gainsaid.

"I don't know about that. You hear such stories."

"What stories?" Mrs Markle snapped back.

"You know… indecent stories… about them… and their… appetites. I'm sure, Mrs Villiers, you don't want me to draw you a picture."

"Oh, for God's sake!" expostulated Sally. "You don't really believe those tales, do you? They'll be saying next that they've got horns and tails and carry toasting forks."

"Quite," said Mrs Cadwallader. "It's just this sort of rumour that makes young girls either fearful or… well, dare I say it, curious… and that, I am sure, is not something we would want to be seen encouraging."

"Curious about what?" asked Agatha Wills ingenuously.

"Never mind, dear!" snapped Mrs Cadwallader. "Really, this discussion is taking a most prurient turn—"

"It's all very well for us to say as how they're no danger," said Mrs Foster, "but we don't know, do we?"

"I saw one in the post office the other day and he looked

most smart and spoke very politely to young Amy Richards behind the counter," said Lucy Bland. "I'm surprised you've never seen any of them in there, Mrs Foster."

"Well, I haven't. And perhaps I should be keeping a good eye on Amy Richards."

"And I've seen them about town," said Agatha Wills, "and they seem very well behaved and not at all the sort of people one should worry about."

"But how do we know what they're like when they get a drink inside 'em, eh? It's a well-known fact some races just can't take it like whites—"

"I dunno about that," said Lucy Whiteley, "the number of times I've seen Sam Westwood rolling through the town after closing time."

"Well, Major Bellucci knows them," Mrs Foster went on, "and he says they're a danger to every decent woman, and he should know."

"That's ridiculous," said Sally. "It's perfectly obvious the major is prejudiced against them. Half of them still think of them as slaves, and Bellucci's one of them. For God's sake, I thought it was the British way to give folk the benefit of the doubt."

"Please don't take the Lord's name in vain," admonished Mrs Wills, bizarrely raising her hand as if in blessing. "But we could hold a dance for them; there'd be no alcohol, and we can ensure only the most proper girls are invited. Really, we should be ashamed of ourselves to speak about them in this way."

"Quite right," said Lucy.

"Speak for yourself," said Mrs Foster. "I ain't ashamed. It ain't shamin' to look out for your own girls."

The meeting getting out of hand, Mrs Cadwallader raised her beringed appendage in an attempt to call order.

"Please, ladies. We've had quite enough of this unseemly talk. We might in due course, through the good offices of Reverend Villiers, arrange a dance for the blacks, and as Mrs Wills says, the girls will be carefully vetted, as they are for whites. For my own part I think we should let matters lie for the time being… give the blacks a chance to settle and… see how they fit in, and then consider what we can do for them."

"I for one would be more than happy to invite one to tea now," said Mrs Villiers.

"And so would I," said the Misses Lightowler and Blake almost in unison. Agatha Wills plaintively agreed with them.

"And I," said Mrs Knight. "That's the sort of thing that broadens the mind."

"Well, we all want broader minds in this town," said Sally.

"Mrs Burns, please. This is not helping," Mrs Cadwallader admonished.

"One aspect of this we have not considered," said Mrs Markle, "is how our good Major Bellucci would react were we to invite the blacks to our little gatherings. Prejudiced against them he undeniably is, and in that he might be quite mistaken. Nevertheless, we don't want to do anything to cause offence. To rock the boat."

"You mean make things more difficult for your husband," interjected Mrs Foster.

Mrs Markle, as behoved the wife of a lord mayor, haughtily ignored the interruption and carried on:

"We should all realise just how beholden to them we are."

"I doubt the invasion of Europe will fail for want of our snubbing the blacks," said Mrs Villiers.

And more intemperately, Sally:

"So we have to kowtow to them in everything, do we?"

"No," said Mrs Cadwallader emphatically, "what we have to be is circumspect and judicious. And not take precipitate steps that might cause offence among our American friends."

"With that I am in accord," said Mrs Villiers, "but as Mrs Burns says, we should not allow our allies' prejudices to dictate our behaviour… nor, indeed, to prejudice us."

"Quite," said Mrs Cadwallader, "we shall do something for the blacks, but let us, pray, give it time. They've been in our midst for only a few weeks."

Yes, thought Sally, *let's wait until they are due to be shipped overseas, and we can conveniently forget about the problem.* But for once in her life, she did not voice the thought. Instead, she said:

"I think we should vote on it."

Vote upon it they did, and as usual Mrs Cadwallader's influence swayed opinion, although on this occasion by a greatly reduced majority than she was used to enjoying.

"And," Mrs Cadwallader added by way of coda, "I would be most grateful if you younger ladies would stay behind and assist with bringing the children's desks back into this room. Mr Barclay the caretaker and his boy are both away on a Home Guard exercise. The desks are in the storage room."

Mrs France, Mrs Foster, Lucy Bland and others trooped out in obedience to this request, as Sally Burns found herself standing, staring at the blackboard which depicted a crude family tree of the House of Tudor.

"Mrs Burns, will you not assist?"

She turned. Mrs Cadwallader faced her with a look of entreaty to which she was unable to respond.

"Now, now, my dear. We cannot always have our own way."

Still Sally did not move.

"Come, come, let us be adult about this. We are a democratic organisation after all."

"Desks," she said absently.

"Precisely. Young backs, strong arms, that's the ticket," said Mrs Cadwallader with her best gym-mistress vivacity.

"I can't."

"Oh really, Mrs Burns. Let's not sulk when there's work to be done."

The insult did not even register in Sally's consciousness.

She was stumbling through the debris of the school, Arthur at her side, frantic, her eyes roving desperately, despairingly, for signs of life amid the chaos, while she barked her shins on fallen masonry, screaming like one in a delirium to that air laden with brick and plaster dust and tinged with the stench of burnt timbers from the fires the tenders had been unable to contain. Wardens and police bringing bodies or pieces of bodies out covered in sacking, or else shouting for anything to cover the bodies with, while others shouted at them to keep quiet while they listened for any survivors.

"Ma! Ma! Don!"

She pulled at pieces of plaster, at tiles and bricks, conscious of the futility of her efforts, knowing that her family, if they were there, would be far deeper than her feeble efforts could plumb. Deep down, in the cellar. They were strung out before her, firemen, ARP wardens and civilians who may or may not have been searching, as she was, with heart clenched in a tight knot of fear and foreboding.

Sally wanted to howl out her anguish, scream to the skies her frustration. Her mind tried to force its numbed neurons to construct a plan of the school and work out where the cellar would be. Not here, on the crumpled and broken tarmac of the yard. There, over there where those men were, in the lee of the wall that, she was sure, had been the outside wall of the main corridor. Yes, she remembered that window that was now merely the fraction of a frame, its sandbags blown outwards.

"Here, here!" she called to Arthur. Then:

"Ma! Ma!" she called.

"Save your strength for digging," he counselled.

And she both hated and loved his practicality.

Her feet rocked on a piece of plaster and she almost fell.

Her throat choked with dust and dread, her fingers and nails torn and bloodied, she pulled free brick after brick and hurled them heedless behind her. The stretcher parties, with the tell-tale SP on their helmets, arrived, treating some on the spot, carrying away others on stretchers, and when the stretchers ran out, on doors or planks, decorated with luggage labels or, in some instances, just marks on their forehead detailing their injuries – these to be taken to the nearest first aid post for assessment and transfer to hospital. The mortuary vans, usually requisitioned grocers' or bakers' lorries, carried away the bodies under shrouds of sacking or torn curtain, some of the remains no more than a headless torso or limb or the shapeless lump of innards that was not so much human as butcher's offal.

It was the man in front. It may have been Jack Fletcher, she could not remember. Big spatulate hands, like a boxer's, gloved in dust and blood, that tore free the plastered bricks and revealed the desk. The wooden top, the groove that would house the pencils, the hole, still containing its porcelain ink well. You lift it from the bottom, the hinge goes up and there are your books. So he lifted.

It was a boy. Perhaps six or seven. His face a plaster cast of itself save for a rent across the temple through which one could see bone, even whiter than he was, and tissue that was rose-pink, and a greyish thing that may have been brain. His school cap lay under his head, at a jaunty angle to his brow, but the William Brown face it should have overlooked was replaced by a serenity no schoolboy should know.

"No, no!"

She found herself shrieking, her legs quaking beneath her.

And she was not screaming at Arthur or Jack Fletcher, she was screaming at Mrs Cadwallader, pushing her ample bosom away as if she were the very Devil, come in bourgeois matronly form, to claim her soul. She was rushing through the door, and out into the yard, where the air, so fresh and wholesome, made her head spin, and she had to cling to the bicycle stands for support. Her throat spasmed and she brought up a watery bile.

Her hearing must have been better than the others'. It wasn't a screaming just a soft plaintive crying such as a teething child might make. She pulled at the pieces of shattered plaster to reveal a torn and scraped knee, a leg. Moving up to where the head should be, she pulled away the debris. A girl's face. Nine, ten, no more. Suddenly the startling blue eyes.

"I want my mummy. Get my mummy."

"I will, sweetheart. Let's just get you out of here first and then we'll find your mummy. What's your name?"

"Prissy."

"Well, don't you worry, Prissy, I'll—"

"It hurts."

The voice seemed weaker now, as if all her remaining strength had been expended on revealing her presence.

"Don't you worry. I'll go and get help."

"No! Don't leave me! Don't leave me, please!"

"I won't."

She shouted for help. Some navy lads on leave got Prissy out. She was taken in an ambulance that was an old horse box with a sack over the back. She heard later that the girl had died.

They spent well over a week with men of the light and heavy rescue squad, or 'ragged trouser brigade' as they were known, directed by the War Reserve Police, using a block and tackle or simple crowbar to raise the masonry, and descending into the crater where the school had been, listening for signs of life, returning speechless and numb, bringing out what they could, which was always death. The official death toll was seventy-three, but the real one was much more. Rumours circulated that the buses had gone to Camden Town instead of Canning Town, or simply that the authorities didn't give a damn for the people of the East End. In the end they had given up digging and just put quicklime down.

The bodies were taken into the school shed. She saw men, under direction from the mortuary officer, going to and fro with bucket and sponge, washing the faces of the dead before they were wrapped in shrouds and labelled. Some were just parts of bodies – arms or legs or feet still clad in stockings and shoes. It must, she thought, be like doing a jigsaw puzzle to put them together. Every so often one of the men would come out and throw up on the concrete.

They never found her mother or Don or little Edie, but their names duly appeared on the list of casualties posted on the town hall wall. She went time and again to the temporary mortuary they set up in Romford Road baths, to see whole families laid out on trays in the empty pool. Later, they brought her the things they had found. Her mother's handbag, her brother's penknife, and Patch's lead. She opened the bag, rifled through the lavender-smelling handkerchiefs and then opened her mother's compact. She breathed deeply of the powder, of the mother smell, and collapsed on the floor of her kitchen.

Sally stood, bent from the waist, a clammy sweat on her forehead and a sour taste on her tongue. How could she convince the authorities she could cope with a child if she threw her guts up whenever she saw a child's forehead or heard a child's cry. She and Arthur had been trying to adopt a child ever since they had arrived in Chalford. Arthur had been reluctant at first but, to give him credit, he was always sensitive, and would never have accused her of wanting to do so for the selfish motive of filling the void left by her mother and brother and sister, or, worse, using it to assuage her guilt. And those were the things that, when she examined her motives closely, she accused herself of.

How could she consider, as she had, adopting the evacuees taken in by the Villiers? Desperate as she was to provide comfort for these little ones in particular, how could she cope with hearing their cries every night? What toll would it take on her when she was summoned to their room to relive the terror of the Blitz, to see their pale faces peeping out not over the counterpane, but out of a heap of rubble, asking in vain for their mummy? How could she give them comfort when she had none for herself? How could she accompany them to school and, to avoid showing herself up, wait for them at the gates when everybody else's mother had gone inside to admire their child's work on the wall and make sure their cap and coat were on?

With shaking limbs, still feverish and with frantic heart, she eased her way around the pillars at the entrance to the playground and out into the road.

CHAPTER TWENTY

"Hiya, Joycie."

Emily waylaid her friend outside the Midland Bank where she knew Joyce went every Thursday morning to bank her wages.

Joyce looked up from her open handbag with surprise on her spotty face.

"Em… I haven't seen you in ages."

"Ages, listen to yourself."

"Well, a month or so."

Not for the first time, Emily reflected that poor Joycie could do with getting herself a job in munitions so she could take advantage of the special rations of quality face powder those women enjoyed.

"You still workin' for Mrs Potter?"

"Yeah, until my call-up."

"Then what you gonna do?"

"Oh, I dunno."

That was Joyce all over. She had to be poked and prodded into doing everything. She was like a sheep that wouldn't go anywhere without the sheepdog to compel her.

"Gotta make up yer mind, my girl. Seen anything of Lucy these days?"

"No. Haven't seen her for ever so long. She's always out with that Yank with the funny name."

"Luigi."

Emily knew as much. She was only making conversation before slipping in her material question.

"Say, you fancy goin' to the Astoria tomorrow night?"

She was pleased to see the delight spark in her friend's eyes.

"Are you not goin' with – what's his name, Larry?"

"No. Can't anyway 'cos it's not whites night."

"Oh, they changed it, didn't they, 'cos of the blacks."

"Yeah. And I wanted to see my old friends again, go out with you and Lucy, but it looks like it's just us. We gals should stick together, shouldn't we? Shouldn't go everywhere with fellas on our arm," she said disingenuously, flattering the girl and hoping to inspire in Joyce the gratitude of she who would be lucky to ever have a fella on her arm.

For once in her relations with Joyce she felt a curiosity that approached the border of sympathy but failed to make the crossing. Was poor Joycie aware she was only asking her because she had no-one else to go with? Joyce must know she would prefer to go with Lucy. But there again, would she? She had never considered it before, always thinking that two good-looking girls were more likely to attract than one good-looking and one ugly. But perhaps that latter combination was to be preferred, as highlighting her own attractions by way of contrast. She found herself almost feeling gratitude towards her plain friend.

"Oooh," Joyce cooed, "that would be nice. But isn't it blacks night?"

"But we gals don't have to be black, do we?" Emily produced a discordant giggle and was uncomfortably conscious of revealing something of her tension. What a situation for her to be reduced to, having to virtually beg the likes of Joycie to accompany her to a dance.

She felt a rising tide of bitterness against Larry for having deserted her. It was as the old wives' tales said: he had had his way, and now he was producing excuse after excuse not to go out with her, and the latest was the arrival of these blacks; he had, he said, to police the segregation and make sure there were no whites trying to sneak out on black nights and vice-versa, and that 'the niggers wouldn't give no trouble to decent white folk'.

The last straw was when she had been reduced to hanging round outside his barracks and button-holing the first man who went in asking him to take a message to Larry. The response had been swift and terse: he was working hard and could not spare the time to see her. Well, if he wouldn't go out with her, she was damned sure she wouldn't stay in. And who knows, she might find herself a fella who would be proud to walk round town with her on his arm, and then Larry would come begging to her door, not the other way round! And would she go back to him? She didn't know. But she would show him.

Yes, if he was policing the blacks, let him look in on the Astoria and find her in the arms of another man.

"Do you think it'll be safe?" Joyce asked, as Mrs Wills brushed past, giving them a hostile glance, no doubt for what she saw as their hogging the pavement.

"Safe? We ain't been bombed since…"

"No, I mean… the darkies."

"Oh, they're all right. I seen them about town. There's no harm in them."

"But what about at night?"

"Lor, Joycie, they ain't vampires."

At this the two girls laughed.

"So are you up for it or not?"

And Joyce, as Emily knew she would be, was.

CHAPTER TWENTY-ONE

"Whadya think?" Errol asked.

Grover was apprehensive.

They stood at the entrance to the Astoria ballroom at the foot of steps that led up to big double doors. From inside they could hear the strains of rather more genteel dance music than they had been used to in the jazz clubs back home. It sounded like the tenor sax of 'All Too Soon'.

"It don't look like the sort of place they'd let niggers in," Grover said.

"They said it'd be all right."

"You sure someone ain't shittin' us?" said Leroy Clark.

"Well, it's supposed to be our night, ain't it?" said Mitchell Wiley.

"Yeah," said Clark, "but what we does in the streets ain't the same as goin' into places like this. Mebbe we shoulda gone to that – whaddya call it, pub – and see what sorta welcome we got there afore we come here."

"Well, you boys can either turn round and go back where you come from, or yous can follow me, 'cos I's goin' right on in there," said Errol.

Not for the first time Grover found himself lost in admiration for his friend. He did not want to brave the peeling-stuccoed portico, but if Errol was going in, then he was going with him. He did not want to lose face in his friend's eyes by being one who deserted him. He was reminded of the Bible story of St Peter thrice denying Jesus.

"Come on then," said Wiley. "They can only kick us out on our black asses."

Errol was first through the double doors and their blackout screens, and as Grover followed he found himself facing a cashier's window in which a spotty-faced young girl looked up from her magazine, her eyes expanding with surprise. The gentleman in the tuxedo guarding the inner door looked as if his face was about to evince a similar emotion only to be held in check by rigid jaw muscles.

Nobody spoke, until the girl said lamely:

"Hullo."

"Hello, miss," said Errol. "Folk tells us we can get ourselves a dance here."

"It's one and three," she said through a mouth that suggested one commencing its recovery from a peculiarly numbing dental injection.

"I beg your pardon, miss?"

"One and three."

"One and three of what?"

"She means the money," Wiley said.

"One shilling and threppence. Each," said the girl.

Her eyes were still wide. Grover was used to that expression. He had seen it often enough walking about town. At first it had been intimidating. But he sensed almost from the beginning that the emotions that lay behind it were ones of surprise and curiosity, with perhaps a hint of fear. But there was nothing of the loathing and contempt with which whites would regard him walking down the sidewalk in Atlanta.

When he and Errol had first ventured into the market square, one drizzly Thursday afternoon, the only hostility that had been evident was that in the eyes of white Americans. The locals appeared in a state of shock. All stopped what they were doing, frozen in mid-stride: women hefting shopping bags; the butcher clad in his apron, lowering his awnings; his boy frozen in the act of loading a parcel onto a bicycle that loudly proclaimed 'Bob Alder butcher'; the schoolboy gnawing on a pencil, frozen in mid-chew. A queue of women outside a grocer's shop turned their heads like dancers in a chorus line. Grover's senses, perfectly tuned as a diviner with his rod, felt for the tension in the air, but there was none.

Grover was in the process of asking Errol what the line of women standing outside the shop meant, when a boy of eleven or twelve approached Errol and asked:

"Hey, mister, are you always that colour?"

Some of the locals burst into laughter at this, but one middle-aged woman, clad in a floral headscarf, exited the queue calling behind her, "Keep my place, Elsie!", and approached and admonished the forward child.

"Don't you say things like that, Tommy Arkwright. That's rude, that is. Don't your mother ever teach you…"

"Don't you worry, ma'am," said Errol. "The boy done no harm."

"Come on, Madge, we're movin'," the woman Elsie called to her friend.

"Sorry," said the woman. "They got tomatoes, and if I lose my place they're gorn faster than a rat up a drainpipe."

"You ain't got no tomatoes?" Errol, asked, as if unsure he had heard correctly given the difference in pronunciation. But the woman had regained her place in the queue. Errol turned back to the boy who stood by his side, staring up at him like a loyal hound.

"Yes, son, we's always this colour."

"Even in winter?"

"Even in winter."

"Don't it come off?"

"'Course it don't," said another boy, slightly older but still in short trousers, with the loose-limbed swagger of one affecting maturity.

"Bet it does."

"No it don't. Or they'd have had it off us long ago… But you can try if'n you wants."

Both Errol and Grover bent their faces down to the boy's level. The second boy reached out damp fingers and pummelled his cheek. He turned satisfied to the other who was doing likewise.

"Told ya," he said, standing smugly with his hands deep in his pockets.

The butcher was now advancing on the two boys.

"Clear off, you two horrors. Let the poor man be."

"They ain't no bother," Errol said.

The butcher, still clutching his pole and with a face as ruddy as any of the beefsteaks he may have sold before the war, regarded Errol and Grover with grave appraisal. He then snapped out a succulent hand to both in turn.

"Bob Alder. Town butcher and captain of the Chalford

Home Guard. Don't you mind them kids. They ain't seen a black man afore. None of us has."

"That's quite all right," said Errol, with a winning graciousness that Grover had never seen in him before. "And what is the Home Guard, if you don't mind me askin'?"

Grover could not help but grin at his friend's unnatural politeness.

"It's what was set up to guard these shores from the Germans if they invaded. Blokes like myself, older blokes what's too old for call-up, and them young 'uns as is waitin' for their papers, like. 'Specially blokes like me, as seen service in the last lot. Back in '40 we wus expectin' them Nazis to parachute in in their thousands."

"Last lot?"

"The first war. But now we seen them Nazis off, and with you fellas here I guess we ain't gonna be needed no more. But that don't mean to say as we's not glad to see you. And the Chalford Home Guard'll always be ready to do their duty until they's told they's not needed no more."

At this another two men, dressed in overcoats and caps, came over to shake their hand, and a middle-aged woman also, swinging her shopping bag into her left hand and declaiming with her right hand outstretched.

"I hope you lot give them Nazis what-for."

Grover looked uneasily at Errol, not sure what this 'what-for' was that was demanded of them.

"Ma'am," said Errol, as suavely as before, and clearly unwilling to disabuse the lady of her belief that they had a combat role, "we'll bring that there Herr Hitler back here and you can put him in that there thing (he indicated with his finger a wooden board with holes that stood in the middle of the marketplace) and whup him 'til he's good and lathered, yes sir."

This was clearly the response the people hoped for, and as she beamed the men slapped both of them on the back.

But they were not in the town square in broad daylight now.

They entered the ballroom just as the MC, a thin, papery-faced man in his forties, with what remained of his hair brylcreemed to his pate in glistening strands resembling black seaweed on a rock, was announcing:

"Mary Clark, you are my next partner and the dance is the foxtrot."

His hand, presumably reaching out for this Mary Clark, froze in mid-air. The couples on the dance floor turned as one towards them. The band struck up with 'The Man I Love', the clarinet leading with barely a stutter in the progression of notes.

Only two couples, one middle-aged, the other young, joined the MC and Mary Clark on the floor, and it could not be said that they had eyes only for one another – rather on the black interlopers who remained frozen just inside the door.

Grover scanned the faces, many of whom stared back at him, although others, displaying what he had already identified as a characteristic British reserve, looked away at the floor, the band, or the dancers.

The clientele were overwhelmingly young women; and that, he reckoned was only to be expected, but it was unnerving nevertheless. The women were sitting or standing by the walls – white faces without exception he noted with disappointment, but immediately interrogating himself as to why he should have expected anything else. White faces stippled with light and shade from the fragmented lights, muted and modest before a backdrop of pastel Art Deco colour. He instinctively dipped his eyelids, like the headlights of a car hooded in the blackout.

There were some couples, mainly older, and a few single young men who must be unfit for active service or on war work. He tried to avoid the gaze of the women as he had been used to doing at home. He sent a glance, as humble as he could make it, in the direction of the men, and saw that some were staring not at them but at the women as if awaiting their reaction to the new arrivals and – what? – daring them to make any sort of contact with them? But for the most part the emotion to be read on the faces of the men was simple curiosity.

"Well, what we waitin' fer?" Errol asked. And for all his bravado, Grover felt his friend's anxiety to be, if not the equal of his own, then not very far behind it.

He tensed, suddenly conscious that one of the men, a middle-aged man in a grey double-breasted suit with a navy-blue bow tie, was striding across the dance floor towards them, casually tamping tobacco into the bowl of his pipe. He awaited the confrontation with tiny currents of apprehension, and a feeling that he struggled to recognise but eventually identified as disappointment.

The man's arm shot out towards them, and to his surprise, Grover saw that he was offering a handshake. The lady the man had been sitting with, a woman clad in a black dress whose figure belied her age, was following in his wake. Grover tore his gaze away from the woman. The man swivelled, as if uncertain which of the three black GIs to approach, and then, as if instinctively adjudging Errol to be their leader, thrust his hand at the latter's midriff.

"Hello, you chaps. You're very welcome."

"Well, thank you kindly," said Errol, displaying a tenebrous version of that southern courtesy whites prided themselves on but reserved solely for their fellows.

"Alfred Appleby, town clerk," the man said. "And this is my wife, Elsie."

"Mighty pleased to meet you, ma'am. I'm Private Errol Gideon."

"Ooh," said the lady, "like the actor. My sister's got the most awful crush on him. As far as she's concerned we can't have too many Errols in Chalford, isn't that right, Alfred?"

She gave a forced laugh, some notes of which verged on the hysterical, betraying her nervousness. Errol introduced them in turn.

They offered their hands to husband and wife as Mrs Appleby chattered on, as if to camouflage her discomfort.

"Ooh, Leroy, how *very* transatlantic. Life in Chalford is getting more exotic by the minu—"

She cut off her speech with another nervous little laugh and dipped her blushing cheeks.

Mr Appleby, who appeared not to notice his wife's discomfiture, went on:

"Come on in, you chaps, and make yourselves at home."

He turned as if to lead them further into the ballroom. As they moved in his wake, it was as if the eyes of the whole company were upon them.

"Do you own this join—?" Errol asked.

"Good Lord no. We're just occasional visitors. When the urge to tread a measure takes us."

It was as if this reception had broken some ice. Another man, hollow-cheeked and with somnolent eyes, proffered his hand, introducing himself as:

"Derek Chalmers. Good to have you chaps here."

Errol responded, as complaisantly as before.

Another, a swarthy, curled-haired fellow whose manners were more down-to-earth, slapped Grover on the back and whispered in his ear:

"Cheer up, mate, you look as if you've found sixpence and lost a tenner. Ted Barkiss. You got any spare nylons or boxes of chocolates I'm yer man. I'll pay top whack. There ain't nobody can beat my prices."

When Grover appeared surprised by the man's suggestion he added:

"Come orn. You know the score. That bleedin' big army of yourn ain't gonna miss a few gallons of petrol or a few tins of peaches, eh. 'Course it ain't. Any time you want me you just ask Tom Curtin behind the bar of the Black Bull."

"Here, don't you go leading these young lads astray, Ted Barkiss," said Chalmers, who by now had been joined by a tall, delicately featured woman in her late thirties.

"What do you mean? I was just extending a warm welcome to our brethren from across the Atlantic."

"Well, you can clear off now."

"Charming. Keep yer pecker up," said Barkiss as he slouched off towards the far corner and a group of three female admirers who quickly closed around him, as if to protect him from the judgement of an over-censorious world.

Another man, with a battered grey pipe dangling from his mouth, approached them and said:

"Looks like you blokes mean business, eh?"

When Grover turned to face him with alarm at the thought that the words must refer to their designs on local girls, the man, with an expression of youthful, ruddy eagerness that suggested an overgrown child on Christmas morning said, in an accent so thick that Grover struggled to understand:

"You know… (here he nudged them with the patched elbow of his jacket) the Second Front. Can't be long now, can it? Take it to 'em is what I says!"

"Oh, I don't know nuthin' about that. They don't tell us nuthin'."

"You're just being modest, I'm sure," said Chalmers.

"No, he's right," said the man with the pipe. "That's the army all over. Don't tell you where yer goin' 'til you got there… or what yer dyin' fer."

At that last he had second thoughts, and with a guilty smile added:

"Don't mind me. Had a couple afore I got here."

Grover, increasingly dismayed by the differences an apparently common language camouflaged, and who did not know what the 'couple' he had were, smiled wanly as the man, swaying gently, eased his way back through the dancers, and Chalmers said:

"This is my wife, Elaine (he nodded towards the tall lady at his side). You must come to tea at our house sometime. We'd be most delighted to have you."

"Of course," said his wife in a languorous trill, like that of a songbird grown bored of its song, "we can't treat you to anything special these days, not like you're used to back home. But if you give us plenty of warning, we'll save our coupons and give you something more than National Loaf and a few oxtails."

"Coupons," said Errol. "Is that what they call rationing?"

"That's right," said Mrs Chalmers after the manner of a schoolmistress whose pupil has correctly conned his lesson. "It's ever so hard, when we think back to what we had before the war. I can't remember the last time we tasted chicken, or real eggs. But it's only right that we should all pull together and suffer the same privations as everyone else. We invited one of your white friends to tea the other week and he was amazed at what a family had to live on."

Grover said nothing. Even if he had had the courage to speak, how could he explain to these people how life had been for blacks across America in recent years?

In Georgia mechanised cotton picking had made labour redundant so that thousands of black sharecroppers were driven from the land to the cities. The whites shouted, "No jobs for niggers until every white man has a job." Jobs for blacks were scarcer than a snowflake in August. The Klan marched again behind the whip and the noose. Black firemen on the railroad were murdered so that whites could take their jobs. Black women were forced into the 'slave market' to work for whites.

Roosevelt's New Deal did little for blacks. The President opposed anti-lynching legislation, and the

NRA[6] and social security did not apply minimum wages to unskilled labour. Grover's mother continued to work as a cleaner for whites at starvation wages. And in Harper's Textile plant where Grover worked, his job was reclassified to a lower-wage code to avoid NRA rules.

It was no wonder so many turned to the Communist Party, particularly after it saved the Scottsboro boys from execution, and got Angelo Herndon released from the chain gang. The party set up labour unions, organised rent strikes and hunger marches, and prevented Grover and his mother being evicted. But they could do nothing when Grover lost his job, as the company came under pressure from unemployed whites. They could no longer afford the rent, and his mother had to live with their sister Anastasia, while Grover and his brother Carl were forced to live in a tented camp known as Rooseveltville.

The birth of federal assistance in 1933 did little for the prospects of the brothers, as the city could not afford to provide employment for more than a few homeless. Each day saw them queuing at the Baptist church soup kitchen in Acacia Gardens. The Unemployed Citizens League got them some work cotton picking in exchange for food, but Grover had no paid job until 1937 when the Works Progress Administration put him to work on the Birmingham highway for six months.

The poverty they experienced drew the blacks of Atlanta more closely together, and there was ever-greater ingenuity in devising strategies for survival. Grover and Carl worked their own vegetable garden, did odd jobs

---

6   National Recovery Administration, established by President Roosevelt in 1933.

on cars and boilers, fished for their evening meals and, when lucky, sold the surplus. Grover was a runner for the numbers game for a while. Their mother took in sewing in exchange for cast-off clothes. Folk rarely used money, bartering their crops and fish. Stoves and wash boilers were used in common. But they often went hungry, and parents went hungrier still giving what little food they had to their children. It was usually the children that died, from typhus, or dirty water. What public aid there was through organisations like the Federal Emergency Relief Administration went mainly to whites.

But despite the heroic efforts of the Committee for Industrial Organizations, which tried, in the face of Klan and company violence, to organise the blacks into trade unions, Jim Crow persisted. Where work was available, the AFL refused to work on a site where there were negroes, so the blacks had to go. And Grover, who got no legitimate bouts as a boxer, and refused to take part in the bare-knuckle fights between blacks beloved of the white betting fraternity, did not work again until after Pearl.

"That's right kindly of you, ma'am. But we'd have to ask permission of our commanding officer 'afore we could accept invites o' that nature, you understand," said Errol.

"Of course," Mrs Chalmers trilled. "But I'm sure he'll have no objection."

Grover endeavoured to modulate the bitter cynicism of his smile.

"And," said her husband, "I don't know which religion you gentlemen profess, but whatever it is you are all welcome at our Methodist chapel. You'll find it just off the high street behind the Masonic lodge. Services are Sunday morning, ten thirty. Please tell your friends."

"I didn't think it would take you long, Chalmers," said Mr Appleby. "Might I put in a word for the Church of England. St Edward's. You can see the tower from anywhere. The times for Matins and Evensong are posted on the church door. Can't let these low-church wallahs have it all their way, what?"

"Well, we're most grateful for your welcome," said Errol.

But his words were belied by his gaze, which was directed towards a group of three men in worn sports jackets slouching against a wall who were looking at them with at the very least dismay, at the worst downright suspicion.

Chalmers followed their gaze.

"Don't you worry about them. They're only worried about the competition you chaps represent. Thought they'd have the place to themselves when your white 'buddies' (he pronounced the word with an emphasis that may have been ironic or simply denoted its unfamiliarity in an English mouth) are not allowed out. Their chances of a dance or something more have diminished with your arrival."

"Don't be coarse, dear," his wife admonished.

Chalmers simply gave them a knowing look, startling his eyes from their natural hibernation.

"So," he went on, "you've got the girls virtually to yourselves. What's the matter, old chap?"

They must have been looking dubious, as indeed were some of the girls, clinging like leeches to the lemon-coloured walls so that you could imagine having to use force to dislodge them. For once Errol appeared lost for words.

"I... I dunno... we doan wanna make no waves."

"Oh, don't mind those chaps (he nodded in the direction of the three young men). They may look daggers but they know the score. Your white buddies have put them in their place."

"But we's black," Errol pleaded with an impotence that verged on the pathetic such as Grover would never have expected to hear from him.

"Take my advice, old chap," Chalmers leaned close to Errol's ear in a gesture of male confidentiality, "the female of the species prefers silk to homespun. Witness the success of your white friends. You chaps are more exotic still. You could put a—"

Here Chalmers stopped abruptly, and Grover was pretty sure he had intended to say something like 'put a monkey in a US uniform and the women would be all over it'. Realising now what the 'couple' were that the other man had had, Grover wondered whether Mr Chalmers had also had a couple.

An embarrassed silence was explosively broken as Chalmers burst out again:

"You take it from me, just give those gals ten minutes to get used to the idea and they'll be all over you."

"Derek!"

Mrs Chalmers delivered a curt admonishment that was not without some resigned good humour.

"Well, what am I standing here for when I've got a beautiful young lady to attend to! Elaine, let us take to the floor."

His wife's face, with its appearance of long-suffering solemnity, suddenly dissolved into a girlish giggle, and she allowed herself to be seized by her narrow waist as the MC announced that he would partner Margaret Dawson in the quickstep.

Grover and Leroy took their lead from Errol who seemed inclined to take Mr Chalmers' advice literally. So they stood, Errol glancing repeatedly at his watch, as the couples wound past them, the Applebys glancing amiably in their direction, the three men sending them ever more hostile glances, and the women regarding them with looks that seemed just as suspicious, sometimes curious, one or two even downright lascivious.

Two of the hostile young men exchanged brief words then approached the girls for a dance. At first they were rebuffed only to succeed at the second time of asking.

"I think we should just go," said Leroy. "We ain't welcome here."

"'Course we's welcome here," Errol replied. "Ain't that what the man said?"

"Well, if we ain't gonna dance..."

"Sure we's gonna dance. Like he said. Just give these good folks time to get used to us. Ain't no hurry."

But Errol's demeanour belied his apparent calm. He grew increasingly twitchy, lighting Lucky Strike after Lucky Strike, shooting questing glances in the direction of the women, and dragging his index finger around the inside of his shirt collar. It seemed to Grover that he was feeling the pressure of being their leader, of having to make the first move towards the women, and timing that move judiciously, or else lead them in a humiliating retreat.

Eventually Errol lost patience. To his amazement he seized Grover by the arm and said:

"Come on, boy, you and me gotta show these folk how blacks dance."

He launched into the throng that were engaged in a quickstep and set off round the room. After his first halting steps in which he felt as if he was dancing on soft sand, Grover's natural grace took over, and he found his feet flowing in a familiar cadence that was restrained only by the need to match his steps to those of the slower Errol. When the music stopped, they found that some of the dancers had done likewise and were staring at them in astonishment. Abashed, Grover let go of Errol, leaving the latter standing, arms still raised and embarrassment clouding his habitual exuberance. They slunk from the dance floor.

Following their display, the tension only seemed to grow. It was as if people were waiting for them to repeat the performance. They resumed their nervous scan of the room, and Errol produced his packet of Lucky Strike once more, his throat hauling on the smoke.

But the decision was taken out of Errol's hands. Grover had been gazing at the picture of connubial bliss represented by the Applebys, and reflecting on his own relationship with Doreen, and how she would never stare into his face as Mrs Appleby was doing to her husband without her eyes wandering, with no attempt at discretion, over the other men in the room, appraising them as much for the quality of their jacket as their physical attributes, when he was conscious of being approached by a blonde girl, a cigarette in her hand and a desperate look of challenge on her face.

Behind the girl her friend, with ashen complexion in which spots flared down her nose, appealed:

"Em, you can't."

The blonde girl turned abruptly back to her and said:

"Can't I though?"

She turned to face them with a brazen stare whose recklessness was unsettling. Standing a couple of feet from the small arc formed of their three bodies she said:

"If you blokes are gonna dance with each other we gals might as well bugger off home."

Grover felt as if he had been slapped. His fear returned with a vengeance. He glanced around Leroy's shoulder at the three young men who were oblivious to what was taking place.

The girl said:

"I've asked Charlie there (she indicated the MC) to play a quickstep and make it a 'ladies excuse-me', so come on."

She grabbed Errol by the hand and led him into the throng of partners wheeling around the dance floor. One of those couples was the Chalmers, and Mr Chalmers smiled conspiratorially in Errol's direction. Grover scanned the other dancers, anticipating a reaction, but there was nothing to alarm him, and where notice was taken of the newcomers it was usually glances of ironic amusement. The exception was provided by some of the girls, who looked darkly at them. As one older couple left the dance floor, Grover heard the woman say, with no attempt to moderate her voice:

"Brazen hussy. Young girls nowadays. Before these Americans arrived, they wouldn't have dared…"

The centrifugal termination of the dance deposited Errol and the girl directly in front of Grover, who started on their sudden arrival.

"Lor!" said the girl. "I thought all you Yanks could dance. I won't be able to walk for a week after you been steppin' on me feet!"

"I do apologise, ma'am," said Errol at his most suave. "But this here guy is the dancer in our party. Ain't that so, Grover?"

"I… I can dance."

"Can dance," said Leroy, "why he's the best goddam – beggin' yer pardon, ma'am – dancer you ever did see."

"Well, I'll dance with him then. And you (she spoke to Errol) can dance with my friend and break her toes. Joycie!"

The spotty girl crossed the dance floor, as dutifully unenthusiastic as a tired dog called for his walk. Her eyes grew wide in the face of her impending doom.

"You can dance with this bloke, and I'll dance with you."

At this the girl seized Grover's arm, and as the MC announced a chrysanthemum waltz led him prematurely onto the floor.

As they launched off amongst the other partners, Grover made sure he made no eye contact with the girl, and being unwilling to gaze downward, which was his natural inclination, for fear of being thought to stare down her cleavage, gazed instead over her left ear, scanning the room for hostility. But beyond one of the young men, scowling at him over his cigarette, all the other couples were either dancing happily or chatting amongst themselves.

"What's the matter with you? Expectin' to see a ghost or what?"

"It's just… I never danced with a white woman afore."

"Don't you like white women?"

"It ain't done where I come from."

"Where's that?"

"Atlanta, Georgia."

"Georgia."

"You heard of it?"

"Yeah… *Gone with the Wind*."

"I never seen it, but I guess."

"Well, who's best then, white or black dancers?"

"Oh, I dunno," he said, still staring, but now at the revolving lights hanging from the rafters. "You're good."

He was surprised an English girl would be so forward. From what he heard they were reserved. This girl was behaving almost as if she were drunk, but whatever she was drunk on, it was not alcohol.

"You gotta car?" she asked.

"No," he replied, surprised by the randomness of the question.

"I thought all you Yanks was rich."

"Not us blacks ain't, miss."

"Well, you aren't like the whites, are you?"

"How's that, miss?"

"Full of theirselves."

"No. I guess we ain't."

"But you're light on your feet, I'll give you that. Not like that other bloke."

He couldn't help but laugh at that.

By the time the music ended Grover was feeling quite

relaxed. They rejoined Errol, Mitchell and Leroy, the former having just parted from the girl with the spotty face who stood looking about her with some desperation for her companion.

"Well, that wasn't so bad was it, Joycie?"

Joycie didn't seem convinced. Whether that was because of Errol's dancing or his colour, Grover could not say. But the girl maintained a diplomatic silence.

"Well, you ain't seen nutin', miss," said Errol. "Wait 'til you sees this guy do the jive… You heard of the jive?"

"'Course I have," said the blonde girl, sounding annoyed. "I've danced the jive many times."

"Pardon me, miss. It's just that the music here sounds… kinda old-fashioned, if you get what I means. It ain't got no beat to it, know whad I mean?"

"They're dreadful old fogies in this town. Straight out the pages of Dickens. We want something to liven us up."

"Do you think that if I was to speak to that there guy (Errol pointed towards the MC, who was mopping his brow with a handkerchief) he'd give that there band of his a kick in their tails?"

There was the glitter of something reckless in the girl's eyes and a vibrato to her sweet voice as she replied:

"Give him the fright of his life, then we might get some decent music in this place. Somethin' folk can really dance to."

"I sure will."

Errol smiled at Grover, and he felt a thrill at the thought of jiving with this girl.

Errol approached the MC whose eyes grew wide with a sense of insult that slowly modulated. The MC walked over to the band, and there was some discussion in which the clarinettist grew particularly heated, making chopping gestures with his hand. Errol spread his lips in a triumphant grin.

"You get them pins of yourn movin', Grover. This is your moment, courtesy of the golden tongue of your friend Errol here."

The band began to play the first notes of 'Don't Sit Under the Apple Tree', and Grover glanced shyly at the blonde girl, whose face lit up, reckless and wilful and icily beautiful. She seized his hand.

"Let's see what you can do then."

The dance floor had all but cleared, there only being one middle-aged couple standing by the far seats in some bewilderment at this rude incursion into their sedate evening.

Grover allowed the girl to lead him to the dance floor. He felt terribly exposed with all those eyes upon him, but the girl seemed to relish the prospect. She seized his hands, and they began to move back and forth. At first Grover's movements were stilted and wooden, disturbed as he was by the proximity of this strange female of a type he had previously only respectfully cringed from, by the dew of her palms mingling with his own, and the smell of her scent mingling with her sweat in a dreamy intoxication. And then he began to forget who he was dancing with, or rather imagine it was Doreen in one of the dives in Atlanta, an illusion he tried to encourage in order to dampen his anxiety, and his feet began to flash with the fleet precision of memory, the silken song of their instinct, and he wove around the girl, pulling and tugging and throwing her like an icy glowing moon about his dark sun.

He moved in and out of her orbit, around her, with the fluidity of a stream fed by a raging downpour, weaving through her embrace, clasping and throwing her, and his mind was wild and exhilarate to rediscover something he thought he had left behind on the other side of the Atlantic.

'Don't sit under the apple tree with anyone else but me.' Yes, that was him, in the song, though it was written for whites not the likes of him. But Doreen would not be waiting for him. She would be under the apple tree before his ship even cast off. He dearly wished that a girl who could display the song's constancy was waiting for him; a girl who had seen him off from the dock, waving her tear-stained handkerchief, and who would welcome him home on his return, without apple trees or lanes in between. Instead, he had been seen off at the dock in New York only by his mother. Was there such a girl in all of America? he wondered.

Throughout his reverie he had been intermittently conscious of the other people in the room, of Errol and Leroy clapping and shouting, of the English, clapping likewise. And of the occasional banging of the door as people left and arrived. It was only as the last trilling notes of the clarinet faded into diminuendo that he saw him, standing by the door, a look of satirical hatred on his face.

It was Sergeant O'Rourke, and for the sergeant there was no-one else in the room: no band, no English, not even Errol Mitchell or Leroy. He was staring at Grover and Grover alone. Or at least at Grover and the girl. As he drew on his cigarette his lips parted in something like a snarl. For all his breathless sweating exertion, a shiver like a drop of cold water trickled down Grover's spine.

The Irish were always the worst.

CHAPTER TWENTY-TWO

Sergeant Michael O'Rourke arrived by jeep at the camp early next morning – a misty morning, perspiring with dew.

As he wanted to speak to one person in particular, and that person was not on guard duty, he drove into the compound and made straight for the MPs' hut. Here he found Larry Schultz (the person he sought), Luigi, Stan, Duke and Mickey Reilly in various stages of undress, and in the case of the latter, sitting bolt upright on his bunk, blowing smoke rings from his cigarette.

"Why, Sergeant O'Rourke," Reilly said, "ain't one of your niggers hidin' under our bunks."

"If so," said Stan, "he's a brave man can stand the stink of your socks."

"Niggers don't mind none. Everybody knows their noses is nearer their ass."

O'Rourke stood in the doorway, but pushed the door gently closed behind him.

"I come to give you guys fair warnin'. I don't mean nuthin' by it, you understand. You guys know yer job, I knows that."

Stan walked over and turned off the wireless, curtailing Sinatra's crooning of 'Body and Soul'.

"Just so long as Gene didn't strip search you when you come through them gates," said Luigi, proudly displaying the product of an excavation of his right nostril.

"I'm serious. My niggers wus out on the town last night, and I made it my business to see what they wus up to. 'Cos there's stoopid dumb Limeys in this town ain't never seen a nigger before, and don't know what he's capable of. So like I said, I follows them. To that shed they calls a dance hall, and whaddo I find? I finds me niggers dancin' with white gals, and them dumb Limeys lookin' on like it was hunky-dory."

"Shit," said Schultz. "But they don't let us go breakin' their heads. If them dumb broads is stoopid enough to get involved with niggers it's their look-out – and their town's, if there's gals wheelin' prams full of little niggers in nine months' time."

"They wasn't smoochin', was they, Sergeant?" asked Luigi.

"Not that I seen. There was only four of them: Errol Gideon, Leroy Clark, Mitchell Wiley and Grover Carson. Gideon, he thinks of hisself as some kinda smart nigger. But was the last was the worst. Thinks hisself a proper Fred Astaire. Was showin' off, throwin' this English gal about like a bale o' cotton. Thinks hisself a proper smart nigger, and all the gals'll throw theirsels into his arms. Didn't have no respect nor decency."

"And you want us to keep an eye out for this guy?" Duke asked.

"For all those guys. Shouldn't be hard. They goes round like the Three Stooges, 'cept there's four of 'em."

"But it's like Larry says, Sarg," said Luigi, "they's allowed to go out. Major Bellucci's spoken to the folk hereabouts, and if they's stoopid enough to…"

"I think I should point out something here," said O'Rourke, turning to face Schultz. "You's Larry Schultz, yeah?"

"What of it?"

He sounded surprised O'Rourke knew his name. He was going to get an even bigger surprise.

"Thing is, this gal this uppity nigger was pawin' was a blonde gal. Looks to me she's the same gal I seen you out and about with. Kinda like Veronica Lake only bigger."

O'Rourke beamed with satisfaction at the response his revelation provoked. The muscles around Schultz's jaw and cheekbones became visibly taut, his blue eyes steely and alert. He did not speak.

"That her?" O'Rourke asked, though he did not need to.

"Might be."

"Was with another gal. Ugly, spotty face."

"Yeah, that's her," Schultz replied, the words laden with significance.

"That nigger bin pawin' yer gal?" Duke asked, insensitively.

"You can't let him get away with that," said Reilly.

"Okay, okay!"

O'Rourke took a piece of paper and a small pencil from his jacket pocket and licked the tip of the pencil.

"What's this gal of yours' name?"

"Emily France," Schultz said absently.

"So the way I sees it," O'Rourke went on, "is, yeah,

they's allowed to go about town. But they's still gotta behave theirselves. Still gotta stay sober, not cause no trouble, be back for curfew. And it's the job of you guys to make sure they don't step outta line, you get me?

"And if you think they's gone and done just that, you can do whatever you wants with them, give them a beatin', throw them in the cooler. Nobody here's gonna take the word of a goddam nigger agin yours. And I sure as hell ain't gonna come knockin' on yer door to complain if one of ma niggers gits what's comin' to him, no sir. So I advise you to think on that, and keep a close eye on that nigger and his buddies when next they's out on the town.

"I advise you to pay one of these local hillbillies to keep an eye out and note down the names of those gals that dances with them. Keep a list. Pass it round camp so everybody knows not to dance with those nigger-lovers.

"I'm sure you fine body of men'll do what's right. I give you good day."

With that O'Rourke pulled open the door and strode out.

As he drove back to his own camp, O'Rourke reflected on a good morning's work.

The nerve of those niggers pawing decent white women. Taking advantage of stupid dumb Limeys that didn't know no better. There was only one thing that would lead to. It was a well-known fact that niggers couldn't keep their hands to theirselves where a white woman was concerned. Sure, white men have their lusts, but they had the brain power to keep those lusts on a tight leash, whereas niggers, they didn't have no self-control at all. They was no better than beasts in their lusts, on account of not being as developed, as mature a species, as whites were.

And letting them become soldiers! Hell, didn't everybody know niggers was just children, that lacked initiative and would panic under fire. They was also suggestible, and hysterical, like women at their time of the month.

The sergeant felt poignantly the indignity of having been put in command of these negroes who, like children, could never be allowed anywhere near a real battlefield. He was insulted. And angry. And the only ones he could take his anger out on were the niggers theirselves.

They had to be put in their place. Otherwise they would cause havoc, and that would only serve to distract them from the task they had been sent here to perform: to win the war.

Yes sir, so far as that was concerned, he had done a good morning's work, and that uppity nigger would sure as hell get what was coming to him.

CHAPTER TWENTY-THREE

Emily took the noonday Dorchester bus to the crossroads, still lacking its fingerpost in order to confuse German invaders. That should give her enough time to walk the quarter mile to the American camp and arrive after the time she knew Larry was due on sentry duty.

She disembarked to a glance of some suspicion from Mrs Todd who was making her weekly visit to her son in Lanton, and who must have known where she was going.

As she walked the newly laid tarmac that had replaced the dirt track that had existed before the Americans' arrival, and that still exuded a bituminous smell in the midday sun, she reflected that the growing confidence she had felt these last weeks was now to be tested to the utmost. Confidence – was that what sex brought in its wake? The feeling that now she was a real woman, not some slip of a girl. But the man who had made love to her was now, she feared, intent on deserting her. She had to stand up for her rights. For he was rightfully hers. She had slept with him; she was now due her reward of possession. That was the bargain, wasn't it?

As she rounded the bend in the road by the telephone box, the gates of the camp came in sight, with the guard post to the right, and two MPs standing by the barrier, rifles at port, their white helmets and belts a beacon to her frustrated possession. She regarded the midday heat with some dismay, finding she was sweating and exuding a sultry aroma of sweat and her scent. She hoped that her lipstick, Cyclax's 'Auxiliary Red', would not run.

As she walked along the verge of the road, she felt her legs grow weak. She had thought her anger would be sufficient to support her, but now she was not so sure. And in her head she rehearsed the competing possibilities with which she had tormented herself for the last fortnight. Did he have someone else? Was he some Lothario wooing and bedding local girls? Had she said something that offended him? Did he find some fault in her that had not previously been apparent? Had he lied when he said he had not slept with anyone else, and been disappointed in her in that department (an all-too plausible scenario given her rabbit-caught-in-headlamps reaction to the deed)? Was she doing the right thing by confronting him, or should she 'play hard to get'? They always said that was the best way to a man's heart. But the risks were great. He might lose interest if she were too distant, particularly as there were young girls only too willing to walk out on the arm of a handsome Yank.

She wished she had been able to discuss her predicament with someone. But Lucy was happily ensconced with that Luigi, and her natural reluctance to describe her humiliating position, even if she didn't disclose sleeping with Larry, was compounded by the fear that anything she said would get back to him. And it would be just too humiliating to reveal her unhappiness to Joycie, being convinced that the plain girl she had always condescended to would rejoice in her state.

She felt herself quailing as the distance between her and the guard post lessened and she saw the hardness in Larry's face. This was not the loving remorseful welcome she had dreamt of in her bed last night.

When she was a few yards from him he turned to the other man, the tall man called Stan, and said:

"Go smoke a cigarette."

"You know I can't leave the post. I'll be up on a charge—"

"Just for a minute. For me."

Reluctantly, and with a backward glance in her direction that was, she thought, rather rueful, Stan went and stood in the roadway fifty yards away. Larry turned back to her. She had not imagined the hardness in his face. It was implacable and accusatory. Is this how he regarded her now, as pestering him?

"You come all this way to see me?"

But there was no hint of gratitude.

"I had to, didn't I?"

"Why?"

"Why? Because you've been avoiding me in town."

"You get by, though, don't you?"

"What does that mean?"

"From what I been hearin'."

"What have you been hearing?"

"I've been hearin' you bin out on the town. Dancin' the night away—"

"Well, what's wrong with that?"

For all her former resolution she was now in combative mode and certainly not inclined to demonstrate the penitence he obviously expected of her.

"A girl can have a bit of fun, can't she? Especially if her fella is avoidin' her and don't seem to want nothin' to do with her."

"That's what you think, is it?"

There was a barely controlled anger in his tone now, his mouth taut and pinched, the muscles in his jaw vice-tight. For the first time in their relationship she felt afraid of him. But she was in the right. She was damned if she would back down and let him see her fear.

"Well, what's wrong with that?" she said petulantly. And then, gaining confidence with her own growing anger:

"You got someone else, is that it?"

"What does it figure if I have? You got someone else yerself."

Something pierced her bewilderment, something like hope. He was jealous, and if so, he must still care for her. But jealous of whom?

"That's rubbish. You been listening to gossip. It's that April Knight, isn't it? Vicious little piece. She's always had it in fer me."

"You was seen dancin' with that nigger."

"What? Oh, him. That was nothing. It was just a dance. I mean, we weren't, we didn't do anything else… it was just a dance."

She stared hard into his face, seeking in vain for the reassurance she hoped her words would inspire.

"You danced with a nigger."

"Is that all?" she asked incredulously.

"Is that *all*?"

"Well, all right, but... what does it matter?"

"What does it matter? Are you crazy or somethin'? Ain't you been to dances and seen them gals lined up along the wall? Ain't you never wondered why we don't dance with them? It's 'cos they's bin seen dancin' with niggers, that's why? And you say why does it matter. Like you got no sense at all."

"But it was just a dance. Don't you believe me?"

"Stop sayin' that! I know it was just a dance. But it was a dance with a nigger. Can't you understand? It ain't done. Nice white gals don't dance with niggers."

"I didn't know—"

"Ain't no gal of mine gonna dance with no nigger."

His words, angry, even furious though they may be, yet held out to her a scrap of comfort.

"But I'm still your gal, aren't I? I mean... (she wanted to say again that it was just a dance, but his prohibition stopped her)... it was nothing. I didn't mean any harm by it. It was just 'cos you was avoidin' me. That's the only reason I done it."

She stopped short at confessing she had wished to make him jealous; that, she felt, would have been too demeaning.

"You still don't get it, do you? I won't have nothin' to do with a gal that dances with niggers. Do you get me?"

"But... you don't mean that..."

"We're finished, you get me?"

"But you can't mean that. Not after we... you know. Not after that. Not just because I danced with..."

"I do mean it. Where I come from ain't only one sort of white woman dances with niggers. I don't want nothin' more to do with you, you hear me?"

At that the dam that held back her tears burst. Her chest heaving, she angrily wiped the shameful drops from her cheeks.

"Is this how you mean to treat me? Is this what a… southern gentleman does to a girl?"

"A southern gentleman, as you put it, doesn't consort with women who paw negroes."

"I didn't paw him! It was only…!"

"That's enough! I won't hear no more. You get outta here now, or I'll call the guys to throw you out. You want that? You want that to get around town?"

At that there was nothing left but for her to walk forlornly back through the stale lemon midday light to the crossroads, stopping only briefly to search in her handbag for the handkerchief she used to wipe the tears away.

The only consolation that was left to her was the thought that the bus back to Chalford was not due for another hour, which would give her plenty of time to compose herself. If she didn't, and people noted the direction she had come from, they would certainly know the cause, and the word would be around town in no time. But beyond that the landscape of her future was irredeemably barren.

CHAPTER TWENTY-FOUR

"I thought you said this English beer was watered down."

Grover whispered the comment into the ear of Errol as they stood at the bar of the Black Bull, not wishing to cause offence to the landlord, who was rushing red-faced hither and thither to satisfy the demand for his product.

"That's what that guy told me."

"Well, it sure must be stronger than beer back home."

"Well, we come out to git ourselves drunk, didn't we?"

They had good cause. For all the paucity of black newspapers in their camp, and the complete absence of the *Atlanta Daily World*, the news of the race riots in Detroit, Michigan, had got around. The situation was the more poignant for them in that one of their number was from Detroit, and feared for his family, not knowing whether they numbered amongst the dead and injured.

"Our war is at home," Errol said, portentously, referring not only to Detroit but also the riots in Texas, Ohio, Massachusetts and Harlem. "We're fighting on a different front. And instead of where the action is, we is a thousand miles away in another country."

Leroy agreed.

"I'd rather kill me some of them ofay[7] than Germans."

It was the blacks' day to go into Chalford. Nobody actually said, 'Let's go into town and get drunk', but it was an unspoken feeling. Errol, eloquent as ever, came closest to articulating what they felt:

"I got a bad taste in my mouth. I needs some English beer."

Which was ironic, since the last Grover had heard from his friend on the subject, it was the English beer that gave him the bad taste.

It was the first time they had set foot in that particular pub, and the welcome they received was mixed. Errol ordered the beers in undiscriminating fashion, pointing to the two men at the bar nursing pints and announcing, since he had no idea what bitter or mild were:

"We'll have what they're havin'."

As he did so Grover stared wide-eyed at the exposed wooden beams of the roof, wondering why no-one had thought to complete a building that appeared to be so venerable.

An elderly man with an unshaven chin sitting on an uncomfortable-looking wooden bench, shouted at them:

"When you Yanks gonna do some proper fightin' then? You ponce about town, seducin' our women. What you waitin' fer? The Russkies to do the job for yer?"

---

[7] Derogatory term for a white person

Errol, as equable and urbane as any black could be having just heard the news from home, responded:

"I'm sorry, sir, we don't do no fightin'. And they wouldn't tell us anyhow."

"You'd be good at it, you blacks," another elderly man said. "'Specially at night. You got the camouflage already!" He expelled a spittly cackle.

"What you talkin' about, you don't do no fightin'? What the hell you here fer then?" asked the first.

"Black soldiers ain't allowed to do no fightin'. Only whites does that."

Grover took his first sips from the warm, flat, frothy beer, and tried to remember the cold sharpness of the American product.

"What do you do then?" asked the old fellow, tamping a wad of tobacco into the bowl of his pipe, his tone ameliorated into something approaching curiosity.

"We does the fetchin' and the carryin'," volunteered Clark Endean.

"'Black man fight wid de shovel and de pick Lordy turn your face on me,'" Errol sang in his fine tenor.

"Funny bloody way to fight a war, if you ask me," said the old man.

"Nobody did ask you, Sam Westwood," said the middle-aged man standing next to them at the bar. "Don't mind him. Your white friends took his land off him, so we haven't seen hide nor hair of his usual good temper this last year."

"What you doin' proppin' up that bar, Tom France, when you should be out there enforcin' the blackout."

"I don't need to, Sam, 'cos I's got you all so well trained, ain't Oi?"

As Tom France introduced himself with the denomination of 'ARP warden' that inspired some looks of bewilderment, the man behind Grover, wearing a checked sports jacket and sporting a freckled face and ginger moustache, pronounced:

"I dunno what you're moanin' about, Sam Westwood. You'd think you was the town martyr the way you talk. If you ask me you're better off out of it."

"That's easy fer you to say, George Rule."

"Maybe it is and maybe it isn't. But I knows this: you don't have to deal with the War Ag no more. I got directives comin' outta my ears. And you ain't had them come round threatenin' you with eviction 'cos yer yield's too low. Too low! Says who? Says they, who don't know a blind thing about workin' the land."

"Well, you ain't had yer land took off you, like they done my da, have you?" said the young man sitting next to the other and wearing some British Army uniform.

"Don't you mind those two. They'll go at it all night," said the landlord, who had already introduced himself as Tom. "Nice to see you coloured chaps in here. Only don't go criticisin' my beer for bein' warm like the whites does. I tells them, 'I bin in this trade all me life, and that's the way beer is.' It's not meant to be froze. 'Tain't nat'ral, an' beer is a nat'ral product, it is. Folk hereabouts think you Yanks is the same as us 'cos you speaks the same language. But you ain't, and that's a fact."

"It's the best goddam beer I ever tasted in ma life," said Errol, his urbanity sounding rather less than sincere on this occasion.

"Best in this town. Don't let that Dan Taylor at the Swan

tell you different. Best in Devon, I says. They guidebooks talks about the Twin Compasses in Honiton, but they's writ by folks in London, and their beer's made with water straight out the Thames."

At this point another elderly man, with long, straggly, grey hair and sunken, denuded cheeks, who had been sitting opposite the other, rose from his seat and walked towards the door saying:

"You can say they's welcome, Tom Curtin, but you won't be sayin' the same when these blacks is walkin' out with yer daughters on their arm. Think on thaaat."

Tom Curtin said under his breath:

"Don't you mind. That's one less miserable bugger we got in tonight."

"We don't want to cause no trouble," Grover said.

"You won't cause no trouble now Barkiss is gone. Westwood's bark's worse than his bite."

The landlord looked up from washing a glass and saw Grover staring at the metallic and leather things stuck to the wall.

"Horse brasses," Tom said and went off to serve another customer leaving them none the wiser.

Later, the atmosphere improved when a party of men and women, the men wearing British air force uniforms, came into the bar, the foremost among them, in a smart well-pressed uniform of blue loudly announcing:

"Well, chaps, bit of a bind, it's not the White Heart at Brasted, but it'll do if it's Tommy's local."

Those behind let out a loud cheer. The men, seven in number, wore uniforms that seemed the same to Grover, but some of which were of poorer quality, and five of them had girls on their arms, three of the girls dressed in smart civilian attire, the other two in blue uniforms.

"It didn't take you land gals long to find the fly boys, I see," shouted the man they called Westwood from his corner seat. "I hope they've washed the pigswill off."

"Have some respect for the few!" called out a dapper man wearing a sports jacket with shiny gold tie pin in a far seat. "We've had to take it for four years, and now our lads are taking the fight to the enemy. Gawd bless 'em."

"Yes, old timer," said one of the new arrivals, "or we'll kidnap you, take you up to 8,000 feet and walk you out."

The airmen, the girls squealing on their arms, hit the bar and placed their orders with the injunction, given at a volume which Grover, with his limited knowledge of the war in the air, imagined them using to communicate between planes.

"Open a tab for us, landlord, there's a good chap. And as it's Tom's birthday, you can give him two for every one of ours."

Some of the locals came forward and clapped one of the airmen, who looked impossibly young with his ruddy, freckled cheeks and wavy, brown hair, on the back.

"I wus wonderin' what you boys from 87 Squadron was doin' so far outta your way," Tom Curtin said.

"All so we could take our young friend to his local, and he could throw up on his native sod. What more could true friends do."

This man, of medium height with unruly blond hair and a pipe stem protruding from his jacket pocket, seemed a bit older than the others, and appeared to be their leader.

"Well," said another, tall, thin flyer standing at the

man's side, "we could keep quiet about him bein' downed by a Heinkel!"

"Yes!" the other roared. "Don't mention it! You hear that, boys, don't mention Topper's getting downed by a Heinkel."

"We won't," the others chorused in no less volume.

"Aha, what have we here?" the first said to Errol in a clipped, languid voice. "Yanks, I'll be damned."

Grover was astounded to see that the man had, within a minute, downed more than half the beer in his bevelled glass.

Errol, as suave as ever, introduced himself, Grover and the other two.

"I hear you Yanks have all but taken over this part of the world. Leave some of the gals for us, there's a good chap, eh?" The man gave Errol a wink and nudged him with his arm. By this time he had downed the rest of his beer and said:

"Can I get you chaps one?"

"Get some more cans in, Steve," said another.

"Well..." said Errol.

"Come on, drink up. Time waits on no man."

He proceeded to give his order to Tom Curtin, who looked as though all his Christmases had come at once. As he did so, Errol asked the airman to explain the great joke.

"Don't you get it, old boy? One is not expected to get shot down by a bomber. A 109, fair enough."

The attitude seemed rather callous to Grover, who asked:

"Was he hurt?"

"Sprained his ankle. Couldn't walk for a fortnight. Serves him bloody well right."

Again, they all laughed, including the victim of the incident, who appeared to be struggling to keep up with the alcoholic intake of the others.

Grover had never met anyone like these airmen. He was attracted and yet a little repelled by their insouciance. He wondered if it was the fact of flying that produced this gung-ho attitude. How must it feel to trust your safety to less than an inch of metal, to soar above the clouds, to look down on the earth below, and see what was of such significance to us as the merest petty thing? The sense of freedom, of not being tied by earthbound law, earthbound prejudice. And yet be so vulnerable. Like a crow to the shotgun pellets.

Articulating his thought before he had even formed the intention to do so he asked the airman:

"What does it feel like to fly?"

He immediately regretted speaking, conscious of how naive he sounded. But the man replied with enthusiasm.

"The greatest feeling in the world, old chap. The sense of freedom. Not just freedom, but lawlessness. It's like being a cavalry charge in the air. We're like the Musketeers, 'all for one and one for all'. Because we're all dependent on one another, and what's more you know the man you're dependent on, he sits at your side, not like in the army."

"And the chances of promotion are better," added another.

"Oh, that's mundane stuff. When you see a Kraut plane, it's like a hunt, you're stalking your prey. And when you get one in your sights and pull the trigger and see it going down in smoke, there's nothing better. When I got my first, I couldn't think about anything else for days. Woooow! The exhilaration! In the air – I don't mean bombing, there's no skill in that – it's the only part of this war where a man can meet his foe face to face in fair combat, like the knights in the lists of old. Sitting in a trench and shelling someone a mile away, that's murder. It's only in the air that there's still some chivalry in war."

"Where's all the rest of the Yanks then?" asked one of the girls.

"Oohh," said her male companion, who in comparison with the others was dark and swarthy, "don't you go bailing out on me, Sheila."

"It's just us. The whites have their night when we're not allowed out, and they aren't allowed out tonight," Errol replied.

"Bloody good job, if you ask me," said the dapper gent. "The girls in this place have Yank eyes."

"And they think theirselves better 'n' us," said France. "I hear they been goin' around laughin' at us 'cos we's not got 'phones and washin' machines and such like. Looks down on us, they do. No offence to you blacks, of course, I ain't heard nuthin' bad about you."

"We don't look down on honest hard-workin' folk," said Errol.

"Well said," said the airman. "So you're not allowed out with the whites, is that right?"

"That's right, sir," said Leroy.

"Well, I'll be damned. Not like the old 87. We all mix in. Officers and sergeant pilots and all. We might have separate messes back home, but here we're all one, and we stick together."

"Well said, old boy," said one.

"And as far as I'm concerned you chaps are all our allies. And I must say I admire you if you hope to keep pace with us RAF chaps (he waved his pint glass). Many have tried, old boy, none have succeeded."

"I think," said the blond airman, "it's time for a good old sing-song. I see you have a suitable instrument in the corner (he nodded towards a piano standing by the unlit fire). May we make use of it, landlord?"

"That's what it's there fer."

"Dodger, you haven't had so many you can't tinkle the old ivories, have you?"

"Can't I have a go, Rusty?" asked one of the younger fellows.

"No, you bloody well can't. You tinkle the ivories like you were giving a Kraut a squirt. Dodger, go to it. Let's have 'Roll Out the Barrel'. And I hope you Yankee chaps are in good voice."

"I's known as the Black Sinatra," said Errol, in whom alcohol consumption had a tendency to produce the boastful.

"Anybody hits a wrong note'll get a ducking in the water barrel! Come on, you chaps in the snug, come and join us!"

And so they began, with 'Roll Out the Barrel' and continued with 'Bye Bye Blackbird' and 'Boogie Woogie Bugle Boy'. Their repertoire included a bizarre song called 'The Lambeth Walk', that involved an extraordinary strutting dance that four of the airmen and their girls performed to a thunderous chorus of applause. Grover noticed that even the cantankerous old Westwood and his son were joining in.

All of a sudden one of the girls, with chestnut hair and a fierce red lipstick, who had been imbibing freely, grabbed Grover by the arm and dragged him towards the others.

"I don't know how to do this," he complained.

"It's easy!" the girl screamed unnecessarily into his ear.

"Kick yer legs in the air, and after everybody says 'Lambeth Walk', stick your thumbs up like this and shout 'hoy!'"

So that was what he did, watching the others closely to see that he was doing the same as them, at the same time as trying to prevent the girl falling, and stopping himself from laughing too much. Eventually it all became too much for his dancing companion, who, after one sideways lurch too many, he had to let go to slump into one of the settles where, after cracking her head loudly on the wood, she nevertheless fell into a deep sleep.

Grover's head was swimming, he was sweating profusely, and would have been glad of an opportunity to sit down. It was at this point that he became aware of a low keening that suddenly rose to a terrifying scream.

"Aaaahhh!"

It was the young lad whose birthday it was, the one they called Topper, who was lying with his head against the wing of the settle, in a drunken stupor.

Grover was standing beside the blond flyer, who was talking to another man:

"I was just waiting at dispersal when—"

The lad screamed again.

"Dusty! Dusty! He's burnin', I can hear him over the R/T! He's burnin', I tell you!"

The blond flyer strode swiftly up to him and grabbed him roughly by the shoulders, shaking the young lad, whose glazed eyes rolled in his head.

"Shut up! Shut up, Topper! We don't want to hear that! You can't take the juice you go outside and dip your head in the water butt!"

"Sorry, Dutch, I didn't mean—"

"You didn't mean, but you did. Don't lose your wool. Remember, stick, search, report. Remember."

Another said, with shocking callousness:

"Shouldn't have joined up if you can't take a laugh, old boy."

The blond flyer, still supporting Topper, turned to the bar and asked the landlord:

"Do you have a back room where he can sober up?"

The landlord led the blond airman, who was dragging the drunken lad, his feet trailing over the bare stone flags, behind the bar.

Grover, who had been partially startled out of his drunken reverie, found himself standing next to Errol and a short, stocky airman with a ginger moustache, through which he whistled and muttered:

"Bad show."

"Hey!" said Errol. "He ain't got no cause to be so hard on the young lad."

"What do you know about it?" the airman said, and his anger – as had the fury of the blond flyer – surprised Grover.

"I'm sorry," the airman said. "You chaps can't know…

Dusty was his friend. Went for a Burton last week. Kite caught fire over Dungeness. It's bad show to talk about things like that."

"Yes," Grover said. "I'm sorry."

"I said, we don't talk about it."

The man turned to the rest of the company and shouted:

"Come on, chaps, let's have another chorus of 'Roll Out the Barrel'! Dodger, get to it!"

There followed an even more lusty performance of the song, together with an encore in which two airmen attempted a version of the jitterbug with a couple of the land girls, one of whose legs, flying through the air, knocked a stool to the floor. The performance ended with a loud roar, during the coda to which the blond airman returned with the lad Topper, ashen of face, clinging to his arm with something approaching desperation. There was an embarrassed silence as those in the bar looked anywhere but at the new arrivals. Grover felt even more confused by these people.

Demonstrating on this occasion not so much anger as an avuncular concern for his young charge, the blond airman gently lowered Topper onto one of the settles, easing the comatose girl's legs to one side.

It was at this point, just as the man at the piano was starting to tune up again, that Leroy, who was standing unsteadily against an oaken beam by the window, shouted:

"Hey, what those snowdrops want?"

Leroy looked out the window.

"They're comin' here."

Grover glanced over his shoulder to see four MPs, who had disembarked from a jeep, approaching the front door to the pub.

A second or two later and the first of them, tall with a fringe of blond hair visible beneath his white helmet, burst through the door, which smacked against the wooden partition behind it. His right arm bore the MP brassard and insignia of two gold-crossed Harpers Ferry pistols, and in his right hand he carried the MP's lead-weighted baton. He pulled up short as three more MPs followed through the door, colliding with him. His blue eyes scanned the bar and came to rest upon Errol, Grover and Leroy.

The blond one shouted:

"Hey, you niggers! I want you outta here this second, you hear me!"

Without allowing them time to respond, he walked straight up to Errol, pulled the glass roughly from his hand, slammed it down on the bar so that its contents leapt out to lie in a frothing pool, grabbed him by the sleeve and began to frog-march him towards the door while his other hand brandished the baton in threatening fashion.

Errol only had time to expostulate an ineffectual:

"Hey!"

Then the blond MP barked:

"What's your name, nigger?"

"Errol—"

"Take him!"

He pushed Errol behind him to where the other three MPs stood.

"I ain't goin'," Errol said, pushing the MPs away from him.

The blond MP turned on him, a look of hooded fury in his blue eyes.

"You do what I says, nigger. Or you suffer for it, y'hear."

Then he turned back and barked:

"Which one of you niggers is Grover Carson?"

Grover's stomach plummeted within him like a faulty elevator.

It was at this point that the RAF men, who had been staring wide-eyed at this intrusion, seemed to come to an awareness of what was happening. The one called Steve said:

"Hey, steady on! What do you mean by this?"

The blond MP turned on him the look of fury still igniting the icy blue of his eyes.

"It ain't none of your business. This is US Army business."

"See here!" the other said. "There's no call for you chaps to come barging in here – what do you mean by it, eh?"

The MP looked as though he would have liked to strike out with his baton at the airman but thought better of it.

"We had a call these here niggers was causin' a disturbance."

"Balderdash. They've been good as gold, and we've just been having a quiet drink, so your informant—"

"What was that noise we heard?"

"What noise?"

"That rucus afore we come in."

"Oh, come on, old chap. We were just having a sing-song."

But the blond MP simply ignored him.

"Which one of you niggers is Grover Carson? I won't ask again."

Grover felt himself quaking. So they had come for him. For him in particular. But he had no idea why. He had to speak in case this madman took out his rage on one of the others.

"Here." He stepped unsteadily and queasily forward.

The blond MP stared at him, his face a livid coal of fury.

"Just look at you, soldier. You're drunk and incapable. Your tie's not done up, you're improperly dressed. You're a disgrace to the United States Army, you goddam hoboe. Let me see yer pass."

As Grover fumbled in his pocket the MP uttered a jeering:

"You ain't got it. You ain't got it!"

The tone of almost hysterical triumph in which these words were uttered terrified Grover all the more, and he lost all control over his fingers.

"Yessir, I got it... I got it right here."

Still he could not find it, his frantic clumsy fingers fumbling in his inside pocket to no avail.

"That's it! I'm takin' you in. Takin' you all in."

"He ain't done nuthin'," Clark protested.

"Take him out!" the blond MP screamed to the two who had hold of Errol. He then turned back to Grover, seized him with his free hand and pulled him towards the door. The force he applied was such that the intoxicated Grover was almost yanked off his feet, and was staggering to right himself, when he, and the MP, were brought up short by two of the airmen and the man called France who said, with all the authority these ARP wardens seemed to possess:

"You ain't got no call to take him. They done nuthin' wrong."

"Quite right," said the airman. "You're being heavy-handed and I've a good mind to report you to your commanding officer. Let these chaps go on with their drink in peace. We don't want any trouble now, do we?"

The last sentence contained just enough of an edge to bring the MP up short.

"I don't want any trouble in my pub," Tom Curtin echoed from behind the bar.

"You got no right to stop us doin' our dooty," said the blond MP. "We're takin' them now."

"You ain't takin me, snowdrop," said Leroy.

The MP turned at the words and found Leroy, his legs planted unsteadily apart and swaying slightly, an empty beer bottle held by the neck in his hand.

"You wanna fight, nigger?" said one of the MPs who was unencumbered with Errol or Grover, planting his feet and holding his baton at the ready.

"I want no fightin' in my pub," said Tom Curtin. "If you wants to fight go outside."

"I'll teach you a lesson," said the MP.

He advanced on Leroy, bringing his baton down in a sharp smack on the bottle, which shattered into fragments, some of which flew in the direction of an ATS girl who screamed.

"Come on!"

The blond MP hauled with his free hand on Grover's arm. But Grover was determined to stand his ground for as long as he could in the hope the RAF men might make the MPs see sense. The last thing he wanted was to be left alone with the MP in this mood. When the latter realised what he was doing he raised his baton and brought it down with a crack on Grover's knee.

Raw pain exploded up Grover's thigh and lights flashed in his head. The leg collapsed under him, and he found himself falling to the floor as the MP's grip loosened. A cacophony of noise rang through his head. When he was capable of looking up, he saw through tear-filled eyes the blond MP surrounded by four men: two airmen, the ARP warden and the son of the man Westwood, who was shouting:

"You can't come in 'ere hittin' blokes what've done nobody no 'arm."

In the background the two MPs were wrestling Errol through the door. Errol was trying to prevent them by bracing his right leg against the door jamb, while one of the MPs was trying to stretch out his arm far enough to strike Errol's leg with his baton. Another thick-set young man in a cap and patched pullover had the MP who had struck Leroy by the arm and was pushing him against the bar in the face of the landlord's vociferous protest.

Grover half rose, pulling himself up by his hands on the bar, his right leg quivering under him. He laboriously straightened himself, with his back to the bar and facing the blond MP. The latter turned from the men surrounding him and glared at Grover.

Instinctively Grover, already in the partial crouching posture dictated by the searing pain in his right knee, raised his fists to defend himself.

"Go on, Joe Louis!" Errol yelled from the door, which was banging to and fro as the MPs tried to manhandle him through it.

"Oh, the nigger figures hisself a boxer, does he?" the MP jeered.

"He is a boxer, so you better watch out, snowdrop," said Clark, who had retreated to the end of the bar and was eyeing an escape through the back of the pub.

"We'll see about that."

One of the MPs ran to cut Clark off and the blond MP advanced with his baton raised.

One of the girls screamed.

"Tommy, do something!"

At this point the airman and the younger Westwood each grabbed the MP's arms, and as he swung round he struck Westwood on the hip with his baton, causing him to lose his grip. The airman threw a punch at the MP but missed and was pushed backwards so that he fell into a table of glasses and bottles that cascaded to the floor.

"Goddam Limey bastard," said the MP, a malicious grin on his face.

He then advanced on Grover, chopping down with his baton on his raised knuckles. He screamed, feeling as if his arm was cleaved in two. Pain flared in his skull, and he was conscious of nothing save that pain and the sensation of being dragged, his legs useless under him, towards the door. He could hear tables being knocked flying and glasses and bottles shattering, but his head was held in a vice that was slowly being tightened as waves of pain migrated up from his hand to his jaw.

The cool night air was as a bucket of water in his face. He found himself falling on the cobbles. In his head he heard the voices of Errol and Leroy calling to see if he was all right. As he turned in the direction of his friends' voices his head swam, and he caught a glimpse of them being tossed into the back of a lorry before he passed out. The next thing he knew the blond MP was pulling him upright from the cobbles and draping him over a bench and table that he knew stood on the forecourt of the pub. The man was standing over him, his voice a malevolent hiss accompanied by spittle in his ear.

"I'll teach you to make love to my gal, nigger."

The MP switched his baton from his right to his left hand and with his right punched Grover full in the jaw. He must have passed out again because when he awoke there was a tidal wave of people issuing from the pub, and one of the younger men had the MP by the arm, restraining the baton, and another was punching him in the face.

The blond MP fell to the cobbles, a trickle of blood issuing from his mouth. At this two of the other MPs jumped out of the back of the lorry and advanced in threatening fashion on the locals, batons paused to strike. The crowd, with three airmen, the younger Westwood, the ARP warden and the man called Rule, began a wary retreat back into the building. By this time the blond MP, spluttering and dabbing at his bloodied lip, was beginning to rise.

"Goddam Limey bastards," he hissed.

He glared at Grover, who was still on the ground, and barked at the other two snowdrops:

"Take him!"

They seized him roughly, an arm each, and hauled him to his feet. They had to drag him over the cobbles as he was unable to move his right leg.

The blond MP ordered:

"Temple, throw those other men out! We'll take this one."

At that the tailboard was let down and Errol, Leroy and Clark were thrown bodily out of the back of the truck to land, hands splayed, on the roadway.

Grover was gripped by terror. It was bad enough were they all to be carried off by the MPs, but for him to be at their mercy, without the support of his fellows, without them being present to witness what the MPs intended to do to him, was the stuff of nightmares. He made a bid for freedom. He was held by only one of the MPs, the man called Temple, and that by his left hand only since the man clearly thought him disabled.

Grover jack-knifed, ripping his left hand free of the man's grasp and delivering a swift punch with his still partially numbed right to the man's solar plexus. Temple doubled up, retching. Grover looked towards the pub as towards salvation. If he could get in there, and maybe go through the bar, get out the back while the locals blocked the MPs from getting to him. But he knew it was futile as soon as he kicked off. His right knee crumpled under him, he stumbled, and slipping on the cobbles and stretching to right himself, fell backwards. He managed to regain his feet, but one of the MPs had him round the throat, pulling back on him, another yanked on his arm, and they dragged him back to the lorry where the furious Temple punched him in the guts.

As he doubled up, winded, the blond MP brought his face up close to his, and, hissing bloody spittle, said:

"You'll pay for this, nigger. You're gonna wish you'd never come to this goddam country. That I do swear."

CHAPTER TWENTY-FIVE

Emily was making the familiar journey: the noonday bus to the crossroads and then the walk to the American camp, but the tentative hope that she had experienced on her last such visit was entirely absent, to be replaced by a consuming dread.

That which remained optimistic in her had about it the stubborn rather than the hopeful. It stood not in the auditorium of her mind but in the wings, and not so much prompted sanguine thoughts as heckled the dreadful ones. They spoke not with the conviction that Larry Schultz was a decent man who would do the decent thing, as almost to dare him to do otherwise, or to dare her mind to think that he might do otherwise.

It was not the warm, sultry day it had been when she made this journey three weeks before, but a blustery one that disarranged her hair and leaked a steady drizzle upon her disarray. But she cared not for her appearance. If he was to be true to her, it would not be for the sake of her beauty. Rather, she felt, it would be for pity of her and her condition; if indeed, there was any pity in him.

He was at his post by the sentry box, a martial silhouette like a toy soldier. When she caught sight of him, she found that she was no longer the humble supplicant who had disembarked the bus to the disapproving looks and knowing smiles behind the shopping bags. She was no longer bent and crying beneath her disordered locks. She was ramrod straight. She was a woman bent on claiming her due from a faithless swain. She was the incarnation of every avenging female she had encountered between the pages of a book or on the silver screen. She possessed that cold, glassy, superior mockery of Katharine Hepburn in *The Philadelphia Story*. She just needed, she thought, as she stared at him across a strip of asphalt and flower-dusted roadside verge, a bit of steel in her spine. She was sure she possessed glassy mockery, but did she have the steel?

When she reached him, the other man had already been dismissed. Larry stood alone, behind him only a group of six playing baseball on the square.

"I thought I told you I didn't want to see hide or hair of you agin," he said. "Whaddyou come here fer?"

She knew what she had to say, but now that it came to it, she had no idea how to begin. Her tongue cleaved to the roof of her mouth – a mouth that was dry and adhesive.

"There's somethin' you should know."

Her voice was steady, but it was the steadiness of one standing on the edge of a precipice.

"I dunno what you think you gotta say to me that's gonna be worth me hearin'."

"Don't you?" she said significantly.

He did not seem to get the point. Or if he did his

expression did not change, and when he spoke it was with a level unconcern.

"Okay then, out with it."

"I think I'm with child."

His face evinced no shock. The immediate concern, the sympathy, that should have appeared, even if only by way of simple human reflex, was absent. Instead, his lips, those lips that had once been so eager to taste her own, stretched in a smile whose cynicism verged on derision.

"Oh, that's yer game. That's how you plan to get me back, is it?"

This was not how it should be. It was for her to be haughty and mocking. He said:

"Why the hell should I believe that, eh?"

"It's true."

"You been to a doctor?"

"No."

"No, so you're just guessin'. Hopin'. Is that it? Or mebbe makin' the whole goddam thing up."

She felt anger swelling like another new life within her.

"I missed my time of the month."

"So what? You bin sick?"

"No."

"You been eatin' funny?"

Of course, she had cravings; they all had cravings. She dreamed, like they all did, of bacon and eggs and lashings of fried bread, of chocolate and cake and bananas and oranges. Her dreams were culinary orgies. But she didn't have cravings for stupid things like beetroot with sugar on or some such. What could she say in reply to that?

"I eat me ration, dunn I."

"So you're just guessin'. Mebbe you're sick or sumthin'. Or… or mebbe it's 'cos you Limeys ain't got no decent food to eat."

"A woman knows."

Even to herself she sounded less than certain. Could she just be ill, could she just be depressed? Was there, after all, an element of wishful thinking to her conviction?

"Yeah, and women make up stories. Women have ways of snarin' a guy."

"It's true, I tell yer!"

"What if it is true? How do I know it's mine?"

"What!"

The incredulity made her head swim.

"For all I know you bin with any number of guys."

"How can you say that? You know fine well… You must know you were the first."

"Honey, I don't know any such thing."

"You bastard! You're gonna turn your back on your responsibilities…?"

"My responsibilities? For all I know you bin sleepin' with that there nigger of yourn, and you gonna have yerself a little coffee-coloured baby."

"You can't… How can you be so cruel?"

"No gal o' mine's gonna throw herself into the arms of no dirty goddam nigger, pregnant or not, you hear?"

Despite every resolution to the contrary the tears that welled in her eyes escaped their breakwater, compounding her shame. The only response that was left for her was anger. Furiously wiping away the tears with a gesture that was more like a slap to her own cheeks, she rounded on him.

"You know what, Larry Schultz, I don't know why I come here. I don't know because, whether I'm pregnant or not, I don't care, because I wouldn't have a bastard like you if you was the last man on earth."

"It's not what you was sayin' a few weeks ago, babe," he said, complacently malicious.

"Well, a few weeks back we wus both sayin' different things, wasn't we? You wus sayin' how you loved me and wanted nothin' so much as to make me yer wife. And you might think no man's gonna have me now. But you're wrong. And any man's gotta be better than you. I hope I never see you again as long as I live."

With a gesture that swung her bag so that it whipped around her body and struck her breast on the other side, she turned smartly and walked back towards the crossroads. She did not turn back to see his reaction. But she felt his gaze burning into her back all the way until the road turned. She never wanted to see him again.

But as she sat on the bus, she was no longer sure. Convinced she was pregnant, she could not accept that Larry would not wish to see and acknowledge his child. Perhaps he just needed some time to get used to the idea.

And she in turn couldn't afford to be so choosy as to shun the father. If she had Schultz's baby, nobody else would take her on. There was Tom Dawkins, who was sweet on her and would do anything to get a ring on her finger. But would even he take her on if she was with the child of some Yankee soldier? That was, if he was still alive.

When she arrived home her parents were out, her mother no doubt at the WVS meeting and her father at work. Eric was at school. She went into the kitchen and put the kettle on the Aga. She needed a cup of tea and a fag to calm her nerves. She sat nursing her tea at the kitchen table, staring out at the roof tiles of the terraces opposite.

What had changed between her and Larry? It must be more than his having had his way and now wanting shot of her. There was real anger. All because of one dance with that stupid black feller. Hadn't she said she never intended to see the man again? Or had she said that? She couldn't remember. But he must know it was only a dance. However much he hated blacks he must know that.

Or was this whole black thing just an excuse to get rid of her now he had slept with her? He had been playing hard to get ever since their visit to the hotel. But he had been genuinely angry.

There was a knock at the door. Was that Eric gone to school and forgotten his key again? They should just leave the door unlocked like they used to. It was only with the arrival of the white Americans that her father had suggested they always lock the front door, and with the arrival of the blacks, begun to insist upon it.

She put down her tea, walked out into the hall and, after first checking her face for tear smudges in the wall mirror, opened the door. And stared, disbelieving.

"Hello, Em."

She opened her mouth, but before she could speak, she collapsed in a faint. She did not feel the arm that gently held her and prevented her falling to the lino.

CHAPTER TWENTY-SIX

Tom Dawkins approached 27 Acacia Lane, a nineteenth-century weaver's cottage, and applied his hand to the tarnished brass knocker. The door was answered by Mrs Climpson, a flour-doused pinny about her ample waist, hair in a floral scarf.

"I… I was looking for Eric, hopin' he might be home, like."

"It's Tom, isn't it?"

"That's right."

The last time Mrs Climpson had seen him he would have been no more than twenty. A lot had happened since then. To what extent was what he had been through written in his face? To what extent had what he had seen erased the shy, optimistic and impulsive lad he had been?

His da must have noticed but said nothing. They had never talked much, and still less could the younger Dawkins discuss what he had seen in North Africa with a father who never referred to his own service in the first war.

He was suddenly struck with something that was very like panic, almost terror, at the thought that he would never be able to return to that lad of nineteen; that that young man was lost for ever, like so many others, left to mummify in the sands of the desert.

"I just thought he might be back."

Eric Climpson, his boyhood friend, fellow apple scrumper in the Cadwalladers' Dovecote Park, and later drinking companion, was a stoker in the Merchant Navy.

"No, lad, he's not... we haven't heard from him... well, he's overdue getting in touch."

Yes, Tom saw it now. That tautness of the flesh about neck and cheekbone, as if preparing to flinch from the blow that was anticipated. Best pretend that everything was normal.

"Oh well," he said cheerily. "Sorry I missed him... I'm done with soldierin' now... The leg..." He glanced down at his left leg. "When he gets hisself some leave tell him I'm back, and if he wants to share a jar or two..."

"You... you couldn't find out could you... if he's still... all right, you bein' in the army, like?"

"I'm not in the army no more... and even if I was, they don't tell us nothin'. I'm sorry... When you see him, tell him I called..."

Best get away as quick as possible. He turned to put it behind him but felt it burning into his back all the same: that look on the mother's face, the envy, the blame, the question, 'Why couldn't it be my lad back for good, even at the price of a gammy leg?'

He limped away. It was nearly a week since he had been discharged from the Joint War Organisation-run home in Hinchingbrooke Castle in Huntingdon. He had been at the castle for two months, with regular visits to the Clifford Rehabilitation Centre for physiotherapy, and remedial exercises supervised by an army PT instructor.

He had suffered a fracture to the bones of his left leg, and the doctors performed what they called reduction on it, with the leg put in plaster. He then had skin grafted from his buttock onto his calf before being discharged from the army into the care of the Red Cross.

He continued to have pain, both in his left leg and increasingly in his right. He walked with a gait that, even after physiotherapy, was part limp, part hobble. He had been provided with a stick but would not let himself be seen walking about town like an old man. Still, at least they didn't need to take the leg off, even though its pocked, fiercely reddened appearance and dry lifeless texture were constant reminders of the trauma he had undergone.

But he did not need his leg to remind him of that. His doctors might concentrate on his body, but instinct told him that it was his mind that was the more crippled. He had, he guessed, for nobody had ever said as much, what they called battle exhaustion.

Most nights he would waken and hear again, not the crashing artillery and staccato machine guns, but the screech of tank wheels and the piercing scream of his friend as the armoured beast ground Jack's body into the sand. And he would feel himself standing, shaking uncontrollably on the edge of that abyss of unnatural platinum blond night, booming with menace, slashed with tracer, fearing that he would be unable to step off. He would wake drenched in sweat, and his father at the door asking:

"Are you all right, lad?"

Now the experience had become so common his father never left his bed.

At times such as this he sought refuge in his memories of Emily; she was the hope that beckoned to him, hers the cool loving palm that, placed on his skillet of a forehead, would soothe all.

He had always intended to visit Jack's widow. He just delayed the journey. He told himself that this was to give him time to make as complete a recovery as possible, and to renew his relationship with Emily, but wondered whether he would ever be well enough to face the question that would be posed by the haggard face:

"Did he suffer?"

The same applied to the parents of Stevie, who had been killed by enemy mortar fire at Mareth. That would be easier, for Stevie had been killed instantaneously, but he could not visit the one without the other. *There is*, he thought, in uncharacteristically philosophical terms, *more than one kind of courage, and more than one kind of cowardice.*

But he had discovered that fact in Hinchingbrooke Castle. Amongst the casualties there had been badly burned airmen. These poor bastards had already undergone prolonged surgery at Queen Victoria Cottage Hospital in East Grinstead under a man they referred to as 'Archie', who they all seemed to idolise.

The first time he had seen one of these unfortunates he had been horrified. The man who he later learned was Frank Heyhoe, a pilot officer with 92 Squadron, was sitting in a deckchair on the lawn. Tom was walking past and, as he had left his fags behind in his room, asked Frank, whose back was turned to him, for a cigarette.

Frank turned to face him. That face was like some creation of Lon Chaney, archetypical Hollywood horror. It was a particularly gruesome death mask, painted in livid colour, and illustrative of one who had died in agony. His right eye was a pinprick in a crater of dead flesh. The other eye was deformed with the lid burned away to reveal the inside of the eyelid, raw and livid. The mouth was twisted into the worst hare lip he had ever seen. The flesh of the left cheek was pockmarked like one who had survived smallpox.

Those nightmares that haunted Tom Dawkins were largely of situations about which he had no control. But that which haunted him after he first caught sight of Frank Heyhoe possessed an added dimension of guilt. Could he ever rid himself of the guilt he felt for his reaction to seeing Frank? He did not faint or cry out, and the reaction was entirely involuntary, but the revulsion he felt, the feeling that he was looking at a monster, must have been writ plain on his face, and although he would later come to see Frank as a friend during their brief time together, he could never be comfortable in the man's company, not for the hideous sight he presented, but for the shame of his own reaction to it.

And his admiration for this man had little to do with the courage he had displayed in the face of his injuries, the twenty-one operations he had undergone, the saline baths, the grafts that involved production of a skin flap from his thigh which was attached to his arm, then from arm to face with a tube like an elephant's trunk; it had little to do with the fact that he had lost sight in his right eye and would never be able to smile again. It was because Frank never bore Tom any grudge for his reaction, and never, save for those occasions in which Tom found him sitting with tears falling from his left eye, bemoaned his state. Rather constantly cheerful, he regaled him with stories about the East Grinstead hospital, of them having showgirls brought up from London to practise chatting to, of being invited to people's houses for tea. The only abnormal thing was that they were not allowed mirrors, Frank said, his face impassive, as if this were just some form of administrative eccentricity.

Getting to know Frank had helped him through the trauma of the wounds, and he was able to face the prolonged medical interventions with gratitude rather than self-pity.

But what sustained him more than anything was the thought that soon he would get to see and hold Emily again. She was the light at the end of his tunnel. And he could greet her at their reunion conscious that he was, at least on the outside, and as long as he did not try to walk, the same Tom Dawkins that had boarded the train from Chalford a year and a bit ago.

But when he saw her, he immediately realised that it was a terribly dim light – dim in her eyes now and in his own. And he was beginning to wonder if it could ever be rekindled.

The reunion had not been as he had pictured it. True, she had fainted away, and that is what women are supposed to do at the return from the battlefield of the loved one. But when she had come to, after he had assisted her to a seat in the parlour, she had not welcomed him in the manner he had anticipated. There were no tears of joy, no greedy kisses, no clinging arms that refused to let go of his neck. Just a dazed seeming indifference. And those questions, as if she was making idle chit-chat with the milkman – How was he? How much leave had he got? Was he injured? Was he now discharged from the army? – and the words 'it must have been awful for you' spoken in that colourless tone that could have been referring to his dropping a fiver down the drain, and spoke more clearly than anything of her indifference.

In the end he could bear it no longer. He wanted to scream at her: 'Don't you care for me anymore!' He was angry, of course he was. There he had been, risking his life, fighting to prevent Nazi jackboots marching down the high street, taking girls like her as they wished.

Of course, he had feared something. He had received no letter from her since January. But he tried to explain it away by that mad rush across the desert, and then his injury and transfer from hospital to rehabilitation. But other blokes got their mail. He had not believed it. But now… And so he was angry. But most of all he was sick to his stomach.

He had expected her to see him the next day; to call and apologise, or at least send him a message and ask to meet. He was damned if he would go chasing her. It was best he let her make the next move.

But maybe he was being too harsh. There was the shock of him turning up on her doorstep like that. They had been walking out for almost a year before he was called up. And although they had never gone too far, there was a clear understanding that she was his girl. He could have proposed, or even married her, before leaving. He thought hard about that, but in the end decided it was best he just imply – he could not remember the words – that he would do so on his return if he was still in one piece (this latter was his own qualification which he thought best not to spell out). It would, he thought, be emotionally easier for her to lose a lover than a fiancé or husband.

She had seen him off at the station at the end of his embarkation leave with tears in her beautiful eyes, and he thought, love in her heart. But fifteen months was a long time for lovers to be apart.

And maybe he should have brought her something. Flowers, maybe. Yes, at the very least he should have brought her a bunch of flowers!

His reflection in the shop windows in North Row: something bent, concave, as if forever breasting a stiff wind. He stopped in front of a jeweller's. There were some nice bracelets. That gold one with the strands intertwined like rope. But that was nearly a fiver. He could not afford anything much, not on his army pension. As he was over twenty-one he got 34s2d per week, which was all very well as long as he didn't go splashing it about on jewellery. And if he was going to have to fork out for a ring… He scanned the prices of the rings with misgiving. They were so much more expensive than he had imagined. He wouldn't be surprised if the bastards had put up the prices with the war being on, with more people wanting to get wed. He smiled. Such a thought would never have occurred to him before he met Jack and Stevie.

"Excuse me."

He gave a start, catching a glimpse of the reflection of a woman behind him. For a second he thought it might be Em come to apologise. But this woman was a brunette and smaller. He spun sharply round, and the pain scythed into his knee, so that his leg almost gave way beneath him. He bent double, holding on to the knee. He had not yet learned, especially when caught off guard, that he could not make the sort of movements he would have made before his injury. He looked up.

It was… He recognised the button nose, the slightly buck teeth. But he could not put a name to the face. The Knight girl.

"Tom Dawkins, isn't it? You probably don't remember me, no reason you should, but…"

"It's, er…"

"April… April Knight. Yes. I'd just like to say how sorry I was to hear you was injured—"

She spoke fast, pert and briskly business-like, but his anxiety to denial still managed to interrupt her.

"No, it's no—"

"I'm sure you don't want to talk about it. I just wanted to say – on behalf of the town – how much we admire you and all of you, and what you've done for us."

"Well, thanks."

He was touched and felt a warm glow of pride. Nobody had said anything like that to him since his return. Surprised moreover that this vote of thanks should come from a girl he had barely spoken to and had regarded as rather snooty.

He was about to move off when she stopped him with a gloved hand on his arm.

"There's a lot of us here in this town as don't like the way those Yanks go on."

"I'm sorry," he said, nonplussed. And then thought, *What the hell am I apologising for?*

"It ain't right gals throwin' themselves at them, just 'cos they looks the part. It don't make a soldier, does it? Looks?"

"No."

"That's what I says. What's better about them than our own lads? I says. It's unpatriotic, that's what it is, when our men are away fightin'."

"Yes."

"And them Yanks don't seem to wanna do any fightin'. All they're interested in is chewin' gum and eyeing up the women."

"Yes." He was becoming embarrassed at the thought that this was all he had to say.

"Bad enough if the gals don't have a beau. But where they's got a fella already, one of our own, doin' his bit, fightin' to keep them safe, and there they goes gallivantin' about with some Yank. It ain't right, and you'll not find many as thinks it is."

He was uncomfortably conscious that this conversation was turning into a harangue, and one, moreover, with something ominous about it. Her very elusiveness endowed her words with significance.

"I don't get what you mean."

"Well, I thought I made my meanin' plain enough. We's all behind you. You and those like you, all in the same boat... And if you've thrown her over there's none in this town is gonna say a word against you, and that's a fact. We admire you. Oh, don't get me wrong – I got my own fella. A WOPAG, he is… No, I just wanted to say…"

"I don't know what you mean." There was an edge of hysteria to his voice now.

She closed her green eyes slowly like a cat, and then opened them as if with reluctance.

"You've bin back a few days, haven't you?"

"Four days."

"And she hasn't told you?"

"Who?"

"Emily France. She's your gal, isn't she? Or was."

"Told me what?"

"Well, if she hasn't told you it ain't for me to go spreadin' tittle-tattle. If I thought you didn't know I would've kept my mouth shut. I just wanted you to know we're behind you."

"Told me what?" He couldn't keep the edge of anger out of his voice.

"It ain't for me. Ask her yourself."

"Ask her what?"

"Ask her what's been goin' on while you been fightin' fer King and Country… and the likes of her."

She made to walk off, but he detained her with a none-too-gentle grip on her forearm.

"Hey!" she screamed in protest.

"What do you mean? You can't say things like that then just walk off."

"What do I mean? You ask her. About her and the Yank. The tall blond fella… Larry… some German name. As bad as the Germans if you ask me… I ain't sayin' no more."

And with that she walked off, her high heels tapping on the pavement, a tattoo of misery that punctuated his shock.

CHAPTER TWENTY-SEVEN

Emily met Tom on the riverside path just beyond the bridge, the same path she had walked with Larry Schultz ten weeks previously. She had insisted they meet there rather than he call for her, because she did not trust her mum and dad to keep quiet about Larry. It was just possible she might still be able to keep her relationship with the American from Tom. If she got back together with their blue-eyed boy, her parents would surely see the sense of keeping mum about what she had been up to when he was in Africa.

It was not that she wanted to walk out with Tom again. After Larry he seemed pale and bland and well… so English. She had enjoyed him doting upon her a year or so ago, but she was at an age when time moves with frightening speed, and the Emily she now was regarded being worshipped by a farmer's son as a silly schoolgirl's gratification. Tom had been useful in an abstract sort of way when he was in the desert. She liked the idea of having a soldier who fought not for King or Country, but for her. She even found herself fantasising from time to time over Tom Dawkins dying some heroic death and his body being found with her photograph clasped in his hand.

But walking out with Tom again may be the best thing for her. She still had not had her period and was becoming more and more convinced she was pregnant. If so, and people knew, she would be a scandal. Would her parents still want her, or would they throw her out on the street? It had happened to Lily Flitcroft a few years ago. Would Tom want her? Would any man? She would have to leave town, that much was clear. That might not be such a bad thing as she was fed up with the place. Her horizons stretched further than Chalford, ideally all the way to Georgia, USA. But she would have to make her own way in the world, with no relatives elsewhere, with nothing to her name but a case with her clothes and a baby on the way.

She was on tenterhooks, awaiting more fervently than did any Indian farmer the Monsoon, the first tremblings in her lower abdomen that would be her reprieve. And if they did not come, if she was pregnant, what then? She would have to snare Tom and get a ring on her finger as soon as may be. And get him to bed before the wedding. She dare not wait much longer if she was going to pass off any baby as his.

But all her careful planning would come to naught if someone in the town spilled the beans. It need not be someone like April Knight doing it out of malice. It could as easily be silly little Joycie letting it slip. Or someone who had seen them walking out together. But no. If someone said something it would most likely be malicious. And they would be queueing up to do it; she had seen the sanctimonious old fogeys giving dirty looks to girls with

GIs on their arm. If she did get Tom into her bed and into church, they would have to live elsewhere. Even if Larry was shipped out sharpish, she could never feel safe in Chalford. The thought of moving away from her parents and all she had ever known both thrilled and terrified her.

She debated with herself how she should play this first tryst with her former love. Should she be passionate at the outset? If so, how could she explain her previous coldness? Shock at his return? Yes, that was it. On the other hand, she did not want to tie herself lifelong to the likes of Tom Dawkins if she were not pregnant. To become a farmer's wife...? To live in that tied cottage where the kitchen served as the living room, with Tom and his da. She must not do anything that implied commitment until she was absolutely sure she was with child.

As she caught sight of him labouring up the path towards the bridge dragging his leg with a swinging movement, she felt an intense resentment. It was as if she were being blackmailed by his war service. She hadn't noticed his leg when he called at the house. When she came round, he was sitting in the armchair. Her parents had returned and she was lying on the sofa, Tom explaining that she had passed out with the shock of seeing him. And while her mother fussed over her, Tom declined to stay and have a bottle of Bass with her father, and beat a hasty retreat.

He called upon her the next day when she was still in bed, and because she had not got her thoughts straight she told her mother she was ill and could not see him. She it was who had arranged this tryst. Calling upon him the previous day at the farm and finding him out, she left a message with his irascible father, who laced his disrelish with a hawking phlegm-laden cough.

Tom hauled his body, which had once seemed so lithe and fluid, but now suggested a man bearing a heavy load on a creaking frame, out of the shade of the elms and into the strong sunshine. He stood, hardly looking at her, and for what seemed to her an unnaturally long time, waiting to cross the traffic of lorries and drays heading to Chalford market, an attraction that seemed at once both denuded and lent a greater significance by the exigencies of war. Was this what war did to a man? You would think someone who had faced battle would be rendered fearless rather than timid.

"Tom," she purred and manufactured a smile.

"Em," he said, a little guardedly.

"Well, aren't you gonna give a girl a kiss?"

"I didn't know you'd want me to."

"'Course I do. What does any girl want when her fella's come home safe from the war? A nice hug and kiss."

She moved towards him, and his arms enfolded her, spread round her waist, but without applying any pressure. She held her head back and her lips slightly parted and closed her eyes to await his kiss. When it came it was the merest tentative brush followed by a quick stab and retreat. There was something wrong, she was sure. Was it her cool reception of him, her failure to rush to his side once she had recovered from the shock of first seeing him? Or did he know? She would have to be careful.

"Gosh, you know how to sweep a girl off her feet! I'm sorry I didn't give you the welcome you must have been expectin'. The sort of welcome you had a right to. But it was such a shock. I haven't been meself lately. Gone down with somethin', I suppose. And then you turn up on the doorstep, without any warning (she could not resist the subtle criticism), well… it's enough to make anyone pass out!"

He remained mute. That dumb inscrutability that had once led her to label him the strong silent type, now only served to aggravate her.

They eased into the shadow of the trees where the coolness of the water was like a smell of freshness after the hot-tarmacked and dung-fragranced streets.

"Are you back for good now? You been discharged?"

"Yeah. The gammy leg."

"What happened?"

"I don't want to talk about it, Em."

"Of course not," she said, breezily. "But you can walk all right, can't you?"

"Sure. It might affect my work about the farm but not much, I hope."

"Well, you got me to look after you now, haven't you."

"Have I?"

Again, the same blank inscrutability.

"Shall we walk on? Down the path. You'll be all right with your leg?"

"I'll be all right."

She slid her arm into his, and they turned their backs on the burnished bow of the bridge, walking through the tunnel of shade formed by the elms and willows. And with it the memories of her prideful stride with Larry on her arm. Less happily, the thought occurred to her that she might bump into April Knight. If so, the harpy was sure to say something about Larry. She wished they had gone elsewhere, but she could not suggest they go back, not without some explanation. And it was safer to walk down the path than to parade through the town or sit in Dorothy's Tea Shop. God, was this what her life was going to be like? She felt like one of those spies in occupied France.

"It's lovely to have you back safe and sound," she said, holding out the words, to see how he, so reticent and inscrutable, would bite.

When he spoke it was a shock.

"I hear we got ourselves a bunch of them Yanks here now."

"That's right," she said, guardedly.

"My old man won't give them time o' day. But I guess everybody don't see it the same way."

"What do you mean?"

"What do you think of them? Yanks?"

"Oh… they're a bit fresh… thinks a lot of theirselves, they do."

A cold shiver was trickling down her spine. He must have heard something.

"I expect there's lots of rumours," he said, significantly.

"I dunno what you mean."

"It's only what I heard—"

If he was to go on in this roundabout fashion her best tactic was to seize the nettle.

"What? About me?"

"I bumped into someone. They was sayin' how you was friendly with one of them."

She had a flash of inspiration. He was sure to be referring to April Knight. And if so, she could use the fact to her advantage. Even someone as dull and introspective as Tom knew what a reputation girls had for bitchiness. But first of all, she would test the water.

"What did she say?"

"She said as how you were seein' this Yank fella. Blond."

So it was a she.

"It was that April Knight, wasn't it? Little minx! From the word go she's had it in for me. Thinks herself a cut above the likes of us, she does."

Tiny inspirations of cunning were sparking in her brain.

"Don't get me wrong. It weren't nuthin' I was gonna keep from you. It happened this way. The three of us, Lucy Watson, Joycie and me, goes dancin'. At the hall. And these Yanks shows up. Showin' off, flashin' their cash and their fags all over the place. Lucy's seein' one of 'em now. Anyway, this blond MP, name of Larry Schultz – they was all MPs – takes a likin' to me. So I said I was spoken for, nat'rally. But he keeps on at me. So I dances with him. You don't like to offend them, bein' our allies. Got to show them hospitality, or we'd have old Markle knockin' at our door. But it weren't no more'n that."

She was in her stride now. Until that moment she had never realised what a fluent liar she could be.

"And then he gets to bumpin' into me in the street. Well, first time I said I had to be off. Had to get somethin' to eat. But he insists on followin' me into the British Restaurant."

She instinctively realised the importance of sticking as close as possible to the truth when lying. Especially in a town like Chalford where there were so many eyes and ears. God, talk about German spies; they had nothing on the English in a small town. Careless talk costs lives.

"Well, what could I do? I insisted on paying my own way, mind. And the next dance we're at, he's there. And when I goes for a walk down by the river, he follows me, and it's 'why don't we walk down thatta way'. Well, again, I didn't want to give offence, so I walks with him. Made sure it was somewhere there was plenty of people about, mind. I know what reputation these Yanks has got. And that was where I was seen by April, who don't miss a trick to stick the knife in... I dunno what she got against me, thinks herself too good by half, that one... And I guess the whole thing's made me a bit jumpy and not me usual self, you know what I mean? So, I says, thank God you're come back. He can't do nuthin' no more now you're on my arm... You do believe me, don't you?"

There was a delay in his response, but she did not know if it were long enough to be of significance. He was often slow in articulating his thoughts.

"'Course I do, Em. I know you wouldn't go behind my back."

She turned to face him, to see if she could read the truth of it in his face. But he was looking straight ahead and up, as if at a dragonfly that hung in the air above him, and she could not see his eyes.

Would it make any difference if she could see his eyes? There had always been something dumb and slow in him, as if familiarity had imparted to him something of the character of his dad's cattle. And his eyes. Had they always been this dead? There was no life or sparkle in them; nothing of the azure light in the eyes of Larry, that mirrored the sky, that mimicked the sun on the summer sea, but at the same time knew so much more than either in their arch and worldly glamour. Tom's eyes were not like sky or sea, things that moved and changed with the light, with the capricious charm, with the life they contained. His eyes were like the earth he ploughed, brown or grey, she did not know which, but heavy, immobile, lumpen.

"Well, that's good then," she said, as cheerily as she was able, pulling him closer.

"Now that you're come back I don't need worry about no Yanks sniffin' around. You and me we gotta make the most of things now you're back. We gotta see more of each other, like we used to. What do you say we go dancin' tomorrow night, eh? One of them Yanks tried to show me how to do the jive. I didn't much take to it, all that throwin' about. But now that you're back it'll be different. You can still dance, can't you?"

"I dunno," he said indifferently.

"Well, even if you can't move the way you used to, you can still throw me about any way you want. To hell with the war. We'll have ourselves a good time, what do you say?"

He said nothing. He was staring blankly in front of him. Hadn't he been listening to a word she said? She felt like slapping him.

"Tom!"

"What?"

He looked down at her. With horror she saw there were tears in his eyes. He made no attempt to conceal them. And when they started to fall, he wiped them smartly away with his palm, apparently unconcerned, and not in the least ashamed.

"Are you all right?" she asked, and it came out with less concern and more accusation than she had intended.

"It's just the war."

She felt like saying, 'Well, for God's sake snap out of it', but instead pulled herself closer to his side and said with her best attempt at sympathy:

"What's in the past is in the past. I'll help you forget about the war."

CHAPTER TWENTY-EIGHT

Grover sat on the backless wooden bench in the field that contained what was known locally as the Chalford Barrow, until, still suffering considerable pain about the ribs and buttocks, together with that emanating from head, knee and arm, he subsided onto the grass, with his back to the amputated metal fence that surrounded the monument. He stretched his legs to relieve the pain in his knee.

After lighting up two Lucky Strikes, and handing one to the injured man, Errol joined him.

"What is this thing?" Grover asked, twisting his head to nod in the direction of the baulk of earth behind him, one of the few actions he was able to perform without being lanced with shards of pain.

Errol got to his feet and read the signboard at the entrance to the barrow.

"It do say it's the East Chalford Long Barrow, dating to 3000BC and excavated by Mortimer Wheeler in 1929… 3000BC, Jeez, that's, like, 5,000 years old."

"5,000 years old, whaddaya know about that," Grover said in a tone of wonder, turning to look at the earthen walls and immediately regretting it as the pain sliced through his side. When he had got his breath back, he said:

"I didn't think there was folks on the earth that time."

"Not in the States there weren't. 'Cept injuns."

"And there was people here in that time?"

"That's what the man says. It say, 'Before the mound was begun a rectangular mortuary chamber of wood was set in place and into this were placed the bodies of the dead adults and children.'"

"A cemetery?"

"I guess."

"Five thousand years," said Grover in the same musing tone. "I can't even think how long ago that was. And they's the granpappies of the folk what live here now?"

"I guess. Way back."

"To think they's livin', talkin', workin', and here's their kin what died all them years since buried here… Ain't no wonder…"

"Ain't no wonder what?"

"Well, it sure enough gives them somethin' to fight for."

"Why, Grover Carson, you's got mighty philosophical since…"

Errol's voice trailed off in embarrassment.

Grover went on:

"I's just thinkin'. We's got ourselves nuthin' like that. Where was we? I guess we come from Africa," he said, although it did not sound like him; his speech still sounded strange in his own ears, on account of the sibilance imparted by the loss of teeth.

"Guess so. They brung us in them slave ships and dumped us in the States to work their plantations."

"So we don't belong anywheres."

"We sure don't belong in the States. I guess we belongs in Africa."

"I don't know nuthin' about Africa."

"I guess we's nomads. You know what that is?"

"No."

"It's folk what don't have no home. They just wanders from place to place. But there agin, the ofay they just the same – in the US – they don't belong. They just thinks they does, 'cos they took the land from the injuns. And those whites, they comes from places like this is. So I guess these guys is some of their ancestors."

"I think if I come from here I wouldn't wanna leave it."

"Not on a night like this is, boy," said Errol, his wide white eyes scanning the field appreciatively.

It was a lovely evening. A light breeze from the south, that contained the merest hint of ozone, teased the leaves of the mighty elms that flanked the field, while swifts swooped for insects and wind-blown grass, coming in with piercing screeches over hedgerows in which the memory of May was being supplanted by dog rose and bindweed. The expanse of grass on which they sat, which was tinged red with sorrel and had clearly not been grazed for some time, was decorated with daisy and buttercup and clover. The fading sun made the sky the colour of peach, and cuckoos called to one another from the high branches.

"You heard of the Romans?" Errol asked.

"No, I guess I ain't."

"Well, they come from Italy, a thousand years back.

And they had this empire, ruled the whole of Europe, like the Germans does now. And they had slaves. But their philosophers, the guys they looked up to, bein' the cleverest, they believed it was in men's souls whether they wus slaves or not. What wus inside them. A guy that wus rich and powerful, he could be a slave inside, and a slave, he could be free if that wus what he was like inside."

"I guess that kinda makes sense," said Grover. "But I dunno how it would work... 'ceptin' maybe you's like that."

"That's what I like, boy, flattery." They laughed.

"And we's the first black folks that ever set foot in this here island," Grover mused.

"Ain't that somethin'. I guess we's pioneers like them first whites in the US."

"Can't see why they'd wanna leave it," said Grover, still in that musing tone, his forefinger tracing, as was his newly acquired habit, the space in his jaw where two of his premolars had been prior to their visit to the pub.

"I don't rightly know. Maybe this place just got too small for them."

And then he asked:

"There ain't nuthin' you miss about the States?"

"Sure I do. Fer all we gets back home. Sure I do."

"It's all you've ever known, son. Ain't no mystery in that. What you miss? Your gal?"

"Doreen? No, she's no good. Always got her eye on other fellas, know what I mean? Likes a drink – don't get me wrong, she ain't no lush. But yeah, I do miss her. She won't be missin' me none, though. No, I miss things. Molasses and oranges and cold beer, things you can't git here. And just, like, the hot summer nights. This is nice, but I miss those hot nights, and all the gals'd be out on their stoops givin' you the eye… but I guess I got me some good things here I don't have there. I like the folks here. They's just like we wus, back home, never havin' proper food to eat… Only difference is they gotta roof over their head."

The pain in Grover's face could not prevent his facial muscles expressing their admiration as he looked at his friend. He dimly recalled the older man's distress when his body had been dumped at the gate of their camp, the board simply let down so he could be rolled off to fall to the ground. And one of the MPs sending him on his way with:

"Back home you'd be swingin' from a tree fer what you done, boy. Think yerself one mighty lucky nigger."

The jarring of the fall winded him, and as he fought to breathe, the twisting ground on his rib bones, so that he felt as if his insides were one mass of broken glass.

Errol and Mitchell Wiley were standing remonstrating with the guard. And then Errol swooped down upon him, his big tender hand reaching out for Grover's cheek which had swollen so much as to partially obscure his vision.

"Man, you's beat up," Errol said. "Get the MO pronto!"

And after that it was pretty much of a blur, though he could remember Errol shouting:

"Give him somethin' fer the pain, can't you!"

And whatever they'd given him sure worked. The next day or two was nothing but a dream, with him lying on his bunk but feeling as if he were floating two feet above it. But he was not allowed the period of recuperation he needed. As soon as he was back on his feet Sergeant O'Rourke was detailing him to join the others in carrying boxes of ration packs. Errol, who was gently supporting Grover by the arm, remonstrated:

"Why, Sarg, this man ain't in no fit state to go liftin' and carryin.'"

O'Rourke turned a furious face on Grover's friend.

"Well, he'd better or I'll have him on a charge, and don't you go doin' his work fer him, yer hear?"

In the end O'Rourke was forced to see sense when Grover collapsed in agony with pain in his ribs, and the MO had to be called, interrupting his morning's fishing. As he gazed down at Grover in his bed, he turned a severe expression upon the sergeant.

"This man is in no condition to lift and carry, and will not be so for a week at least. Please ensure that he is detailed to administrative tasks only. I don't want to be called out again and find his injuries haven't been given a chance to heal."

The ill temper that resulted in the sergeant led to the fit men, Errol in particular, being driven with peculiar severity for the next few days, but Grover was detailed to clerical tasks only.

Grover said:

"That snowdrop sure must've been stuck on that English gal."

"Don't figure," Errol replied. "He'd just as soon have laid into you if you wus with any white gal. With some old white mamma come to that."

"I don't think so."

"Well then, he don't like the idea of a dirty nigger touchin' what he's touched."

"She didn't mind none."

"Well, I guess she didn't know no better."

"You think I done wrong?"

"Well, I done the same, didn't I? Neither of us wus to know O'Rourke'd come in. When he done that he was bound to tell tales. And then..."

"How can they do it?... In this country... what they done. It ain't the way of folk here."

"Don't mean nutin'. They thinks they can do what they likes, and I guess they can."

"But you wouldn't want to give it away, though, would you?" he said, his thoughts straying again to the bodies in the mound at his back.

"What?"

"You would want to fight all yer could to stop them Nazis gettin' their hands on the soil where your folks is buried."

"Yeah, you's mighty philosophical," said Errol. "Ain't but one cure fer that. You gotta come to the pub with us. Maybe them fly boys'll be there agin, and they can tell us what it's like to be up there with them there birds."

Errol raised his eyebrows to reveal startling opals that swivelled in the direction of the swifts, swallows and house martins that swooped and dived in pacific mimicry of the Spitfires and Messerschmidts that had fought to the death in those same West Country skies.

"I can't."

"Come on, man, what you mean you can't?"

"I..."

He wished Errol did not press him to put things into words. It was all right for Errol, he was good with words.

How could he describe the shame he felt? The insult to his pride of having to just take it. But there again, niggers weren't allowed pride. Pride was a language they'd never learned, on account of being kicked into the gutter from the day they was born. But the anger and the hate remained, stillborn within him. And would remain with him, and eventually die with him, having never been able to escape their prison.

"We gotta show them British flyers they can't drink us under the table like they is always saying they can."

"I dunno... I been beat on before. There was a time some of us got us jobs as tile setters, and we wus set on by these three carloads of AFL guys... but that was a load of us. This was just me."

"We wus there, wasn't we?"

"Not..."

"You ain't scared them snowdrops is gonna come back fer you?"

It was as if Errol had given him the excuse he hoped for.

"Why shouldn't I be scared?"

"Man, they learned their lesson. The locals chased them out."

"They still done what they wanted to, though, didn't they? Fact is, is what you said, the ofays is in charge here, nobody can stop 'em."

"Well, we ain't gonna let them, we—"

"You can't stop them, Errol. You go into town if you wants to, I—"

"Hell, I don't want to now. Now you ain't goin."

"Well, I'm a-tellin' yer. I'll make my way back to camp

once I've drunk in this night... It's just like springtime back home, ain't it? Before it gets too hot and sticky, and you just wants to lie down in the dirt like some old dawg with its tongue hangin' out..."

"Lyrical is what you is... And the gals all comes out on the stoops and gives you the eye, eh?"

"Let me enjoy it."

"Well... if you wants shot of me."

"No, you knows I don't. But I wants me a bit of peace. And you wants a bellyful of beer, even if it is that English stuff. So you go into town and I'll make my way back to camp."

Grover watched his friend go, his spindly legs picking their way between the molehills that mined the field and crushing the daisies beneath his boots. For a while he sat on, staring through the clouds of midges and ghost moths, breathing in the heady musk of grass and meadowsweet. Admiring the dog roses in the hedgerow, like a white girl's lips, kissing-pink. A skylark rose high, pouring down upon him its bubbling song.

Then he rose, and his gaze surmounting the yellow and white screen of cow parsley and gorse, he briefly surveyed the fields of wind-combed wheat beyond, and those in which the drying hay stood in stacks or lay in pale undulations on the greener sward.

He crossed a couple of fields and came out onto the minor road on which a cartful of hay pulled by a horse was being led by two land girls in fawn-coloured dungarees. The creaking of the wheels died away in the fragrant twilight, leaving only the churring of the nightjar and last cooing of the pigeons. The sun was fading with the green and gold of the fields, the trees etched against the last light; in the west the sky was pearly pink.

He met the main road and ten minutes later came within view of the camp gates, and was surprised to see two jeeps parked, and, to his dismay, an MPs' lorry. There were no MPs to be seen, but as he got within fifty yards, he saw the two guards were talking with three other men, one of whom was Sergeant O'Rourke. One of the sentries spotted him and spoke urgently to the sergeant. The next thing he knew, they were advancing, rifles raised and pointing at him. He froze in fear. The urge to run fought within him, but his mind held him rigid; he knew he wouldn't get more than ten yards before a bullet took him in the back.

The sergeant advanced, the pistol that hung from its lanyard drawn and held before him. When he was three yards from Grover, he barked:

"Grover Carson, you are under arrest for murder, you follow these men back into camp now, y'hear, so's I can read you yer rights. Make a run fer it and I'll shoot you down like the dawg you is."

He took Grover roughly by the forearm, igniting the pain in his ribs, and began to frog-march him towards the camp gates. He said, under his breath:

"You're gonna swing fer this, nigger. Sure as God made them little green apples, you's gonna swing fer this."

CHAPTER TWENTY-NINE

He'd been out since Bob Alder the butcher had lowered the awnings on his shop and Mr France, Em's father, had brought in the wooden trays of marrows, carrots and potatoes, and the heat of the day still lay heavy and soporific over the town, confined between the terraces, but according to that morning's *Chalford Echo* there were still three more hours before blackout. Would he be able to stay on his feet for those three hours? Tom Dawkins wondered, bending to massage the pain that was spreading up the front of his thigh.

He leaned back against the wall of the Primitive Methodist chapel and lit a Woodbine. It was the first he had smoked since coming out. That was a measure of the anger he felt for that blond American redcap, an anger that had driven him out of doors and rather than abate had festered in the open air. And the images his mind played back to him, of silhouetted forms advancing into a haze of desert, of human body parts lying like the discarded belongings of fleeing refugees, of men emerging from brewed-up tanks consumed by flames, and, worst of all, the piercing screams of Jack Ferris as he was squashed beneath the tracks of the tank, had served to stoke his anger to the restless thing it was, itching to discharge itself in some cathartic act.

He gratefully accepted the support the wall of the chapel afforded and watched the smoke from his cigarette disperse. He had been walking for an hour, covering the town, speaking to the occasional passer-by, including Dan Squires, the garage mechanic, who asked if he knew anything of Eric Climpson.

He made no mention of the fact that he had seen Mrs Climpson that morning at the war memorial, bent like a willow in a storm with spasms of grief. Either she knew something definite, or that uncertainty that was perhaps worse had overcome her. But now he had something on his mind of even more moment than the fate of his friend.

When he received his call-up papers, America was still neutral. And while they were fighting for their lives, their loved ones, in the desert, Crete or Italy, thousands of pampered Yanks were strutting about their streets doling out nylons and seducing their women.

Was this the price we had to pay? We might not be able to win the war without them, but we could keep the Germans at bay, and the Russkies would bleed them white on the eastern front and maybe even beat them. If this is what they were about it was better Churchill had never invited them. What was the difference, Nazis or Yanks?

He thought back to the first time he had really seen Emily. He hardly knew her, save as the daughter of Mr France, the grocer. She was standing with Joyce Foster outside the Gaumont looking at stills from the picture. He even remembered the picture; it was 'Lost Horizon'. He recognised Joyce, but not the girl she was with. And then they started down the steps, discussing the relative merits of Ronald Colman and Gary Cooper.

Perhaps it was the contrast with the lumpen Joyce that brought out that quality in her friend, that blonde lissom grace that made her seem almost ethereal, as if she were floating down the street, wafted on the breeze. There was nothing of weight, of form, about her, so that even her skin seemed petal-thin and diaphanous.

And then they were in front of him, and he reaching for his cigarettes, speaking to Joyce, trying to appear nonchalant, offering them both a Player's.

"And who's your friend?"

The words exploded from him as if they were the climactic, and damning, question of an interrogation. Her smile was vaguely nostalgic, perhaps a little wistful like one remembering a long-dead loved one, but as the left corner of her lip moved upwards, he saw that they were not lips made for smiling, or talking, but for kissing. And that hair, with its impossible lightness and delicacy, that he longed to tease through his fingers like a freshly washed fleece.

And what was it all for, the pain, the suffering and the fear, if not for her? Perhaps he should have realised their separation, and the difference in him that was the product of war, would draw them apart. But he had always regarded what they had as something permanent. He knew she had travelled from him in his absence, although he did not know how far. But he possessed both the determination to fight for her, and, co-existing uneasily with it, the belief that he, who had fought to save the country, and the lives of those like her, should not have to.

When he had been with her by the river it was as if they were strangers. He had not known how to talk to her. He did not know how to judge what she told him. Was that some change in her, or the result of what had happened to him? But if he did not believe her, either silently in his own heart or with a frank accusation, there was no future for them. And after all he had been through, he did not think he could face a future without her. What else was there for him: to work on the farm, in the face of the mute frustration of his father who would never feel able to voice the thwarted future he contemplated in the comparison of the son who had gone away to war and the one who had come back; to give his orders to the silly land girls who laughed at him behind his back? No, he had to have Em, and if that meant accepting what she told him without further enquiry, he was happy to make the bargain.

He had not come out looking for Schultz to interrogate him as to what he had got up to with his girl, he had come out to warn the American off, and make sure Em would have no further distractions from the life he had planned for them.

He knew American MPs patrolled the town on the night when the blacks were allowed out. This he had learned from Constable Reg Anstruther, who he had waylaid outside the police station.

He had been doing a circuit across the green by the war memorial, along the high street, then past the Gaumont and the Astoria, reasoning the cinema and dance hall would be prime destinations for the blacks, and taking in the Swan and Black Bull on the way. So far he had seen small groups of blacks hanging about, waiting in the queues for the cinema and dance hall, and had but one sighting of the white helmets the MPs wore. There had been two of them scanning the queue to the dance hall, but both were dark.

His leg aching, Tom subsided onto one of the benches by the stocks. He rubbed vigorously at his thigh. Perhaps it would have been better had he done this at the outset, waiting for the Yankee redcaps to pass him. If they were patrolling the town, they were sure to pass this way.

And he hoped the blond Yank would be on his own. He had assumed this to be the case, naively expecting they would behave in the same fashion as a British bobby. But of course, even redcaps often went around in pairs, and he had no plan to deal with a group of them.

Tom had to wait twenty minutes before he caught sight of two men in uniform with white helmets and cross belts crossing the road towards Hopkins Street and the allotments that had been the public park before the need to 'dig for victory'. One was tall and dark, the other was tall and blond. He rose, rubbing his thigh to relieve the cramp, and set off in pursuit.

He felt frustrated that there should be two of them. He was sure he could handle Schultz on his own but did not want to have to confront two men armed with truncheons and pistols; men who, by virtue of their calling, knew how to handle themselves. Would they stay together, being ordered to patrol in twos for reasons of safety? On the other hand, he had seen them walking about singly.

He crossed the road, cursing the cobbles for the pain in his leg, following them at a distance of one hundred yards. He stayed behind them at roughly this distance, allowing them to turn corners and then speeding up until he was at the corner, looking around to make sure they were still in sight, and waiting again until the requisite distance separated them.

For the next half hour, he followed this routine, going through the square, up Simpson Lane and past the Gaumont, now minus its queue, and returning again to the green. The Americans went up Charles Street, and stopped briefly for a smoke outside the Astoria, as if debating whether to enter. But they moved on, and catching sight of a pair of blacks, they walked ostentatiously down the centre of the pavement towards them. The blacks stepped off the pavement, and the shorter man held out an arm to stop them. There followed a brief altercation before the MPs issued a dismissal and the blacks went on their way.

Now in considerable pain from his leg, a fact which only increased Tom's anger, he followed on, wondering for how much longer he could maintain a pursuit that appeared fruitless. As he followed the redcaps past the queue for the chip shop he was hailed by Joe Harper, who he had gone to school with, and who suggested they 'go to the Bull' and celebrate his leave. Tom was tempted to give up the pursuit, the desire to subside onto a settle almost overwhelming. But he knew he had to speak to the American and warn him off Em as soon as he could, and this might be his best opportunity.

He was vacillating between these alternatives when, from the periphery of his vision, he saw the Americans stop, the tall blond slap the other on the forearm and gesture down Landless Lane, and the two parted. Feeling a burst of exhilaration he declined Harper's offer, and crossed the street, conscious of only a peripheral sense of his own churlishness.

He followed the American for two more streets, increasing his pace as much as he was able to catch his quarry up. Then the MP turned into Charles Street and stopped and drew back into the doorway of Dawson's Tobacconist's, drawing a pack of cigarettes from the top pocket of his tunic and lighting up. He stood staring down the street in the direction of the Astoria ballroom, like some private eye in a Hollywood movie.

Tom hobbled across the street, so that he was on the same side as the tobacconist's, determined, for some reason he could not explain, to come upon the American by surprise. He rehearsed in his mind what he was going to say, repeating the words he had used many times in his head, but which now started to elude him, breaking up like so many Scrabble letters tossed into a box. As he approached the doorway, he could see nothing of his quarry save the edge of his helmet, shoulder, arm and white belt, and the smoke from his cigarette. Tom's stomach knotted, while the anger that had begun to seep away from him under the influence of his tiredness charged his body with a renewed energy.

He was little more than a yard away when the Yank, hearing his footsteps, turned to face him. He was tall, good-looking in a haughty, officer-like way, and with a tan as if he, and not Tom, had spent the last year in the desert. Tom stopped, planting, almost stamping with his bad leg that throbbed with the pain. The Yank turned on him a look of enquiry that seemed to mock him as if he was some inferior being. His lips cracked to reveal white teeth.

"Larry Schultz?"

"Whaddya want, buddy?"

The man's hand made an abortive move towards the truncheon in his belt, but the smile that bordered on contempt showed he had judged Tom to be no threat. Maybe, Tom thought, he considered him some poor local trying to cadge a cigarette. The anger flared again.

"You Schultz?"

"Yeah, what of it?"

"I'm Tom Dawkins."

"Who's Tom Dawkins? Don't mean nuthin' to me."

"I hear you bin seein' my gal, Emily France."

"Oh, Emily."

A smile appeared on the American's face. The sort of smile Tom didn't like.

"I hear you bin pesterin' her."

Again, the American's hand made a slight movement towards his belt, but he clearly decided this opponent did not merit the drawing of the truncheon. Tom imagined he could smell burning: the pork roast aroma of a man caught in a burning tank.

"I wouldn't say that," said Schultz. He gazed down at Tom's right leg, which was now beginning to tremble involuntarily. Again, the same contemptuous smile.

"What would you say?"

"My advice to you, buddy, would be to just walk away."

Was it Tom's imagination or was there a barely perceptible pause before the word 'walk'?

"I don't want none of your advice, and I ain't your 'buddy.'"

"Well, I'd say as how she come to me for somethin'… somethin' she couldn't get hereabouts."

Tom had to fight to resist asking what that 'something' was.

"On your way," the American advised, with a sneer. "You're missin' valuable drinkin' time."

Was that what he thought of him? That he was some local drunk?

"You bin pesterin' my Em. And it's gotta stop, do y' hear?"

"Don't threaten me, you Limey sonafabitch."

Who did he think he was? Did he think he was in charge here? In their country?

"I won't have it, y' hear."

"Yeah? And what you gonna do about it?"

"I just won't have it, y' hear?"

"You already said that."

The American scanned Tom Dawkins from head to foot, the same contemptuous sneer tugging on the corner of his mouth. Tom's fist balled, his bicep muscles tightened. But the American was speaking again.

"But if you want to know the truth, I'll tell you. I owe you that much, I guess. And I owe her."

There was malice now in that long, lazy drawl; that which had been homely and affable in the dialect banished, the words manufactured of venom and, maybe some bitterness.

"She come to me, see. She come to me."

"What for?"

"Whaddya think? You say I bin pesterin' her? She's bin pesterin' the life outta me, but I don't want nuthin' more to do with her, see. But she still comes to my camp, beggin' and cryin'. You her fella, out in the desert?"

"Yeah."

"Yeah, well, I tell ya, she ain't bin thinkin' of you overmuch lately, buddy."

Here he dropped his cigarette stub onto the pavement and screwed it out with his hobnailed boots.

"Well, I'm back now," Tom said, painfully conscious of how ineffectual he sounded.

"I guess you is."

The contempt was overt now. Tom's fist balled and he felt the nails biting into his palms.

"But I'm at liberty to tell you that you'll have no competition from me."

The smile like a snarl.

"That's good."

"Yeah, ain't it. 'Cos I don't want nuthin' more to do with her, see."

"Good."

"Yeah… 'cos I's had what I wanted."

Tom's whole body tensed. He felt the blood rush to his temples, a roaring in his ears. His head swam as if he were about to faint.

The Yank went on, clearly now enjoying himself.

"Ain't you worked it out yet? Well, if you didn't give that gal what she's bin askin' fer afore you went to Africa, I got in there afore you, son. And right pleasant it was, though she didn't know a whole lot about what she was meant to be doin'... but now she do, so I guess I done you a real good favour there."

"What?"

"You Limeys sure is slow on the uptake."

The American barked a short contemptuous laugh and went on:

"And you know, if'n she hadn't thrown herself at that nig..."

The punch caught Schultz off guard, but he still managed to avoid most of the impact, arching his back, riding the blow, which impacted on his chinstrap, and falling back onto the sill of the shop with the rim of his helmet catching on the metallic 'Capstan' sign. As the helmet fell to the ground Schultz was up in a flash, catching Tom by surprise and drawing his truncheon. Tom's left hand clamped down upon the American's forearm, preventing him raising the weapon.

Tom charged Schultz, pushing him back against the facade of the shop, driving his back into the corner of the sill. As the American tried to reach for his pistol, Tom switched his grip from right to left hand, so that Schultz was now free to use the truncheon. The American, his mouth contorted into a snarl, pushed Tom back, and swung his arm to deliver a blow. As the truncheon swept towards him Tom's instinct told him he had no time to manufacture a full punch, and he delivered a short arm jab with minimal backswing, into the American's midriff. Schultz was momentarily winded, the truncheon halted in its progress, the arm that held it sagging down. Tom drew back a little to give himself room and then unleashed a punch that had all the weight of his fury behind it, that caught the American full on the jaw, splitting his lip, and he fell backwards, striking his head on the corner of the windowsill. The truncheon clattered to the ground, and the arm that had wielded it lay enervated.

Briefly Tom stood, impotent and frustrated above the prone body of his opponent. His fury was unabated and still longed for something to vent itself upon. But the American lay still, unconscious. Blood seeped from a cracked lip, and there was a rosy tinge to his blond hair. Helmet and truncheon lay on the pavement.

Tom, his legs planted and his hands still raised in vain fists, began to feel the stupidity of his position. He glanced about him. At the far end of the street, crossing and with his back to him was an ARP warden, helmet disappearing round the corner. The American MPs might soon be on the scene. He didn't want to be caught by a group of them and sustain the sort of beating they had recently handed out to one of their blacks.

With one last baleful glance at the victim at his feet, he moved off nursing his hand, and as swiftly as he was able, and becoming newly conscious of the ache in his thigh, crossed the street, and made for home.

CHAPTER THIRTY

The pain was thrust into Grover Carson's oblivion. It stabbed at him with multiple points and from all directions at once as if he were being assaulted by a whole battalion of bayonets. His arms were seized and all but wrenched out of their sockets. His body hung limp, dragged by those arms, and in an arena of pain. He had never known, even after the beating he had received outside the pub, that pain could come in quite so many forms. There were stabbings, sometimes by tiny needles, singly or in clumps as if a porcupine were being pressed into his torso, sometimes by bayonets or lances, and then there was the constant numbing pain, sometimes cramping like that which held his head in a vice, sometimes glowing as if that part of his body were being toasted over an open fire.

This was what they had done to him, the men who met him at the gate to the camp and, when shouts went up that the nigger was there, those others that came running, some with truncheons at the ready, others only their fists and boots. He passed out, coming round briefly to a consciousness of being hauled through a metal door, a cold, dark cell, with a low bed and a bucket covered by a cloth in the corner, and the cold gritty concrete upon which he was thrown down.

They dragged him through the door and along the corridor. He tasted blood in his mouth, which felt empty of teeth. His left eye was all but closed; that was the one that had been damaged by the blond MP, but it was now so bad he could see nothing out of it but a chink of hazy artificial light.

"You're gonna be interviewed by Lieutenant Beston, nigger, so you'd best tell the truth, y' hear."

Beston was the platoon commander of the MPs.

"Don't make no difference anyhow," said the other, whose breath reeked of stale tobacco, "they's gonna string you up good and proper, and I just hope I's gonna be there so I can throw somethin' at you while you's a-hangin'."

He spluttered a vile-smelling chuckle.

They pulled him through another door into a room with a desk and three chairs. He was thrust down upon one of the chairs. There were two snowdrops in the room, apart from the guards that had brought him in. Both, one squat and swarthy, the other tall, pallid, with glasses, stood with their backs to the wall.

Grover's mind, stunned both by the beating and the startling turn of events that led to it, tried desperately to work out what it could be they thought he had done. He tried to clear his throat, that tasted coppery with blood, before asking them what he was supposed to have done, but at that point an officer, with a round face and flat nose that radiated pugnacity, entered the room, glanced at him with undisguised hostility, then swept round the table and drew up the other chair. A captain, portly and balding and carrying a writing pad, entered in his wake, and drew up a chair sitting at right angles to Grover and the first man, before drawing a ballpoint pen from his jacket. The first man barked:

"Right, let's git down to it. I'm First Lieutenant Beston, commander of this here platoon, and I find that one of ma men has been murdered, and I'm damned if I ain't gonna get to the bottom of it right here and now in this here room, you hear me? So you better answer my questions and you better answer them quick and true, and no shilly-shallyin', you hear?"

Grover could only nod, an action that sent his head spinning and made him feel, for a brief second, as if he were about to pass out.

"So let's start by you tellin' me where you was this evenin' from… say, six 'til you was caught walkin' into the compound by my men."

The man sitting on Grover's right started to scribble on his pad in a kind of shorthand.

"Shouldn't the suspect be advised of his rights, sir?" asked the tall, fair MP who had until this time been staring fixedly at the ceiling lights as if neither Grover nor the lieutenant were present.

The lieutenant rose from his seat with an ominous deliberation, and stood facing the MP, his head right back on his neck so that he could stare into his face.

"Deacon, isn't it?" said Lieutenant Beston. "Well, I ain't in the habit of askin' the opinion of privates when I'm conductin' an examination, you hear? This is one of our own that's been killed, and there ain't nobody on this whole goddam base but thinks this here nigger done it. And what's more I understand that the deceased was your personal friend. So don't you go givin' me a mouthful of legal rights. There ain't no Article 31, there ain't no 5th or 6th Amendment in this room when one of our own has been murdered, you understand me!"

"Sir," said the tall man, still gazing fixedly at the light fittings, "it's just that any failure to do so might compromise any conviction, especially if he doesn't know who he's suspected of killing, sir."

Meanwhile Grover was wrestling with the intelligence that he was suspected of having murdered an MP.

"I will not be told how to conduct an interrogation by one of my subordinates! You swallowed some legal textbook or what? Goddam it! One more word from you and you are on a charge, you hear me!"

"Yessir."

The lieutenant fell into his seat in an emphatic fashion.

"As if he doesn't know who we 'suspect' him of killin'. For the record, Carson, it's Private Larry Schultz of the Military Police. So let me advise you of your 'rights,'" he said with heavy sarcasm.

"You do not have to answer my questions or say anything. Anything you say or do can be used as evidence against you in a criminal trial, got it? You have the right to talk privately to a lawyer before, during and after questioning, and to have a lawyer present during questioning. The lawyer can be a civilian you arrange at your own expense, or a military lawyer detailed at no expense to you.

"But let me tell you before you goes gettin' any ideas of counsel and amendments to the constitootion into that black head of yourn. Those things are fer people that has somethin' to hide, you understand, guilty people. People with nuthin' to hide don't need no lawyer. People with nuthin' to hide ain't got no reason not to answer simple questions. You don't answer our questions and I'll want to know why. Because these fancy rules ain't fer niggers that murders MPs. This is just you and me and these here men, and we want the truth out of you, and we's gonna git it one way or the other. So I'm gonna ask you here and now, and you better think good and hard about your answer… Don't you write that last bit down, you hear?"

These latter words were directed at the clerk sitting on Grover's right hand.

"Yes, sir," Grover croaked.

"Do you understand your rights, Carson?"

"Yes, sir, I think so, sir."

"You think so. Yes or no?"

"Yessir."

"Do you want a lawyer? Think carefully now."

"N…o."

Grover was not sure if the answer he was giving was the correct one. It was certainly the one the lieutenant wanted to hear, but was it best from his own point of view? However, he feared the response to the affirmative more than he feared any nebulous adverse consequences to his decision.

"At this time, are you willing to discuss the offence under investigation and make a statement without talking to a lawyer?"

"I... I guess so."

"Good. You sign or make yer mark on this here waiver certificate."

The lieutenant produced a form from the pocket of his tunic, placing it on the table, smoothing down the creases. He thrust a pen into Grover's hand. The latter extended his right arm, but the fingers were numb and unable to grip the implement, which slipped down between thumb and forefinger. He reached for it with his left hand, staring all the while at the paper, which consisted of a series of boxes headed 'Rights warning procedure waiver certificate'.

"Sign at the bottom if yer can. Where it says, 'Signature of interviewee.'"

"I... I don't think I rightly can, sir."

"You refusing to sign!"

"No, sir."

"Don't make no difference anyhow. You've stated you understand your rights and have orally waived your rights. Give that here!"

The lieutenant snatched up the paper and scribbled something on it.

"So let's hear it, Carson, where you bin since you left your compound? Give it me straight now."

Grover had to fight to reply. The fear that gripped his chest only served to exacerbate the stabbings that were provoked by any attempt to expand his lungs.

"I... I went for a walk, sir."

"Why of course, you went for a walk," the lieutenant mocked. "'Cos you's in England now you can behave like some country gentleman. You sayin' you didn't go into town like the other niggers?"

"No, sir."

"And why not, pray?"

Grover didn't want to say he was afraid to do so. It was too demeaning, and he doubted it would be believed in any event.

"I... I didn't want to drink, sir... I just wanted to take me for a walk in the fields."

"You niggers... You think we's stoopid, boy!"

"I did," Grover croaked. "Can... can I have a drink of water?"

"No, you cannot have a drink of water. A week ago you had a fight with Private Schultz outside that pub – what's it called, the Black Bull, ain't that so?"

"It weren't no fight, sir."

"What in God's name was it then?"

"He come an' arrested me."

"What fer?"

"Sir, I don't rightly know... It may be he says we was improperly dressed, but that weren't the real reason—"

"You sayin' one of my men – a man that's now in the morgue – was lyin'? You got the nerve to blame a dead man!"

The lieutenant was halfway across the table now, red in the face and with spittle flying from his lips.

"No, sir... I don't say he was lyin'. I guess he had good reason to arrest me fer somethin'."

"Well, what the hell you talkin' about then?"

Grover didn't know whether to tell the lieutenant of the fact that O'Rourke had seen him dancing with the English girl and had told Schultz, who was sweet on her. If they knew he had been dancing with a white girl, it would only make it the worse for him. So he simply said:

"I dunno, sir."

"You dunno. And is it true you resisted arrest on that occasion? Remember I can git me witnesses to prove it and it'll go the worse fer you if yer shown to lie."

"I... I guess I did, sir."

"Yes, I guess you did. You was seen throwin' a punch at Private Schultz, that right?"

"I..."

Grover found himself looking at the tall MP who had spoken earlier, in the most forlorn of hopes that in that direction some relief from his nightmare might lie. But the man stood impassive, staring resolutely at the ceiling lights.

"Don't look at him!" the lieutenant bawled, showing his teeth. And Grover thought of 'Mack the Knife'. And he keeps them pearly white.

"I didn't throw no punch."

"You's lyin', nigger, and remember I can prove it." There was a smile of cruel satisfaction on the mouth that showed the shark's teeth. "You threw a punch at him and you threatened him with a broken beer bottle, ain't that right?"

"No, sir, that were..."

He was about to say that was Leroy but didn't want to get the other man in trouble.

"That was what?"

"I didn't threaten him with a beer bottle, sir, and I didn't throw a punch. I raised ma hands to defend myself."

"So you intended to resist arrest and throw a punch?"

"No, sir, I... I didn't know why I was being arrested."

"But you just said you'd been informed you wus bein' arrested for bein' improperly dressed."

"I... I can't rightly remember."

"And you's a boxer, ain't yer?"

"I do box, sir."

"Sure you do. So you raised your hands. Well, I'm sayin' you threw a punch and resisted lawful arrest by a military policeman. And so he had to use force to arrest you. Lawful force, ain't that right? And after that you bore that man Schultz a grudge, and now a week later, when you niggers is allowed back on the town, you goes lookin' fer him and you finds and kills him, ain't that right?"

"No, sir... I never seen him."

The lieutenant's doughy face seemed to glow with an inner satisfaction and a carefully nurtured malice.

"We got evidence, boy. We got ourselves a doctor can say Schultz was killed by bein' beaten and punched... punched hard. Ain't no ordinary punch can kill a man, you understand. That's the punch of a man who's a boxer. Ain't nobody else had reason to kill Private Schultz. Nobody but you, boy, so you might as well admit it."

"I... I wasn't there, sir."

Despite himself Grover's voice took on a pitiful pleading tone as he realised the situation he was faced with. And all the while the man on his right kept scribbling away, each symbol seeming to serve to incriminate Grover the more. It was as if every stroke of the pen were digging his grave.

"You wasn't where?" the lieutenant asked, in a sneering, insinuating tone.

"I dunno."

"Where?"

"I… I dunno where."

"Yes you do, boy."

Again, the smile of satisfied malice, as if Grover had been caught out in something.

"I was with my friend, nowhere near…"

"Nowhere near where it happened, that what you wus goin' to say?"

Grover looked around him, forlornly seeking a means of escape. His heart was racing, and he was leaking sweat from his armpits and groin.

"No, I…"

"How you know where it happened if you wasn't there?"

"I… I was walkin' in the fields with a friend, he can tell yer."

"This here friend, he wouldn't be another negro by any chance, would he?"

"Yes, sir."

"Well, fancy that… 'Course he's gonna say you was somewhere else."

"His name's Private Errol Gideon, and he wus with me the whole time."

"He swear to that?"

"Sure… Well, not with me the whole time."

"So he weren't with you the whole time."

"Well, most of that time… We just sat and talked then he gone off to join the others in town."

"And how do you know what time that was, boy? If you didn't have nuthin' to do with the killin' of Private Schultz, how you know what time he was killed, eh?"

"I dunno… I was…"

"I think you do know, boy. I think you's lyin' through yer teeth."

Not that Grover had many teeth left to lie through.

"No, sir... It were just afore I walked back to the camp and they grabbed me."

"Well, it don't matter none anyways, 'cos nobody's gonna believe the word of a nigger friend of yourn who's gonna say whatever you wants him to say so's you can git away with it. You think any judge gonna believe what he says? If so yer dumber than you looks, boy."

"His word's good as anybody else," he said forlornly, fully aware of how untrue that was. He felt tears start to his eyes, tears of pure frustration, and anger welled up within him that these men might think they were tears of fear.

"That what you think, is it? You think that just 'cos you's arrested you can murder the guy what arrested you? You think you's so mighty powerful now you's in the army and out here where the goddam Limeys don't know what you people are capable of? Think again, mister.

"Ain't nobody gonna believe you now or any time. You better just admit what you done and save us the trouble of a trial, 'cos whatever happens, you're gonna be found guilty as hell. So if you confesses here and now, and we don't have to waste our time with this when we got ourselves a war to win fer these Limeys that can't fight their way outta a paper bag, it might just go a bit easier with you. But if you don't, and you sticks to yer story, that's as full of holes as my pappy's old shed, you're gonna swing fer this, you hear?

"You killed this man, didn't yer?"

Grover hesitated. If he said he had done it, would that mean they wouldn't kill him? He wanted to believe it, but he couldn't. Best to deny it, and then he could talk things over with Errol. Errol would know what to do. He looked up to see the lieutenant staring at him with a satirical smile on his face. The lieutenant had interpreted his indecision as evidence of guilt.

"No, sir, I did not," Grover said, as decisively as his terror would allow.

"Oh yes you did, boy. Ain't nobody else had no reason to kill Schultz but you. Even a dumb nigger can see that. So say it, say you killed him."

Grover shook his head.

"You wanna say it, don't you? I can see it in your eyes. So go on, say it. It'll go the worse fer you if you don't."

"No, sir."

"Well, on your own head be it, Carson. So, just so's you can understand it, you's gonna be charged with the murder of Military Police Private Larry Schultz in – what the hell's this tumbleweed town called…"

"Chalford, sir," said the clerk, not looking up but continuing to scribble away.

"Chalford on the 2nd day of July in the year of Our Lord 1943."

"Take him away."

As the two military policemen grabbed Grover by the forearms and yanked him to his feet with a searing pain tearing his torso, the accused was dimly aware of the lieutenant turning to the clerk, who was still writing, and saying:

"I wanna see that when you're done, son. And you better explain to me everything you've writ."

CHAPTER THIRTY-ONE

Emily France had just finished applying the gravy browning from the cup of warm water to her legs and was slipping into the grey utility suit she had worn to her first date with Larry, when her mother arrived home, banging the front door behind her. She looked at herself in the full-length mirror on the back of her wardrobe door and felt the merest pang at the recollection of her former love. She dismissed it with worldly nonchalance. She must look to her future now.

She had still not bled and was more than ever convinced she was pregnant. She must secure Tom Dawkins and lay with him as soon as she could, and that evening's visit to the pictures would be the first step on what for her would have to be a moving staircase. Was it her imagination or was her belly protruding ever so slightly? It couldn't be because she was overfed. But it might of course be wind; small wonder with all that bloody stodge they had to eat these days. She smoothed down the dress at her hips, her lips canting approvingly. A bit of soot around her eyes and the paste made up of her ground ends of lipstick to provide a bit of rouge, and any doubts Tom might still entertain would be – what was it the Yanks said? – blown away.

She considered whether she should wear lipstick. On the one hand she felt naked without it these days. On the other it might look tarty and serve to confirm any prejudices he still harboured about her. What the hell, she would risk it. Better that she feel good in herself; that way she felt she could overpower his reservations with the confidence in her own attractiveness, and would possess the mental agility to wriggle out of unwelcome situations.

Tarty? Well, how did she know he hadn't been with those tarts in Cairo? And then she surprised herself by wondering whether it mattered to her what he had been up to. It didn't. Just so long as she could hook him and preserve her good name, not have her family disown her, and everyone in town, particularly that bitch April Knight, looking down their prim noses and saying, 'I told you so.'

She was confident of her ability to get Tom into bed in short order, and if she could do so she was sure she could dupe him into thinking the baby was his. She couldn't imagine him counting the weeks on his fingers. And he had no mother to look suspiciously at her stomach and tell him otherwise. He had a father, but men were ignorant in these matters. And farmers were no different; they might know sheep, but of women they knew nothing.

Perhaps if she was pregnant it wouldn't be such a bad thing. As long as she could fool people. Her ma and pa might blame her for jumping into bed with Tom, but if she were to marry him before the kid was born, what did it matter? Even their generation did it. What was more, if she gave birth, she wouldn't have to go into the ATS;

no tinkering with oily engines and driving snooty officers. On the other hand, some of those officers… No, she was being naive, they would just be looking for a bit on the side.

Emily was almost ready. But she should have something to eat before Tom called, even if it was only a slice of bread and dripping. She went downstairs. From the sitting room she could hear the wireless; a man with a deep portentous voice like Valentine Dyall was reading from some murder mystery. Her mother was in the kitchen putting the knitted tea cosy on the pot.

"I've just made some tea, dear. There's enough for two if you've got time."

"Go on. Pour me one, will you."

Emily pulled up a chair to the table, being careful to keep her hands on her lap to avoid the smear of jam on the oilcloth.

Her mother took the other chair and subsided into it with a sigh, easing her right foot out of her shoe and massaging it.

"Have you heard the news?" she asked.

"What news? It's not somebody gone and got theirselves killed again, is it?" Emily said absently.

"Well, it is – not that you need worry about that no more, not with your Tom being back home. No, it's one of them Yanks has got hisself killed. Terrible it is. They come here to fight the Hun and they end up gettin' killed in the street."

"Yanks!" Emily felt herself start back in her chair. She snapped back the question. "What sort of Yanks?"

"Well, what sort is there? I dunno."

"White? Black? Soldiers? MPs? What?"

"I think they said it was one of them policemen."

"What happened? Tell me." She was unable to dissemble or contain her urgency.

"Oh dear Lord," her mother said, putting her hand to her mouth. "You're not thinkin' it was him you was walkin' out with? I never thought..."

"Just tell me what happened."

"Well, it was Mrs Hardcastle told me, you know her as has got the husband that's not all there. And she had it from Tom Curtin's wife, 'cos the constable was talkin' about it in the pub. It were him that found him. Beaten up and lyin' in a shop doorway with his head clean stoved in... Oooh!"

Here Mrs France gave a little start, seeing the effect her enthusiasm for lurid gossip had produced in her daughter.

"I'm sorry, love."

She leaned across the table and attempted to put her palm over Emily's stricken hand as it pawed the oilcloth, but the latter drew the hand angrily away. "You've gone white as a sheet, you have. Listen, don't pay no heed to me. I'm sure it weren't him. Anyway, you got your Tom back now, haven't you?"

"What was he like?"

And when her mother looked blankly:

"What did he look like?" And then as an afterthought, "What was his name?"

"I've got no idea, love. Really. Tom didn't say—"

"Tom!"

"Tom Curtin. And I don't know what he looked like neither."

At this Emily jerked up out of her chair and ran back upstairs, as much out of a desire for some physical expression of her distress as to avoid her mother witnessing that emotion. She banged the bedroom door behind her and flung herself down on the bed.

A few seconds later, her mother knocked tentatively on the door.

"Don't take on so, Em. Look, here's yer tea. Drink up and you'll feel much better."

That was typical of this country. Bombs falling all around, people dying left right and centre, and everybody thinks a drink of tea is going to put everything right.

"I'm sure it wasn't him."

"How do you know!" Emily screamed through the door.

"Oh, Em, I'm sorry. But you got Tom now, remember."

The words of supposed comfort were as a branding iron laid upon her back.

"Just go away, will you!"

Emily's hands fiercely clenched the eiderdown, and then as suddenly she leapt upright and began to stride about the room, her fists still clenching. A panic gripped her, like a weight lying on her chest, making it difficult to breathe.

Her first instinct was to get the bus to the camp and ask if it was him. But the buses were only one an hour, on the hour. She wouldn't have time to get the bus, walk to the camp, then get back home for 6.45 when Tom was to call. By the time she got back he would be long gone. The first feature would be started, and he wouldn't enter the auditorium on his own. She mentally cursed Tom Dawkins.

But she was compelled to pursue him; and, what was worse, she could not afford to incur his displeasure by even so trivial a dereliction as non-attendance at the pictures.

There was also the dread possibility of her turning up at the camp gates, dishevelled and distressed, seeking news of Larry, only to find him marching across the parade ground, staring at her with a smile of pity and contempt. Even if he were not there, the news that she had called, and wanted to assure herself it was not he who had been killed, would get back to him.

Could she tell Tom she was ill, then go and ask someone who might know? Tom Curtin? The constable? But it might leak out. And what would she say? There was also the fact that she could not afford to waste one night with Tom. She needed to hook him as soon as she could. Her hand went instinctively to her belly. If she cried off now, he might think she was lukewarm about resuming their relationship. Oh damn! She stamped her foot.

And then she began to think that perhaps her mother was right after all; she was frightened for no cause. After all there were... well, she did not know how many American MPs there were. There might be hundreds. On the other hand, why would they want hundreds of MPs here? She did not know. She did not know why Larry and those others were here. There was so much she was ignorant of!

Her mother was probably right and she had got herself into a state over nothing. But still, she felt uneasy. Damn that Tom Dawkins. If it hadn't been for him, she could have gone to the camp. She felt uneasy, not only, she thought, because of her fears for Larry. There was something else. But it remained tantalisingly out of her reach.

CHAPTER THIRTY-TWO

By the time Tom Dawkins called at 25 Cavendish Lane, Emily was composed. She had had a cup of tea, and a slice of bread and jam. When the knock came, she mentally girded herself to greet Tom with all the enthusiasm she could muster.

That she did with a swift kiss on the cheek, seizing him by the arm and dragging him into the sitting room where her father sat reading the newspaper, Eric was fiddling with the dial on the wireless, trying to get dance band music, and her mother, the only one who knew of her distress, was fussing about the table and behaving with such excessive complaisance to the new arrival as must, Emily reflected, arouse suspicion.

"Hello, Tom," said her father. "How're you doin'?"

"Not so bad, Mr France."

"Terrible shame about General Sikorski and them Poles, gettin' theirselves killed in a plane crash."

"Oh yeah."

"Do you want a cuppa, dear?" her mother asked.

"No thanks, Mrs France. We gotta be away if we're gonna catch the show."

"What yer gonna see, lad?" Mr France asked.

"*We Dive at Dawn* with John Mills and Eric Portman."

"Oh yeah, John Mills. He's very good. Sally likes the old 'uns, don't you, Sal? Robert Donat and Ronald Colman."

"They're not old."

"Well, you young 'uns have yerself a good time. And mind yerselves in the blackout."

Mr France raised his right eyebrow and produced an arch smile.

"We will, Mr France," said Tom, smiling in return, "we know there's not gonna be any lights showin' when you're on duty."

"Woe betide any who are, son, woe betide 'em."

As soon as they were over the doorstep, Emily took Tom's arm in a fiercely proprietorial grasp, and they walked off down the street towards Laurel Avenue. For once in their relationship, their habitual roles were reversed: she, the talkative one, remained mute, and he, usually so taciturn, was voluble. He said, speaking with that gruffness, that rasp in his voice, that she did not remember from before the war, as if the desert sand had scoured his throat:

"Seems a shame to be sittin' inside on a night like this."

The air was almost still and lay on them exhausted of the daytime heat, but with a heady perfume of high summer: meadowsweet, lime and the merest hint of cut grass. Testimony to the heat was the melting tarmac at the edge of the road, a smooth black plasticine. The shutters on the shops reflected the declining sun, and in the doorway of Dalton's Hardware, a tortoiseshell cat lay stretched out like an embodiment of the day's lethargy.

"We can go for a walk instead, if you like," she suggested helpfully, although her original plan had been to get him inside the darkened auditorium where there would be no need to make conversation, and with the subtleties of scent and proximity of her body, draw tight the strings that bound him to her.

"No, it's all right. In the desert I would dream of nights like this. I'd dream of grass and trees and the smell of the blossoms."

She was tempted to say, 'and did you dream of me?', but it was too early. She would work up to that.

"Don't they have no grass or trees there?"

"In Cairo they do, and in the Delta. But it's all palm trees and gum trees."

"Sounds lovely, Cairo."

"Well, it don't smell lovely. Smells of spices and what not, but it stinks of camel dung, and everywhere you get mobbed by packs of kids wanting baksheesh."

"What's that?"

"Money off yer. But out there there isn't the... smell of the earth. Here you feel as if the earth beneath you goes all the way to the centre, down to Australia if you dig far enough – that's what they say innit. When I was a kid I'd dig and try to get meself there; dig so long I could hardly stand."

Here there was a slight crack in his voice. But he carried on, speeding up as if to camouflage the emotion.

"Out there it's just a – whaddya call it – veneer. And in the desert, there's plants like, but it's like it begrudges them life, where here, there's life everywhere, earth and insects and you can put yer hands in and part the soil and see the water come up, and you know there'll be life."

Emily's heart sank within her. Was this what life with Tom Dawkins was going to be? Talking about the filthy, dirty earth as if it were something wonderful. She should never have got herself mixed up with a farmer. But now she had no other choice.

"Lor, Tom, I never knew you talk so much. Is this what that desert's done to you?"

He turned and said:

"It's what you've done to me, Em."

He smiled, shyly, but as if both embarrassed and proud at the same time. He had never looked so gauche, even when she first set eyes upon him. How could a man go through a war and still look so naive?

But she knew she had him now. A glow spread through her that was tempered only by her contempt of him. And also something else: that same sense of misgiving, even of dread she could not shrug off. But she must drive home her advantage.

"I hope none of them Egyptian women caught your eye out there, what with all that belly dancin'."

For a second he did not reply, and she feared she may have struck the wrong note, anticipating a response to the effect that she had played while the cat was away, so why should not he? Instead, he simply said, with that same overgrown schoolboy smile:

"You know there's nobody for me but you, Em."

He looked away, and it seemed as if his embarrassment was mutating the schoolboy into the man, drying out those plump succulent cheeks with the desert sun, causing them to implode into the cavity between jawbone and cheek, carving little deltas of wrinkle about both eyes, burning the rich chestnut colour from his hair and making him look like a faded photograph of some ancestor of Tom Dawkins.

He said, as if to camouflage his embarrassment:

"But I'm surprised you want to see a film about submariners."

"I'd see anything so long as we can be alone, away from Ma and Da and Eric lookin' at us. I thought we could snuggle up in the back row."

She took him even more firmly by the arm.

"Besides," she said, "ain't it my patriotic duty to watch John Mills and Eric Portman?"

He laughed. They were passing the allotments, where leeks and potatoes sprouted and, behind their wire, chickens squawked and fluffed up their feathers. Emily dimly remembered these plots being thick with sunflowers and hollyhocks and honesty.

She was rudely wrenched out of her reminiscences by the sight of Reg Anstruther, the constable, riding by on his bike. She felt the sudden urge, that for a second appeared irresistible, to launch herself at him and beg him to tell her who the MP who had been killed was. But she could not, and once again cursed the man on her arm.

Instead, she gave way to a different urge, that some part of her grudgingly acknowledged to be akin to a death wish.

"You heard the news?" she asked, a rasp in her voice. The dread trickled down her back, and she was conscious of something loathe in the question.

He snapped back:

"What! It's not Eric... is it?"

"Who?"

"Eric Climpson… His mother hasn't heard from him."

"Oh," she said indifferently. "No."

"What is it then? The Russians…? Everybody says there's gonna be a big battle—"

"No, not that—"

And now it came to it she didn't want to speak at all. Her suspicion, that thing she could not name, and hardly acknowledge even as suspicion, now seemed ridiculous, and if it was Larry… she didn't want to talk about it.

"One of them Yanks. Got hisself killed last night."

"Killed…?"

They were within sight of the end of the cinema queue that stretched like a giant tongue protruding from the marble classicism of the facade.

"How?"

"What do you mean?"

"Well, was he shot or what?"

His response startled her, but the urgency of his questions chimed in with some premonitory feeling that rose like a spectre before her. When she spoke it was tentatively, each word the wary step of a trespasser.

"He got beaten up."

"Where?"

"Here… in town…"

He was remorseless.

"Where in town?"

"I dunno… I dunno, Tom…"

But he was not listening. He turned now to face her, and she was shocked how haggard and drawn he looked – a suffering face, but one guilty in its suffering.

"Who found him?"

"The constable, I think."

"Which one? There's more than one, isn't there?"

For the first time in her life, she felt terror. But did not know its cause.

"Reg Anstruther... Tom... what—"

"I gotta go. I'm sorry, Em. I gotta go..."

And with that he simply turned and walked away from her, and she stood there, watching him hobble off down the street, past the cinema queue, past the faces that were staring at her and must have been thinking he'd stood her up.

She should have walked away, dragging her shame behind her. But she stood stock-still, constructing something of her dread, something that blamed Tom and explained his guilt.

But if Tom was guilty, then the dead man must be Larry Schultz.

CHAPTER THIRTY-THREE

It was after nine o'clock, and the fading light in the western sky silhouetted the Victorian tower that had been built onto the Anglo-Norman church of St Edward's, and from which the Union Jack hung limply in the still air, as Tom Dawkins approached the vicarage.

For the last hour he had been in the police station, a red-brick building that consisted of one reception room and two interview rooms, and a cell large enough to accommodate the one man it was anticipated would have committed a crime at any one time in Chalford.

He waited for forty-five minutes, fortified by two cups of tea, for the appearance of Reg Anstruther. Constable Mason was manning the desk in typically lugubrious fashion and sent baleful glances from beneath his fulsome brows as Tom sat on the settle by the door.

Tom had considered asking Mason for the information he wanted. But he was not confident Mason would tell him anything, he being a stickler for a protocol in which reticence was an integral part. Reg Anstruther was the more approachable, and it was he who had found the body of the Yank MP.

Rumour had it that Reg would turn a blind eye to Bob Alder, the butcher, keeping 'a little something under the counter' for favoured customers. Likewise, his own father when, the previous year, he slaughtered three pigs instead of the permitted two, and Mrs Anstruther found herself cooking bacon and eggs more often than the letter of the law provided for.

Reg would tell him what he wanted to know. The only problem was what questions the constable would ask in return. This was not something Tom had considered when, in a state of distraction, he arrived at the police station to announce that he 'wanted a word with Reg Anstruther' and was not prepared to say what that word was. On being informed that the latter was on patrol, he subsided into the settle and smoked three Woodbines in a row, punctuating each with a series of perambulations the last of which provoked a 'for gawd's sake sit yerself down can't y" from Mason.

His mind, like a spooked horse, indiscriminately racing to and fro, reasoned for his innocence whilst at the same time being confounded by the coincidence that would be represented by that innocence, namely that he had fought with Schultz whilst at more or less the same time another Yank MP was getting his brains beaten out.

But that was just it. He had not beaten the Yank's brains out. They had a fair fight, that was all. He had seen such fights in the desert. The heat, the flies, the fear, it just got to you. He only hit the Yank with one punch. You can't kill a man with only one punch. If you could, half the boxers in the country would be pushing up the daisies. Yes, it must all be a coincidence.

But how could he ask? What excuse would he have for coming to a police station, to ask about the identity of a total stranger? What would he say if Em's dad walked in, fresh from his ARP round, only to see Tom, who was supposed to be at the pictures with her? He was considering leaving and weighing the benefits of doing so against the not knowing, when the door creaked open.

Reg Anstruther walked in and straight to the counter, where he began to speak to Mason, who interrupted him and nodded his head towards the settle. Reg approached Tom with that impossibly wide smile on his pockmarked face, a face that suggested the not-standing-upon-ceremony welcome of a house with ever open door and skimpy pebble-dashing.

"Well, Tom, good to see you, lad. You enjoyin' yer hard-earned rest, eh?"

And then, not receiving the cheery response he had clearly anticipated, the constable asked:

"What can I do fer you?"

"Can we talk?"

"Sure we can," said the constable, not taking the hint and disinclined to move from the spot.

"In private."

"Well, certainly," said Anstruther, although his tone implied the eccentricity of the request.

He led Tom into one of the interview rooms, the one with a view through the sash window to the town hall, its clock catching the last fitful luminosity of the sun.

"What can I do fer you, young lad?" Anstruther asked, pulling back the chair so Tom could sit, with the exaggerated courtesy of the non-combatant for the wounded man.

"I was just passing, like (his excuse was beginning to sound lame already), and I heard that somebody'd been killed yesterday, and I wondered if it was somebody I knew. They said you'd found the body."

Reg Anstruther regarded him with a good-natured smile, the sort of credulous response Tom had anticipated in one in whom the piercing stare of pitiless detection was as foreign as, well, Inspector Maigret or Hercule Poirot.

"There ain't no call for you to worry. It was one of them Yanks. No-one you'd know."

"Well, I did know one or two of them. Just seen them about. Them MPs, I think it was."

"Well, it were one of them MPs now you come to mention it."

"Oh," said Tom, impressed with his own cunning, "I hope it weren't one of them I knew."

"Well, that's war, ain't it. I 'spect you seen plenty in the desert. You don't expect it to happen in yer own town though. But I dare say they gets into fights between theirselves. There was one with our lot in the Black Bull. These MPs – I ain't got time fer them meself, thinkin' they can throw their weight around in m… our town. Right hoo-ha it was, I don't mind tellin' you. But we can't do nuthin'. It's not like the Canadians and Aussies. The Yanks don't let us touch their people, oh no. Law to themselves, they is."

"What did he look like?"

"Who?"

"The dead bloke."

"I dunno. Had all the MP gear on. Typical Yank. Big. White teeth."

Tom wanted to ask if he was blond but did not feel he could go so far in prompting a response.

"Was he outside the pub?" he asked disingenuously.

"No. What makes you think that?"

"You mentioned the pub."

"You got yerself a job on the *Echo* now, Tom Dawkins?"

Tom had indeed considered consulting the *Chalford Echo*, but as it only came out once a week, did not feel he could wait that long.

He smiled with the best counterfeit of innocence he could summon and did not press it further. But thankfully the policeman went on:

"He were in the street. Just outside Dixon's shop."

Tom felt the blood drain from him. He immediately rose in order to hide his discomposure from a policeman who, however credulous and willing to give the benefit of the doubt to people he had known all his life, was not stupid.

"I'd better be on me way."

He turned swiftly to hide his face and made for the door.

"Take care, young Tom," were the words Anstruther left in his wake, containing just a hint of the dubious.

Once outside, Tom had to steady himself by holding on to a streetlamp. He clung to its fluted surface for what seemed a long time, feeling so light-headed he did not trust himself to let go, despite an awareness that he should move on lest Anstruther exit the station.

There was just enough light for him to walk to the vicarage. As he did so, keeping to the verges lest he be surprised by cars, he justified his decision with the reflection that it was not something he could discuss with his father. The latter would ride roughshod over the nuances of morality that conflicted Tom, draw the pipe out of his mouth, trailing spittle, and stab the stem towards his son's chest with the words:

"You keep yer mouth shut. Ain't nuthin' to do with us, and nobody knows different."

It was only as he walked up the vicarage drive, the gravel crackling beneath his boots, newly polished what seemed like a lifetime ago for his date with Emily, and was cheered by the sight of a faint light in the fan window above the door, which meant the vicar had not retired to bed, that it occurred to him that one of the Yank officers was billeted at the vicarage. If he could not talk in private to the vicar he would just have to leave, that was all. He seized the ornate knocker and rapped.

To his relief it was the vicar who opened the door, having doused the light, standing in short sleeves and braces, slippers on his feet, the blackout curtain draped around him.

"Tom Dawkins, isn't it? Are you all right, Tom?"

The vicar's concern told Tom all he needed to know about his physical state.

"I… I'm sorry to call on you so late at night, but I need your help."

"Of course."

"I need to ask you something."

"Do come in."

As he wiped his feet first on the boot-scraper and then the doormat, the vicar went on:

"My wife is upstairs looking after young Arthur."

He must have looked blank for the vicar added:

"The evacuee."

He led Tom into his study and pulled up a button-backed armchair before the lit fire.

"Is the Y... the American in?" he asked.

"Colonel Bellucci? He's up in his room working. We don't see much of him."

The vicar's tone seemed to hint at the fact that the Villiers family was not unduly inconvenienced by the major's absences.

The vicar pulled up a chair opposite Tom.

"But of course, you must have witnessed traumatic events in your time in the desert. Children, they can cry and throw tantrums and we try to comfort them, but a grown man has no such outlet for his emotions, and if he appears distressed we often lack sympathy. He is supposed to 'keep a stiff upper lip'. I am not only willing to listen and bring you what poor comfort I can but am indeed most anxious to do so."

Tom was nonplussed by the vicar's ramblings, but it then occurred to him that Mr Villiers was under the impression he wanted to talk about his wartime experiences. True, he did suffer from nightmares, but it had never occurred to him to discuss them with anybody.

"Can I offer you a cup of tea, Tom?"

"No, thank you."

"Or something a little bit stronger. I myself rarely partake but keep a supply for purposes of hospitality, you understand."

Tom was tempted by the prospect of a whisky but felt that any delay in getting out what he wanted to say would only make it more difficult.

"I'm all right, thank you, Vicar."

"Please feel free to talk."

"Is this like what Catholics do…? I mean, if I said anything to you, it wouldn't get reported?"

"I can assure you, Tom, that in this case anything you say to me will be treated with the strictest confidence."

Having said that, he did not know how to begin.

The vicar said encouragingly:

"What is it that is troubling you? For I see something is troubling you most grievously. Speak freely. Regard me as your friend. I shall endeavour with His assistance, to bring the comfort Our Saviour offers to all suffering mankind, to you."

"What it is… Before I went away, I had this understanding with Em – Emily France, the daughter of the warden. I wanted to make her mine, get spliced an' all."

"Oh yes, indeed, a very pretty girl."

"And… well, I comes back and I starts to hear things… about her and this Yank."

"That she'd been seeing an American serviceman?"

"Yes."

"Ahhhh," said the vicar, as if the story was one with which he was familiar.

"An MP he was, name of Larry Schultz. So I asks her about it and she says no, he was the one what was pesterin' her. They'd just been dancin' the once, and then he follows her about town. And now I was back, I didn't want no more of that goin' on, did I? So I thinks, I'm gonna see this Yank and tell him it's gotta stop.

"So last night I hangs about town and sees if I can see him. 'Cos it was the blacks' night on the town, and them

MPs gotta be on duty. Then I sees him. Hanging about in the doorway of Dixon's the tobacconist. And I goes up to him, see, and I tells him it's gotta stop. And he says it was Em what was pesterin' him, and he didn't want nothin' more to do with her.

"And I was mad by this time, but I didn't do nuthin'. And then he says… This won't go no further, will it?"

"Of course not."

"…he says how, she and him… how they slept together, and he's laughin' at me, sayin' I was too slow, and I should've got in there first… and we had ourselves a fight, and I punched him. Just one punch, and I knocks him out cold. And off I goes.

"And now I'm hearin' how there's a Yank been killed. So I goes to the police station and speaks to Reg Anstruther, and he tells me this Yank's an MP what was found in the doorway of Dixon's… so it's gotta be him, hasn't it?"

"Are you saying," asked the vicar, "that you think you may have killed a man?"

"Well, yes, sir. That's about the size of it. But I can't see how I could've. I mean, I just laid one punch on him. You can't kill a man with just one punch, can you? Otherwise it'd happen all the time, wouldn't it? It don't make no sense."

"I'm afraid it can happen, Tom. I've heard of such cases, rare though they are. I think it may be to do with the way the man falls."

"Not the punch? So I didn't kill him after all?"

Even to himself Tom sounded like a drowning man clutching at a straw.

"I don't say that. The law would still regard you as the

guilty party, even if it may not be murder. It would be manslaughter if you had no intention to kill the man."

"I didn't, I swear it. I just wanted to stop him seein' Em, and then he goes and says what he said, and I thumped him one. Well, any bloke would've done the same, wouldn't they?"

"I'm sure you're right, Tom, but in the eyes of the law you're still guilty."

"So you think I should go and tell Reg Anstruther what I done? Even after I done me duty for King and Country in North Africa. 'Cos if I kept mum nobody'd know any different, would they? They'd just think he fell and 'it his head. Nobody'd know it was me."

"Just you and me and Our Saviour," the vicar said musingly.

Mr Villiers rose and stood with his hand resting on the mantelpiece, poised like a specimen of unheroic but thoroughly English statuary.

"Reflect, Tom. Whether you meant to do it or not – and I'm sure most people would believe you did not – your actions have led to a man losing his life. That is not something that is easy to live with. And live with the knowledge you must, for the rest of your life. That is a great burden for a man. One day he may find it too much to bear, may feel compelled to reveal all. And the later he does so the greater the shock to all who know and care for him. But there is more to it than that, I'm afraid. But before we go into that, how does Emily react to these events?"

"She doesn't know nuthin' about it. Okay, she knows he's dead – she it was what told me – but she don't know that I done it."

The vicar had withdrawn his arm from the mantelpiece and, reaching for his jacket that lay on the back of his chair, was withdrawing a tobacco pouch from the pocket.

"She does not suspect."

Striding to the dining table the vicar picked up a pipe and began to fill the bowl with tobacco.

"No."

"Are you sure?"

"I dunno. When I run away and left her after she told me about it… I dunno."

"Does she care for him, do you think? The dead man?"

The vicar was tamping the tobacco down into the bowl.

"I don't think so. She was just her normal self when we was goin' to the flicks. Laughin' and jokin'."

"So it seems there was nothing serious between them, even if this Larry…"

"Schultz."

"Quite, even if his story were true. Did you believe it, by the way? Was that what drove you to strike him?"

"I dunno."

The vicar was again hunting in the pocket of his jacket before withdrawing a box of matches. He proceeded to light his pipe.

"Yes, I suppose you could have been angry because you believed what he said, and perhaps equally so because of the calumny against your intended's name."

Mr Villiers drew deeply upon the pipe stem as if the fumes were an aid to his cogitations. He went on:

"I'm afraid there is another aspect to this matter which may make your silence upon the subject less viable

– indeed may make it imperative you speak out. As you are aware, Major Bellucci is billeted here, and we heard from him today that the Americans, who regrettably have sole charge of investigating the matter, have a black serviceman in custody, and seem determined that this man, this innocent man given what you've told me, is the guilty party."

"They think this black done it?"

"Apparently there was a fist fight in the Black Bull, and it seems this MP was involved in an altercation with this black soldier, and the conviction of the Americans is that this black went looking for revenge on the first night he was allowed out."

"So he could've done it after all?" said Tom, a different straw appearing within his grasp.

"I don't think so, my boy. As you yourself said, he was found exactly in the spot where you had your fight with him."

"But he could've got hisself up and then this black came upon him."

"Well, that is a possibility, but I think a very remote one. To some extent the American's train of thought is logical. This black was the only man they know of who had a grudge against this Larry… and no doubt his being black made them suspect him the more. And indeed, makes it more likely they will seek to impose the harshest punishment upon him. They will throw him to the lions, I fear, unless something is done to stop it. And you, my dear Tom, are the only person who can do that."

Panic exploded in Tom's head.

"You mean, give myself up to the Yanks? For murderin' one of their own. They'll have me swing for it!"

"No, I don't say that. I don't know what the legal niceties are, but I would think that as you are a British citizen you should be tried by our own courts."

"But either way I'll hang fer it, won't I?"

Tom had risen without any clear intention of what he was to do, desperate to escape the place that had seemed his refuge and that he now found his prison – indeed, his condemned cell.

"No, I cannot say that you will not, but I believe our system of justice is more merciful than that, and you will be given the benefit of the doubt, as one culpable of manslaughter not of murder, and the extreme provocation you suffered at the hands of this man will go in your favour."

Tom subsided back into the chair but was no less distraught. He felt somehow betrayed, and angry at the vicar.

"How can you ask me to do it? You that's known me all me life, and when I come here an'... You're askin' me, when I fought for me country, when I gone out there to that desert and seen me mates blown to pieces, and I gets all wounded and shot up, to give meself up and like as not get a noose put round me neck!"

"No, Tom." The vicar raised a placatory palm. "I do not believe that will happen. But what I'm sure of is that if you don't speak up, an innocent man will be dealt with for this crime, and I have no doubt the Americans will execute him as an example."

"Won't the judge want to execute me as an example?"

Tom felt his voice rise an octave, straining at the pitch of hysteria.

"No, I don't believe so. The example I mean is that of a black American serviceman striking a white one. The actions of a British national are entirely different... Come, Tom, let me pour you a little brandy."

The vicar rose and strode over to a roll-top drinks cabinet, poured the fortifying liquor and offered it to Tom, who accepted meekly and downed it in one swallow that scoured his windpipe and left him gasping.

"Whatever you do should be done with due reflection. I do not ask, let alone require, you to go now to the police station. Think about it. Go home. Ponder what I have said. Discuss the matter with your father. Then come and see me tomorrow morning at whatever time is convenient. Major Bellucci leaves the house at eight. I shall make sure there are no other calls upon my time."

"You'll say nothin' to the Yank major?"

"Nothing. You have my word upon it. And do not neglect to discuss it with your father. He, after all, is your closest relative."

"Thank you, Vicar."

Tom rose to go, steadying himself on the arm of the chair as a wave of light-headedness made him feel as if he were about to black out. It was as if he were experiencing the wound to his thigh once again, but this time he clung on to consciousness.

The vicar took him by the hand.

"Take care of yourself, my son. And seek the guidance of Our Lord in prayer. If you wish, we shall pray now and ask Him to show you the way."

"No, sir... I'll..."

"Of course. Then tomorrow perhaps. In a situation

such as this, it is vital that we endeavour to ascertain His Will. Will you be able to find your way home safely in the blackout?"

"Yes... I'm used to the desert."

With that the vicar took Tom by the hand and said:

"God be with you, my son. Let Him look after you tonight and always."

As the door closed upon him, and Tom Dawkins found the gravel drive crunching beneath his boots, his mind was as numb as an organ whose blood supply has been cut off – white and drained and utterly useless. He walked off along the verge of the road, feeling with his right hand along the dry-stone wall, only dimly aware of the direction in which he was headed.

CHAPTER THIRTY-FOUR

It was nine the following evening that Mr Villiers, having just returned from visiting Martha James, whose son Donald had been killed on Crete, and anticipating an hour or so listening to the wireless before bed, stood at the hall stand divesting himself of his walking cane, overcoat and hat, only to be approached by Major Bellucci. From the stealth and vigour of the approach, the vicar gained the impression the major had been waiting behind the door to the dining room, in ambush.

"Good evening, Reverend," the American said. "Listen, can we talk somewhere… in private?"

The vicar, feeling such a precaution quite unnecessary, whatever one's view of his wife's discretion, since Mrs Villiers retired early these days, to be on hand in the event of any disturbances in the sleep of their evacuees, led the major into the study. He was conscious of a feeling of apprehension.

"Will you take a drink, Major?" the vicar asked,

having convinced himself, perhaps through watching too many American gangster films, that the question was an indispensable preliminary to any conversation with someone from across the pond.

"Thank you, yes. Scotch, if you've got it."

As he pulled back the roll top of the drinks cabinet and reached for the decanter, Reverend Villiers' mind returned to that morning when he and Tom Dawkins had been ushered by a sergeant into the office of the major.

There they had found Bellucci, his close-cropped head with its snowplough of a brow framed by a wall of maps, together with the United States flag, a photograph of President Roosevelt, and a series of lists of personnel with ticks in columns, that may have been duty rosters.

"Well, what can I do fer you, Reverend?" the major growled.

"May we have a word with you, Major… in private, if you don't mind."

Nevertheless, the major looked up sharply, as if conscious of an impertinence.

The major stated:

"I am a busy man, Reverend."

"Oh dear me, yes, Major. Please be assured I would never have dreamt of trespassing upon your valuable time were it not absolutely imperative."

The major, for the first time, regarded Tom, and did so with some suspicion, that drew down his brows and etched runnels of wrinkle at the sides of his grey eyes. The vicar was reminded of a sky before a thunderstorm.

"This is my parishioner, Tom Dawkins, who has performed sterling service for his country in the Western

Desert and suffered grievous wounds. He has come here of his own free will and, I should add, against the express wishes of his family."

The vicar forbore mentioning that that opposition, from Mr Dawkins senior, took the form of the declaration, 'I won't have no son of mine throwin' his life away for some Yankee black', and attempting to lock his son in the farmhouse. To the young man's credit, he was able to overpower the elder and present himself at the vicarage with the asseveration that 'I don't want nobody to suffer fer what I done.'

But even Mr Villiers' conviction of the rectitude of his proposed course quailed before the bleak look of incipient terror on the young soldier's face. The vicar had never so appreciated the literal truth of that old cliché of one's heart melting, and he found tears spring to his eyes. His unmanning was not assisted at this point by his wife exiting the dining room, and, putting down the egg cup and plate she was carrying, grasping the young man by the shoulders and saying in a voice choked with emotion:

"My dear Tom, I am sure that neither you nor any of those other brave boys could have acted with more courage in facing down those Nazis than you do now. It is the bravest thing I've ever seen."

With this, and the merest squeeze of the vicar's arm, she beat a retreat to the kitchen, where young Arthur had commenced howling, "I want jam!" and banging on the kitchen table.

The vicar, who had turned away to hide his own emotion, gave a quick glance at Tom who was standing stricken in best Sidney Carton fashion in the hallway, before guiding him onto the drive.

"If it's a complaint about one of my men I would—"

"No, Major, nothing of that sort, I do assure you. Tom has something to tell you about the assault on the military policeman."

"We got us a nigger in custody fer that, Reverend. You may not have heard."

"Indeed I have," said the vicar, finding, against his will, his hackles rising at the major's throwaway use of the term 'nigger'. It was one thing for the ignorant to talk in such terms, but he felt it was most unbecoming of a representative of the US armed forces. "That is precisely why Tom has come here today. Although I do not say that he would not have come otherwise, you understand. It is precisely to forestall a grave miscarriage of justice—"

"Can you come to the point, Reverend, please."

"You should speak, Tom," said the vicar, glancing at Tom as he stood kneading the brim of his hat. The boy (for so the vicar still regarded him) watched him with the intensity of a dog greedy for any mark of favour.

"Well?" said the major, looking at the young soldier with a resignation that suggested he regarded this being as having been created solely for the purpose of frustrating his work.

"I… I done it," Tom said.

"You done what?" Bellucci barked.

"I killed that MP."

"Well, just how do you think you done that, son?" the major asked, disbelief and sarcasm dripping from every syllable.

"I punched him. Knocked him out. We had us a fight."

"And where and when did this happen?"

The major's tone suggested a confidence he could catch the young man out.

"In the doorway of Dixon's the tobacconist's, about eight o'clock night before last. He was just standin' there."

"And why did you choose to pick a fight with an MP that was standin' in a doorway mindin' his own business, a guy I guess you'd never set eyes on in your whole life?"

"He was makin' up to my gal."

"Makin' up?"

"Pesterin' her. That's what she told me."

"How'd you know he was the one?"

"She described him to me… Blond he was. Name of Schultz."

"And what's the name of this gal?"

Tom hesitated but for only a second.

"Emily… Emily France."

"'Cos, you see… if you's tellin' the truth…"

Here the major rose from his seat and turned his back on them, staring straight into the face of his president on the wall.

"…we gotta check everythin' out… 'cos there's people, people that ain't right in the head – I'm not sayin' you's one of them – that goes about confessin' to things they never done. And we got this nigger locked up, and he's got hisself a good reason to kill Schultz 'cos he had a fight with him no more'n a week before. And you say you never set eyes on this guy before."

In fact, Tom had not said that, but he still nodded meekly.

The vicar asked:

"You don't want to take Tom into custody, Major?"

Major Bellucci turned to face them, a quite uncharacteristic uncertainty on a face the vicar had never known to express anything less than unshakeable confidence.

"Er... no, Reverend. Not... as yet."

"Should we inform the constable?"

"No... I would ask you to tell nobody at this stage."

"But you will appreciate, Major, that we wish to arrange legal representation for Tom."

"Please, Reverend, do nothing for the time being. Let's just keep this between ourselves."

"And Tom can go home?"

"Yes."

"But what do you propose we do about this?"

"What I propose," said the major, a trifle irascible now, "is that we tell no-one about this for the present. I will discuss it with my colleagues in the Military Police and we will speak to you again once we have made our decision."

"Well, this sounds most irregular. Young Tom here has come to you in perfect good faith and laid out the facts of the matter. It seems perfectly clear—"

"Yes, yes, Reverend. Just you do your job and let me get on and do mine."

The vicar left the meeting with a feeling of considerable unease.

"What did he let me go for?" Tom asked as they stood at the parting of their ways by the village green. "Ain't they gonna put me in prison?"

"It seems not. At least not at present. I am sorry I

cannot provide you with the certainty you crave, but that is the way it stands."

When he later discussed the interview with his wife (the vicar had already informed her of the situation and did not consider in any event that the major's injunction should apply to a spouse), Mrs Villiers was of the opinion that Major Bellucci seemed happy for an innocent man to be punished for this crime. The vicar rejected so uncharitable a view of their house guest, but his unease could only increase as a result.

The vicar replaced the silver stopper in the many-faceted crystal decanter, purchased by his great-grandfather who, by all accounts, made considerable use of it, and handed a glass to the major.

"Will you not join me, Reverend?" the major asked in the nearest approach to bonhomie that he had ever displayed in his host's company, although one less charitable than the vicar might reflect that it was Mr Villiers' own whisky he was being generous with.

Indeed, the major's whole demeanour was bizarrely and disturbingly contrary to what the vicar had come to expect from him. The close-cropped aggression with which the major headbutted his way through opposition in the name of the American constitution had mellowed into something that touched on humility. It was unnerving in the extreme, and unnerved the vicar most certainly was as he poured himself an infinitesimally small whisky and invited the major to take a seat. As Bellucci did so, subsiding into it with a creak of complaining timber, the vicar appropriated a wing-backed chair, and looked enquiringly at the American.

The latter took a mouthful of whisky, smacked his lips and began.

"It's like this, Reverend. I bin thinkin' things through. You know how things stand in this here town. Relations between us Americans and the townsfolk ain't good. I don't blame anybody fer that. Seems to me when any town gets a foreign army camped on its doorstep there's gonna be friction. But we don't want those problems gettin' any worse."

"Oh, that's nothing more than high spirits, Major. I think you underestimate the goodwill between your servicemen and our townsfolk. Your men have gone out of their way to tell me how much they enjoyed the hospitality our ladies have been able to provide. It was only at Evensong that—"

"You forget, Reverend, that there's been two fist-fights in the pub this month. And your local farmers have taken to stampedin' their cattle through my men's tents. That's more than high spirits. For the sake of the war effort, we have to try and improve things. Neither of our governments is gonna want the situation to get worse."

The major took another sip of whisky, that rippled a throat supported by formidable buttresses of neck muscle, pursing his lips before proceeding.

The vicar was regarding him closely and was beginning to wonder whether there was not something almost shamefaced about the constitutionally gung-ho major.

"Fact is, Reverend, we have us in custody a black who got hisself into a fight with the dead MP on account of him, the nigger, molesting a white woman."

"Molested a white woman? I heard nothing of this."

"I dare say you ain't, Reverend. But it's a fact. And this black, he's handy with his fists. An ex-boxer. Anyone'll tell you that. The MP tries to arrest him fer it, the black resists and the MP has to use force to restrain him. That's what the fight in the pub was about. You see how this gives this nigger one mighty grudge against Schultz. And if anyone can kill a man with one punch it's a nigger as is handy with his dukes."

"I beg your pardon?"

"Been trained to box, Reverend. This nigger he's a disruptive influence. A danger to his colleagues and to your congregation, particularly the women. The thing is, Reverend, these blacks they ain't got no control where white women is concerned. They just got animal instincts, and they ain't learned to control them, you know what I mean? The last thing we wants is fer him, or any of 'em fer that matter, to… make advances to your good ladies. That's gonna make things a whole lot worse, and our masters in London and Washington ain't gonna be impressed. Fact of the matter is, we thinks an example's gotta be made… You see what I mean?"

"I'm not altogether sure I do, Major."

The major sighed.

"We thinks we should keep this just between ourselves and let things as they are."

The vicar rose from his seat and strode over to the French windows from which he had a view of the lupins and peony roses in the borders. He did not turn to face the major (in fact he was not sure if he could ever bring himself to face the man again) as he said:

"Are you seriously suggesting we allow an innocent man to be punished, Major?"

"First off, Reverend, we ain't sure he is innocent. He's as sure as hell ain't innocent of pawin' white women."

The vicar prided himself on being a mild-mannered man whose experience of the emotion of anger was limited and not at all recent. But he now found the emotion being stoked within him, and he was distressingly conscious of the need to prevent it gaining mastery of him.

"Well, perhaps all of us are guilty of something, Major. But the question here is his guilt or innocence of the killing of this Schultz. That is all that matters in this case."

The major smiled a warped smile that was like a wince from a blow.

"You gotta look at the bigger picture, Reverend."

The vicar was conscious of a quite uncharacteristic flush to his cheeks.

"I do not think our governments would want us to connive at the conviction and, conceivably, the hanging of an innocent man. Both our countries are justly famous for their strict adherence to the rule of law—"

"That's just where you're wrong, Reverend. Fact is nuthin' matters 'cept winnin' this war. There's been plenty innocent men sacrificed in that cause already, and there's gonna be a helluva lot more. My advice to you is to let things take their course. It's better for the town and the war effort. Think on it. Your people are gonna be mighty riled and anti-American if one of your own gets hisself hanged fer protectin' his woman from a Yank. I ain't so stoopid I don't know there's a lotta bad feelin' about our boys chasin' your women. You can't blame them fer that. But folks don't like it. Nobody's gonna thank us fer bringin' that poor lad to justice, not your people and not mine, who wants to see things run smoothly in this here town."

"But... but this is a grave injustice..." stuttered the vicar, who had not been so lost for words since 1935 when Herbert Lapworth, his churchwarden, announced that he did not believe in God.

"You're pre-judging things here, Reverend. Who knows what's gonna happen. A court martial might be convinced by this black that he had nothin' to do with it. Somebody might provide him with an alibi, we don't know."

The vicar remained silent, not out of stubborn opposition but because he simply did not know what to say.

"Have a think about it anyways," said Bellucci. "And while you do, don't go tellin' anybody any of this. Rumours is liable to get right out of hand and take off with all kindsa outlandish things being said. You think on it, Reverend, and you'll see what I suggest is the best for all concerned."

"Not for the young black man."

"Like I said, Reverend. This is war. What did the man say, you can't make an omelette without breakin' eggs. Your parishioners sure ain't gonna thank you if young Tom swings."

With that Major Bellucci retired to his room. And for a long time afterwards Reverend Villiers did not move, but simply sat at his desk staring at the gleaming whisky glass on the desk, a urine-coloured smear remaining in the bottom.

CHAPTER THIRTY-FIVE

It was early next morning with his breakfast of bacon and powdered eggs still lying undigested inside him that Reverend Villiers approached the Jacobean manor house that now served as the town hall for Chalford. The morning sunlight flashed off leaded panes and gilded the glossy leaves of the evergreens flanking the drive that debouched in a car park occupied, in these days of petrol rationing, by a single Austin. Mr Markle, who lived in Goodrich Lane only a few hundred yards away, preferred to walk to work – perhaps, as his enemies mocked, an attempt by this latter-day Stanley Baldwin to appear a 'man of the people'.

The vicar's conscience was sufficiently disturbed to provide justification for ignoring any injunction to silence laid upon him by Major Bellucci, or at least, to confine in his interpretation, the undertaking to one of universal publication only. He had already, over breakfast, having dismissed the two evacuees to break their fast with the maid in the kitchen, discussed what the major had said with Mrs Villiers. His good lady was even more appalled than he was.

"Oh, my dear," she said, reaching across the butter dish with a vain arm not long enough for the purpose of furnishing tactile comfort, "what a perfectly frightful position for you to be in. Can the major seriously believe that we would keep mum about such a thing?"

"Apparently so. He seems to think the appeal to self-interest will prove a strong one."

"Self-interest? What can you mean?"

"He seems to think I will be swayed by the desire not to offend the parish by unmasking Tom."

"Then the major, my dear," said Mrs Villiers, vehemently conjugal, "does not know who he is dealing with!"

It was indeed Mrs Villiers who suggested that the vicar pay this visit to the mayor, as early as may be before the cares of office began to weigh upon his time.

The vicar approached the reception desk, as snug in its recess of oak panelling as to suggest that in a small but select country hotel. A young man with dark hair polished to a bright sheen with brilliantine faced him.

"May I see Mayor Markle? I regret I have been unable to make an appointment, but it is most urgent. Reverend Villiers."

The receptionist spoke on the telephone, and a mere minute later Mayor Markle was advancing to meet him, his watch chain swinging from his waistcoat.

Mayor Markle was a shortish man with a pronounced paunch, whose face with its expression of doughy good humour would, when required by the dictates of office, reset itself, like a jelly transported to a more severe mould, into one of civic responsibility. When welcoming the vicar, however, a man decreed an amicable and deferential reception by virtue of his calling, there could be no suggestion of severity.

"Frederick! What can I do for you? Please come into my office."

He was led into an office fully as panelled as the rest of the building. The mayor's desk was flanked on the one wall by a bookcase housing volumes of the *All England Law Reports* and *Halsbury's Statutes*, and on the other by a quincunx of framed photographs of the mayor's predecessors.

Mayor Markle turned to face the vicar with the air of an orator, his right hand on the lapel of his jacket like Cicero clutching the clasp of his toga.

"What can I do for you, Frederick? I can only give you half an hour before the Finance Committee meets, I'm afraid."

The vicar had always been on cordial terms with the mayor, who was of course one of his parishioners, although the two men had never been close. Nevertheless, the vicar had the utmost respect for the courage the then Mr Markle had demonstrated in sailing his boat to the rescue of stranded soldiers at Dunkirk. In that history of resolution and rectitude resided the vicar's hopes for a principled stand against Major Bellucci.

"Then I'll be brief."

The smile that tickled the mayor's lips seemed to suggest that he would believe that when he heard it.

"It is about this unfortunate killing... of the American military policeman... You'll have heard of it."

"Of course."

"The Americans have, I understand, arrested a black serviceman for the crime—"

"I quite understand your concerns, my dear Vicar. And I have, if truth be told, been rather anticipating representations of the kind. It's the sort of event that can only serve to increase disquiet so soon after our granting the blacks freedom of the town. In light of the incident, it's imperative I have a meeting—"

"No, Henry. You don't understand."

The vicar described as quickly, and with as few circumlocutions as his nature was capable, the confidences that had passed between him and Tom and his conversations with Major Bellucci. While he did so, the flesh of the mayor's face settled into its severe mould. The latter spoke.

"Well, Frederick. I'm afraid you may have come to the wrong man. Remember that I am not a private person. Were it only my own feelings I had to consider I would sympathise wholeheartedly. It seems the most grave injustice. But I would also sympathise with Tom Dawkins. Like many I've been concerned that some of our young women seem to be throwing themselves at these Americans. I, like them, would not want to see Tom hanged for doing what every red-blooded man in town would do. Nor would I wish to see an innocent man suffer for his wrong.

"But I am also the secular representative of this parish in the same way that you are its spiritual representative. I cannot, so long as I wear the chain of office (here Mr Markle touched his chest, though he was not in fact wearing his chain), indulge my own private feelings.

And it seems to me in my capacity as mayor that Major Bellucci, whatever my own feelings about the man, has it right in this instance.

"The powers that be would not be happy if this got out. They would see it as likely to stir up animosity towards the Americans not only in this town but in those others in which there has been friction. If Tom Dawkins were to hang, which God forbid, would not be the case, for protecting his girl from the advances of the Americans (here Mr Markle held up a chubby hand, boasting an engraved signet ring, to forestall the vicar's interruption) – and whatever the rights or wrongs, that is how our people would see it – there would be discontent, or worse. We must consider our responsibility towards the war effort.

"It is also the case that the affair would not reflect well upon the American military who have jumped to hasty conclusions..."

"It will be a lot worse for them if they convict an innocent man."

"Well, that must be their concern, likewise the fact that the prosecution must expose to the public gaze a widespread hatred between the races in the US military. No, I regret I cannot help you Vicar. I must put the interests of the town and the war before everything else. You do see that?"

The vicar nodded despondently. He was not a man given to uncharitable thoughts, but for perhaps the first time in their relations he wondered whether the selfless concern for the inhabitants of the town with which the vicar had always credited Mr Markle was not, whilst genuinely held, also a cloak for more personal ambitions.

"But if I am prepared to lay my larger responsibilities aside in this case, can you not see your way to doing likewise?"

"Secular and spiritual are two different things. You are answerable to a higher power, but so am I. You cannot know how your Superior views matters—"

"Excuse me, Mr Mayor, but I think I can."

"Well, I am answerable to Westminster, and in these times there can be no doubt they take a dim view of anything that undermines our relations with our allies."

"You – and all of us – are also answerable to God."

The mayor carried on as if oblivious to the vicar's interruption.

"The government, for good or evil – no doubt they did not have any choice – have seen fit to allow the Americans to rule their own roost, and if they choose to do this to one of their own men, who are we to gainsay them?"

"But, Henry, it's perfectly monstrous, don't you see that? What is the old saying? If you would sup with the Devil, you had better have a long spoon."

"We are in a cleft stick. Tom Dawkins is one of our boys. Those we represent would think it outrageous if we handed him over to American justice. If the Americans are determined upon charging this black serviceman with the crime, it's in the interests of Tom and the town as a whole that they handle the matter. Indeed, we should rejoice that we have no say in it."

"I cannot," the vicar said with a slight quaver in his voice, "sit idly by and allow this injustice to take place."

"Please don't misunderstand me, I sympathise with your position. This situation is, I think, less clear-cut for one of the cloth than it is for myself. Speaking in my capacity as civic representative of this town – the only capacity in which I can speak on this matter – I reiterate that it is for the American military to decide the case. Whatever you choose to do must be without overt assistance from me. However, I shall not take any steps to hinder you unless I consider your actions likely to harm the town, or unless ordered to do so by some higher power. And, for what it's worth, Frederick, you have my best wishes."

As he left the mayor's office, the vicar gave one brief glance back towards Henry Markle. The mayor was standing with his back to him, staring out of the leaded window. But the vicar saw not the mayor's suit, straining at his shoulders, rather a gleaming white toga. 'He took water, and washed his hands before the multitude, saying, I am innocent of the blood of this just person.'

After his meeting with the mayor, Mr Villiers knew he had to think, wishing if at all possible to avoid that alternative of last resort his wife had suggested, and to which he had tacitly agreed. He therefore strode off along the old drovers' path towards Depton. Here, hemmed in by high hedgerows and stands of cow parsley at which the vicar, with uncharacteristic vigour, thrashed with his cane, and walking in the ruts of generations of farm carts, he pondered his predicament.

Or at least endeavoured to do so. But he was conscious of little save the perfume of newly mown hay, the rustling in the oaks beyond the hedge, and the breeze stiffening from the west that flowed in welcome relief over his heated cheeks.

What Major Bellucci had held out to him like a crudely tied fly for his confounded mind to seize upon, and that which he had heard from Mr Markle, a man he respected far more, and that was perhaps a more ingeniously tied lure, was a temptation. His surroundings being what they were, he could not but compare his situation with that of Jesus, tempted in the wilderness, uncomfortably conscious as he did so of the blasphemy inherent in comparing himself with the Saviour of mankind.

Why should he not then do as they suggested? To allow a matter of discipline in the American forces to remain as such. No harm would come to Tom, who would not even suffer damage to his reputation. The townsfolk would live in ignorance of the possibly inflammatory knowledge that one of their own was being punished for defending his woman from American advances.

Offset against these benefits was the unjustified accusation of this black man. He cursed himself for not enquiring as to the man's name. Or had that reticence stemmed from a desire on the part of his subconscious not to know the name, thereby relegating the victim to one cell in the corpus of an alien race, and mitigating his own guilt? That was what they said, wasn't it, these psychoanalysts or whatever they called themselves? He had always regarded it as an unnecessarily demeaning, and even pagan philosophy. But perhaps in this case…

What would happen to this black chap? The vicar possessed no knowledge of the American justice system save that it was based on English Common Law. But that availed him little as he did not know what punishment Tom would receive at the hands of English courts. They surely could not hang him, could they? He should have asked Bellucci: but he was not sanguine that he would receive a truthful answer from that gentleman.

When he had been a young curate, the case of John Turner, one of his fellow Divinity students, had been something of a cause célèbre. This young man, being of an unworldly tenor of mind, had reported his vicar to the bishop for embezzlement of church funds. But the affair was hushed up, and poor John never received the parish and stipend that should have been his. At the time, Mr Villiers had wondered what he would have done in John's position.

Now it had arrived, his time of trial. He did not know what view the church authorities might take of what he was contemplating. More importantly, he would surely offend the sensibilities of his parishioners. He may even be regarded as behaving unpatriotically. But as he regarded the clay ruts at his feet, he kept seeing John Turner's face, with its shy, lopsided smile.

John was too innocent a being to have doubted his own rectitude. Perhaps that quality of innocence, that was a pale shadow of Our Lord's own unworldliness, was the only true goodness in this cruel and self-seeking world. If so, Frederick Villiers feared he could not match it. But he could do something. If he possessed the courage.

He risked alienating his congregation. And now that his interview with Mayor Markle had come to naught, the alternative suggested by his wife was fully as daunting. But there was John, and there was his wife, resolute and implacable in her tweed skirt and sensible brogues, like some spirit of Britishness against which the hordes of

Nazis and the inducements of the Americans would break in vain, urging him on.

Nevertheless, he could not but blanch at the prospect. His wife had said it, in response to his question of what they would do if Markle was not prepared to assist:

"And if you get no joy with Mr Markle, my dear, I am very much afraid there is only one person left to go to."

He ventured Mrs Cadwallader.

"Oh dear me, no. I do not say she would be unsympathetic. But she too would have the communal interest at heart and prove unwilling to risk offending the townsfolk… There is only one person who wouldn't."

The vicar had been tested in the wilderness and not been found wanting.

CHAPTER THIRTY-SIX

"You got fifteen minutes. No more, y' hear?"

Thus spoke the warder, his full lips canted in a sneer, as he admitted Leroy to Grover's cell.

The latter sat on the trestle bed, staring absently at the toilet and washstand fixed to the wall opposite. The only other furnishing the cell possessed was a bedside table upon which a toilet roll and testament stood.

When he looked up, Grover's face was transformed by a smile. Leroy felt as if his heart were being squeezed in his chest with the thought that Grover must have believed his friends had deserted him. Nevertheless, the smile of welcome was a qualified one, and the stretched lips sank back into a more relaxed posture as the prisoner stared over Leroy's shoulder. He had expected to see Errol.

"Hey, man," Leroy said with a forced cheeriness that he knew would fool nobody, "how you doin'?"

"Okay… Good to see you."

Grover's eyes flitted from wall to wall, as if he were searching for the comfortable armchair that was the normal appurtenance of this accommodation, before shuffling his bottom along the bed and patting on the mattress for Leroy to sit down. Leroy felt the springs creak beneath him.

"Don't you go thinkin' we didn't wanna see you," Leroy said, anxious to forestall his friend's anxiety. "They wouldn't let us. We bin at them time and agin, but they say no visits. I only got in here 'cos we's threatened to report them to the NAACP."

The National Association for the Advancement of Colored People was the mouthpiece of the African in the United States.

"They still won't let Errol come and see you, though he's been a-bangin' on their door most every day."

"Why not?"

Leroy got the impression that the interest in Grover's voice was no more than a spark from an otherwise ashen and abandoned hearth, nevertheless it seemed to flare brighter at the mention of Errol.

"They say 'cos he's a witness. That's right, ain't it, 'cos he was with you that night."

"Yeah."

"So he's not allowed to speak to you, case you goes and tells him what to say."

"As if I could tell Errol what to say."

They both laughed.

"Yeah."

Leroy studied Grover's profile. His friend was still staring at the toilet and washstand, but there was that guardedness, that told he knew how closely he was being observed.

Did the poor sap know what they had in store for him? Leroy wondered. Once the whites got that scent of black blood, they knew no mercy. His cousin Scooter had a rabbit. The white fella up the road he had a pack of hounds, and one day they got into the rabbit's cage and tore that beast limb from limb so there wasn't nothing left but a bit of skull. A white MP had been killed and a black would have to swing for it.

Grover couldn't expect anything else. Even Leroy, who knew his friend's pacific nature, was impressed by the coincidence that the self-same white man who had fought with Grover a week before was found dead the next night blacks were let out. And apparently the snowdrop had been downed with punches only. If it had been a gunshot or knife wound Leroy would never have believed Grover guilty. But punches... and he a boxer... Not that he would have ventured such an opinion in front of Errol; he would see it as a betrayal, not just of Grover but the whole black race. Errol never doubted for one minute Grover's innocence, and it was on that basis that Leroy had been briefed.

If it had been up to Leroy, he would have asked the question at the outset: had Grover done it? Then there could be no misunderstanding. But he didn't know how to ask without offending. If Grover was claiming to be innocent, he would be insulted, and whatever morale he possessed would be injured at being doubted by his friend. But maybe he could get at the truth in a subtler way.

"Was he there with you the whole time?"

"The whole time what?"

"The time this snowdrop was killed."

"I dunno what time that was."

There was something almost simple about Grover. This was a man who could, Leroy thought, kill in a fit of temper, with his fists, but he would not have the sense to cover it up. And there had been no attempt to cover it up. The body had lain in the street.

"I left him. Then I sat there for a time, then I come back to camp, and they done grabbed me."

So he must be saying he was innocent. Leroy found himself articulating his thought.

"So who else coulda done it?"

"Dunno."

That was Grover, absent, slightly wistful, as if he had never asked himself that question.

"Errol, he say you gotta write to the NAACP, and 'cos you's in here and you ain't much good with writin', he done it fer you. And he says when they gets the letter they'll take it to the *Daily Word*, and all hell'll break loose, and they'll let you out faster'n one of Joe Louis's right hooks. Whaddya think of that?"

Leroy had expected some enthusiasm on Grover's part, but the prisoner turned to face him with another of those blank stares.

"Then they's gonna have to do it fast. They're gonna have me up before a court martial in the next week."

"Well, that's just what he says. You gotta git yerself an attorney."

"I got me one."

"What? A real one? One that ain't from the army?"

"No, he's from the army. A captain."

"White?"

"Yeah."

Leroy didn't know if that was good or bad. A white captain wasn't going to have much sympathy with a black private accused of killing a white MP. On the other hand, a white court wasn't going to set much store by what a black lawyer said. One thing them whites hates more than a dumb nigger, is a smart nigger.

"Well, Errol, he says you should git yerself a –what did he say? – a private lawyer, one as ain't in the army."

"How'm I gonna pay?"

"He was hopin', if the NAACP was to help us, they'd raise the money."

"They ain't gonna have the time to raise no money and send it all the way across the ocean."

"Well, Errol, he says, don't you go givin' up hope now. The NAACP's got theirselves some power."

"Ain't what he said afore I got thrown in here."

The spark that had been in Grover's face was now gone, and Leroy desperately sought some words that might rekindle it. He said:

"Us blacks is an important part of the army now. They don't wanna go offendin' us..."

"It's just the same," Grover said bleakly.

And he was right. Now they were at war, the whites looked at them with even more loathing, like they was some sort of – what did they call it? – fifth column.

"Don't you go givin' up hope now, y' hear," said Leroy, squeezing Grover's arm. The muscle in the forearm tensed suddenly like a flinch.

"It were that white gal, weren't it?" Grover said. "What she wanna go botherin' a nigger like me fer? Back home in Georgia no white gal'd do that."

"She took to yer dancin', I guess."

"She never even seen me dance. Why she do that?… I wish I never come here."

Leroy did not know what to say. But Grover carried on:

"Funny thing is, they's sayin' I's a boxer, and that's how come I can kill a man with my own bare hands, ain't they? But it don't figure. When I wus fightin', Cyrus – him what called hisself my trainer – he'd say, 'Grover Carson, you ain't never gonna amount to shit in the ring. 'Cos you ain't got the killer instinct.' Killer instinct. That's kinda funny, ain't it? But fact was I never did like fightin'. 'Cos that other guy in the ring, he'd hurt me and I'd get riled, but then I'd think to myself, he's same as I is. His life ain't no better'n mine is, mebbe it's worse. And I didn't want to hurt him no more. And that ain't good fer a boxer now, is it?"

"I guess."

Grover reached under the bed, picking up off the floor a metal mug which was attached by a chain to the wall, as if the authorities in this place were plagued by petty larceny of their drinking vessels.

"Well, that's got to be in your favour, ain't it. No killer instinct," Leroy said.

"It's just my word fer that though, ain't it?"

Grover drank deep of what was in the mug, but kept it in his hands, cradled between his knees as if they contained a baby bird he was saving from a predatory cat.

Tears fell from Grover's eyes. Leroy turned away, not wanting Grover to see that he had witnessed his shame. And he thought this man, however angered he might have been, could never have killed another with his fists.

Or at least he could not have beaten him to a pulp. But one punch... No, if Grover had done it, he would have admitted it.

"Don't worry, we're working to git you outta here. You know what Errol's like."

"Do you think they's gonna shoot me?"

Grover's voice was a crippled version of what it had formerly been.

"Hell no," Leroy lied. "You think an educated nigger like Errol's gonna let his buddy... Well, he ain't. If anybody can git you outta here, he can."

"There's times I tell myself I don't mind none. What I gotta go back fer, eh? More of the same we had before. And then I gets to thinkin' I got my mom and little brother, that's allays looked up to me though he never had cause to. And I think o' them hearin' I bin shot fer a murderer. When you gits back, you and Errol, you go tell them how it was – I'll write you their address. You'll tell them, won't you?"

"Sure, but—"

"And my mom won't have no grave to shed tears on, 'cos I's halfway round the world."

"Look," said Leroy, but he could only lamely repeat, "we're gonna git you outta here, y' hear?"

Then, to change the subject he asked the question Errol had told him to ask.

"Did any folks see you? The night you wus out with Errol. The night the snowdrop was killed. Some farmer mebbe?"

"No. I seen two of them – whaddya call 'em – land girls, with a cartful of hay."

"Well, that's good. We can speak to these gals and git them to say that, and you's gonna be free as a bird, my friend."

But Leroy knew it would not be that easy. And when he rose to take his leave, the look in his friend's big eyes made him want to weep. It was not an imploring look, there was nothing of hope in it, simply the forlorn look of one being cast adrift on a desert island for the boat that was taking the last human face he would ever see into the sunset.

CHAPTER THIRTY-SEVEN

"I want to raise a matter of morality."

That got the attention of Mrs Villiers as she pondered how best to approach the querulous Mrs Burns – indeed, of all the ladies of the Chalford WVS.

The words were spoken by Betty Absolom, the wife of Tom Absolom, the town blacksmith. They had reached that part of the meeting where Mrs Cadwallader called upon the ladies for 'any other business'.

"And what is that, Mrs Absolom?"

"'Twere last night. I was comin' back from seein' our Marjorie when I sees him chasin' them land girls – not that they needs chasin' – ready, willin' and able, they is."

"Chasing?" said Mrs Cadwallader, in a tone that suggested she agreed with Mrs Absolom that the need for any such pursuit was so unlikely as to verge on the incredible. And it was true, Mrs Villiers thought, that the behaviour of some of the girls was getting out of hand.

"I don't say chasin'," said Mrs Absolom, despite that being exactly what she had said. "But you know, makin' up to 'em."

"And who precisely are we talking about?"

"Well, that... negro," Mrs Absolom said as if it were obvious.

"One of the Americans then."

"Well, I don't know of any blacks besides them, I'm sure."

"This negro was..." Mrs Cadwallader struggled for the correct terminology, "...was flirting with the land girls?"

"That he was, and I don't mind sayin' I think it's disgustin'. No self-respectin' gal – but of course they don't have no self-respect."

"So he was not pestering them?" Mrs Cadwallader interrupted in a tone that suggested some frustration at having to thus tease out the facts of the matter. "They were not unwilling, to be so addressed?"

"Not at all. Brazen, they was. I says, 'You should be ashamed of yourselves, you should.' But they wasn't ashamed, they just gave me lip. I wouldn't be surprised if their folks wouldn't blink twice about them carryin' on with one of them blacks. It'd be different if they turned up on their doorstep with a pramful of chocolate-coloured baby."

"Really, Mrs Absolom," said an increasingly impatient Mrs Cadwallader, "you need not make your point in so unseemly a fashion. So you gave them a piece of your mind."

"Much good it did me. They just brazened it out, smug as you please. 'We wusn't spoonin', you know,' they says, and laughs their heads off. Well, spoonin', have you ever heard the like? And then they flat denied they wus up to anythin'. The nerve of it."

"Well, what was a negro doin' talkin' to land girls if it weren't for that?" asked Lily Foster, the postmistress.

"That's my point," agreed Mrs Absolom. "But they come out with some cock-and-bull story about him askin' if they seen him or his mate on some night or other."

Mrs Villiers, whose attention had wavered somewhat, now sat bolt upright, her eyes fixed on Mrs Absolom's ample frame.

"And what was he doin' on that night he was so worried the girls'd seen him?" pursued Mrs Foster, sensing, if anything, an even greater scandal.

"Somethin' about his mate havin' murdered somebody. There ain't been no murders here fer hundreds of years!"

"He must mean that American MP," said Mrs Cadwallader.

"Oh, I didn't think o' that."

"In that case he wasn't doing anything wrong," Mrs Villiers said.

"And he wanted to know if these girls had seen it?" Mrs Cadwallader asked. "Heavens! Was he threatening them?"

"It's bad enough them Yanks come over 'ere, without their bringin' their blacks and their gangsters as well," said Mrs Foster. "We'll be like Chicago before long."

"I don't think he was threatenin' them exactly," said Mrs Absolom. "Leastways they wasn't frightened. Just asked if they'd seen him when he was supposed to be murderin' this bloke."

But, Mrs Villiers reflected with some frustration, Mrs Absolom wasn't one to be deflected from her agenda of immorality by anything as mundane as facts.

"They'll concoct any story, these girls. Sly, that's what they is. Sly and brazen."

The complement of ladies fell silent, as if contemplating what a combination of brazenness and slyness would amount to. Mrs Villiers, however, was intrigued. Who was this black? He must be a friend of the accused man.

"I don't think this amounts to sufficient reason to report their activities to the War Agricultural Committee. No doubt you'll continue to keep a close eye on them, Mrs Absolom."

"Close eye. You gotta have a very close eye fer them. Sly is what they is."

"I'm sure you have their measure."

It was as the meeting broke up, and they were walking down the path, that Mrs Villiers approached Sally Burns, at first obliquely, she having noticed an uncharacteristic silence on the part of the latter during the meeting.

"How are you, my dear? I heard you'd been unwell."

"Just a bit of a funny turn, that's all. I still get them."

"Of course," said Mrs Villiers sympathetically. "You've been very brave. We Chalfordians can have no idea. But I like to think that Mr Villiers and myself might have a better idea than most, having seen the effects upon our young charges."

"How are they?"

"Better. Do come and see them. They've become quite the village children. It's just at nights, you understand."

"Yes."

"You've been very brave. And most principled, if I may say so. Not one to be brow-beaten by public opinion and those in authority into doing something she doesn't want to do, if I may venture that far."

"It's very kind of you to say so."

"And it was for that reason," Mrs Villiers hurried on, as if frightened that any stalling of her speech might prevent her reaching her desired goal, "that my husband and I felt that you were the one to turn to in the dilemma we face, having exhausted all official channels. Because this is a most delicate situation we find ourselves in. A situation in which we may find our powers ranged against the townsfolk of Chalford, and in which emotions could conceivably run high. Moreover, one in which the life of an innocent man may be at stake. And if you're unable to help I am sure I can nevertheless count on your discretion. Can we walk to the park and talk there?"

Mrs Burns nodded her assent. Her uncharacteristic taciturnity made Mrs Villiers wonder if she had picked the right time to approach the firebrand.

There was a row of four wooden seats. One was occupied by an elderly lady who was feeding pigeons from a paper bag. The pigeons of Chalford must, the vicar's wife reflected, have had a lean time of it lately.

Mrs Villiers looked over the two seats furthest from the lady and, hopefully out of earshot, and selecting that which possessed the most meagre complement of bird droppings, subsided into it. As Sally joined her and they sat facing the somewhat dilapidated swings, slide and roundabout on which generations of Chalfordians, dating back to Mrs Villiers herself, had beguiled their childish hours, she patted the councillor's wife on the knee and commenced her narrative of the events arising from Larry Schultz's death. Some minutes later she wound up the tale with the following:

"No-one but ourselves and Mr Markle knows anything of this. And were it to get out I have no doubt people would take Tom's side – not that Tom is contesting any of it, rather he seems quite passive, poor chap – and would want us to leave it up to the Americans. You can see how our involvement could turn people against us, and indeed threaten my husband's position as rector of this parish. That would not be a happy result. We have no desire to move from the town where we had imagined we would live out the remainder of our days. You see our predicament."

But Sally Burns' response was a tangential one. She said:

"So those land girls must've been telling the truth to Mrs Absolom when they said the negro was asking them about his friend."

"I suppose so."

"And the court martial, or whatever you call it, is entirely in the hands of the Americans?"

"Yes. I don't think our police have any jurisdiction. One would think they would want to put the blame on one of our people, but it's quite the reverse."

"They decided from the outset the negro was guilty?"

"Yes, because he had been involved in a fracas with the MP concerned."

"And because of his colour, let's not forget that."

Sally sat back on the bench, pursing her lips, the act of contemplation imparting to her still, pale features an added gravity. As the old woman, after shaking out her paper bag, rose and walked away from them, Sally said:

"So we must somehow get word to this man that Tom has confessed."

For the first time it occurred to Mrs Villiers that there might be something of a conflict of interest between her and her husband and Mrs Burns.

Although she had no desire that Tom should come to harm – rather the reverse – in the interests of justice she wished that Tom's confession should come to the notice of the accused man, so that he had the opportunity to make use of it. And, ideally, she would wish that knowledge be imparted without the involvement of herself or the vicar. They had judged Sally the only one capable of doing so, and if word of that fact got out, it would be Mrs Burns who would incur the censure of the village. A part of Mrs Villiers, that the vicar's wife had hitherto been unaware of, argued for the fact that Sally Burns was an outsider who would not lose as much if her involvement in the affair became public, as would she and her husband. How much of herself that was craven and selfish would she reveal were she to ask, as she must, that Mrs Burns keep their involvement a secret?

Mrs Burns meanwhile was thinking aloud.

"But he's in custody. We must find this friend and give him everything we know. It's a pity we don't have his name. Or a description. I could ask Mrs Absolom or the land girls at Westwood's farm, I suppose. They might know something more."

Another unkind thought was stirring in Mrs Villiers' head, which was the reflection that all this was very easy for Mrs Burns, who no doubt viewed it as one of her matters of principle; another crusade for which she could don her shield and unsheathe her sword. Because she did not know Tom Dawkins. He was just a name to her.

But Mr and Mrs Villiers had known Tom since he had first come to Sunday school, a small, reserved lad forever picking his nose, who had no doubt grown up in the shadow of that maxim of being seen and not heard that she imagined a particular favourite of Farmer Dawkins.

She felt compelled to speak, despite being oppressed by the ineffectuality of her words.

"Of course, we don't wish for Tom to come to any harm."

"Oh no," said Mrs Burns, with something that hinted at indifference in her tone, and augmented Mrs Villiers' misgiving. "But justice must be done."

This conversation was turning into something of a moral inquisition for Mrs Villiers, and she herself the Torquemada.

For she did not necessarily agree that justice must be done. Rather it must have an opportunity to be done. She did not want anyone to hang for the murder of this philandering MP, but if someone must, she would rather it were the anonymous black man. What she wanted, she realised for the first time, was not justice, but the salving of her own conscience by passing the responsibility of her knowledge onto another. She wondered if Frederick, normally so discriminating on any point of morality, felt the same, and if so, whether he had attained the same degree of self-knowledge on the subject as she.

Mrs Villiers was uncomfortably conscious that in broaching the subject to Sally Burns she may have let the genie out of the bottle, and the cork was nowhere to be found. But there again, she thought, with a degree of mortification, she may already have done so when she first mentioned Mrs Burns' name to her husband, effectively binding him to the course of action she was now intent upon.

"We must get word to him somehow," Mrs Burns was saying.

"Who?" the vicar's wife asked, having entirely lost the train of thought Mrs Burns was pursuing.

"The black soldier who was asking questions," Mrs Burns replied, surprise in her tone. "I'll speak to those land girls. Assuming he got no joy out of them, the likelihood is he'll come back, asking other folk in town. The most direct route, of course, is to go to the prison and ask to see this man, but I don't even know his name, and if I say I want to see the black accused of murder they'll slam the door in my face. We could write him a note, but I doubt that anybody bar this friend would pass it to him. And we don't know who the friend is."

Meanwhile Mrs Villiers was calling in aid every resource at her disposal, and the one which came most readily to mind was flattery. She put her hand on the heavy serge of Mrs Burns' skirt above her knee.

"I was sure you were the right person to bring this to. Your sense of justice is exemplary. However, you do appreciate the delicacy of this situation, do you not? If the town were to get wind of it, they might... Well, they might put the wrong construction on things, you see what I mean?"

But Mrs Burns clearly did not.

"But surely they'll see that what we are doing is right?"

That 'we' made Mrs Villiers more uneasy still.

"They are more likely to see... someone who is trying

to get Tom Dawkins – the Tom Dawkins who has gone to their school, drunk in their pub, and fought for their freedom – put to death for the sake of some negro—"

"Oh, that's it!"

But Mrs Villiers was adroit enough to forestall Sally Burns from embarking upon another diatribe.

"Man then! His colour does not matter. To most it'll be simply a question of one of ours or one of theirs. They would not embark on any fine discrimination of morality. So I beg you, keep this between ourselves, and go about your business as circumspectly as you are able. Speak to the land girls, if you wish – they don't mix with us locals – but I would caution against speaking to Mrs Absolom. You saw what she was like at the meeting. Tell her and you may as well broadcast it with a microphone. And please, I beg, for the sake of our position in this community, do not mention our involvement. Can I rely upon you?"

She turned to scrutinise Sally Burns. The pale face, that had at the outset of their conversation appeared drained and wan, was now lit with a zeal for the cause, the cheeks blushing with the circulation of her fervour, the speckled grey eyes sparkling and inspired. But the look that was returned was one of shrewd contemplation, and beneath its gaze Mrs Villiers felt uncomfortably shabby. *Is this how Our Lord must have looked upon the worldly, the selfish and the cowardly?* she wondered.

The vicar's wife was conscious that she had in the last few minutes abdicated all power of direction over the matter, and they were now entirely in the hands of a woman who possessed many qualities Mrs Villiers admired, but who was inclined to episodes of passion that she, with her middle-class upbringing, viewed with some suspicion. And there was, she suspected, a degree of something in Mrs Burns that she attributed to her experiences in the capital, and which she could only describe as instability.

Moreover, Mrs Villiers had the horrible suspicion that it was not just the town that would see matters as 'one of ours or one of yours'. Mrs Burns, who knew neither man, for whom there was nothing at stake, may be driven to pull out all the stops to save this negro, not out of a concern for justice, but purely because of his colour; that it were better in her eyes that the white man be sacrificed than the oppressed black. That she, with the contempt she had frequently evinced for her fellow whites, may even feel that the only good may reside in the black.

"I'll try and keep it as quiet as I can. I see no need to mention your names."

That was the assurance Mrs Villiers had wanted, although she was uneasy about the qualification. Furthermore, she noted in the tone in which it was delivered something almost approaching disdain, and before which the vicar's wife had an urgent desire to retreat.

"But I do thank you for choosing me to confide in," Mrs Burns was saying, as if qualifying an unspoken and most cutting criticism. "I shall do all in my power to be worthy of your trust."

"Well, good," said Mrs Villiers, rising and drawing her jacket about her. "I'm sure that that young negro can have no more determined advocate in his corner than you."

And with that Mrs Villiers, as confused in her metaphors as in every other aspect of this meeting, took a hurried departure, directly over the tarmac play area between swings and roundabout, and, without looking back (perhaps even feeling that she may thereby be turned into a pillar of salt) regained the high street.

CHAPTER THIRTY-EIGHT

"He's checkin' the cans of bully beef, Sarg," said Private Luwitski.

Sergeant O'Rourke scowled.

"I don't care if he's countin' the colonel's balls, get him in here pronto. And when he arrives, post two men to stand outside the door. I'll need an escort for him."

O'Rourke smiled at his own witticism as Luwitski departed the office and, easing his chair onto its rearmost legs, rocked back against the wall, under the Stars and Stripes and the team photograph of the Boston Celtics, to await the arrival of Private Errol Gideon.

It was a mere thirty minutes since he had departed the office of Major Bellucci, the scene of a profoundly uncomfortable interview in which he had been on the receiving end of the major's wrath. The sergeant now looked forward to venting his own spleen upon the cause of his discomfiture, Gideon.

The sergeant had anticipated nothing of the storm that was about to break when he received the summons to the infantry camp. He flattered himself that he and Major Bellucci saw eye to eye on many matters. They had both come up through the ranks, and they looked on the world in a broadly similar way. In addition, if there had been any cause for complaint about the way he, O'Rourke, carried out his duties, then it was a matter that should be addressed by Captain Harris, not by the major himself.

On being admitted to Major Bellucci's office, O'Rourke found himself facing not only the major but also 1st Lieutenant Beston, the MP platoon commander, and 2nd Lieutenant Toth, the executive officer. He barely had the leisure to note the presence of these latter, being immediately aware of the major's fury, and the fact that he seemed to be its unwitting cause.

The major was crouched over his desk as if to pounce upon the first person who came through the door, intervening furniture notwithstanding. The shaven head was held rigidly to attention by neck muscles that seemed to strain against some threatened delinquency on the part of that organ. The major's face was the colour of a rich red wine, not much diluted. The brows narrowed as O'Rourke entered, and held him in his sights, while the private closed the door behind him.

"What the hell is goin' on in your camp, Sergeant? What sort of ship are you runnin' there when any nigger can come and go as he pleases, and question the Limeys about this here Carson?"

Lieutenant Toth, a small man with the mournful countenance of a mortician, and the pallor of one of the latter's subjects, nodded as if in approval of this invective, while Beston kept his head down like one anticipating a ricochet.

"I don't know what you mean, sir."

"Here's what I mean. One of your men, Private Errol Gideon. That Limey farmer, Westwood, thinks he can walk straight in here 'cos it's his land and his folks has farmed it since George Washington was in diapers, he says this here Gideon's been comin' onto his land girls. So my first thought is we got us another nigger can't keep his monkey paws offa white flesh. That would be bad enough. But here I finds these gals tells Westwood he's bin askin' about his friend that's charged with murder, and did these gals see anything of Carson on the night of the murder.

"This here private of yourn is gonna stir up a hornets' nest good and proper if you don't put a stop to it, y' hear?"

O'Rourke wondered why the major had not waited to take the matter up with Captain Harris when he returned from Dorchester later that day. But he said:

"I sure will, Major."

"You're goddam tootin', yer will. How come he's runnin' around askin' these questions?"

"I guess it was the niggers' time in town, sir. Me and the captain, we didn't think to stop 'em on account of Private Schultz."

O'Rourke was not sure that that was what the major had intended they should do, but it seemed to be implied from his words.

"Well, you should've thought. That's what you's a sergeant fer, ain't it?"

The unfortunate object of this tirade reflected that, on the contrary, it was not the responsibility of a sergeant to think a great deal. Rather, thinking was something he expected to leave at the door of a superior officer, and if the major wanted the niggers stopped from going into town, he should have given that order. In the absence of any order, O'Rourke was, he felt, entitled to abide by the policy allowing blacks access to the town. It was true he had his doubts about that policy, and felt that, already having incurred the major's wrath, he might as well voice them now in mitigation of his offence.

"Fact is, Major, I was thinkin', on account of this whole business bein' started by the niggers goin' after white women, whether it wouldn't have been better to stop them goin' into town altogether. I said the same to Captain Harris."

"Well, why the hell didn't he stop them?"

"He felt it would have – what did he say? – an adverse effect on the morale of the blacks."

O'Rourke had no compunction about telling tales so far as Harris was concerned. The latter was one of those West Point-trained, Ivy League-educated officers who, O'Rourke felt, looked down on the likes of him.

"Morale of the blacks!" Bellucci exploded dismissively.

"He said 't'weren't right to keep them pent up in camp, 'specially when the whites was allowed to go into town same as allays."

"I was brung up to believe niggers did what they wus told, Sergeant. If we thinks it ain't safe to have them wanderin' around town, we don't have to take into account their precious feelin's in the matter, y' hear?"

"I guess so, sir. But fact is Captain Harris, he don't think that way."

"Well, what way does he think?"

"Like we gotta… keep them happy, I guess."

"And what about keepin' the folks of this town happy? Ain't he thought about that, when niggers is roamin' about, lookin' to satisfy their animal lusts. And stirrin' up trouble about Schultz."

"But that don't matter none, Major. This here Carson's gonna be shot fer it, ain't he? Ain't nuthin' gonna change that."

"Now you listen here, Sergeant, and you listen good and hard. And this is between you and me, yer hear: it's not to go outside this room. This here Carson ain't confessed – not that that'd make much difference. But I'll tell you somethin' your Captain Harris don't know. Couple of days ago I had the parson come to me with a lad by the name of Dawkins, and this Dawkins he says Schultz was runnin' around with his gal, and the night Schultz was killed he comes on him, and he lays Schultz out on the sidewalk. So he thinks he's killed Schultz, you get me.

"Now this ain't good. This here Dawkins, he's a local boy, bin fightin' in the desert, so the locals see him as some sort of hero. They ain't gonna take kindly if we wades on in and puts him on trial fer stickin' up fer his gal, 'specially if we shoots him. Our bosses ain't gonna like it neither. They ain't gonna give a shit if a nigger is shot, but if one of the Limeys swings fer Schultz it's a different ball game, y' get me? They're gonna start askin' questions. Questions like how come we didn't keep an eye on what our men was doin', you get me?

"Them uppity niggers back home get wind of this, they'll wanna know how come we picked on Carson. It don't matter that until we found out about this Dawkins only Carson had a motive fer killin' Schultz on account of the beatin' he give him. Our superiors is gonna wanna know the same thing, and they's gonna accuse us of underminin' morale by drivin' blacks agin whites. Blacks back home has too much power these days, and our superiors is pussy-footin' around tryin' not to rile them. They're gonna blame us fer damagin' relations with the Brits.

"'Cos we take notice of what this Dawkins says, we gotta shoot him, and all fer protectin' his gal.

"So we gotta keep the lid on this, and I don't reckon from what I've seen of him, yer Captain Harris is the man fer the job. So I'm lookin' to you, Sergeant, you hear me?"

"Yes sir, but—"

"Best thing all round we just let this nigger swing. You agree?"

"Well, I don't want no come back on me, Major. After all, I was in charge of the camp when Captain Harris was away, and as you yerself said, the finger's gonna be pointed at me, and questions is gonna be asked."

"No they ain't. We shoot a nigger fer what we all knows niggers does, ain't no questions gonna be asked 'cept of them that sent them out here in the first place. We said no good'd come of it, them of us as knows what these people are like. This'll show 'em we wus right all along, and niggers ain't got no place in a white man's army, and good men like yerself what was just doin' their dooty ain't got no call to fear. You was told to let 'em out, so him that told you should shoulder the blame. It don't make no difference that Harris was away, he was in charge of the camp, you get it?"

O'Rourke agreed with what the major was saying but could not help an uneasy feeling that the responsibility for killing Schultz was to be laid at the door of one of the men he had charge of. He cared nothing for the injustice of it so far as Carson was concerned. Niggers like Carson were not entitled to a white man's justice. But he cared about the possible injustice of him being blamed for Carson's supposed offence.

"I'm sensing the sergeant has some reservations here, Major," Lieutenant Toth said, his voice sounding terribly urbane in comparison with the machine-gun delivery of the major.

"Do you? Do you, O'Rourke?" the major exploded.

"Perhaps he has reservations about sacrificing one of our own to save a Brit," Beston added, helpfully from O'Rourke's point of view as he had no wish to reveal his real reservation.

"He ain't one of our own, he's a nigger," the major corrected with the ponderous emphasis of one well used to the didactic.

"I guess I agree with you, Major," said O'Rourke.

"Sure you do," said the major, a sudden shocking emollience in his tone.

"So just how we gonna keep the lid on this?" asked Toth, his suavity sounding almost satirical.

"I been givin' it some thought."

Bellucci sat forward, his forearms on the desk, the fingers of both hands raised in a point like a steeple. "We gotta get this Gideon outta here or stop him contactin' folk in town, leastways until his nigger buddy swings."

"We can't have him transferred without Captain Harris agreein', sir," O'Rourke said.

"Here's what I bin thinkin'," said the major as if he had not heard the sergeant. "You get this nigger alone in yer office, y' hear. And you say he's hit you. Put the bastard on a charge fer strikin' a superior officer and lock him in the cooler. Make damn sure he stays there 'til this business is over, you get me?"

"What happens then, Major?" Lieutenant Beston asked. "He could come out and ask awkward questions all over."

"What fer? When his buddy's just bin shot?"

"He might still want to prove he was innocent."

"He don't know nuthin' about this Dawkins. And we sure as hell want to keep it that way. We might just have to get the whole goddam lot of 'em transferred. But at the minute what worries me is if Gideon's banged up, he might still get his buddies on the outside to do his dirty work fer him. So this is what you needs to do, O'Rourke. You go to your Captain Harris and tell him you had complaints off the locals about the behaviour of some of your niggers when they's about town: drunkenness, pawin' white women, stuff they gets up to anyhow. So you think the only way to deal with it is fer them to be confined to barracks fer the duration, you get me?"

"But I ain't had no complaints, Major."

"Sure you did, O'Rourke. You think hard on it. Sure you did. Say they was anonymous and that way yer captain has no way of tracin' them."

"What if he asks to see the letters?" asked Lieutenant Beston.

"Letters?... Well, say there was no letters. Say these folks, they just come up to yer in the street. Say you don't know no names. You hear that, O'Rourke?"

O'Rourke who, given the volume at which the instruction was delivered, would have had to be severely deaf not to have heard, nodded his assent.

"Get to it. And I don't wanna hear no more of no niggers playin' Sam Spade, get it?"

O'Rourke got it all right. And the more he thought about it the more sense it made, that the life of one goddam nigger hardly weighed in the scale compared to the reputation of their military and their good relations with these Limeys. The truth wouldn't get out, just so long as he could keep Carson's buddies out of circulation. This Dawkins wasn't going to rock the boat, because it was his neck on the line.

What concerned O'Rourke was his own position. But, as the major said, it hadn't been on his authority these niggers had been allowed to wander the streets. He was responsible for them when they were in camp, but he wasn't required to nursemaid them when they came to town. He had gone beyond the call of duty in observing their behaviour in the dance hall. No, if heads had to roll for this, they must be more elevated heads than his own. But it was a well-known fact that those in power were adept at passing the buck onto subordinates.

There was a knock on the door and Gideon was ushered in. He stood to attention before O'Rourke's desk, and the sergeant waited until Luwitski exited. He regarded Gideon's face, his nigger complexion shiny as a black pool ball.

Of all the men in his charge, O'Rourke liked Gideon least of all. The man had that – what would you call it? – bearing, insolence, arrogance, that O'Rourke was happy to respect in a white superior, even to tolerate in a white inferior, but was damned if he would abide it in a nigger. The only quality he expected in a black was that of a becoming humility.

At bottom was the uncomfortable consciousness that this nigger was cleverer than he was, and although Gideon had the good sense never to demonstrate as much by talking back to O'Rourke, the Irish sergeant always felt the man was laughing at him behind those pearly white teeth. The fact that Gideon never talked smart to him was doubly aggravating, as it gave O'Rourke no excuse to punish the nigger for the mockery he sensed in Gideon. Gideon was, in short, too clever for his own good.

"So, Gideon," he said, through lips taut with anger and distaste, "I hear you bin makin' a nuisance of yerself."

O'Rourke held out the words like the lure he might use for a catfish back home on the Ogeechee River, awaiting the smart-alec response, his anger tensed like biceps for the pull of the line. But once again the nigger denied him.

"You hear me, boy?" he barked.

This time the response came.

"I don't know what you mean, Sergeant," Gideon said.

There it was. Polite and respectful the words might seem to an observer, but they contained sufficient insolence when viewed through O'Rourke's eyes to provoke the sergeant.

"Don't you go givin' me yer nigger lip, you hear me, boy? You bin goin' round town, pesterin' folk on account of that murderin' friend of yourn."

Gideon stiffened at that, and O'Rourke was pleased to note that his own barb, the calculated use of the word 'murderin", had struck home. Gideon had reckoned without O'Rourke's cunning. Now it was the smart nigger who was struggling to contain his emotions. Maybe O'Rourke would after all goad the nigger into hitting him. Not that it mattered, since there were no witnesses.

"Don't you deny it now."

Gideon was silent. He had the sense to know when speech was useless. But his silence goaded O'Rourke even more. Gideon should be weeping and wailing like the craven nigger he was, saying, 'No, massar, I didn't do it, massar.' Instead, he just stood to attention, staring at the Stars and Stripes that peeped over O'Rourke's back.

"You think we's so stoopid we don't know what our niggers is doin' behind our backs? Well, maybe you thinks we is stoopid. Maybe you thinks we's stoopid enough to let yous git drunk and go pawin' white women, then we's stoopid enough fer anythin'. But this is where it ends, Gideon. Your buddy's gonna be shot and there ain't a goddam thing you nor anybody can do about it."

O'Rourke rose, his heavy, bow-legged frame edging around the desk with as much lateral as forward motion, to stand in front of Gideon. He stared slightly up at the negro, into the twin barrels of those nostrils that flared in a flattened nigger nose, and thrust his face towards the private.

"Too bad you ain't gonna be here to see it. 'Cos this is where your interferin' ways is comin' to an end. You hear me?"

O'Rourke's face was a mere couple of inches from that of the negro. The latter's head sprang backwards, as if O'Rourke had spat at him, and the sergeant smiled his satisfaction.

"I got me a right to ask folk, respectful-like, if they seen anythin' that might help my friend, ain't I, Sergeant?"

"No, you ain't."

"But that's only justice, Sergeant."

"It ain't justice. It ain't justice," retorted O'Rourke, so infuriated now that he hardly knew what he was saying. "And it's gotta stop."

Suddenly aware of the temptation to strike Gideon himself, O'Rourke stepped smartly back, the backs of his thighs striking the desktop, and bawled:

"Luwitski! Luwitski, git yerself in here!"

The door opened promptly, without the preliminary of a knock, and Luwitski's boyish face appeared flushed as if anxious he had been caught out doing something he shouldn't.

"Take this man in charge, Private! He's guilty of striking a superior officer."

O'Rourke glanced at Gideon, at the same time moving his hand upwards with the half-formed intention of touching his cheek to add verisimilitude to his accusation. But the hand stopped, froze and dropped to his side. He had expected Gideon to deny it, to beg forgiveness like a nigger who knew his place should, or even to react with indignation like the barrack-room lawyer he was. But he just stood stock-still and stared at O'Rourke, the hint of a smirk about his lips. O'Rourke, who had been savouring his triumph, suddenly felt himself overcome by a wave of emotion he had never expected to feel: shame. And that shame would only be compounded were he to counterfeit the struck man.

O'Rourke was unused to feeling shame. True, he had

on rare occasions been remiss in his duties and felt duly repentant in the face of the censure of a superior officer. But to feel shame before someone who was not his military superior, was something he had not felt since high school. And what was worse, he felt ashamed before a nigger: one who was so far beneath him, one who should be cringing before him, instead of looking straight into his head and smirking about what he saw there.

O'Rourke blazed with an anger so uncontrollable, that had Luwitski not been present he would have laid into Gideon with his own hands. He felt tempted to do it now. But again, O'Rourke instinctively realised that for him to do so would represent yet another victory for the nigger. The best thing he could do was get the man out of his presence as soon as possible before he was tempted beyond endurance.

"Take him to the cells, Private. Solitary confinement."

"Yes, sir."

Luwitski seized Gideon by the arm.

An inspiration struck O'Rourke.

"Oh, and Luwitski."

"Yes, sir?"

"Bread and water until I say different, y' hear?"

CHAPTER THIRTY-NINE

The earth of the path was baked hard by many days of summer sun that had preserved foot and hoof prints impressed upon the mud some months previously. The rutted surface was something Tom Dawkins had not reckoned with when he decided to strike out across country to the American camp rather than take the more circuitous metalled road. Nor had he anticipated the effects of the two pints he had downed in the Black Bull. Normally he could drink two pints of even pre-war ale and feel no ill effects, but these drinks had been consumed in little over half an hour, and the legs that swayed on the ruts and brushed past ferns, brambles and thistles threatened more than once to pitch him flat on his face. But the ale was his Dutch courage.

He had reached the area of heathland known for reasons lost to posterity as 'Barney's Meadow', when the thought brought him up short, so that he stood, breathing in the musty fragrances of summer, and swaying slightly amid the gorse, their black pods popping around him like detonations from the cap guns of boys playing cowboys and Indians. What if she was pregnant?

He had lain with her in Parson's Wood, in the hollow formed by a dry stream bed where one of the trees had fallen, concealing them from sight from one direction, and with a holly bush performing that office in the other. He was surprised how keen she was. And she was wearing her blue overcoat. There seemed little need for an overcoat when the air was mild and the clouds in the sky, a mere dusting of scaly cirrus, threatened no rain. She dropped her coat on the springy earth and they lay upon it. When she took it up again, afterwards, she spent ten minutes removing pine needles. So she had intended they do it from the moment they left her house.

That was what he had longed for. What else but the dream of making love to Emily France had guided him through treacherous minefields and bombardments of random death, had sustained him during those nightmares in which he relived the horror? But not like this. He had imagined himself having to woo her, and infinitely slowly, calling in aid those attributes that were alien to him, but which he might put on like stage makeup, the macho confidence of Clark Gable, the suavity of Robert Donat, he wore her down. She would give herself, half desirous, half fearful, always coy and gauche, as the utmost expression, teased reluctantly from her, of her love for him. He could never have dreamed of the cold-blooded calculation with which she now approached the deed. Nor the knowing lust with which she undid the buttons on his shirt and tugged free his trousers; the passion that yet had something counterfeit about it, like the enthusiasm of a prostitute.

He was all the more bewildered to find this passion coming in the wake of what he interpreted as a reluctance for his company, what at times seemed a positive shrinking from him. This emotion at least was all too explicable. Of course, it was never hinted at, indeed Schultz's death never alluded to, but he felt she must know and blame him for it. The very fact that she had not approached him for an explanation for his extraordinary conduct when he heard about Schultz's death, the fact of her silence in a matter in which speech would have been most natural, was proof in itself she must know of his involvement. She must have expected him to confess. Was she dismayed that he did not do so, had he fallen in her estimation as a result? Or was she glad, hoping he would hold his peace? Or had she heard about the black man suspected of the attack? If so, did that mean she believed him innocent?

Why then this coolness towards him? Was it not proof there must have been something more between Emily and Schultz than she let on? Or was it the natural shrinking from one whose hands had taken a life? And yet if so, he would have expected her to confront him with it, blame him, say that she never wanted anything more to do with him. She was so utterly baffling. His mind reeled before his attempts to read her.

No, she had wanted him, but not, he was sure, for reasons of lust. And in the coupling, the smell of the pines and the earth, that should have been sharp and fragrant and optimistic in his nostrils, was rather as the rankest weeds and the most fetid ripenesses of autumn, with all their connotations of decay and ill omen. If this was how their life together was to begin, what future did it hold? Because the decay was that of all trust between them.

He lay on her exposed lower body, white and bony, and her flesh gave and opened to him not, as some romantic novelist might describe it, as the flower that opens before the sun, but with a ripeness that was more like putrefaction. It was not so much the making of something beautiful as the breakdown of something. He lay on her and she was cold, and when he rolled off her onto the soft, downy earth it was warm. Their bodies, young and taut and lithe, were nevertheless infected with the virus of mistrust, and he feared the prognosis was terminal. He should have been able to give himself to her with love and gratitude, and instead all he felt was the shame of one who goes with the cheapest of whores. He lay back replete, not with satisfaction, but with an overwhelming consciousness of having been used.

Yes, he was convinced there had been more between Emily and this Yank than she let on. Had she lain in the woods with the Yank on top of her? The thought tormented him. He had not believed the American when he'd implied there had been something physical between them. He had even half forgotten the words, attributing them to jealous spite. And here he was now trying desperately to remember them. He had given her what she wanted. Yes, that was what he said. He had tried to bury his suspicions of her, but now they resurfaced with a vengeance. The Emily of his imagination could not have behaved so. But what of the real Emily?

He looked at her as she sat pulling up her stockings and saw how he had been duped. She was not the dream he had aspired to. She was not the Emily whose face appeared to him in his darkest moments. Hers were not the lips that willed him to survive and come back to her. Those lips were the innocent lips of a girl; these beetroot red and cheap. And until that moment he could have backed away from her approach, turned his head aside as she beckoned to him from beneath the lamplight. Now he had gone too far. He may not have been the first to have her, but she had made sure he was the last. She had snared him, and he felt helpless and dirty as much as spent; used and deceived as much as replete.

Was this the reason for this attack of conscience? Did he wish to escape her toils; the debilitating consciousness that when she held him her arms were without love? The awareness that his life hereafter was one of a double entrapment: by her, and by the knowledge of what he had done; that he had allowed an innocent man to be punished for his transgression.

Whatever his reasons for doing what he was now about to do, and they remained obscure from him also, what he had not taken into account was the possibility that he may have made her pregnant. They had taken no precautions to avoid it. He of course had no idea she would lie with him. But she had been entirely careless of the risk. He wondered about that. For all her shrinking from him, she nevertheless wanted to bind him to her, and her indifference to consequences was proof of that. He was not so innocent as to be ignorant of what a woman did when she wanted to claim a man. And she knew he was not the sort of man to turn his back on his responsibilities.

What then of the child? For his mind, having accepted the possibility, now converted it into a fact. Could he carry on to the American camp and confess what he had done, thereby depriving a child who had barely been conceived, and who was entirely innocent of the circumstances of the conception, of the support a father could provide? All for some black man he had never met.

Or was a part of his mind revolting from the actions of a body literally walking towards its own destruction and tempting him with a reason to justify to himself, his turning round and walking back to the pub for a third pint of mild. No, face it for what it was, Tom Dawkins: fear. It was fear that had conjured up this non-existent baby; that had, like the Devil of the Bible in his temptation of Christ, known just what to dangle before his eyes. 'Get thee behind me, Satan,' as the vicar would say.

He trudged on, along the path that wound through flat mats of bilberry and now purpled heather, its springy roots catching at his boots as if it, indigenous as it was of this land that had nurtured him, were anxious to prevent him sacrificing himself for some alien being and principle obscure.

He saw her again, as the last time they had met, after their coupling in the woods, she taking her leave from him with a kiss bestowed upon him as if for form's sake. One who saw them would never have imagined that a momentous union had taken place. She left him like one clocking off from a shift at the factory, he thought bitterly, drawing her pine-needle-free coat around her and clopping off along George Terrace. It may be, if he now went through with what he planned, that that would be the last he would ever see of her. And to his surprise, he felt no dismay.

What would she say if she knew what he was doing? Would she, like some damsel in a Victorian melodrama, throw herself at his feet and beg, her pale, tear-streaked face lifted to his, him to turn back and spend his life with her? He really had no idea. He was that ignorant of the woman whose face had haunted his adult life, and with whom his future, what there was of it, was now inextricably tied.

Once through the copse of alders, the path crossed, by means of stepping-stones, the River Otter. Here he stopped, for it was his last opportunity before the road. He stood on the stones, surveying the tea-brown water. Three white stones partially protruded from the surface, underneath shadowy, coated in moss, like the shipwrecks of stones. How ironic, that he had walked into the hellish bombardments of Alamein and Tunisia and survived, had anticipated a long life that ended lying beside Emily in his own bed, only to find himself walking into a noose.

He thought of his surrogate father. What would Jack say about the sacrifice he was now intending? Would he applaud his selflessness, the principle of not letting another suffer for his own actions? Or would he say he had already done his bit, and he should get in the ambulance and leave the battlefield with those other casualties? He did not know.

He climbed onto the minor road once known only as that leading to Forecombe, but now forever associated with the American camp, whose lookout tower appeared over the hedge. He had as a child been fascinated by Chalford Castle, his schoolmaster Mr Edwards explaining that it was the means by which the alien Normans maintained control over the Saxon population of England. And he had always equated the Germans with those 'alien Normans'. To some the American base represented glamour, but to him it was little better than the repressive motte and bailey from which Norman knights once rode out in their mailcoats to oppress the English peasantry and take what they regarded as their rights amongst the local womenfolk.

He was on the road now, his eyes straying down the fringes of hedge, of young hawthorn berries and bindweed, a last glimpse of freedom before prison walls separated him forever from the flora of his native land.

He found his legs carrying him up the path at an alarming rate. There were two men on guard. The man on the right was swarthy as an Arab. It was the man on his left who caught his attention: tall, angular, blond, and for a moment he thought it was Schultz come back to haunt his killer, or else, in a moment of fleeting self-delusion, that he was not dead at all, and it had been nothing but a nightmare. But this was not Schultz. Quite apart from the spectacles, this man had a softness about his spare frame that was at variance with the other's sardonic tension, and a quizzical look that examined him, not with satirical contempt, but the absent-minded bookishness of his old teacher Mr Meadows, who was known to break off a lesson to dash to the window if a butterfly flew past.

"Hey, feller! You can't come in here! Whaddaya want?" the swarthy one asked.

"It's okay, Doug. Let me deal with this," said the tall blond. "You all right?"

The look of alarm on the American's face told Tom all he needed to know about how he must appear to them.

He opened his mouth and tried to speak without quite knowing what he was going to say, but his tongue clove to the roof of his mouth, and all he could do was stare like some kind of halfwit.

"What is it you want? Because we can't let you in."

For a fleeting second Tom felt outrage. This was his country after all. And then the outrage faded, overtaken with frightening rapidity by a sense of nostalgia for any such feeling. He said, huskily, like an old, loose-dentured, slack-jawed version of Tom Dawkins:

"I came about that bloke. The one what was killed."

He had the full attention of the man, who had up to now been treating him with the offhand indulgence of one dealing with the retarded.

"Larry Schultz."

"Yeah. I come about him. You still got that black bloke locked up for killin' him?"

"I'm not sure I should be telling you that."

"Why not?"

"You ain't some newspaper guy?" the swarthy one asked.

Ignoring him, the blond said:

"I don't know that I have the authority."

"You gonna let him go?"

"Look, feller. It weren't me that told yer, but no, we ain't. He's gonna be court martialled."

"If he's court martialled, what's gonna happen to him?" Tom persisted.

"If he's found guilty, shot, I guess."

"Or hanged," Tom said absently. And he had a sudden terrifying vision of the hangman placing the rope around his own neck, tightening the knot, and then placing the black bag over his head, the fabric lowered slowly, deliberately, so that his eyes strained downwards until it was painful, clinging desperately to that last sliver of light, that last needles-eye glimpse of the world he was about to leave. He felt the sweat gathering in his armpits, leaking out down his spine, its oily texture caressing the vertebrae. His legs began to tremble.

"The guy's smashed. Send him on his way," the other MP said.

"I... I gotta go," Tom said, and turned unsteadily, his head swimming, so that he feared he might fall in a dead faint.

"You know something about this feller?" the blond asked.

Tom wanted to say no, but he did not have even the courage to lie. How could it be that he had the courage to face down Rommel's Panzers, walk into the Germans' stonk, the hail of small arms, but not admit what he had done? He turned and stopped but remained mute.

Part of him did not want to go, because once he had gone there was no going back. If he stayed, even if he stayed silent, there was still a chance he might speak. And part of him wanted to speak. But the skin on his cheeks still tickled to the touch of the cloth bag, and he could feel the hempen fibres pressing against his Adam's apple.

The tall blond was saying:

"If you know anything, you should speak."

But he could not speak. He could not move and walk away, but he could not speak either.

"Did you see anything on that night?"

"Send him on his way!" the other said.

"No!" barked the tall blond. "If you did… if you did, fella, then it's your dooty to speak up. A man's life is at stake here – it was Wednesday last."

Yes, a man's life was at stake. His own.

With dismay, Tom Dawkins found himself walking down the path. Behind him he heard the forlorn pleas of the tall MP.

"Come back! There's folks here might wanna talk to you. The guy's attorney…"

But Tom was already at the road, and wondering how long it would take him to get to the pub.

Behind him the swarthy MP was asking his companion:

"What you botherin' with that stoopid Limey fer anyway, Stan?"

The other replied:

"Somethin' ain't right, I tell yer."

CHAPTER FORTY

The *Chalford Echo* may have been, as the gold lettering on the window of its office proclaimed, 'the voice of Chalford', but, Sally Burns thought, to judge by the size of that office, its voice was little more than a whisper. Hemmed in between Thomson's the tobacconist's and Lavender's Hardware, its frontage could easily be missed by one in a hurry to impart the sort of tidings its readers awaited in every Thursday issue. These, having once been little more distressing than the sad demise of so-and-so's Pekingese beneath the wheels of the number 22 bus, had taken on an altogether more sombre note, most lately by the news of the death of Eric Climpson.

Sally Burns entered through the narrow door, squeezed between a small window and a poster that read 'Freedom is in peril, defend it with all your might!' and entered upon a spacious reception, with a row of chairs down one wall, and a receptionist behind a desk. Facing her another door opened onto an even more spacious area with printing presses and two men in shirtsleeves tending them. The impression the organisation gave was that of one very large man behind a monocle.

The receptionist looked up with harassed competence. The girl could have been no more than twenty, her bright lipstick as if designed to pre-empt any 'You are young to be doing this job!' But that was the war. Everyone seemed so much older before 1939. Now it was as if the young were running the country, and the middle-aged, perhaps even those of Sally's own age, were put out to pasture, even if most had not recognised the fact.

"Yes?" drawled the girl. Whatever it was that had got her the job, it was not manners.

"I would like to see the proprietor – the editor, I mean," said Sally, momentarily nonplussed in this alien environment.

"That'd be Mrs Lacey."

She had heard of Caroline Lacey, and she liked what she heard. 'Campaigner' was the most common epithet applied to that lady, although when used in WVS circles it tended to acquire negative connotations. And being a 'campaigner', Caroline Lacey was surely a kindred spirit for Sally Burns.

"Who can I say wants to see her?" the receptionist simpered.

"Mrs Burns… Sally Burns."

A somewhat intense interval, in which the receptionist stared at her as if she wished to preserve Sally's features on her retina until the day she died, was relieved by the girl taking a lengthy telephone call from a paper supplier.

Sally felt tense, and to relieve that tension kept flicking the hair from her forehead in nervy gestures. She was surprised at the importance this affair of the black US serviceman had assumed for her. She kept telling herself the man was nothing to her; she had never met him, and he was not as important as the principle his case represented. But there was more to it than that. The man was a symbol of the way the United States treated its black citizens, a symbol moreover of all the downtrodden of this benighted earth.

And something more personal still. Sally had been unable to save her mother and brother and sister, and those others who died in the ruins that had once rung to childish laughter. And in her eyes that fact condemned her life to one of failure. But Mrs Villiers had unexpectedly handed her a chance of redemption. She could not save her mother and Donald and Edie, but she could save this black American. She, an insignificant woman, who had failed so many, could do a small, perhaps unregarded thing, that would strike a blow for the principle that all races should be accorded the respect one human being should accord another.

The rear door opened and Sally found herself facing a squat, middle-aged woman with a strikingly beautiful face and piercing hazel eyes.

"Caroline Lacey."

She strode up to Sally and thrust a hand at her midriff, at which Sally snatched defensively, half fearful that if she missed, she would be seriously winded. The woman was dressed in sober tweeds, with brogues on her feet, and eschewed makeup. It was as if she were making a statement denying her sexuality; indeed, as if she felt she needed to do so in order to command the position she held in this work environment. Sally recalled that Caroline Lacey had been sub-editor until the editor received his call-up papers.

"Can I get you some coffee?"

Sally was about to decline, but when Mrs Lacey said, "real coffee", she assented.

"Some coffee please, Irene."

The receptionist scowled at her with a look eloquent of 'Haven't I got enough to do?'

Sally was led by Caroline Lacey through the rear door, and up a flight of stairs to a metal gangway that looked down on the printing presses, past the composing department, whose window revealed a man crouched over a typeface, and then into a small office. Caroline Lacey subsided into the seat behind her desk, indicated that Sally take that opposite, and asked:

"Well, Miss Burns, what can I do for you?"

Sally narrated the story as she had it from Mrs Villiers, omitting only the latter's involvement, and stopping when the receptionist entered carrying a tray with coffee pot and cups, and dispensed with it a look of reproach for Sally's too-obvious discretion. When she had finished, Caroline Lacey rose, taking her cup and saucer with her, and strode over to the window.

"Grover Carson, a sad story indeed," she said. "And what is your interest in the matter, if I might ask?"

Grover Carson. So that was his name.

"Justice," said Sally. "I want to see justice done."

"No. Talk of the law by all means, Miss Burns—"

"Mrs Burns."

"I'm sorry, Mrs Burns. Talk of the law by all means, but do not talk of justice. In this instance, and whatever the outcome, I cannot see that justice is served."

"Well, it's not served by an innocent man hanging,"

said Sally, her hackles rising at this lack of sympathy for her cause.

"If that is indeed what the United States army do. He is their man after all. And it is their rules and regulations."

"But he is innocent!"

"Is Tom Dawkins then guilty?"

"He's guilty of something."

"He's guilty of doing what every red-blooded man would have done in his situation, and, it has to be said, what every woman would want him to do."

"That's just what—"

Caroline Lacey raised a quizzical black eyebrow.

"Never mind. He's one of yours. So you won't help me then."

"There are, I'm afraid, many reasons why I won't, and even if I would, can't, help you. And that is the least of them.

"First of all, we are a newspaper for this town. We are its voice. We stick up for Chalford, against Whitehall, the War Ag, against all-comers. And we stand up for its citizens. We do not condemn and throw them to the wolves – the wolves in this case being the US Army."

"So that's it. You're afraid for your circulation figures," Sally said, making no attempt to conceal her contempt.

"You may choose to put it like that. But to print what I imagine you want us to print would be to deny our raison d'être as a mouthpiece for the citizens of this town, by condemning one who has family and many friends here. After that, who would want to read the *Chalford Echo*?"

"You'd be out of a job," Sally sneered.

"I don't care for your tone, Mrs Burns. If you want to look at it like that, there would not just be me. This newspaper puts bread in the mouths of a number of families. And the town would have no voice. We stick together in this town, Mrs Burns. If you want to stay here, you would do well to remember that."

"That sounds like a threat."

"Merely friendly advice."

Caroline Lacey's tone was superficially amicable, but there was no mistaking the hard edge.

"Well, Mrs Burns, there's the rub, I'm afraid. If it comes to a contest between the town and justice as you call it, we have to pick the town every time. If on the other hand the cause were justice *for* the town, you would find we would be the first to man the barricades."

"Well, if that's all you've got to say," said Sally, rising from the chair.

"Please, Mrs Burns," said Mrs Lacey, who had now regained her own seat and was making a subsiding gesture with her palms. She said:

"Even if I wished to help you, I regret it's quite beyond my power. None of us are masters of our own fate in this war, not least the newspapers. We're in the hands of the Ministry of Information, in particular the Department of Home Intelligence and the Press and Censorship Bureau. All our newspapers are monitored by scrutineers at the ministry. You're not so naive as to believe we can print what we like, regardless of whether it damages morale or aids our enemies?"

Sally was not entirely sure whether the question was rhetorical, so remained silent.

"Let me explain," Mrs Lacey went on. "We're given guidance from our masters in Whitehall on what topics may be subject to censorship and are invited to submit stories that may be subject to a Defence Notice. In a sense it is merely voluntary…"

"So—" Sally interrupted.

"No, please, Mrs Burns, do not suggest what I think you are about to. A story that is not passed for censorship can leave us open to prosecution. In a time of war, it's a most serious matter."

"But this isn't a matter of grand strategy, it's not about troop movements or anything of that sort."

"The Americans – love them or loathe them – are our allies, and anything that jeopardises our relationship with them damages our morale and aids the enemy. You do not think that Herr Goebbels and Lord Haw-Haw make these insinuations about American troops and British girls for the fun of it, because they have a sense of humour. I can assure you they do not. They wish to drive a wedge between us and the Americans.

"The constraints under which we act do not allow us to publish articles concerning disputes between the US forces and British civilians. Nor those which would give the enemy grounds for thinking that differences exist between us. The Americans have a similar system."

"So much for the freedom of the press. For the freedoms we're supposed to be fighting for," said Sally petulantly.

"Oh please, Mrs Burns, don't be so naive. When our very existence as a country is concerned, we must curtail certain freedoms we've taken for granted, and make…

accommodations that would otherwise be regarded as unwelcome."

"Accommodations, is it? It seems we have made so many 'accommodations' the Americans all but rule this country now."

"That, I'm afraid, is the way it is. We can only hope they give us our country back when the war is over."

"Well, there's no more to be said then."

Sally pushed her still largely full cup of coffee from her and stood up, smoothing down her skirt with brisk, angry gestures.

"What do you propose to do now?" Mrs Lacey asked.

"What can I do?"

Sally was disappointed to note there was a forlorn fall to her voice.

"Believe me when I say I have some sympathy with you. There have been occasions when I've felt the same frustration you're feeling. And it is for that reason I caution you to do nothing that would incur the displeasure of the authorities."

Sally gave a little guffaw, looked down at her feet, but then rallied, looking Caroline Lacey full in the face.

"I don't need a newspaper to publicise things, do I?"

"I'm not sure what you mean."

"What about the case of Henry Woods?[8]"

Henry Woods was a black soldier attached to the 3914 Quartermaster Gas Supply Company based in Somerset, who had been a regular customer of a local woman whom he paid for sex. On one occasion, he not being in funds,

---

8   A fictional character based upon the case of Leroy Henry in 1944.

she accused him of rape. Having been court martialled, he was sentenced to death. However, a local baker started a petition and obtained signatures from 33,000 people, as a result of which the case was thrown out.

"I cannot see you getting 33,000 signatures in Chalford if it means condemning Tom Dawkins to hang. Let me give you some advice, although I doubt you'll take it. Do not allow your emotions to cloud your judgement. And I beg you don't act without taking matters through the appropriate channels."

"Do you think I'm frightened?"

"Oh, I'm sure you're not. But you're quite settled in this town, are you not? To do what you propose would make life difficult for you and your husband. I need not remind you of his position on the council."

"Are you threatening us?" Sally asked belligerently.

"Not me. But there are many others you would annoy. Think on it."

"This town…" Sally struggled for words to express her contempt. "I never thought I'd see the day this town, this country, valued truth so cheaply."

"Somebody," said Caroline Lacey urbanely and without the slightest discomposure, "once said that truth is the first casualty of war. We in the press have learnt that the hard way."

But her words were wasted, as Sally Burns was already exiting the door and negotiating her way back along the gangway, her heels sending back their crisp morse of disappointment and anger.

CHAPTER FORTY-ONE

Lionel Forbes Cameron 111 stood in the doorway of the canteen of the US base at Norton Manor Camp, now appropriated for the purposes of Grover Carson's court martial, smoking a Lucky Strike and watching as Carson was led, chained to two guards, back across the parade ground from the cells where he had been treated to what was doubtless a much inferior lunch to that which Cameron had enjoyed in the commandant's lodgings.

A light drizzle was falling, and it seemed to the watcher as if the weight of those lowering skies was concentrated upon the form of the black man, and the strength that it took to keep them at bay had rendered him hunched and sunken. How must it feel to be so close to death? Cameron wondered. To know that you would almost certainly not see another Christmas or Thanksgiving?

He tried to imagine what he would feel in such circumstances. But imagination failed him, as it must fail us all. Our lives are predicated upon our survival. Even in this time of war, he had never really faced the possibility of his own demise. When he had embarked at New York, and taken leave of his parents, it had felt little different from when they had left for a tour of Europe in '36.

Carson glanced up at him, his eyes startling cameos of misery and fear and, perhaps, resignation. Yes, if he understood what was happening to him. Cameron had to look away rather than face the man he had been charged with defending; the man whose life was in his hands, if one was prepared to take so optimistic a view as to imagine that anything Cameron did might influence the outcome of proceedings.

Cameron doubted it would. That assumption was some comfort to him. He did not want to think there might be something he could do to save this man's life, and, through neglect, or incompetence, failed to do. If he did fail – and he was sure he would – then the least he could say, was that it would not be through indifference.

Cameron ('Cam' to his friends) had some sympathy with Grover Carson. No doubt there were attorneys who loathed their clients, but Carson was a man who was easier to like than to loathe.

Cameron stood to one side while Carson and the two MPs passed into the building, the accused man still with eyes lowered. Cameron's acquaintance with blacks was limited, but he liked to think he knew the breed, having been in his youth quite close to Joseph, their butler. His was the sort of family where children were often closer to their servants than their parents.

Cameron was a WASP: a White Anglo-Saxon Protestant – a classic example of that elite breed of Republican who made up America's greatest families. He was related through his mother to the Forbeses, through a cousin to the Harrimans, and, no doubt, to most of the other clans who made up the untitled aristocracy of the United States. His parents were listed in the Social Register, which advertised the top one per cent of the population. He had grown up in Boston, and majored in law at Princeton, hence his eligibility as defence counsel.

Yes, there was something about that wistful look of Carson's that took him back to his childhood, and to the sticks of candy Joseph proffered but withheld until Cameron had performed his afternoon walk in the park. There was something straightforward and downright about Carson that reminded him of Joseph, who was not afraid to speak his mind to young 'Masser Cameron', particularly where Lucille, the untrustworthy maid, who boy and servant both loathed, was concerned.

But the man was guilty, of course. Only he had a motive to kill Schultz. That was something Cameron could not quite square with the Grover Carson he knew, albeit that theirs was a short acquaintance, the attorney only having ten days, from notification of his role, to interview Carson and prepare his case. He had applied, but his motion to delay the proceedings for two weeks was rejected out of hand by the trial judge.

Of course, Carson could be dissembling. But Cameron had never known a negro who possessed the intellect to successfully dissemble. Yes, if there were violent tendencies in his client, they were well hidden. He had, playing the Devil's advocate, tested Carson as he would be tested in court in the hope of producing an angry response, to no avail, succeeding in eliciting only a sullen resignation. But Carson had been a boxer, and one who engaged in that profession could easily, Cameron reasoned, produce the violent response much as the tap of the hammer will elicit the knee jerk. That was an interesting point. Could pugilism instinctively provoke the violent response in the otherwise pacific? If so, was Carson really responsible for his actions? But that was too speculative. In any case, it was Carson's choice to become a boxer.

The case mattered to Cameron not only because of an instinctive sympathy for the accused, but because the very idea of capital punishment revolted him. He regarded it as primitive, retributive in a way that sat ill with the modern USA, and he would save Carson from it if he could. But he could not see how.

This was the first court martial Cameron had been involved in, and a man's life depended upon the outcome. The awesome nature of that responsibility diminished as Cameron became acquainted with the facts. The case against Carson was purely circumstantial. On the normal standard of criminal responsibility, a court should not convict. All the prosecution had was evidence of motive and absence of a credible alibi.

But Cameron was convinced the court would convict. The brutal truth was that this was a military tribunal investigating the killing of one of its own, and it demanded blood. The only blood it could have was that of Grover Carson, because he was the only one who possessed a motive to kill Schultz. And, as a pugilist, and, it had to be admitted, a black, he fitted the bill admirably. The best Cameron could do was an argument for self-defence.

Nevertheless, Cameron wanted his conscience to be clear in that he had done all he could to present his client's case in the best possible light. It did not help that he, someone who had never conducted a court martial (did anything suspicious lie behind that?), had so little time even to familiarise himself with the *Manual for Courts Martial 1928*.

Cameron had been allowed two interviews with Carson, both taking place at Norton Manor Camp to which Carson had been transferred with what seemed to Cameron suspicious precipitation. The gentleness, even timidity, and transparent honesty of the man was quite at variance with the vision Cameron had formed of him. Carson did seem a little lacking in intelligence, and repeatedly and with an enthusiasm that caused his guard to rap repeatedly with his baton on the glass separating client from attorney, urged Cameron to contact his friend Errol.

"You gotta speak to Errol!" Carson insisted. "He'll know what to do."

Cameron understood, from the papers provided to him, that the person in whom such confidence resided was one Errol Gideon.

Cameron made a list of the men he wished to call as witnesses. This Errol was in custody for striking an officer, and although his alibi was partial only, Cameron was forbidden to speak to him. There were the other blacks present at the pub brawl: Clark and Endean. Cameron would also dearly have wished to call the locals who had been present in the pub but had been warned in no uncertain terms by the colonel, as well as Major Bellucci, that no British people were to be approached as witnesses. On querying this he was informed it would have an adverse effect upon relations between the US military and the British.

Cameron had no doubt that the authorities would not wish it known their police had come to blows with 'their hosts'. He argued strenuously against the prohibition, pointing out that the prosecution would use the fracas as the basis for their case on motive, and he had a right to challenge their version of events. In doing so he unleashed the full fury of the major.

"Well, you got the evidence of them other niggers, ain't yer? How much goddam evidence you gonna need, son?"

Cameron was quite taken aback by the vulgar bellicosity of the man. Was this really the standard of major in the modern US military?

Bellucci knew, as did he, that the evidence of black men would carry little weight. But he must abide by that order. If he had been at all in doubt, the major, with what Cameron now recognised as characteristic unsubtlety, pointed it out.

"I hear you got political ambitions back home, son. A dishonourable discharge fer disobeyin' orders ain't gonna look good on your record now, is it?"

Cameron wondered if he should wait until the court martial began, then apply for a continuance for the purposes of interviewing the locals. That would make his request and its refusal a matter of public record. The authorities wouldn't want that, and the consequences for him personally would not be good. In addition, the continuance would almost certainly be refused, and a verdict reached, before he tracked down the locals.

Cameron was even less optimistic when he discovered

that the trial judge was to be Colonel Nathan Etherington from Jackson, Mississippi, one of those officers most vocal in their opposition to blacks in the US Army. He had been hoping it would be Bertie Abraham, a friend of his father from Yale, or Hiram Bosanquet, one of the New Bedford Bosanquets.

The trial judge advocate was Captain Horace T. Atkins, a man notoriously intolerant of laymen's lack of precision in giving evidence. But he was a fair opponent who would allow Cameron to present his case without undue carping.

The court room, having recently been used as a canteen, remained redolent of cooking oil to such an extent that Cameron wondered whether the off-white decor was the result of years of frying. Such frivolous speculation was a welcome distraction from his nervousness, as he stared at the photograph of President Roosevelt, whose benign features seemed to be doing their best to reassure him that he would perform his duties as befitted a US Army captain, and that he could depend upon the impartiality of American justice.

Facing him was Colonel Silas Gorman, a thick-set man who squatted as much as sat over the desk in front of him and could not but remind Cameron of a giant toad. Gorman was the president, the most senior of the five members of the court, the minimum number allowed in a general court martial, who were seated according to their rank on either side of him.

When Grover Carson was led, handcuffed, to stand before the desk that represented the dock, he made a pathetic figure. He shot wary glances about him, squinting at the brightness of the ceiling lights as if the hours of daylight they had enjoyed had never penetrated his cell. There was something pitiably submissive and abject about him, as if, thought Cameron, all that genetic servitude now found expression in his cowed and broken frame. His fearful glances mutated into the bewilderment of the retarded. Could anyone imagine this man capable of murder? And yet it was as difficult to imagine him squaring up to an opponent in the ring, and the man was undeniably a boxer.

Colonel Etherington spoke in a ringing bass, those brows that seemed so ambitious of meeting in the middle, like a bridge constructed from either side of a river, and his green eyes, fixing themselves upon Carson's face with an expression of solemn judicial opprobrium. Cameron was quietly relieved that his client had, on his advice (and Carson was as perfectly malleable as any lawyer could wish), decided against opting for trial by judge alone.

They were ordered to stand as the judge announced the hearing of the case of the United States versus Private Grover Carson convened under Article 8 of the Articles of War by Major General Gerhardt, commander of the 29th Infantry Division. There being no question of the accused's competence, the judge asked Carson who he desired to introduce as counsel. Carson, standing as unsteadily as if he had been hit by a solid right, simply turned his head to Cameron, as if imploring.

"You must answer," said the judge severely. "Do you desire to introduce…" He looked to Cameron with exasperated appeal in his heavy-lidded eyes.

"Captain Lionel Cameron, sir."

"Captain Lionel Cameron," Etherington repeated,

the syllables as if slapped down one by one on the bench before him, like a teacher admonishing an idiot child.

Grover Carson nodded, head heavy and mechanical, and managed to articulate a faint 'yessir'.

After the reporter was sworn, Etherington proceeded to name the members. Apart from Gorman they were all lieutenants. All were, of course, white. He did not know if any were from the south. But there were many places in the north where relations between black and white were no better than in Louisiana.

As defence counsel, he had a right to make a peremptory challenge. But as the court need not sustain a challenge upon the mere assertion of the challenger, Cameron doubted it would be upheld, and may prejudice the court against his client.

He was not, he realised with some dismay, an aggressive advocate, rather one inclined to do nothing if uncertain; but aggression in these circumstances could cost his client his life.

The judge proceeded to the arraignment.

"Private 22179 Grover Carson, you are hereby charged that on the evening of 3 July 1943 in the town of Chalford, England, and while serving in the army of the United States of America, you did feloniously murder Private Lawrence Schultz of the United States Military Police. How do you plead?"

This at least Cameron had rehearsed with his client, and Carson was able to intone, feebly:

"Not guilty."

Each member in turn was called to take the oath to 'faithfully and impartially try, according to the evidence, their conscience and the laws applicable to trial by court martial, the case of the accused'. Three were clearly from southern states, the fourth from the Midwest.

Atkins outlined the prosecution case. In a doleful tone he described how Carson had resisted lawful arrest in the bar of the Black Bull public house on the evening of 26 June. The accused who had, prior to enlisting, been a boxer (Cameron considered objecting, but decided against it), was one of a group of three negroes arrested by Private Schultz and his MP colleagues. It was the prosecution case that several days later, on the next occasion in which blacks were allowed the freedom of the town, while on foot patrol in Chalford, Private Schultz was accosted, and killed by the accused.

No mention was made of the fact that Schultz bore Carson a grudge because of the latter's involvement with Schultz's girl. But Cameron knew the prosecution were intending to rely upon this. When he interviewed Carson, Cameron was at pains to extract as much detail as he could about this. It was clear that Carson and Errol had gone to a dance hall, and this girl had behaved in a forward fashion, dragging first Errol and then Carson onto the dance floor. This had been witnessed by Sergeant O'Rourke who then, presumably, passed this information onto the MP.

Cameron thought long and hard about the implications of this for his case. Even if the court believed O'Rourke, the rules stated that the prosecution might not adduce evidence of previous bad character in order to prove guilt.

The incident at the dance hall certainly gave Schultz grounds for the exemplary beating he had administered to his client, which was at odds with the treatment the other two blacks received. But the greater the beating Carson received, the greater the reason he had to seek revenge. In addition, the incident in the dance hall would inevitably prejudice the court against him. Again, Cameron would dearly have liked to call some locals to give evidence. As it was, it would be a case of the evidence of O'Rourke against the three black men, and Cameron had no doubt as to whose evidence the court would prefer.

Cameron rose and made his opening address, pointing out that the accused was presumed innocent, and the government bore the burden of proving his guilt beyond a reasonable doubt. If there were any such reasonable doubt, it must be resolved in favour of the accused. As the accused was charged with an offence which carried a mandatory death sentence, a conviction required all members of the court to bring in a guilty verdict.

In theory it sounded a high hurdle for the prosecution to surmount given the evidence, but looking at the five men before him, their faces like busts mounted for the purpose of expressing censoriousness, Cameron quailed within.

The first witness called by the prosecution was the doctor, Evan Chilcott, a pasty-faced individual who spoke in an almost incomprehensible dialect that Cameron identified only as northern English. He said that Schultz had died of a subarachnoid haemorrhage (bleeding within the skull, he explained), at some time between 6pm and 9pm on the evening of 3 July. This was caused by bleeding from a ruptured blood vessel into the space between the pia mater and the arachnoid layer, causing the blood to clot and form a haematoma. It would cause an immediate loss of consciousness. Given the circumstances in which Schultz was found, Chilcott had no hesitation in stating that it was caused by a severe blow to the head.

"And the more blows that were inflicted the more likely such an outcome would be, is that right?"

"Do not lead the witness, Mr Atkins," the judge admonished, but went on, "You may answer, Doctor."

"Of course," Chilcott agreed.

When Cameron cross-examined, he made no attempt to ask if Schultz's knuckles were bloodied because he knew, from the autopsy report, that they were not. Instead, he asked:

"Doctor, was there any evidence that the deceased was subjected to a sustained attack?"

It was a calculated risk. They always say never ask a question you don't know the answer to, but he had seen the autopsy report and was sure that if there had been such evidence Atkins would have made the most of it.

Atkins rose in objection.

"Sir, learned counsel must define exactly what he means by a 'sustained attack.'"

Judge Etherington agreed.

"Yes, Captain, you must."

"I mean, Doctor," Cameron said, disappointed he had not been able to phrase the question in a way that was most likely to produce an emphatic negative, "was there any evidence of multiple blows?"

"No, but of course a blow may connect and leave no evidence."

"That is unlikely, is it not?"

"In the case of an adult male assailant, yes."

"So far as appears to you, there was only one blow?"

"Yes."

"Doctor, can you clarify whether one blow alone could have caused the injury?"

"Certainly it could, but one has to be very unlucky…"

"Am I right in thinking that in this case the bad luck arose as much from the fact that his head struck the windowsill as from the blow itself?"

"Well, yes."

"Please confirm for the court record what evidence there was that his head struck the sill."

"There was blood and hair on the sill."

"Am I correct in saying this was on the corner of the sill?"

"That's correct, yes," Chilcott agreed.

"And the ground where the deceased fell, was it hard?"

"Yes, it was paving slabs."

"Can you say whether the deceased would have sustained his injury had he not fallen and struck his head on the sill or the sidewalk?"

"I cannot say that," said Chilcott.

"For the benefit of the court, can you clarify exactly what you mean by that?"

"I cannot say whether it was the fact of the blow to the head or the fact that he struck his head on the sill or, indeed, on the pavement, that caused his death."

"But there was evidence of a contusion on the back of the skull, was there not? Don't you agree that an assailant doesn't usually punch his victim on the back of the head?"

"Sir!"

Atkins was on his feet, his voice heavy with exasperation.

"Yes, Doctor, ignore that," the judge agreed.

"Doctor," Cameron persevered, "is that contusion evidence of a severe blow to the head?"

"A significant one, yes."

Oh, how Cameron hated pedants!

"And was it most likely caused by a blow to the head from a fist, or from a fall striking sill or sidewalk?"

"From the fall. But—"

"So Private Schultz was very unlucky?" Cameron hurriedly interposed.

Here Atkins objected.

"Sir, learned counsel is putting words in the witness's mouth."

"Ignore that question, Doctor."

Cameron persevered:

"So there is no evidence that the assailant intended to cause the deceased serious harm, let alone death?"

Here Atkins shot up again, but even his precipitation was anticipated by the judge.

"You need not answer that, Doctor. The witness is not required to speculate on the accused's intent, Captain. Don't let me have to warn you again."

"Just one more question, Doctor. Did you examine the accused to determine whether his knuckles were bruised or bloodied?"

Of course, Cameron knew he had not, and got the answer he desired.

The next witness Cameron had a chance to cross-examine was Sergeant O'Rourke. Standing straight to attention, buttoned, formal, he was the very type of his rank. What was distinctive in him was the way in which the lips canted, as if in incipient snarl, when cross-examined, as opposed to the respectful formality with which he answered Atkins' questions. This was a man who did not take kindly to having his word questioned, a man who could easily be led into some outburst of temper or injudicious remark.

"Sergeant O'Rourke," Cameron began, "the accused was, according to your testimony, pestering white women at the dance, and making, you said, 'one hell of a nuisance of himself'. Can you tell the court precisely what he was doing when you entered the hall?"

"He was dancin' with a white gal," said O'Rourke.

"And what, in your opinion, is the purpose of a dance hall?"

"Well, to dance. But he was forcin' her."

"But since he was already dancing when you entered the hall, you cannot give evidence as to whether the accused asked this girl to dance or whether she asked him."

"English gals don't do that sort of thing," O'Rourke said with an air of pontification.

"On the contrary, I understand there is something called the 'ladies excuse-me' when girls can ask men to dance with them."

"Well, I may have seen him drag her up."

"But you said he was already dancing with her when you entered."

"Well, he was draggin' her around the floor like she didn't wanna go with him."

"I believe that's the dance, Sergeant. It's called the jive."

"I know what it's god—…I know what I seen, and she didn't wanna be with him."

"On the contrary, I suggest she first of all asked his friend to dance with her, and when disappointed of that man's prowess, turned to the accused."

"I didn't see that."

"Right, Sergeant. You did not see that. Now, you say you knew this English girl was the girlfriend of the deceased, so you felt it was your duty to inform him of this. Why was that?"

"She'd been insulted, hadn't she? By a black."

"Insulted by being dragged up to dance against her will. But she was, after all, in a dance hall. And presumably hoped and expected to be asked for a dance."

"Not by no nig— not by a negro, sir."

"But this was the night when the blacks were allowed into town and whites were not. Who else would she dance with?"

"The English, I guess."

"But she would surely know that most English young men were in the forces, and there would be a significant complement of black troops present. One would think if she was averse to the idea of dancing with them, she would have stayed at home."

At this point Atkins shot from his seat with such precipitation Cameron was convinced he must, at some point, have had both feet off the floor.

"That's pure speculation on the part of counsel."

"Indeed it is," agreed the judge. "Captain, it is the motive of the accused we are concerned with, not that of the witness."

When he regained his seat with a suitably chastened air, Cameron was nonetheless satisfied he had dented the prosecution's attempt to blacken Carson's character and make him appear to conform to the redneck stereotype of his race.

The next prosecution witness was a Private Rudi Dolenz, who had been present at the pub brawl. The man entered the room with a lumbering, unsteady gait. If he had not known better, Cameron would have said the man was drunk, but he was probably just what his Jewish friends termed a 'klutz'.

Dolenz testified that he was a friend of Larry Schultz, and that Schultz had been dating an English girl called Emily. He said he didn't know that Schultz had been told about this Emily dancing with a black soldier prior to the visit to the pub. As to that, Cameron was not sure if he believed him.

Cameron pondered long and hard as to the picture he wished to paint of Larry Schultz. At the moment, his client was saying that he was not present at the time of the assault on Schultz. That, Cameron was convinced, was a defence that had little mileage given that Carson was the only one with a motive. All it had going for it was the evidential hurdle the prosecution had to overcome, and he was convinced this was not as high as in theory it should have been.

Cameron had invited Carson to consider admitting that he was present, and the punch he threw was in self-defence. Cameron could then argue that Schultz had come upon Carson by accident, or better still, had deliberately gone looking for him. When he put this to his client Carson was adamant that he 'weren't gonna tell no lies'. If Carson stuck to his story, Cameron could always refuse to call him to give evidence, as was his right. He therefore determined to see how the morning's evidence went, and at lunchtime try to persuade Carson not to take the stand.

Nevertheless, Cameron had another dilemma. On the one hand, he wanted to portray Schultz as bent on revenge. In doing so, not only might he turn the court against the deceased MP, but he strengthened the case for self-defence. However, the more angry and vindictive he made Schultz appear, the stronger Carson's motive for revenge against the MP. An understandable desire for revenge was not a defence open to his client. His only hope was to suggest that Schultz, having beaten Carson once, went to find him on the first occasion blacks were allowed in town, to repeat the process, and Carson punched him in self-defence. On the other hand, if Carson insisted on giving evidence that he wasn't there, it wasn't in the defence's interests to emphasise Schultz's malice against him. It was a gamble, and in the circumstances Cameron thought it best to keep his cross-examination to a minimum.

"You said the accused raised his hands like a boxer to 'get hisself ready to fight'. Where was Private Schultz when the accused did this?"

"He was... in front of him, I guess."

"And what did Private Schultz have in his hand?"

"Well, just his baton, I guess."

"Try not to guess so much, Private. Did he or did he not?"

"I... yes."

"So the accused's hands were raised in self-defence?"

Again, Atkins shot up from his seat. Cameron could only admire the man's leg musculature. The objection was sustained, but Cameron had said what he wanted to say. He had planted the seed.

The next prosecution witness was Private Eugene Larkins, a wiry, restless man, also a friend of Schultz. The cross-examination proceeded as with Dolenz, and Cameron asked the same question. This time it had apparently been anticipated and Larkins replied that Private Schultz 'went nowhere near him'.

"Which one of you was near him?" Cameron asked.

"None of us. Weren't none of us near him."

"Well, why did he raise his fists? Who was he going to fight with if not one of you?"

"Don't rightly know."

The final prosecution witness was a Private Randy Temple, who had been patrolling in Chalford the night Schultz was killed. This man, like Dolenz, was a big, shambling brute, whose eyes kept flicking to his right side as if suspicious his president might step out from his photo frame (and, indeed, his wheelchair) and spring some cowardly Democratic ambush upon him.

This man was an important witness for Cameron. He had always been puzzled about the patrol on the night Schultz was killed. He had assumed MPs would go about at least in twos for reasons of security. They were not, after all, the most popular military personnel. So why was Schultz on his own? And did he even want to ask that question? No, he did not, because if it was left open, it might imply Schultz wanted a witness out of the way when he went to vent his spleen upon Carson. The explanation could be something innocuous like a call of nature. But it was far better if nothing at all was said about it.

Nevertheless, he expected Atkins to ask the question, and was surprised he did not. This, Cameron realised, could be the crucial moment in the whole trial. If the issue of why Schultz was on his own was left open, Cameron could argue that Schultz had left his buddy to go in search of Carson and give him another beating. On that basis Carson would have been acting in self-defence. There was no evidence one way or the other, but the existence of doubt should be sufficient to find in his client's favour.

Instead of asking the crucial question, Atkins was concerned with timing.

"What time did you and Private Schultz part company, Private Temple?"

"Er... half past six, I guess."

"No guessing, Private. You must be quite sure."

"Yeah, half six, sure as I can be, sir."

"And you were where when he left you?"

Atkins produced copies of a map of Chalford.

"We was on the corner of that street—"

"Which street?"

"The one with the dance hall."

Atkins pointed to the map.

"Yessir, that's where we was."

"And in which direction did Private Schultz walk?"

"He went off towards the pub."

"The Swan?"

"Yessir."

When it was the turn of Cameron to get to his feet, feeling mightily relieved that Atkins had not asked the question he feared, he simply said:

"No questions."

It was better that this witness's evidence was left as open as possible.

The prosecution having presented their case, it was now open to the defence to ask the court to make a finding of not guilty as the evidence was insufficient. Again, Cameron decided against this course, as the chances of it being successful were virtually non-existent, and he did not wish to prejudice the court against his client.

As they adjourned, it was only left to Cameron to convince Carson not to give evidence, leaving open the possibility that Schultz had accosted him in the doorway of the tobacconist's. Amenable as Carson had proved thus far, this may prove a difficult task. Carson had been adamant that he 'wanted to give his side of the story' and he 'weren't gonna lie fer nobody'. Despite Cameron's assurance that he did not wish him to lie, merely not to give evidence, the coloured man regarded him with an expression that made him feel distinctly unclean.

Cameron approached the two MPs who were removing Carson's shackles.

"I wish to have a brief conference with my client before we go back into court."

"You gonna have to wait," said the stocky, chisel-chinned MP, "your baby here wants to go wee wee."

"You take him," said the other MP, the tall blond.

"Aw shucks," the other complained. "I get all the nice jobs. Why don't you nursemaid him once in a while."

"There's a pack of Lucky Strike in it fer you."

Carson and his minder left, and Cameron was turning back towards the door in the hope of a last smoke when he sensed the other MP behind him. He turned sharply, anticipating some threat.

"Can I have a word, sir. In private."

The man must have sensed his apprehension for he added:

"It's about your client. I might have something to help you."

"Sure," said Cameron surprised, his fears not entirely allayed.

They exited the door and Cameron came to a halt just outside.

"Can we go somewhere more private."

The MP glanced anxiously at the canteen window, the upper light of which was open. Cameron assessed the man: tall, with steel-rimmed glasses, rather studious than intimidating.

Intrigued, Cameron led him around a corner to a boiler house with a hill of coke piled to one side of it.

"What can I do for you, Private... er."

"Deacon, sir."

"Well?"

"It's more a matter of what I can do for you. What it is, I was on dooty a few days since at Chalford Camp. I was on guard at the gate, and this guy approaches the gate, an English guy, behavin' kinda funny. He asked if he could see someone in charge, but we said he couldn't and he oughtnta be there. He was real agitated."

Cameron took out a packet of Craven As and offered one to Deacon. As they lit up, he asked:

"What did he say he wanted?"

"Well, that's just it, he didn't. But he did say it was

about this here trial. He asked if he'd hang, this guy, and we said yes, if he's found guilty. But he was real… funny about it. I was sure he knew somethin' he wasn't tellin'."

"What happened then?"

"I tried to ask him, but he just lit right outta there… and I couldn't leave my post."

"Of course not. Did he give his name?"

"No."

"English, you say?"

"Yeah."

"What did he look like?"

"Kinda average. About five nine or ten, dark brown hair, not shaved fer a while."

"Age?"

"Twenties, I guess."

"So he should've been in the forces."

"I think he'd been injured. He had a limp."

"Which leg?"

"Er… his left, I think."

"Have you any idea what he wanted to say?"

"I don't rightly know. But I think he knew something that might help your man."

"Thank you, Private."

"Don't tell anybody I told you, sir."

"Of course not."

"What are you goin' to do now, sir, if you don't mind me askin'?"

Cameron appraised the man again. He was worthy of a confidence.

"I don't know what I can do. I should try and trace this man. There can't be many men of fighting age with a limp in Chalford. But I can't get to Chalford, and unless I ask for a continuance on the basis of the absence of a material witness, this trial's going to conclude this afternoon and my client may receive a capital sentence. Once that happens, I can't do anything more. I'd be sent back to base and won't be able to visit Chalford to get information in support of an appeal."

"I go back to Chalford."

"Could you…?"

"I could ask around, if I can get outta camp."

"Is that likely?"

"Far as I know I got nuthin' else to do."

"I would have to get a continuance first. That might not prove easy. If I could get a day… When do you go back?"

"I'm off dooty at three and the truck picks us up at four, sir."

"Could you ask around in Chalford tonight?"

"Maybe."

"Best start at the pubs. That's where these Brits go. Even if you can't see this guy, if you get a name for him, I could ask for a further continuance and call him as a witness. Of course, I'll be calling him blind, but it may be my client has nothing to lose."

"I'll do my best, sir. I don't wanna see an innocent man hang."

"Of course you don't. I'll give you the number for the camp."

Cameron took an old laundry bill from his pocket and scribbled down a telephone number.

"Ring me if you get anything. Don't give the information to anyone else. I'll make sure I'm around to take the call. That's if I can get the continuance. If we can, my client will be back to the cells in the hour. If not, then we're here until five or six and it isn't gonna matter."

Cameron went in search of his client, who he found sitting in the passage in the company of the other MP.

Cameron took Carson into one of the interview rooms. Seeing him again in close-up, Cameron was shocked at just how denuded he appeared. The bewilderment was still there, and something helpless with it; he was like a child who has lost his mother in a sale at Bloomingdale's. Cameron did not want to get his client's hopes up too much, so he simply said:

"I may have a potential witness, but he's not here at the moment so I'll have to request a continuance."

He had expected Carson to ask who the witness was, but the negro remained mute. And then all of a sudden, it was as if hope sprouted within, like one of those invisible plants that suddenly flourishes in a shower of rain in the desert, and he ejaculated:

"Not Errol!"

"No, it's not Errol."

The hope was extinguished with the rapidity with which it had appeared. A nonplussed Cameron went on:

"If the continuance is refused, we'll have to go on, and I'd like you to think about declining to testify."

"Decl…"

"Not giving evidence."

"But I want—"

There was something pathetic about the man's dependence.

"I know."

"I can't lie. Not to the court."

He was like a child. George Washington would have been proud of him. That or had him clamped in irons and made to work his plantation.

"You don't have to lie. Think about it, please. You were the only person who had a motive for killing Schultz. Do you understand what I mean by that?"

"A reason, yeah."

"The prosecution will try to show you attacked him. And if they succeed you may be executed for it. If we can make them think you may have acted in self-defence, you may only get a few years in jail."

"In jail," Carson repeated as if he had never heard the word.

"Well, that's better than being shot, isn't it?"

"I guess."

"Think about it."

Ten minutes later and Cameron was addressing the court.

"I must request a continuance on the grounds of the absence of a material witness. There is the possibility of a witness to this tragedy, and given what is at stake, I would submit it's in the interests of justice we have the opportunity to investigate the matter."

"What witness?"

This time Atkins got to his feet without his usual alacrity, as if weighed down by a heavy luncheon or the disbelief evident in his tone.

"There may have been a local who witnessed the incident."

"Do you know this witness's name?" Etherington

asked, looking down his patrician nose like a scientist peering through a microscope at some phenomenon that had entirely upset his calculations.

"I don't know the name, sir."

"What exactly do you know, Mr Cameron?"

"I have a description, sir."

"And why have you not called this witness in time for this tribunal?"

"I have only recently discovered his existence. Sir, my client's life is at stake."

"Sir, I object," said Atkins. "The defence has had long enough—"

"Sir, we've only had two weeks. I would remind you of what is at stake."

"How long, Captain Cameron?"

"Could I have three days, sir?"

"And what are we supposed to do, twiddling our thumbs for three days? You most certainly cannot. We reconvene at ten tomorrow morning, witness or no witness, and there will be no further continuances, is that understood?"

CHAPTER FORTY-TWO

It was twenty past eight when Stan Deacon entered the bar of the Black Bull.

The late evening sun made few inroads through the frosted glass of the window, so that in the gloom the two middle-aged men propping up the bar were but hunched sacks of heavy cloth. From a table in the corner came the clacking of dominoes. There was a woman behind the bar, heavily bosomed, wearing a flowery dress whose ill-fitting blooms alternately sagged and expanded with the effort of accommodation. She was chatting to one of the men at the bar, who wore a cap and leant on a stick, a terrier at his feet. The man drew heavily on a pipe whose smoke only added to the gloom.

Deacon moved toward the other end of the bar so there was less chance of being overheard. The woman sent him a glance of annoyance. Perhaps she was thinking that this Yank wanted nothing to do with the locals, that he was what had variously been described to him as 'stuck-up' or, to his amusement, 'hoity-toity'.

On the contrary, Stan Deacon had a great admiration

for these shambling, ill-clad and undernourished folk that were the English. They deserved that admiration, he felt, for having stood up to Nazism without the support of any other country until the Germans invaded Russia and the Japs attacked Pearl.

And he also felt attracted to places like this pub, where the community could come together, and an identity be forged. It was a marked contrast to his home country, in which every instinct to community had to contend with distance and space. In places like these venerable watering holes, one could hope that an instinctive conviviality might iron out the animosities that in his native land hid behind fences and shotguns, and contention find expression only in the occasional fist fight followed by a hop-breathed, bleary-eyed catharsis. Would the British have won the Battle of Britain without the institution of the pub?

"What can I get you, dearie?" the woman behind the bar asked, her big-breasted solidity planted firmly before him.

"Er, a pint of bitter, please."

"Can't get none of that where you come from, can yer?" the old fellow under the cap shouted, displaying a depleted henge of teeth in his upper jaw.

"No," Stan Deacon agreed, although if he was lucky enough to return home to the States, one thing he would definitely not miss was English beer, which tasted to him like bitter soap suds.

The landlady hauled on the pump with an arm on which the flesh sagged like an ill-rigged bowsprit and banged the pint down before him.

"Where are your buddies tonight?" she asked as he

tendered payment, no doubt lamenting the lack of custom, but with an expression that suggested pleasure in having addressed this American in his vernacular.

"It's a bit early, I guess."

"Can't you see he's an MP, Martha?" the man further along the bar, whose hearing was inconveniently acute from Deacon's point of view, bawled. "They's all scared of him."

"There ain't nuthin' to be scared of in this young feller, Si Daley."

"Don't you believe it. I was in the last one. I knows what MPs is like. We was in Bapaume once, and havin' ourselves a bon time of it, but doin' nobody no harm, and they all piles off their lorry, draggin' us this way and that."

"Well, that's just our lot. Any old thug we puts in the MPs. I'm sure it ain't the same in the US Army, eh, dearie?"

"What about what they done here a few weeks ago?" the man mumbled.

Stan wiped the head from his upper lip after taking his first tentative sip of the brew, leaned across the bar and asked as discreetly as he was able:

"Is your husband in tonight, ma'am?"

The implication of discretion was entirely lost on the barmaid, who replied at the top of her voice, perhaps with the intention of that husband overhearing:

"My husband, of course, he's putting his feet up, because he's had a hard day readin' the paper and watchin' me doin' the washin', and cookin' all his meals, so he needs his rest, but I can fetch him for anybody that calls me 'ma'am'. He don't do that, of course. Calls me all sorts else."

"Yes, ma'am, if you could fetch him."

"I'll do it right away, but don't you go hoppin' over this bar and helpin' yourself when I'm gone," she said with a mischievous glint in her eye that may have been an attempted wink defeated by the flabby skin at temple and cheek.

"I might though," said the man Daley, who continued to provide annoying evidence of his acute hearing.

When the barmaid had gone and Deacon was taking another sip of his pint, largely for appearances' sake and the desire to avoid conversation, Daley said:

"See them Russkies has got the Nazis on the run good and proper. You heard that? 'Spect you have seein' as yous got yer own wireless stations, eh?"

"You wanna see me, young feller?"

The landlord was standing before him, a tall man, his head with its sleeked-back black hair gleaming and perfectly round like a bowling ball. He stood upright and immobile as if in some transatlantic competition as to who could appear the most martial.

"Tom Curtin," the man said.

"Er, Stan Deacon."

Stan abandoned all attempts to keep his conversation with the landlord secret. Indeed, there was little point in him doing so. If he wanted to know who the man he had seen was, the more people he spoke to about it the better.

"I'm lookin' for someone. One of your townsfolk—"

"What's he gone and done?" the landlord snapped back.

"No. He's not in any trouble (Deacon felt that the urgency of the situation excused the lie). He just…We may have something belonging to him he may want back."

"What's that then?" the landlord asked.

Deacon was feeling increasingly uncomfortable in the face of the landlord's suspicious questioning but replied as evenly as he could.

"I'm not at liberty to say. In case people claim it that ain't entitled. He's about five nine or ten, in his twenties. Dark hair. And he walks with a bit of a limp, his left leg."

"A limp—" said the landlord's wife.

"Ain't nobody like that round here," said the landlord smartly.

A little too smartly. He had wanted to shut his wife up.

"Are you sure?" he persisted, shooting a quick glance at the landlady before his gaze returned to the landlord.

"'Course I am. I knows all the folk hereabouts. They all drinks in 'ere. I serve a better pint than the Swan and the Dog and Duck, anybody'll tell you that. And I says there ain't nobody like that here."

"Thank you for your help," Deacon said, and after taking another sup of his beer for form's sake, left the remaining half standing in the glass, and walked off in the direction of the other two pubs.

CHAPTER FORTY-THREE

Sally Burns watched out of the corner of her eye as the soldiers, from the Warwickshire Regiment, shot less than discrete glances at the legs of the blonde girl sitting by the door of the compartment. The blonde wore nylons over well-defined calf muscles and smiled in satisfied acknowledgement. Pert lips, red lipstick – the real thing, not beetroot juice. Probably a chorus girl, with some rich sugar daddy. Not all prostitutes came with a red light.

Oh, why was she thinking such horrible thoughts! But she knew why she was being bitchy, and she liked the reason no more than she liked its product. She was jealous that the young soldiers were not looking at her, even though she sat directly opposite. She was no prude. But she did like to think of herself as a respectable, and of course, married, woman, and here was her mind standing on a street corner revealing her suspenders. Of course, the soldiers had probably spotted her ring. What was the matter with her?

She was happily married. She should be glad of it when so many women endured beatings at the hands of their husbands, and here she was thinking like a silly schoolgirl. She had set out to win Arthur, and had, despite the opposition of her father, succeeded.

"He won't never amount to nothing, that Arthur Burns," her father said, thumbs behind his braces, pulling them forward almost to the limit of the elastic's tension, the pose he adopted when in pontifical mode. "What you want, my girl, is a lad with a good solid trade behind him, not some fly-by-night grammar school boy."

They had met at night school where she was studying shorthand in the hope of a career in journalism, he studying bookkeeping. The night school possessed a small clique who were members of the Communist Party.

She was in awe of one of the lads, Peter Bentinck, who claimed to have spent time in Spain fighting with the International Brigades. She would try to put herself in Peter's way, but although he did not ignore her, his gaze was always straying in another direction, perhaps towards Cath Kimber – she of the voluptuous figure.

At first she had disliked Arthur, whose pontifications would remind her of her father, and who made no secret of his dislike of Peter.

"If you tie your colours tight to one mast, you'll find you have no room to move with the wind," Arthur said to her, referring to Peter.

What did that mean? All right, the mast was the Communist Party, every pronouncement of which was retailed by Bentinck as if it were a commandment of God. But Arthur Burns was just saying this for effect. Well, it had the opposite effect to that intended.

"You would think if he had fought for the Republicans, as he claims, he would have had more than enough of the

Communists," Arthur repeated as they sat in the canteen over cups of tea and bread and butter. He was jealous of Peter's good looks and popularity with the girls.

Sally was about to take her tea to another table in order to make her feelings known but decided instead that she would see just how clever Arthur Burns really was.

"Well, the Communists fought Franco, didn't they? It's more than we and the French did."

"The Republicans might have won if the Communists hadn't been more concerned with sidelining or eliminating their allies."

"What allies?"

"POUM, the anarchists, the socialists. When the Communists took over, they always got the worst weapons and were the first over the top in any doomed offensive."

He nodded to where Peter Bentinck stood at the counter, tray in hand, his large head with its waves of saturnine hair breaking on his collar. There was glamour about Peter Bentinck. Arthur Burns possessed no glamour, only a wiry frame, and shrewd, appraising, accountant's eyes – eyes that had never, like Peter's green orbs, expanded to encompass sun seared horizons, but confined themselves to the small print of a mean life.

"What do you believe in then?" she asked, still staring at Peter as he joked with a fellow student.

"I don't believe in following a party line. I follow my own line."

"And where will that lead you?" she said, still moved by a desire to punish him for his portentous conceit.

"To put people first. Not party policy or dogma, but people. The people that need our help: the poorest, the unemployed."

She turned back to face him, and she saw it: something in his eyes that she had never seen in Peter Bentinck's. Behind the steel rims was something steelier by far, something that she sensed lay deeper than the superficial glamour of the hero of the Spanish war. And not just steely resolve. There was a softness there, but a softness that was not twin to weakness, rather expressed from a deep well of compassion.

"Whatever you do," he said, "don't do it only for its own sake or to empower yourself. Never forget who you do it for." His thin ascetic lips broke into a smile of perfect warmth and a charm such as she had never expected to find in him.

She was taken aback by his pretentiousness, still half outraged, and wanting to regain the orbit of Peter Bentinck. But she stayed where she was.

After Stalin signed his non-aggression pact with Hitler, she saw the truth of what Arthur Burns had said, and the glamour of Peter Bentinck faded as the politician in the man rose over the horizon, tying itself in knots to defend the realpolitik he pretended to despise. But by that time, she and Arthur Burns were walking out, and she was warming her hands at the grate of his crusading zeal.

Her mother approved. She knew, as did Sally, that a man should be something more than just himself, he should stand for something. Otherwise, he is little more than an animal whose life is an endless quest for food, shelter, sex, wealth. He whose concerns are entirely selfish is a lesser being than the altruistic. No doubt Mr Villiers would say the latter is the Christian. But to Sally, who could not believe in any supposedly caring deity who would countenance the horrors that were taking place in the world, and who distrusted the social conservatism of churches, the selfless was not necessarily to be equated with the spiritual.

Sally often found her selfless urges frustrated. In her well-meaning attempt to keep her family safe from the bombing, she had caused their deaths. And her guilt augmented her urge to altruism – an urge that now lacked any outlet in this most collective of altruistic endeavours, the nation's struggle to save the world from Nazism. She was no longer able to continue as an air raid warden; she could not bear even to stay in the capital, and they had been forced to flee the sights and sounds that sparked what she called her 'attacks', like the cowardly rich had done in 1940.

But she could not have stayed. Three months after the bombing, she was walking down Queen's Road when a drayman dropped a beer barrel into a pub cellar. She screamed, dived for cover in a shop doorway as two children on the other side of the road laughed at her. When she rose to her feet, she felt a warmth in her groin; she had wet herself. Two days later she saw a couple of children, no more than eight, in small tweed overcoats, walking arm in arm down the street, and she burst into tears.

Each time she heard of another tragedy, particularly an incident in which children lost their lives, she experienced the same debilitating terror, the sweaty armpits, the racing heartbeat.

It was with the utmost shame that she boarded, with Arthur, the train to Chalford, the town being chosen because Terry, Arthur's cousin, worked in the local branch of the Midland Bank and promised him a job. The shame should have been mitigated by the fact that by then the worst of the Blitz was over. But so far as Sally's exacting nature was concerned, she was still running away from her city and people.

Would things have been different had she been able to have children? They had been trying for a child since they were married, only for her hopes to be cruelly dashed by a dose of influenza that caused two missed periods. But would it have been right to bring children into this world? The war hung over them all like a giant cloud, and it was impossible to see through it to some future, to make plans that were not contingent.

At first Sally had been thrilled by the war. Not of course by the killing, but by the scale and overwhelming significance of the struggle, the fact that it was, more than the war that had preceded it, *the* great war for civilisation.

She was desperate to do her bit, and in joining the ARP felt she was doing just that, in a much more concrete fashion than if she had gone into munitions or the WRENS. She was helping to save lives and maintain morale. And the work she was doing was in her local community, so that it was that community, and her people, whose lives she was trying to protect. Only to find the satisfaction of herding her charges to safety was overwritten by her personal failure, and the responsibility became less one of the sheepdog protecting its flock, than the hyena, picking over the corpses, the shattered glasses, the lost sets of dentures.

Now the idea of the war was intimidating, demoralising. Oppressed by the isms and the ocracies, the martial collectives, the inconceivable slaughter, the world in mass, she would shiver and hug her tiny individual barren self. When the world marched away to fife and drum, she had to stand on the pavement, watching, otiose.

Even the moral certainties faded into sepia, like an old photograph of Victorian optimism. Britain no longer had conduct of the war. That had been handed over, in exchange for their cheque book, to the United States, a country whose instincts she distrusted. Britain was in mortgage to a country that, she believed, would not have joined the conflict but for Germany's declaration of war on them, and did not, she was sure, share her moral view of the struggle.

The real task of defeating the Germans was being undertaken by the Russians. And if the Russians triumphed, what then? Stalin and the Communists knew only one law, and that was the law of power – power exercised purely for the savage satisfaction of it. She felt increasingly like the meat in the sandwich between the callousness of American capitalism and the cruelty of Stalinism, and a rigorously rationed meat at that.

Even coming to a place like Chalford, the dilemmas and moral fog followed her. She found herself solicited by people she respected, to join the 'Wings for Victory' fundraising campaign by buying government bonds. These people, even if they didn't have personal experience of the Blitz, knew of the toll it had taken. And yet they now wished their air force to visit that same horror upon the citizens of Germany.

This was no longer her war. It had become not a righteous war of self-defence but one of retribution. She saw it in the faces of men in pubs, of women standing in the queues at the butcher's and grocer's: the hate, the desire for revenge. Dulled, suffering eyes now gleamed with blood lust. Did they understand that that revenge might involve women and children burning to death? Did they turn a blind eye to that fact, or revel in it? Or seek to justify it by saying that modern warfare can no longer be confined to young men on a precisely demarcated battlefield; that the whole nation was complicit in what the Germans had done. True. But if they had only seen what she had seen.

She could no longer do 'her bit'; even if she could, she would not know if what she did was for the benefit of all, or only for those who monopolised power and wealth. How could she know if any of the promises being made, of a national health service, of decent homes and jobs for all, were genuine or just the same old 'homes fit for heroes' lies with which the upper classes had placated those going over the top in the first war?

When she heard of the plight of Grover Carson, it came as a godsend to her. She was amazed by the feelings it inspired, the strength of which even Arthur could not comprehend. Was this the product of a desire to atone for the deaths of her mother and Donald and Edie? Was what she was now doing in visiting the printer in Winchester (far enough from Chalford to avoid complications) about Carson, or about her?

Here was a cause she could incubate in her barren womb. Here was a difference she could make, instead of standing idly by while armies marched past. Grover Carson, even though she had never set eyes on the man, was more to her than a single soldier from a mysterious continent; he was a cause.

Carson was one of the downtrodden of this world, the oppressed in whose name they were supposed to be fighting; those whose rights were being trampled into the earth by jackboots and tank tracks. Those wrongs could be redressed by beating Germany and Japan, and she had no doubt that with the manpower of Russia and the wealth of the United States, those countries would be beaten. But when the armistice was signed, the Carsons of this world would still perhaps end their lives swinging from trees in the victorious land of the free.

Thus it was that Sally Burns could contemplate sacrificing Tom Dawkins, one of her own community – or could perhaps ignore that sacrifice as a motorist drives heedless over a pheasant in the road – because he was white and British and not one of the oppressed of this world; not one of those whose predicament quickened her altruistic womb.

She looked away from the smut-encrusted window of the train and was surprised to see the young soldier staring at her. She dismissed the brief flash of pleasure. But what would this typical product of Britain think if he knew she had gone to Winchester to collect an order for 500 leaflets protesting that an American soldier was on trial for his life for a murder which another man (unnamed) had confessed to, all because he was black, and those leaflets were currently in the battered leather suitcase in the luggage rack? What would he say if he knew she intended to distribute those leaflets (in a manner as yet undecided upon) about the town of Chalford?

Perhaps he would say that she should not sacrifice one of their own for the sake of a Yank – and a black Yank at that. Or perhaps he would, with that sense of fair play for which the British, not unjustifiably, are renowned, applaud her efforts. Or perhaps he would just ask why the hell she bothered when millions were dying in anonymity on the Eastern Front, when their own were dying in Italy, in the ships that ploughed across the Atlantic or up to Murmansk.

But there was a thing called principle. And principle spoke an entirely different language from numbers. It was principle and those who stood up for it that made all the dying worthwhile. It gave her a role in the great struggle, a role that might appear, in the programme, to be at the very bottom of the cast, but was, she hoped, integral to the whole drama, like the maid who unlocks the French windows through which the murderer enters. Some saw it; some did not.

The printer did not. He looked at her with a condescension that seemed to say, 'Have you not got a man whose dinner you should be cooking, kids whose faces you should be washing? Is this all you can do when your country is in dire need?' In a beige overall, pencil behind his ear, he gave her the price with the sort of satisfaction that only the man who knows his services are not worth it can truly experience. But she had her leaflets.

They passed through the hamlet of Lethbridge and ran through the woods, the leaves fading with the weariness of the season, breaking ranks from that uniformity of green and forming that undisciplined rabble of reds and ochres.

Would what she was about to do make it untenable for them to remain in Chalford? If so, it would be a shame. It was not something they had discussed. When, as she knew he would, Arthur gave her his blessing, he must have considered the effect it would have on their status within the town. Perhaps he hadn't mentioned it to spare her feelings. That would be typical of him. She felt a warm glow of love for her husband, augmented perhaps by her shame at the thoughts that had been running through her head since she entered the carriage.

They ran over the points and under the smut-coated glass roof of Chalford station. The soldiers rose, making no attempt to assist her with her case, and after sending valedictory glances towards the chorus girl who received them with bored indifference, alighted in front of her. As she descended onto the platform, its surface etched with curlicue shadows from the station roof, she was surprised to see Arthur.

Her first reaction was one of gratitude that he had come to assist her... then she saw his face.

"Arthur. What is it, dear?"

He regarded her with a gravity that had something rueful about it.

"There's a man been looking for you—"

"What man?"

"He came to the house. When I told him you were away for the day, he said he'd put up at a local pub and return tomorrow morning first thing. He's from London. It's official, I'm afraid."

CHAPTER FORTY-FOUR

"Tell her I'm out," Major Bellucci ordered the sergeant, and, after the door had closed behind the latter, sat at his desk running his sausage-like fingers through the stubble of his crew cut, smiling to himself.

He had successfully sidestepped another interview with Mrs Cadwallader, no doubt an invite to his men to a dance or to 'take tea' at the houses of 'her ladies'.

The smile was elicited by the recollection of his men's comments on their return from these afternoon teas. How many had sat through an uncomfortable silence; how one elderly lady had been tipsy on sherry; how another had fallen asleep. And how Private Champney was convinced that 'the old dame wanted to get her hands in my pants'. And how some had ridiculed the poverty of houses lacking radiators and ice boxes, where cheeses were kept in the 'cool room'.

Likewise the dances, presided over with intimidating respectability by the vicar, lubricated with flasks of stewed tea, and boasting an antiquated gramophone or some old dear playing the piano.

But the major's mood changed abruptly with the call put through from the Black Bull.

"Tom Curtin here, Major, landlord of the Black Bull. I thought you should know we've had one of your MPs in here tonight. Name of Deacon. He's bin askin' questions about one of our lads what's just come out the army."

"Askin' questions?"

"Ay, and we don't like it, zee. He shouldn't be comin' after our lad, what's done nuthin' and has fought for King and Country and got hisself wounded into the bargain."

"Wounded?"

"His leg's buggered."

"Wha'd he want with this soldier?"

"Some cock-and-bull story about havin' somethin' he'd lost. I didn't believe it fer one minute. So look here, we don't like it, zee."

"Did he (the major could barely get the question through a throat that felt rock hard) ask for this soldier by name?"

"No, didn't know who he was. Just described him, like. But we knew who it was all right. What with the limp an' all."

"And did you tell him who it was he was after?"

"'Course I bloody didn't. Do you think I'm stupid or sumfink? I wasn't gonna give up one of ours. And don't you go askin' me neither."

The major didn't need to.

Bellucci wasted no time pondering how it was that Dawkins' existence came to the knowledge of Deacon. But as far as the major was concerned it could not have done so to a worse person. Although Deacon was not under his direct command, Bellucci knew the man to be what he described as 'unreliable'.

Now this Deacon was trying to stir up trouble; and trouble there would be if anyone discovered Dawkins' identity. It would come to light that Bellucci had deliberately concealed Dawkins' confession from Carson's defence team. And if the niggers back home got to learn of it there would be hell to pay. He could, he was sure, rely on the army to hush matters up. He had, after all, acted in the interests of Anglo-US relations. And there may even be long-term benefits if the top brass concluded the behaviour of blacks was such as to warrant them all being shipped back to the States.

For Bellucci the army was not just a group of men, made to don a uniform, taught to fire a gun, and pointed towards the enemy. For Bellucci the army was not simply a force; it was a moral force. And an integral part of that moral force resided in its being white. The very whiteness of the army was a measure of its morality. It was bad enough that they had the draft and had to admit to its ranks lily-livered clerks. But by admitting under pressure from liberals in Congress, blacks into the army, it was no longer the pure expression of all that was best about his country, the greatest goddam nation in the history of the world. Rather it was something sullied. Bellucci was proud he had done something that might, God willing, lead to the restoration of that purity.

He rose from his desk, threw back his shoulders, expanded himself, and looked about him in pre-emptive challenge. He stared at the Stars and Stripes on the wall. As always, the sight inspired a pride that made his chest muscles dilate even further. But it was a pride that was qualified, that was hobbled as you would a proud stallion if you wanted to cruelly curb its exuberant, dominant nature.

The work of defeating the Nazis, work that should fall to the United States, by virtue of its superiority not only in materiel but in moral power over the decadent England, was instead being done by others. True, the US Army was in Italy, but by the time they got to the Alps the Russkies, now they had won at Kursk, might have the Germans on the run back to Berlin.

Bellucci itched with frustration at the thought that the United States might have no more than a peripheral role in the greatest war in human history, that he himself might have no combat role, and others, the hated Commies and effete Brits, would grab the glory of defeating Germany. Of course, it would fall to them to defeat the Japs, but they were not of the same order as the Germans; they were not white for a start. Japs might be all right for a sneaky, cowardly attack like Pearl, but they did not possess the intellect or mettle of the white races.

Bellucci chomped on his cigar in frustration, his blue-shadowed jaws working. He, who should be leading his men into battle, was stuck in this one-horse town worrying about niggers assaulting women. Of what worth was a soldier's life if he did not experience the ultimate expression of his role: combat? A soldier who had not fought, however distinguished, was like a woman who could not give birth.

He jerked the cigar from his mouth, trailing a string of spittle, and swore foully at the image of the person he regarded as ultimately responsible for his ills: Franklin Delano Roosevelt. He turned back to the more congenial image of the Stars and Stripes. The important thing was loyalty to one's country rather than to the man at the helm.

What the army demanded of a man was loyalty. And any American should give of that loyalty freely. What Deacon had done was disloyal. He had gone behind the backs of his fellow MPs, just so he could get Carson off the hook. It was as if the guy was on some liberal pinko crusade, and there was nothing Bellucci hated more than liberal pinko crusaders.

Bellucci had to shut Deacon up before the adjourned hearing. Ever since he had heard of the continuance granted in the Carson case, and the reason for it, that there was a potential witness, Bellucci had been anxious. The witness was obviously Dawkins, and if they spoke to him...

This was the first time Bellucci had had to confront the consequences to him personally if the affair became public. Sure, it would all be hushed up. But what if his superiors took against him for what he'd done? What if they felt he had taken matters too far in hushing Dawkins up? Surely they would not cashier him, or deprive him of his chance to get to grips with the enemy, for something done in good faith?

He would make sure it wouldn't happen. Once Deacon was dealt with, Carson would swing. A white MP had been murdered and somebody had to pay. He would not have minded if Dawkins hanged for it. But it was better for the maintenance of good relations with the Brits, for good order on his watch, and to further tarnish the reputation of blacks in the army, that Carson should pay the penalty. After all, he deserved no better, going after white women.

But first Deacon. The man's fellow MPs, even if they were acquainted with the whole truth, would fail to share his desire to save the nigger who had pawed Schultz's girl.

CHAPTER FORTY-FIVE

A tired and dispirited Stan Deacon returned to his barracks shortly after nine. He was more than a little drunk, having been compelled for proprieties' sake to dispense with his original resolution, formulated on the grounds of personal taste and to avoid compromising his mission, to limit his intake to a sip or two of English ale. As he approached his hut, he was surprised to see it was in utter darkness, no chink of light escaping from beneath the blackout curtains. There was still activity in the other huts, and he could hear the strains of the gramophone – Sinatra singing 'Night and Day'.

He opened the door with his free hand while his left fumbled with his belt and truncheon, stumbling slightly on the threshold. As the door swung back, he was grabbed from behind, his arms pinned behind his back. His helmet was ripped from his head by dark shapes that clustered around him.

He could not see the face in front of him but knew the lazy Tennessee drawl: Temple.

"Where you bin, Deacon? If you was in town, and I

guess you was, 'cos I can smell beer on your breath, how come you didn't wanna take your buddies with you? I call that downright discourteous, you goin' off like that without invitin' us."

"Yeah, Deacon, what you bin up to?"

This time it was Mickey Reilly, sibilantly malicious in Deacon's right ear.

Stan Deacon's tired and alcohol-addled mind struggled to formulate a reply.

"I… I guess I just wanted to be alone."

"I just want to be alone," Temple mocked with a less than convincing impersonation of Greta Garbo's languid Scandinavian.

"That's not what we heard." This was Luigi.

"No," Temple agreed. "What we heard was you bin goin' among them English askin' all sorts of damn fool questions. Why would that be, eh?"

Temple struck Deacon hard on the side of the jaw, sending his spectacles flying. Consciousness receded then suddenly pulsed back livid, with flashing lights and numbing pain and blood in his mouth. A cramping agony rose up through his cheekbones to his skull.

"You wanna tell us? You bin askin' questions to try and get the noose offa the neck of your black buddy, ain't yer?"

"Yeah," said Reilly, "the nigger bastard that done killed yer buddy, Larry Schultz."

"But you got yerself new buddies now, ain't yer," said Temple, his face so close Deacon could smell the stale meaty odour of his breath. "You got yerself niggers for friends, niggers that kills MPs."

Deacon did not see or anticipate the next blow. The fist slammed through his relaxed stomach muscles and buried itself deep in his intestines, driving the wind out of his body, causing him to double up, gasping. The arms behind hauled on him, raising him up against his instinct to the foetal, a scalding pain in his stomach and chest, with a terrible consciousness of exposure.

"And what them English folk tell yer, eh?" Temple asked.

Deacon's eyes were screwed shut with the pain, but he could still smell the unwholesome breath, feel the vile proximity of the man.

"Yeah," said Gene from further away; it felt like a mile distant. "What they say, that nigger Carson didn't do it?"

"Yeah," Temple went on, "and you'd believe them, wouldn't you? On account of how much you admires our black friends, when they's creepin' about 'Yessir', 'n' all the time they's lyin' in wait to attack a man fer protectin' his gal from their dirty black paws. If the English wants niggers go rape their women, they can do what they does, invites them to their houses for 'a cup of tea' (this was another in Temple's hitherto unsuspected repertoire of unconvincing accents: middle-class English), but that there gal was Larry Schultz's gal and he didn't ought to have done it."

"And we don't want no nigger-lover like you tryin' to get the noose from offa his neck," said Reilly with venom.

"So what those folks told you, Deacon?" Temple asked.

"They told me nuthin'," he croaked. It was his voice, but a Stan Deacon aged by forty years.

"Ohh," said Temple sarcastically, "they didn't wanna lie to save their tame nigger, did they?"

The words were spat viciously into Deacon's face, spittle in their wake.

"Shiiit, they must've said sumthin'. Or did they just stand there lookin' at yer with mouths wide open like a shoal o' catfish?"

"They said they didn't know him."

"Know who? What you talkin' about, boy?" Temple rasped back.

Deacon's deranged mind, that felt like a collection of marbles rattling about in his skull, realised they didn't know why he had gone into Chalford. He couldn't let them know about the Englishman. That would make it even worse for him.

"Said they didn't see him… Carson."

"Weeel that's all right then. 'Cos we knows where he was, don't we? He was waitin' fer Larry Schultz so's he could kill him. Ain't that right, Deacon?"

The right hook again, rattling his teeth, igniting sparks in his skull, bruising his brain.

Something hard under him. He was lying on the floor. A boot slammed into his side. He screamed, rolling into a ball to protect his front, nursing the fire that engulfed his ribs.

"Ain't that right, Deacon?"

Some desperate, and at the same time, resigned, desire for survival, managed to summon the strength to croak:

"Yeeesssss."

CHAPTER FORTY-SIX

Cameron drew heavily on his Lucky Strike and looked across the court to the seat that did service for a dock, where Grover Carson sat in handcuffs flanked by two MPs, the coloured soldier blinking as if unable to face the grief of a grey daylight that diffused through the sash window at his side.

The MPs, burly men whose restless gaze chafed against their enforced immobility, were, when their eyes fell upon their charge as he attempted to scratch his head with his pinioned hands, as hostile bookends, radiating malice. It was a smug and portentous malice. They knew. The question Cameron asked himself was whether Grover Carson knew.

He should have known the moment Cameron, who had waited in vain for the appearance of Stan Deacon, informed his client that the witness had not been traced. Carson received the information without emotion, possibly without comprehension. His skin, Cameron noted, had lost that sheen that healthier, contented negroes displayed. His eyes were so blank Cameron struggled to detect even a hint of resignation in them. But resigned he certainly was, his entire demeanour passive and utterly lacking in hope. If it betrayed any expectation, it could only be expectation of the bullet.

Some people would see in this confirmation of the inherent inferiority of the negro. The man was too stupid even to feel afraid. But Cameron's experience of the negro told him different. Who could say whether he, Cameron, would not have exhibited the same impassivity in Carson's position?

Cameron could only assume from the fact that he had not heard from Deacon that the MP had been unable to find out anything. He asked to speak to his client and was granted a ten-minute conference.

The captain had anticipated some opposition from Carson to the suggestion that the negro decline to take the stand. But he simply nodded and said:

"Ain't no bluebirds here."

Cameron wondered whether the man was going out of his mind.

"It says in the song 'bluebirds over the white cliffs of Dover'. But there ain't no bluebirds here. That's lyin'."

"It's called poetic licence. It makes for a better story."

"Errol done told me that. Errol calls hisself a 'learned nigger' (here he gave an ejaculation that only with the best will in the world could be interpreted as a laugh) 'cos he knows stuff. I ain't never been learned. Never had me the chance. I'd like to see a bluebird again. One last time."

This morbid reflection told Cameron that at least Carson had some grasp of the dire nature of his predicament, and that was... no, perhaps it was not something to be thankful for.

"The court may make some adverse inference..." What was he thinking? Was he using legalese to mask the gravity of the situation? He should at least respect his client enough to speak in a way he understood. "The court may think you're not taking the stand because you don't want to be cross-examined – asked questions – by the prosecutor. The prosecutor is not allowed to say that, but the court may think it all the same. But, you're an honest person—"

"I was brung up to allays tell the truth."

"Sure you were. If you go into the box you'll say you never saw Schultz that night. And if you do, the court will find against you. They shouldn't do that, on the evidence. But they'll feel they have to find somebody guilty of the murder, and you're the only person they can find guilty.

"Your only hope is to show self-defence. Now, you won't say you saw Larry Schultz, and he attacked you, will you?"

Carson was staring into the corner of the ceiling.

"Grover?"

It was the first time he had used the negro's Christian name, and although unintentional, it sparked the desired response.

"Yeah."

"You won't say he attacked you, will you?"

"It weren't true."

"So, the best I can do is have you say nothing and try to introduce some doubt in the minds of the court, that maybe you had come upon Schultz by accident and he attacked you, or even better, that Schultz had gone looking for you to finish what he started. You understand?"

"Sure I do."

"Are you happy for me to do that?"

"I guess."

Cameron found himself yawning and trying to camouflage the fact. It might suggest to his client an indifference as to his fate that was far from the truth. In fact, Cameron had spent a restless night reviewing the law and authorities and imagining all the scenarios that might account for the facts. One was the MP Temple, as a result of some private grievance, attacking Schultz. He bemoaned the fact that he knew so little of these men. If he had a bit more time… but they would never break ranks. But one of them had: Deacon. If only he had asked him about the relations between the others and Schultz.

But if Cameron had passed such a night, what sort of night had Grover Carson passed? The man looked outwardly calm, but haggard and – didn't they stun cattle before they sent them for slaughter? – yes, stunned.

When they returned to court, Cameron went through the formality of requesting a further continuance.

"Have you managed to trace this witness, Captain?" Etherington asked.

"No, sir."

"Do you know his identity?"

"No."

Atkins was on his feet, but Etherington raised an admonitory palm.

"The continuance is refused. Please call your witnesses."

"I have none to call, sir." He had been refused permission to call Gideon and had been informed that the other blacks were not available to attend court.

"The accused does not wish to give testimony?"

"No, sir."

"Well, that is, of course, his right."

Cameron did not care for that 'of course', which suggested adverse inferences where there should be none.

"And he doesn't wish to make an unsworn statement in denial, explanation or extenuation?"

"No, sir."

After the appropriate warning was administered to Grover Carson by the judge, the tribunal proceeded to the closing speeches.

Atkins, as Cameron knew he would, made much of the brawl in the Black Bull. There was, he said, quite inaccurately, much 'bad blood' between the accused and deceased. As a consequence, the accused suffered what, it must be conceded (and of course, Cameron reflected, it was only in the prosecution interest to concede as much) was a severe beating.

"Severe it may have been, but it did not leave the accused incapacitated, and on the evening of the murder he was able to leave the camp. Medical evidence puts the time of death at between 6pm and 9pm. That much is not contested. The accused in his statement claims he spent part of that time with one Errol Gideon. The accused gives no evidence as to that alibi, and Gideon is not called to corroborate it, and even were he to do so, the alibi would be partial only. The accused therefore has no alibi for this murder.

"Members of the court may ask themselves whether the injuries the accused sustained were of an extent as to disable him from carrying out the attack that led to the death of the deceased. However, the accused was not examined by Dr Chilcott, nor is he prepared to give evidence as to those injuries… or indeed, anything else."

Atkins paused slightly as if waiting for admonishment from the judge. To Cameron's dismay none came, and the trial judge advocate continued, seemingly emboldened.

"As to the extent of the accused's disability, the court must recall first of all that the accused is a trained boxer, and in boxing as in other activities, familiarity with a task can overcome physical disability. In addition, is the doctor's evidence that 'there was no prolonged beating'. The defence will no doubt make much of this, at least in mitigation, but the court must also remember that the fact militates against any argument that the accused was physically incapable of the assault."

Atkins had hitherto been complacent and smug, addressing the court with hands on hips and only the occasional raised right hand, index finger pointed heavenwards, to emphasise his points. Now he adopted a hectoring tone, bending from the hips and gesturing feverishly.

"Don't let this soldier's demeanour fool you, gentlemen. He may appear placid, even a little slow-witted, but he is trained in a violent profession. He is not above forcing himself upon white women in dance halls – Sergeant O'Rourke is adamant on that point. If he were the sort of individual of whom nothing is hidden, why then does he not take the witness stand and allow us to test his credibility—"

Cameron was on his feet.

"Sir, I object!"

Meanwhile Atkins went on:

"...and character—"

"Captain Atkins!" Etherington bawled, far too belatedly for Cameron's liking. "Objection sustained. Captain Atkins, are you entirely unfamiliar with Rule 120d? We will have no further references of that nature."

Cameron regained his seat. Atkins bowed his head and took a deep breath, apparently chastened. But the damage had been done.

Some ten minutes later, after more in the same vein, Atkins got to the rub of the matter, extenuating nothing, or apparently so.

"Members of the court, you may feel the case against the accused is circumstantial. But that in itself is no bar to a conviction. The accused should not be able to calmly sit back (and Grover Carson was most definitely not calm, his upper body tensed, fists clenching and unclenching in a manner that was unwelcome to his advocate, as tending to remind the court of his physical potential) and, I could say literally 'get away with murder' by virtue of his silen—"

Cameron was on his feet again.

"Captain Atkins, this is your last warning," the judge admonished, but once again Atkins had made his point. The judge's warning was patently ineffectual. Cameron's doubt that he had made the right decision in persuading Carson not to take the stand was now becoming an anxiety.

Atkins went on:

"Don't let the accused escape justice because he had the foresight and native cunning (Cameron did not like that word 'native', which was cunning in itself with its subtle emphasis, but felt that objection would only add to that emphasis) to attack the deceased when there were no witnesses to inform on him."

Atkins was in his stride now, flushed of face and gesturing with the expansiveness of a John Barrymore Hamlet.

"The accused is a man trained in physical combat, long inured to its brutalities. A man entirely lacking respect for the white female. If a man is prepared to force himself upon an innocent girl, of what is he not capable? He is subjected to what we all would concede is a severe beating by the deceased and would not be human did he not have revenge in his heart. And who more capable than he with his pugilistic training?

"The first chance he got, he left the compound, in the company of this Errol or alone. Perhaps this person was his attempt to give himself an alibi, but it failed.

"Let us turn to the deceased. A man universally popular. There is not another soul among the MP contingent, or the local community of Chalford, who had reason to look anything but kindly upon Larry Schultz. One man only bore him a grudge, and that man took his opportunity to exact revenge. We may speculate as to whether the accused lay in wait for the deceased or whether he followed him. It matters not. Nor does it matter that he may not have intended to kill him – we have no evidence from him on that score in any event.

"Members of the court, you can be in no doubt that the accused Grover Carson waylaid the deceased, Larry Schultz, on the night of 3 July and attacked him, thereby causing his death. I submit the only possible verdict is guilty."

Atkins settled back in his seat and regarded the court with a serene confidence on his mottled face.

After taking a deep breath, Cameron rose, his legs trembling ever so slightly. He had compiled a closing speech, working into the early hours of the morning and sustained by innumerable cups of coffee. But he would have to think on his feet and amend it, emphasising some parts at the expense of others, to deal with the points made by his opponent.

"Members of the court," he began, speaking steadily although with a disconcerting quiver that he hoped only he could hear. "We have heard much in the way of speculation and things emotive from my friend. Can I instead ask you to consider the evidence put before you. I will take each witness in turn.

"First of all, we heard from Dr Chilcott. He gave evidence as to the time of death, and to the effect that there was no sustained assault upon the deceased. However, I ask you only to note that the doctor did not examine the accused for injuries such as abrasions to his fists which would have been consistent with my client punching the deceased.

"Sergeant O'Rourke gave testimony to the effect that the accused made improper advances to the deceased's girl. I suggest that such advances were entirely the product of the sergeant's fevered imagination and prejudice against black soldiers. The accused did no more than one would expect to do in a dance hall, and it is his case that the girl asked him to dance—"

"The accused is not giving evidence, Captain," admonished the judge. "You are not to give evidence for him."

"I apologise, sir," Cameron said, slightly unnerved. He paused to regain his composure.

"I beg the members of the court not to allow the prejudice of Sergeant O'Rourke to colour their view of the accused.

"It is clear from the testimony of the witnesses at the Black Bull that all the accused did was defend himself when summarily attacked. The MPs gave no good reason to arrest him and were clearly looking for him personally having been so briefed by the deceased. Please don't get me wrong, gentlemen, I don't seek to impugn the character of the deceased. He was out for revenge for what he saw as an outrage against his girl, and that is understandable. My friend used the term 'bad blood' between the deceased and accused. I submit that any bad blood was on the part of the deceased, and my client can have had no idea why he was being singled out for such treatment.

"We also have the evidence of Private Temple to the effect that on the night in question he was on patrol in Chalford with the deceased, and at some point the deceased went off on his own. It is my understanding of Military Police practice that they patrol in pairs. There is no evidence before the court as to why the deceased left Private Temple, and the matter must therefore remain a mystery.

"In order to prove murder against my client, the prosecution must show the accused brought about the death of the deceased and that he intended to do so. With respect to my friend, he has failed to do either. There is no evidence that places the accused at the scene of the deceased's death. The prosecution rely solely upon circumstantial evidence, namely that the accused had no alibi, and that he had a motive. Other people may, of course, have had an equal motive. The deceased may even have had a chance encounter with someone else, that encounter leading to violence, with death resulting. For remember, it was the doctor's evidence that one punch may have caused death in conjunction with the fall upon the windowsill, and there can be no certainty that the assailant intended to cause serious harm.

"Another possibility is that the accused was in fact at the scene, and there was an altercation, in which my client, in seeking solely to defend himself, threw the punch that led to death. I return to the curious point about the deceased parting company with Private Temple. If we are to place the stress upon motive the prosecution desire, what more natural motive for the deceased to leave his colleague and branch out on his own, with the desire to finish what he had begun a week before, namely hunt down my client and administer another beating? Surely that is the most probable explanation. And if that were the case, then this is not a case of murder, rather one of voluntary manslaughter, which the court will be aware arises out of a sudden quarrel or in the heat of passion.

"Let me draw the court's attention to two cases they may be familiar with. I have transcripts of the trials."

Cameron placed the cases of Danny Shay and Ossian Sweet, cases of self-defence, before the court.

"I would invite—"

"Captain Cameron," said Etherington. "If it is alleged that this case is one of self-defence, why then does the accused not give evidence of that?"

"Sir, I... er... I am not aware of any requirement that the accused give a reason for not testifying."

"There you are correct. But if you allege self-defence, he must give evidence of that."

"Sir, the accused, as is his right, has decided not to give evidence. I simply invite the members of the court to consider the possibility of self-defence and the doubt it raises and would submit in the light of that doubt that it is impossible to bring in a finding of murder against my client."

The judge addressed the members, directing them that reasonable doubt is an honest misgiving not a captious doubt nor one suggested by the ingenuity of counsel (Cameron would have felt flattered were he not so pessimistic) or unwarranted by testimony or born of a merciful inclination to permit the defendant to escape conviction or prompted by sympathy for him (this seemed singularly unlikely given the hostile glances directed towards Carson). The finding should not give reasons, but the court may formulate a statement of reasons for inclusion in the record.

The members retired to deliberate in closed session. Their voting would be carried out by secret written ballot. For a sentence of death to be passed it would require concurrence of all members; for imprisonment of ten years or more three quarters of the members. Any sentence of death had to be confirmed by the President.

As he waited, Cameron shot the occasional glance at Carson, to see him fidgeting, picking his teeth with his handcuffed hands or twisting his head to look out of the window. Cameron reflected that he may not get a chance to see much more daylight. How much of that restlessness was down to the position in which he found himself, and how much to his enforced immobility? he wondered. Withdrawing his gaze, Cameron found he too was fidgeting, drumming the tips of his fingers on the tabletop.

Had he done enough to introduce that element of doubt that would enable some at least of the members to conclude there was insufficient evidence against his client? Had he done the right thing by talking Carson into not taking the stand? If it went badly that decision would haunt him.

When the members trooped back their faces left little room for doubt. Theirs was more than the normal solemnity attendant upon such proceedings. They had been out for forty-five minutes: not long enough. Their verdict was announced from pale lips that split a face of putty: guilty, with a sentence of death.

Grover Carson gave no sign of having comprehended the situation save for a small start or twitch of his eye at the word 'death'. As he was led out of court between his two guardians he did not glance towards his advocate, and Cameron, for all that he feared blame resided in that omission, was mightily grateful for the fact. He loathed himself for the self-pity that told him Carson had the best of it. Unlike Cameron, the negro would not have to live long with the consequences of that verdict.

CHAPTER FORTY-SEVEN

Percival Greaves ('Perce' to his friends in the ministry) was surprised when he stood before the cottage in Woodthorpe Lane where Sally Burns lived. He had expected to see an untended garden, with roses grown to briar and much proliferation of weeds. Instead, there were lupins and foxgloves and nasturtiums. Surprised because reds had little conception of, and no use for, beauty. For them everything was functional, utilitarian.

The cottage itself looked tawdry, with mean little windows peeping out either side of the door, framed by curtains whose floral decoration was faded by the sun. Inside it must be positively stygian.

He opened the gate and, allowing it to sink back on its hinges with a squeal, walked up the uneven brickwork of the path and, resting his right foot upon the scraper, knocked on the door with the aid of the tarnished brass knocker.

It was Mr Burns who answered the summons, balding, moustachioed, squinting through horn-rimmed spectacles. The face evinced no surprise. He knew Greaves was coming, and he had his defensive demeanour already primed for use before the door was opened.

"Ah, Mr Burns. I trust your wife is at home. If so, I'd be grateful for a brief word. I shan't take up much of her valuable time."

He hoped the latter did not sound ironic. He himself was unaware of any such intention, but as Mr Freud tells us, who knows what we intend?

"Come in."

Burns led the way down a short hall, partially blocked by a boneshaker bicycle, past an antique barometer showing fair, and a print of some highland landscape. Peculiar taste for lefties, but perhaps they only rented the cottage.

He was ushered into the front room, fully as stygian as he had expected, and found the lady of the house rising from an armchair. More plain than pretty, lustreless mousey blonde hair done up in a bun, no makeup (there's lefties for you), and a look on her pale complexion he interpreted as guilty apprehension. The *Picture Post* fell from the arm of the chair to lie unregarded on the carpet.

"Mrs Burns," he said in his suavest tone. "Percival Greaves, from Senate House."

"That's…"

For a second he was tempted not to help her out.

"Ministry of Information. Might we have a word… in private."

"Whatever you have to say you can say before Arthur," she said defensively. Like her husband, primed to resist. Then, unexpectedly:

"Would you like a cup of tea?"

He did not, but to refuse would be a mistake.

"Well, you know, that would be perfectly splendid."

"I'll get it." The husband bustled away but no doubt would soon return.

"Won't you take a seat?"

Mrs Burns, the skin of her face still in tight, defensive formation, indicated one of two armchairs. One was already occupied by a tabby cat. He sank into the other one, putting his briefcase on the floor beside the fire irons. Mrs Burns lifted the cat, and sat down upon the other chair, cat on her lap and purring furiously.

Greaves took in the wireless set, an 'economy' set in dark, polished oak with a silk front; the antique wind-up gramophone that had unexpectedly come into its own once again, its portability and clockwork mechanism making it ideal for air raid shelters; and the diploma from the Institute of Bankers on the wall.

"You have a delightful house," he lied.

"Thank you. I dare say you haven't come here to admire the decor."

"Indeed no. To the point. I admire that."

The husband returned bearing a tray. He poured the tea and asked if Greaves took milk.

"A smidgeon, please."

Having performed the ritual, Mr Burns consulted his fob watch.

"I'm due at the bank."

"You just go. I'll be all right on my own."

Mr Burns hesitated briefly, then retreated to the hall and applied his bicycle clips while directing suspicious glances at the civil servant.

"I know why you've come," Mrs Burns said.

Unlike some in her position she made no attempt to mitigate the broad Cockney of her accent. Greaves was inclined to admire her for it.

"Well, that will save us some time," he said. "You will also, being an intelligent woman, know what the Ministry of Information does."

Mrs Burns seemed to wince. Perhaps he had been patronising. You had to be so careful of these reds. They could be very touchy.

"Propaganda."

"If you wish to so describe it. It's not the sort of thing we go in for in this country, as you know, but needs must. In a war, control of information is in many ways as important as control of munitions. The Germans have had a head start on us so far as that is concerned, but we're doing our best to... not catch up exactly, because being a free country we don't want to descend to their level, but... let's say, run a tight ship."

He took a sip of his tea. She was regarding him with a level, pale gaze that was a trifle disconcerting. She had, he realised, an infuriating capacity for making one feel her moral inferior.

But he knew the type. Part of the grand British tradition of the campaigning woman. Like the Suffragettes. His mother had been a suffragette, albeit one of the more pacific of that breed, never having thrown a brick through Asquith's window. He went on:

"Until recently, of course, we were masters in our own home. Now the situation has changed with the various other nationalities to whom we play host – Canadians,

Poles, etc. But more particularly the Americans, who are the least inclined to give way where their privileges are concerned. You will be aware of the Visiting Forces Act."

"It gives the Americans control over their own forces in this country."

"Yes. It allows them to enforce their military justice on British soil. And they guard the privilege jealously. Soon we will invade Europe. Cooperation and friendly relations with our allies, particularly the Americans, who have the money and materiel we need, is essential to bring our plans to fruition."

He did his best to swallow a bile of chagrin that was never to be glimpsed beneath his charm and complaisance. Once we had been a proud nation. Now, in order to keep the tide of Nazism at bay, we had mortgaged our pride, perhaps our very future, to the Americans, with their brazen and brash prodigality; sold our technological secrets to them for a few rusting destroyers in order to survive when we stood alone, and were now in hock to them for how many future generations? Could we have been more abject had we done a deal with Hitler in '40?

"You'll be aware that much German propaganda is devoted to driving a wedge between us, emphasising in particular the close relations between Americans and British girls. That can cause difficulties, particularly in small communities.

"In that regard, the case of this American Grover Carson has come to our attention. We understand a court martial is taking place as we speak, and that he is charged with the murder of an American MP, following an altercation in the local public house where the said Carson was attacked by this MP. I understand the catalyst for this attack was the fact that Carson, a black soldier, had made advances to a British girl whom the policeman was seeing. As you've involved yourself in this affair, would you agree that is a fair summary of the case?"

"Carson had only been dancing with the girl, not making advances. They're all prejudiced against the blacks."

"Regrettably you may be right. However, when a man joins an army – and this applies to any army – that organisation can deal with him as they think fit. We may not approve of the way they go about it, but we must accept it. We don't want the Americans telling us how to run our army, although they will of course be in charge of overall strategy, so we cannot tell them how to run theirs."

"Can I ask how you found out about me?"

"I'm sorry, but I am not at liberty to tell you that."

"Was it Caroline Lacey at the *Chalford Echo*?"

"I'm sorry." He held his palms out, pleading impotence, although she was correct.

"We would call her a snitch at school."

"Please, Mrs Burns, we're not in the playground now."

She seemed to flinch at that.

"Any interference by us with the American forces and their justice—"

"Justice! Let me tell you this. Because this is what you may not know. A man from this town has all but confessed to the murder Carson's charged with."

"What young man?"

"I am not prepared to say that."

Hands clenched in her lap, red mottled hands, husbanding her secret.

"But you know that as well, don't you?"

"Criminal lawyers will tell you many people confess to crimes they didn't commit. The Americans are aware of the existence of this man?"

"Yes."

"Then it's out of our hands. If the man doesn't surrender himself to our police, the Americans have the right to deal with it as they see fit."

"But you're condemning an innocent man!"

"I'm doing nothing—"

"Exactly. You know what these Americans are like, they've just picked on him because he's black and they want someone to blame."

Her pale face had developed a flush that made her almost attractive. With a bit of makeup she might scrub up rather well, he thought. But there was something intimidating, even frightening about her, something he had seen in the women who visited his mother. A fanaticism.

"Are you a Christian?" she asked, momentarily catching him off guard.

"I hardly think—"

"Doesn't it say in the Bible somewhere that what you do to one you do to all… what you do to the least of my children you do to me, something like that?"

"The war is hard on us all. We've all seen things that will remain with us for the rest of our lives, particularly those, like ourselves, who were in the capital during the Blitz."

"You've been checking up on me."

"Oh, please, don't read anything sinister into that. I like to know who I'm dealing with. Call it doing my homework. And you are one of those stalwart women who kept the East End going in that darkest of times... and paid a heavy price. I can only sympathise with you in your loss."

"I don't want your sympathy."

"Nevertheless, you have it."

"So you think me unhinged." The face now pinched with accusation, bloomed once again.

"Not at all. Those who have suffered great trauma are rarely the same as before. I myself, I dare say, am not that carefree spirit I was in the summer of '39."

She directed a look of hostile scepticism at him, as if she doubted he could ever have been 'carefree'.

"Now, about this young man. Have you told anyone else about him?"

She remained silent, obvious calculation behind that wide white forehead.

"Come, come now, Mrs Burns, this is not Nazi Germany... or Russia (a calculated barb he couldn't resist). People don't suffer because of what they know."

"Only my husband and Caroline Lacey at the paper."

"And how did you learn of this man's existence? He did not tell you himself?"

"No."

"Then how?"

Again, the laboured calculation, the pastry-coloured suspicion.

"Mrs Villiers, the vicar's wife."

"Ah, of course. If one is in need of moral counsel... So they, as far as you are aware, are the only ones who know."

She nodded, a resigned gesture.

"I think that wise. In a town like this it wouldn't do to let it get out that you were… how shall we say, pointing the finger at one of their own young men."

"Is that a threat?" she snapped.

"Oh dear me, no. We don't deal in threats. We like to think we perform a not too dissimilar role to the good vicar, providing counsel. Of the temporal rather than the spiritual kind, of course. And we don't wish to see a breakdown in what I understand has been the hitherto amicable relationship between the town and the Americans."

"I wouldn't go that far. There was a fight in the pub."

"Ah well, Americans can be rather abrasive. They lack any capacity for self-criticism, whereas we British, by contrast, have none for self-congratulation. It is a pity it's not the Canadians we must rely on so heavily. But in general, I understand, there's been relatively little friction. And we would like to keep it that way. For a town to feel that one of their own was being sacrificed to save a black American—"

"There you are. You're no better than the Yanks."

"I only state what many would feel. So you see why, in our view, it would be best for all concerned."

"Not for Carson."

"Perhaps not. But we don't know the outcome of the court martial. We must trust to American justice—"

"Hah!"

"It would be better for all concerned if matters were allowed to take their natural course. Do you not agree?"

He could see she did not. They take so long to break down, these fanatical women. He did not wish to have to apply pressure, but it seemed inevitable.

"Have you got the leaflets?"

"How do you know about that?"

"We have our sources."

"The printer—"

"I cannot say." Again, the raised hands, placating, supplicating. She looked at them as if they had just slapped her.

"I beg you, in the interests of your country, in the interests of the war effort which you yourself have done so much to aid—"

"I aided the people that was caught up in it—"

"You don't tell me you oppose the war?"

Greaves was genuinely horrified, having never imagined the woman could have travelled this far from sanity.

"No... I don't say that." For once she looked chastened, the self-righteousness falling from her. That was a victory in some sort.

"Then you will, I hope, sympathise."

"I cannot say that. I cannot accept an injustice like this... How can you sit there and pretend to be so civilised, and contemplate the hanging of an innocent man?"

"For a greater cause."

"Is there a greater cause than justice?"

"Sadly, so many innocent lives have been lost in that greater cause."

"I sometimes wonder what we're fighting for. This is one innocent death we can prevent, one these so-called allies are committing themselves—"

"Is not Tom Dawkins an innocent also? Certainly in a sense. But let me speak plainly, Mrs Burns, and I hope you do not think harshly. Because I understand women such as yourself—"

"What do you mean, women such as myself?"

He raised a placatory hand.

"Campaigning women. Admirable in many ways, selfless—"

"Please don't patronise me."

He did not wish to patronise, but it was time for straight talking.

"It is a matter of choice between two evils. Tom Dawkins, now. The pale Anglo-Saxon is one of that breed that disposes of the world's assets, is he not? And though he be poor, unlearned, disadvantaged by the standards of his own country, he possesses for you none of that vulnerable ethnicity, that provenance of oppression and slavery. Morally, in your eyes, he is the weaker case, the argument that will never sway you. And it will never have occurred to you that in thinking thus, you might be the counterpart, if the obverse, of those you despise: those that look down upon the black as a lesser form of being. Never occur to you that you judge worth by colour in a not dissimilar way."

She looked stunned. For all we should assess each person on their own merits, he reflected, we see them rather as a class, a sex, a race, an aggregate, and we apply to that individual the characteristics we assign, for good or evil, to the group as a whole. There is a kind of humanity that is simply prejudice in disguise, and he – or she – who thinks they are not prejudiced, is the most dangerous of all.

"That's a monstrous suggestion."

And yet the truth of the matter had struck home. Whatever the likes of Grover Carson did or did not do, he would always appeal to this woman over her own kind. She was as prejudiced as these Americans with their hatred of the blacks, the only difference was that hers was an inverted loathing for those of her own breed, their history and culture.

"Oh dear me," he said, feeling genuinely disappointed and regretting the step he was now compelled to take.

"Do you mean to confiscate them?"

"I beg your pardon?"

"The leaflets."

"No... I have no power to do so. Although I could obtain that power... but may I not ask you to reconsider?"

"It's wrong."

"Yes indeed. But necessary... I... (in his shame he found himself stammering and blushing)...I gather you and your husband wish to adopt a child, perhaps a war orphan."

"Yes, but..."

The truth dawned; her eyes grew wide. Yes, she could be attractive.

"No! No, you wouldn't."

"Regrettably, you leave us no alternative. In a time of war, the authorities must be satisfied that prospective parents are, how shall we say, committed to the war effort and not determined upon a course that may, in however small a way, undermine it."

She sat, wide-eyed, stupefied. To his surprise and his shame, tears were starting to her eyes. Such sensitivity was something with which he had not credited her. That is what comes of seeing people simply as representatives of a type.

"I'm sorry, Mrs Burns, I genuinely am."

And he spoke no less than the truth.

"Your sorrow's not worth much."

"Where is the suitcase with the leaflets?"

She rose, brushing down her skirt with an abrupt angry gesture, then proceeding to wring her hands like an actress in a second-rate melodrama. She went and gazed out of the window. From the movements of her shoulders, he realised her chest was heaving. She turned abruptly.

"I'll get it."

With that she walked smartly out of the room.

CHAPTER FORTY-EIGHT

Reverend Villiers stood between the prison chaplain, Reverend Curtis, and Grover Carson's advocate, Lionel Cameron, with his back to the two-storey red-brick extension to Shepton Mallet Prison in Somerset.

This accretion, which looked out of keeping with the weathered grey stone of the wing, had been constructed for the use of the American military as a prison, and the place of execution of American servicemen convicted under the Visiting Forces Act.

The three men stared at the post by the far wall. Villiers found himself shivering in the chill of the early morning, for it was only seven thirty, thirty minutes short of the appointed time, and was glad of the sunshine that lanced over the high wall, even if its warmth did not fall upon him.

There was something sour and judicial about Curtis, something callous about the smell of moth balls that emanated from him. For him this was no more than a job. He no doubt regarded all who came within his purview in the same way he regarded the murderers and rapists that made up the bulk of his parish. He read the majority and extrapolated from it to the whole.

The American, who said Carson had requested his attendance at the execution, appeared appropriately sober and regretful.

"It is the waiting that's the worst," Curtis said suddenly.

Villiers thought that perhaps he had misjudged the man.

"Yes," he replied flatly. Their words echoed between the walls, hollow and empty, devoid of consolation.

And what consolation had he been able to provide to Grover Carson? He fought off, like one holding at bay a wild animal with a brand, the temptation to think it was he who needed the consolation. Never could he have imagined himself in this position. It was just possible a vicar might be required to succour one of his parish faced with the hangman's noose. But this, for all it did not involve... he hesitated to think 'one of his own', for were they not all his own, are we not all each other's own?... this, was worse beyond the power of human imagination. And later, to have to write to his family...

It had visited him the previous morning when he sat in his study, bathed in the early-morning sun that poured through the French windows, and clothed in that blithe happiness we regard nostalgically in the wake of a death of one dear to us. The telephone rang in the hall. It was the Reverend Curtis. Reverend Villiers now imagined he could smell moth balls down the telephone line as he listened to the high, discordant voice that seemed used to minimise its matter with brusqueness.

"Curtis here, prison chaplain at Shepton Mallet. Listen, I've got a chap here asking for you. An American, a Private Carson. The Yanks are going to execute him tomorrow, and my services being offered, he asked to see you. I gather he attended your church."

"He may have done."

"Well, it seems he liked what he heard. Wants to see you before... you know. I tried to give him what consolation I could, but he was adamant he wanted to see you. Sorry and all that. Can you motor up today? It'll have to be today, I'm afraid. They're executing him tomorrow. Coloured – but a nice chap."

Reverend Villiers did motor up to Somerset, and dread worked the gear lever, applied and released the brake, depressed the clutch. But it was right he should go.

He was committed to seeing the pain he was causing. Only by witnessing that pain can one... what? Learn? Not in this instance. But it was cowardly, immoral even, to turn away from the tears in the eyes.

It was late afternoon when he was ushered into the condemned cell, dark, chill, lit by one small, barred window high in the wall. Could they not provide a better view than that? Surely it would not hurt to give a man who would not live to see another day, a last view of the blue sky, the fluffy clouds? Or was it a mercy to deny him those things? But, of course, it was not done with mercy in mind.

One low and surely not very comfortable bed, a toilet and washstand. And the smell of disinfectant he would perhaps always associate with the premonition of death. No, that was not the word. Death was something that came after life, and as a natural corollary of it. It came as the inevitable consequence of ageing or with the randomness of accident. But this was execution. It was done at man's bidding and by his blood-sticky hand. The vicar had often been called upon to console those awaiting their end. But this was not death. It was the abattoir.

But what right had he to condemn? He had known all along what it was, and how little Grover Carson deserved that end. Two of the blood-sticky hands that dealt death were his own, and now he, like some imposter, was here to give comfort. And instead of some biblical parallel that should have sprung to mind, he recalled the nursery tale of Little Red Riding Hood. Carson was the innocent girl, he the wolf sitting in Granny's bed. 'What big teeth you have, Grandma.' His hands were clammy on the goose-bumped leather of the Testament.

Carson was on the bed. The vicar knew that because the negro must be somewhere in the cell, and the hunched silhouette that looked like a sack of coals that was on the bed was the only thing that could be him. The vicar coughed. Carson turned. The vivid whites of his eyes seemed the only living element in that black outline extruded from the lesser blackness as by some emphatic gesture of negation.

"The minister?"

"Yes."

"There ain't no seat. You'd best sit here." Carson shuffled along, and the vicar lowered himself, and kept doing so until he thought he must hit the floor, and his buttocks touched the bed. The sour smell of sweat. The scent worn by those awaiting the noose.

"I bin to your church. You spoke good."

"Thank you." The words stuck in his throat and he had to force them free. "When was that?"

"I dunno. Soon afore I was took, I guess."

"That was…"

Yes, that was the sermon in which he, tentatively at first, hoped to nudge his congregation in the direction of reconciliation with the enemy. A difficult task with Lottie Thomas who had lost her Jim, only eighteen, and the Craig family, who had lost Alfred. Children who would never know their father's voice, see his smile. But it had to be done, resent it as they might. Hatred could not be allowed to fester.

It was James 3.

"Let me find the passage." He flicked through the bible, angling the pages up to the meagre light that penetrated the high window. "Ah, here we are." The relief of having simply to read.

"'But the wisdom that is from above is first pure, and then peaceable, gentle and easy to be intreated, full of mercy and good fruits, without partiality and without hypocrisy…'"

The word 'hypocrisy' set his body and soul resonating like a tuning fork. And another passage of scripture rose to his mind, the one his guilt had been fumbling for in its darkness, from Luke: 'And Peter remembered the word of the Lord, how he had said unto him, before the cock crow, thou shalt deny me thrice.'

The man was shivering.

"What time they gonna do it?"

"Eight… eight in the morning."

"It's cold then, ain't it?"

"It might be."

"I ain't never gonna feel the sun on me agin. The sun

like it is at home, not in the day, in the mornin' afore it's got up, and agin in the evenin' when it's goin' down and it's just layin' on you all warm like a blanket, and you can smell the trees and flowers. Man, they smell sweet. Sweeter than any perfume. I ain't never gonna feel that no more."

The negro got up and started to pace the room, from wall to door, around the basin and toilet.

"My mammy, she'd say, 'Grover my boy, you gotta be glad o' what you got in this world, 'cos some's not even got that. You gotta thank the Good Lord each day fer what you got, and not go thinkin' o' what you ain't.' And the good book, it says you gotta turn the other cheek, so that's what I done. And when the war come, she say, 'Grover, you gotta do your dooty.' And that's what I done. And look where I ended up! And my brother, little Carl, he always looked up to me, he was so proud, though he got no reason be proud o' me. I say to him I fight so's I can get money, ain't no reason to be proud. I can't believe I ain't never gonna see them no more... Do you think, Reverend, I'll get to see them in Heaven?"

"I'm sure you will, my son."

"'Cos there's a lotta things I doan understand. It's like that song – you have it over here? – 'It Ain't Necessarily So'. The Bible ain't necessarily so. 'Cos them white folks they's great church-goin' folk, and they's expectin' to go to Heaven on account of it, but they don't treat us blacks like the Good Book says... and I bet they ain't expectin' to share their Heaven with us, so how is that?"

"I'm sure—"

"I don't wanna die and not see them agin, and have my mom and baby brother thinkin' I done what they said, and thinkin' hows I's a bad man. I didn't do it, you know, Reverend. You probably doan believe me 'cos I's a black man, but I didn't do it. You believe me?"

He sat down on the bed again. Reverend Villiers put his arm around the condemned man and croaked:

"I know you didn't do it, my son."

Oh, how that 'know' lacerated his soul.

"I know it. I know you're a good man, and if you tell me your mother's address I'll write to her and tell her that."

"You will?"

"I'll tell her you didn't do it. And I know you for a good man, an honest man, and the best of the army your country has sent here."

Grover Carson was openly weeping now. Tears were also dribbling down the vicar's cheeks.

"Give me their address," he said, fumbling in his jacket for his pen and some paper, seizing at the mundane as refuge from his emotion. He wrote the address Carson gave him.

"I can't pray, Reverend. I tried. Why can't I pray? That must mean I's wicked like they says—"

Carson was becoming hysterical now.

The vicar took him gently by the elbow.

"We'll pray together."

He eased the condemned man down and they both knelt, the vicar taking him through some prayers. When they rose again, Carson asked:

"Will I get to Heaven, Reverend? 'Cos if it's anythin' like here I don't think I will, when there's that Sergeant O'Rourke an' them others… and here's me, and I ain't hurt nobody in my whole life outside the ring."

"Heaven is not like here. This world is flawed – it's not the way the Lord would want it. But Heaven is, and those that have done wrong in this world will be punished in the next, and those, like you, who are good people, will find their reward."

The vicar saw a form of salvation, not for Grover Carson, but for himself, appear like a destination long obscured by fog, bright in a lance of sunlight.

"You'll be free there… you won't have to worry someone is going to beat you or accuse you. And I'm sure in time – in a time that won't seem long to you, because time in Heaven doesn't run like it does here on Earth – your beloved mother and brother will join you in that paradise.

"God referred to Jesus as his 'beloved son'. But we are all God's beloved. He cares for us all and suffers for us. If we were only to realise that we are uniquely precious to God. Each and every one of us, even those that do us wrong. It's the most difficult thing in the world to believe, especially in times such as this, when evil men appear to triumph. If only those men were to come to that one truth, the most important truth there is, I believe this world could be as Heaven is.

"Let me just read you this passage."

The vicar turned to one of the bible passages he had marked.

But Carson asked:

"Where's Errol? Why don't Errol come and see me?"

"I don't know who Errol is."

There were footsteps, a rattle of keys, and a turning of one in the lock. The negro twitched, and let out a tiny scream, as the door creaked open.

"I can't go, I didn't do it."

He retreated as if to put the vicar between him and the warder. The latter lowered saturnine brows and stared contemptuously at Carson. He dropped a metal plate filled with some kind of stew, like a dog's dinner, onto the floor by the bed, and poured water from a jug into the cup that was attached by a chain to the wall. A shamefaced Grover Carson stood staring down at the plate.

"I'm afraid, Reverend."

Grover began to stride from wall to wall, openly weeping.

"I don't wanna die. I's fearful of what happens when them bullets strike, and it all goes black… I doan wanna die, I don't… Help me, Reverend."

He was on his knees now before Mr Villiers, his hands raised in prayerful attitude.

"Why can't the Lord save me from this?"

"My son, my son." The vicar, openly weeping now, his throat abraded and choked, grasped the condemned man about the shoulders.

"It is but the blinking of an eye. And then it will all be over, and you shall have the reward you so richly merit. Think on what Our Lord Jesus suffered on the cross. For you."

"Then why—"

"Let me read you again what the Bible says.

"'Blessed are you when men hate you, when they exclude you and insult you, and reject your name as evil, because of the Son of Man. Rejoice in that day and leap for joy, because great is your reward in Heaven. For that is how their fathers treated the prophets. But woe to you who are rich, for you have already received your comfort. Woe to you who are well fed now, for you will go hungry. Woe to you who laugh now, for you will mourn and weep.'

"Is that not good, my son? Remember, Jesus said, 'I am the resurrection and the life; he that believeth in me, though he were dead, yet shall he live.'"

Grover Carson was still on his knees.

"I dunno, Reverend. I dunno I's holy enough. I been to church, and I tries to do what the minister say, but I ain't holy like some folks is."

"You know yourself that those that seem the most holy are the least."

"But… you's probably thinkin' I ask you here so's I could say I done it – but I didn't, and now—"

"I know. Do not doubt you will go to Heaven. Those that die for something they did not do are the dearest in Our Lord's eyes. Do not doubt it, my son."

The vicar was on his knees now, hugging the black man, feeling his sobs, feeling their accusation of unjustified punishment reverberating through his own body. They stayed like this for some time. And then Carson said, his voice muffled but the catch in it perfectly audible:

"You know, Reverend, no woman never loved me. 'Cept my mother. Oh, I had me a woman, back in Georgia. But she weren't no good. I knew she didn't give a tinker's cuss fer me. She was just with me on account of the things I give her when I won a fight, or mebbe she thought I could protect her. She'll have herself another guy now, and never think on me no more. I'd have liked to have a woman, one that thinks kindly on me and misses me. Or kids that miss their pappy. But I ain't gonna have that now."

"My son, this world is flawed, and those that most deserve love rarely get it. But have no doubt that what matters is that Our Lord in Heaven loves you with all his heart, pities you and cries rich tears for you, and when this... is over, will take you to his bosom, and all your suffering will be at an end."

The vicar could hardly speak now, stones of pity and guilt occluding his throat.

There was the sound of keys. Behind them the door opened, and eight soldiers were led out behind an officer, all save the officer bearing rifles. Beside the officer was a man in a grey double-breasted suit. The vicar must have been staring at the latter, a balding man with a squint, for the chaplain said:

"The medical officer."

The vicar didn't know why they should need a medical officer, someone whose duty it was to preserve life, when the whole raison d'être of the proceeding was to take it.

The eight men lined up, the officer and medical officer standing to the side, and facing the post. The vicar had been told that one of those eight rifles held a blank round. The blank of absolution, so that the eight could live their lives with the probably erroneous conviction they had no part in the killing of Grover Carson.

Silence descended. It seemed to Mr Villiers that even the birds had stopped singing. The sun had crept down the wall behind him, but the yard seemed more chill than ever. He shivered and drew together the lapels of his overcoat.

Shuffling feet behind him. Grover Carson was led out handcuffed, a soldier at either side. He wore what the vicar took to be his normal uniform, but there were patches at the elbow, and loose stitching that suggested insignia had been removed. Carson's left foot tapped tentatively on the ground as it fell, as if his ankle was sprained. At first, he was looking at the concrete beneath his feet, but when he looked up and saw the post, he panicked, tried to pull away from the men, back toward the door through which he had entered, trying to yank his arms out of their restraining grip. He started screaming:

"I didn't do it, I didn't do it, don't kill me!" The last declining forlornly.

If he had the choice, at that moment, for sheer misery and guilt, the vicar would have taken the negro's place before the post. And a subversive thought entered his head: if he, then why not his God? Why did his God not intervene to stop this atrocity? Was it too glib to think that God was in Carson now?

Roughly manhandled and still screaming, now almost incoherently, Carson was dragged to the post. The men released the handcuffs and proceeded to bind him to the post, no easy task as he continued to writhe and buck. Once this was done the officer withdrew from his pocket and read the contents of the warrant, namely that Private Grover Carson be put to death by musketry. He then turned to Carson, who was tossing his body to and fro against the bindings, frantically twisting his head, imploring them, accusing them with the pitiable wide-eyed innocence of a wounded animal, and said:

"Private Grover Carson, you have heard the sentence of the court which has been duly confirmed by the Board of Review, do you wish to make a final statement before sentence is carried out?"

Howling now, Grover Carson said:

"I didn't do it. As Heaven is my judge, I didn't do it. Why you doin' this to me? I didn't do nuthin.'"

The officer in charge strode up to the condemned man, carrying a small drawstring bag, from which he withdrew a black hood. When Carson saw it he started to buck the more, but swiftly and dexterously the man applied and drew the hood down over Carson's head, although the negro, in a black parody of his life in the ring, tried all he knew to evade that final blow, that ultimate eclipse. When the grim task was performed the officer withdrew from the same bag a circular piece of white cloth, about four inches in diameter. It must have had some attachment to it, for he pinned it, the target, to the left side of Carson's chest.

Withdrawing, the officer began to read from a paper he took from his tunic pocket, intoning:

"At the command READY the execution party will take that position and unlock rifles. At the command AIM the execution party will take that position with rifles aimed at the target on the prisoner's body. At the command FIRE, the execution party will fire simultaneously."

Grover Carson was still writhing, incoherent mumbles coming from beneath the hood.

The first command was given. The vicar's body tensed, twitched as the command of 'aim' was given, then held itself rigid through what seemed an eternity of suspense before the command of 'fire!' was barked out and the rifles exploded, stunning Mr Villiers' ears and mind, hurling a congregation of ravens into the frozen air. The gunsmoke cleared, but the stench of it stuck to the inside of the vicar's nostrils so emphatically as to suggest the peppery odour was permanent.

At the clearing of the smoke, Grover Carson was revealed hunched forward on the post. The medical officer strode towards him, stood in front of Carson, bending forwards and feeling the victim's head. He turned and walked back towards the officer, shaking his bald pate. The officer marched determinedly forward and, passing the medical officer without so much as an acknowledgement, withdrew a pistol from the holster on his belt. Almost before Mr Villiers realised what was happening, the officer pointed the revolver at Carson's head just above the left ear and discharged the weapon.

The next thing he knew, the vicar's head was spinning, the word 'abattoir' setting up an irresistible clamour with the accusatory persistence of a renegade burglar alarm, and he was vomiting the contents of his meagre breakfast into the drain by the parade ground wall. As he lay his fevered brow on the brickwork, his heart pounding to the accompaniment of tramping boots as the firing squad departed, a hand went around his shoulders. He saw a black signet ring; it was the American lawyer. Wiping his mouth with the back of his hand, a sour tang on his tongue, Mr Villiers rose, and the American said:

"Let's quit this place."

Mr Villiers did so without a glance at the group who stood around the body of Grover Carson.

They walked back to where their cars were parked on the grass verge by the main road. The vicar found himself repeating:

"It's barbaric. It's barbaric."

"Sure is," Cameron agreed. "Poor guy. I guess he never had much of a life. His type never do."

"His type?"

"Blacks."

"Of course."

The American seemed to be pondering something.

"I guess you know everybody in Chalford, yeah?"

"Those who attend my church. Not all are church-goers, and there are the Methodists, and others."

"I just wonder what that gal Carson was dancing with feels now. Does she feel responsible?"

"That would be harsh, but… I don't know. Perhaps she doesn't even know. She's getting married in three weeks' time."

"Married, Reverend?"

"To her sweetheart… before. I am officiating."

That, the vicar reflected with uncharacteristic self-pity, was another ordeal he was called upon to perform.

"Her old sweetheart?"

"Yes, he was with Monty's lot, fought at Alamein."

"He have a limp?"

"Yes, how did you know?"

They had reached their cars, and stood, facing one another. And the vicar read it all in the handsome, well-groomed face of the American.

"It's not important," Cameron said, something desolate in his tone.

And it wasn't. Not now.

CHAPTER FORTY-NINE

There was, thought Mr Villiers, an abundance to the wedding reception held in Emily's parents' front parlour, that was only partially an imposture. Tom Dawkins was able to provide eggs and two chickens, to protests from Mr Dawkins senior, whose weather-beaten face glowered at all and sundry. The Frances had saved their ration coupons for butter for the wedding cake, and friends, including the Villiers, had chipped in with theirs, but the wedding had been so rushed, it taking place only a few days more than the statutory twenty-one days after delivery of the Certificate of Notice to the registrar, and a month after the last reading of the banns, that they could furnish only a small cake, minus icing, cunningly decorated with cardboard and rice paper to make it appear larger, and served on deliberately small plates.

The speed with which matters had been arranged had excited some comment, but the vicar had given the rumours no credence until they were lined up by the lych gate for the photographs, and he found himself examining the bride. She wore a cream-coloured skirt with matching jacket and a hat decorated with artificial cornflowers over her new set waves. The bodice was tight, but the jacket had a fringe that was allowed to ride up over the stomach, with unsightly wrinkles above. When one of Emily's friends said, with what appeared to be some disingenuity:

"Oh, do pull your jacket down, Em," the bride reacted with surprising violence, snapping back:

"Mind your own business, Luce! I'm all right as I am."

She appeared anything but all right. She appeared flustered, on edge. Of course, that was understandable on one's wedding day. But there was more to it, he was sure. He wondered whether she was expecting.

As the photographer's lens caught the couple in sharp focus (Ted Barkiss had been able to supply, he was proud to boast, some surplus RAF reconnaissance film) neither the bride nor the groom, in his Eighth Army uniform, gave off intimations prognostic of a lifetime of connubial bliss. As their faces, the bride tense rather than blushing, and the groom hollow-eyed and, did he imagine it, haunted, and both pinched and reddened by the cold wind, were surprised in the camera's flash, the vicar resolved to speak to Tom.

Mr Villiers manoeuvred himself, plate with cake in one hand, cup and saucer in the other, through the other guests. Some relative, a bottle of beer in his hand and his jowly face scorched with its effects, slapped the groom on the shoulders and addressed him with unsubtle bonhomie. Tom winced and his tight lips made a few remarks before he was subject to a gushing approach from a middle-aged woman in worn twinset who levered herself up on tiptoes to receive a kiss, but receiving no assistance from Tom, was obliged to subside. Tom managed to effect his escape, only to run into the vicar.

"Well, my boy," said the latter with counterfeit good humour, "this is the day you have longed for, I know. And well you deserve it, after all your exertions in Africa."

Tom Dawkins looked down at the vicar with a face as desolate as a full moon, pocked and disfigured with a shared intelligence.

"Don't—"

He stopped.

Congratulations were in order. The entire ritual of English social intercourse demanded it. But both knew the tender was entirely hollow.

"Emily looks very pretty."

"Yes." The words were as if spoken in a cave, redolent of voids; of a house that is bombed out.

"You must put the past behind you, Tom. You know I shall always be here for you, don't you?"

"Thank you, Vicar."

"What's done is done. Try to build something you can be proud of. Look to your future with Emily."

When the name was pronounced Tom Dawkins' head snapped up, as if he had been slapped, and his gaze traversed the room until it lighted on the bride, herself looking up as an aunt examined her ring, a half hoop with three stones, as if sensing his gaze. With that one look, desolate and cold on the part of both, so that indifference was the best that could be said of it, the vicar read a lifetime of misery, and a hearth at which no love or trust might warm its feet. When the look was broken an aftertaste of bitterness remained.

Mr Villiers saw it all. The girl was pregnant with the American's baby, and the man she loved was dead, and she was forced, for propriety's sake, to marry another she did not love. Moreover, the man who had killed the man she loved; did she know that? Did Tom know the baby wasn't his? Did he know that she did not love him, and if so, when had the truth dawned? Was it this that haunted him, or the responsibility for Grover Carson's death? What had Tom Dawkins been doing at eight o'clock that cold morning?

Tom must surely blame Emily for the whole situation, even perhaps for that guilt which he would have to bear for the remainder of his life. What sort of perverted, twisted marriage would this be? Or would circumstances force them to a reconciliation, in which their tangled grievances might be laid to one side for the sake of the child? The vicar could only hope that with God's help that would prove so.

There was a sour taste in the vicar's mouth that reminded Mr Villiers of the taste of his vomit after the American officer had shot Carson in the head. He wrenched his gaze from the newly-weds, swilled back his tea in a gulp that almost made him choke, and pushing with a complete absence of his characteristic courtesy through the throng, went in search of his wife as the despairing go in search of hope.

*

Seven months after the ill-omened wedding, the town of Chalford reverberated, quite literally, to a procession of armoured might as the American troops bade farewell to the town on their way to the Channel ports.

They did not have to travel through Chalford, but Mayor Markle and his council lobbied for it, and it was felt by all concerned, given the ties of affinity that had developed between the former colonials and their hosts, that it was fitting they do so.

And so the tanks, the jeeps, the half-tracks and guns, lorries of whites and lorries of blacks, rumbled through the old market square, and cobbles that had once known nothing more concussive than a shire horse shuddered under the impact, and the facades of the Chalford Arms Hotel with its fading climbing plants, and the more plebeian Kings Arms, echoed the metallic aggression of armour.

The schools had been given an afternoon off, and boys in short trousers and caps clung to the market cross or balanced precariously on the far-from-level buttresses to the hotel. This was not only to get a good view of the spectacle that would no doubt live in their memory until they died, but in the hope of benefiting from those volleys of largesse in the form of gum and Hershey Bars periodically ejected from the vehicles. Regrettably for the reputation of the town, in the opinion of those dignitaries on the balcony of the hotel, namely Mayor Markle, Sir Cuthbert Greaves and Alfred Appleby, the spectacle descended into a series of fights between the boys over gum or chocolate.

Beneath the august personages on the balcony cries went up of:

"Good old Uncle Sam!"

Among those looking on were Mrs Cadwallader, on the arm of her husband, Mr Clegg the minister, Professor

Sachs, Dan Squires the garage mechanic, Joyce Foster, Mrs Knight, and Mr and Mrs France. Lucy Watson was one of the not inconsiderable number of women dabbing at their eyes with handkerchiefs, occasionally standing on tiptoe, no doubt in the hope of catching sight of Luigi. Others jumped and waved frantic arms. April Knight looked on, her expression a compound of disdain and smugness. Even the damp-eyed misery of some of these girls seemed to pale in comparison with the look on the face of Tom Curtin, watching forlornly the departure of opportunities that were rather pecuniary than romantic. Likewise, Ted Barkiss, seeing not the departure of an army bound for the front but his supply of nylons, chocolates and surplus 'gas', as he had now taken to calling petrol. His father, Abraham, stood fingering his side whiskers and addressing comments to Sam Westwood that, to judge from the sneering satisfaction on the face of the latter, reflected ill on the martial prowess of the United States military. Bob Alder, his butcher's apron over the Home Guard uniform worn in honour of the occasion, stood in front of his shop. Derek Chalmers climbed on the running board of a car and directed his Box Brownie at the departing army.

The newly wedded Dawkins couple were not present, nor was Sally Burns. Of those present then, it was perhaps only Mr and Mrs Villiers who thought of Grover Carson, the former sincerely hoping that their absence might aid not a forgetting, for that could never be, but some kind of healing at least.

The Americans stood and waved, some directing wolf whistles at the girls, which only encouraged the latter the more. Even one so ungiven to demonstrations of pleasure as Major Bellucci waved, that uncharacteristic smile perhaps suggestive of satisfaction at having neatly sidestepped the mayor's request for a formal leave-taking, and in his words 'an orgy of speechifyin'', calling in aid the tight deadline for embarkation.

The last vehicle departed the square, the exhaust gases dispersed and, some time later, the rumble of their progress receded into the distance, leaving Chalford to a kind of peace.

For various reasons, some of them heroic, others less so, none of the American troops ever returned to Chalford, but the old burgh that had played host to Viking and New Model Army alike, was never the same again.

Sources

'Wartime Britain 1939-1945' Juliet Gardiner
'Dunkirk. The British evacuation 1940' Robert Jackson
'Fighter boys' Patrick Bishop
'The Wartime Farm' BBC programme, and book by Peter Ginn, Ruth Goodman and Alexander Langlands
'Finest Hour' Tim Clayton and Phil Craig
'The People's War' Felicity Goodall.

This book is printed on paper from sustainable sources managed under the Forest Stewardship Council (FSC) scheme.

It has been printed in the UK to reduce transportation miles and their impact upon the environment.

For every new title that Troubador publishes, we plant a tree to offset CO_2, partnering with the More Trees scheme.

MORE TREES
LET'S PLANT A BILLION TREES

For more about how Troubador offsets its environmental impact, see www.troubador.co.uk/sustainability-and-community